THE MORTAL INSTRUMENTS

City of Glass

Also by Cassandra Clare

THE MORTAL INSTRUMENTS

City of Bones

City of Ashes

City of Glass

City of Fallen Angels

City of Lost Souls

City of Heavenly Fire

THE INFERNAL DEVICES

Clockwork Angel

Clockwork Prince

Clockwork Princess

THE DARK ARTIFICES

Lady Midnight

The Shadowhunter's Codex
With Joshua Lewis

The Bane Chronicles
With Sarah Rees Brennan
and Maureen Johnson

THE MORTAL INSTRUMENTS

City of Glass

Book Three

CASSANDRA CLARE

Margaret K. McElderry Books
NEW YORK LONDON TORONTO SYDNEY NEW DELHI

MARGARET K. McELDERRY BOOKS
An imprint of Simon & Schuster Children's Publishing Division
1230 Avenue of the Americas, New York, New York 10020

Also available in a Margaret K. McElderry Books hardcover edition
Cover design by Russell Gordon
Interior design by Mike Rosamilia
Map illustration by Drew Willis
The text for this book is set in Dolly.
Manufactured in the United States of America
This Margaret K. McElderry Books paperback edition September 2015
11
The Library of Congress has cataloged the hardcover edition as follows:
Clare, Cassandra.
City of Glass / Cassandra Clare.—1st ed.
p. cm.—(The mortal instruments ; bk. 3)
Summary: Still pursuing a cure for her mother's enchantment, Clary uses all her powers and ingenuity to get into Idris, the forbidden country of the secretive Shadowhunters, and to its capital, the City of Glass, where with the help of a newfound friend, Sebastian, she uncovers important truths about her family's past that will help save not only her mother but all those that she holds most dear.
ISBN 978-1-4169-1430-3 (hardcover)
ISBN 978-1-4391-5842-5 (eBook)
[1. Supernatural—Fiction. 2. Demonology—Fiction. 3. Magic—Fiction.
4. Vampires—Fiction. 5. New York (N.Y.)—Fiction.] I. Title.
PZ7.C5265Ckg 2009
[Fic]—dc22
2008039065
ISBN 978-1-4814-5598-5 (repackaged pbk)

For my mother.

"I only count the hours that shine."

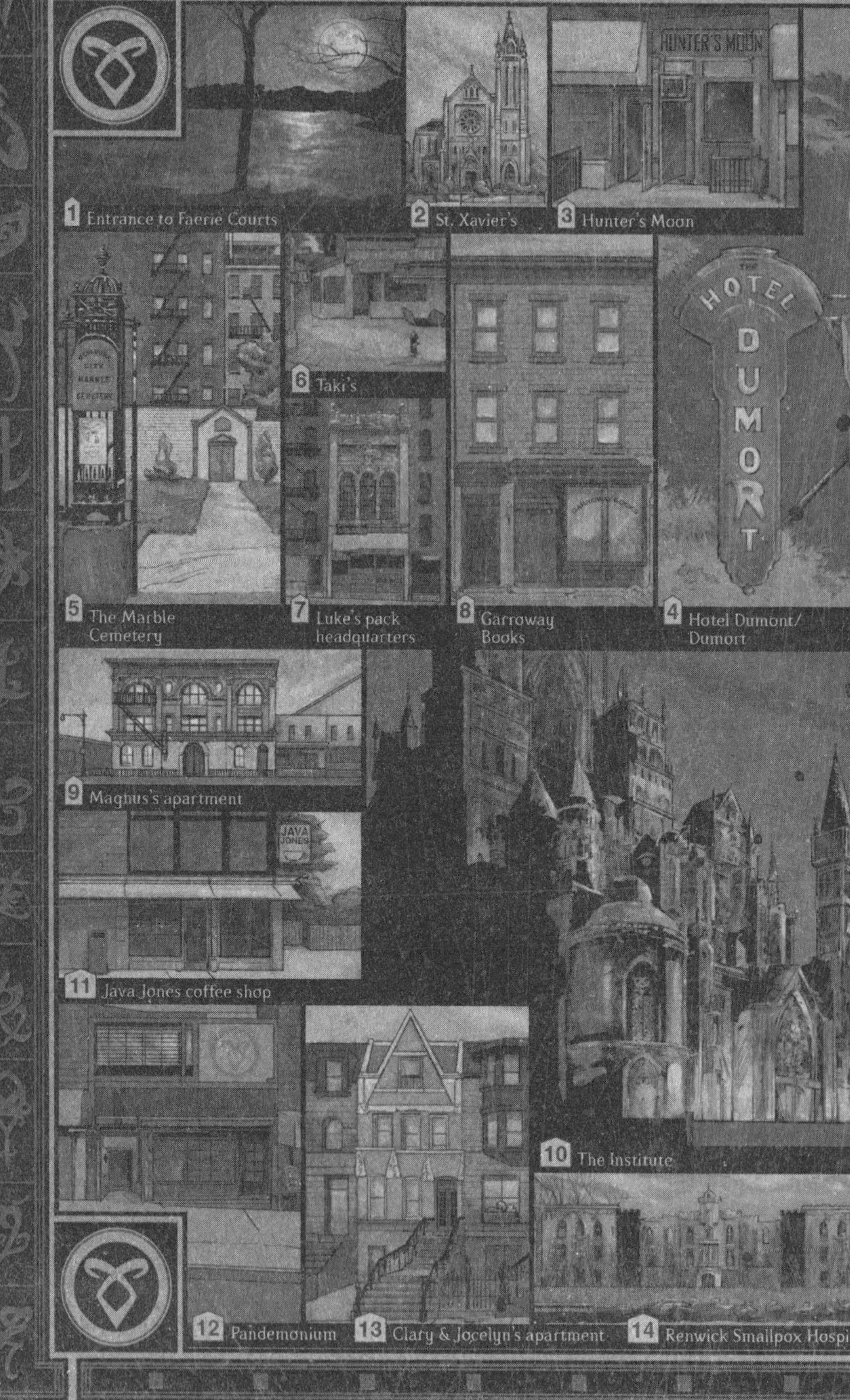
HUNTER'S MOON
HOTEL
DUMORT
JAVA JONES
1 Entrance to Faerie Courts
2 St. Xavier's
3 Hunter's Moon
6 Taki's
5 The Marble Cemetery
7 Luke's pack headquarters
8 Garroway Books
4 Hotel Dumont/ Dumort
9 Magnus's apartment
11 Java Jones coffee shop
10 The Institute
12 Pandemonium
13 Clary & Jocelyn's apartment
14 Renwick Smallpox Hospit

UPPER WEST SIDE
UPPER EAST SIDE
LINCOLN SQUARE
HELL'S KITCHEN
MIDTOWN
MANHATTAN
CHELSEA
WEST VILLAGE
EAST VILLAGE
CHINATOWN
FINANCIAL DISTRICT
ASTORIA
QUEENS
GREENPOINT
WILLIAMSBURG
BUSHWICK
FORT GREENE
COBBLE HILL
BROOKLYN
BEDFORD-STUYVESANT
CARROLL GARDENS
RED HOOK
PROSPECT HEIGHTS
GOWANUS
PARK SLOPE
1
2
3
4
5
6
7
8
9
10
11
12
13
14

Foreword

All the stories are true.

That's what Jace Wayland tells Clary Fray in the first book of the Shadowhunters chronicles, *City of Bones*.

Jace means, of course, more than one thing by this. He means that everything she'd always been told didn't exist—vampires, werewolves, faeries, ghosts, and monsters of all shape, size, and intention—did exist after all and that, in fact, the world is full of them. He means that the stories we believe in our hearts—stories in which we are the heroes, stories in which there are good people who rise up to defeat the evil, stories in which there is always hope—are also true. Clary ends *City of Bones* feeling a true sense of wonder as she flies over New York City, seeing revealed below all the magic and enchantment that had been previously hidden from her.

All the stories are true.

When I set out to write *City of Bones*, I was in love with stories about vampires and faeries and warlocks, but I was also in love with the mythological tales of angels and demons. I was fascinated by *Paradise Lost* and Dante's *Inferno* and Mike Carey's *Lucifer*. I was fascinated with the way that human beings had grappled with the ideas of absolute evil and absolute good tempered with love and free will. I wanted to create a world that was rich in folklore, the tales people tell each other about things that go bump and bite in the night, but which also incorporated the existence of figures of myth—angels so powerful that one look at them would blind you. Demons so evil that their blood could change the nature of your soul from good to evil. I wanted to make real that which is so shrouded in myth and history that it has become symbolic: when Valentine frees Jace from his prison in the Silent City, he carries with him a sword and explains, "This is the blade with which the Angel drove Adam and Eve out of the garden. *And he placed at the east of the garden of Eden Cherubim, and a flaming sword which turned every way.*" Later, Simon comes into possession of the sword of the Archangel Michael. The idea that these objects of immense power and history were real things our heroes could touch and use delighted me.

The existence of angels and demons in the world of Shadowhunters is the ur-myth from which every other aspect of the stories is derived. Shadowhunters were created from the blood of angels. Faeries are part angel, part demon. Warlocks are the offspring of humans and demons. Werewolves and vampires are humans who bear demon diseases. I wanted to create a universe where myth and folklore dovetailed, where every story of magic could be explained.

All the stories are true.

The idea of Shadowhunters came to me in part from the stories of Nephilim in the Bible. The offspring of humans and angels, they were enormous monsters who laid waste to the earth. As writers often do, I adapted what seemed compelling to me from the myth—angels having children, when that is such a human thing to do! (Of course the Shadowhunters are only created from angel blood, but Raziel still seems to have a fatherly interest in them.) The idea of being part angel, partly a symbol of goodness, and yet being beset by all the weaknesses inherent to humanity: frailty, cruelty, greed, selfishness, despair. It seemed a way to take an ancient story and ring a twist on it that would allow any reader to imagine what it might mean to be part divine, to have immense power—and as Spider-Man likes to remind us, the immense responsibility that goes with it.

All the stories are true.

Of course, what Jace means ultimately is that stories are how we make sense of the world. The Mortal Instruments is the story of Clary above everything else: the story of a girl who starts out ordinary and becomes a hero. A girl who first is blind to the magic in the world all around her, but comes not just to see it, but to be able to master and control it. Clary is an artist and a shaper of runes, the magical language of angels, and in using that language she shapes her own story and her own destiny. Clary and her friends are heroes who *make* their stories true—as, in the end, do we all.

Long is the way
And hard, that out of Hell leads up to Light.
—John Milton, *Paradise Lost*

Part One

Sparks Fly Upward

Man is born to trouble
as the sparks fly upward.
—Job 5:7

1
The Portal

The cold snap of the previous week was over; the sun was shining brightly as Clary hurried across Luke's dusty front yard, the hood of her jacket up to keep her hair from blowing across her face. The weather might have warmed up, but the wind off the East River could still be brutal. It carried with it a faint chemical smell, mixed with the Brooklyn smell of asphalt, gasoline, and burned sugar from the abandoned factory down the street.

Simon was waiting for her on the front porch, sprawled in a broken-springed armchair. He had his DS balanced on his blue-jeaned knees and was poking away at it industriously with the stylus. "Score," he said as she came up the steps. "I'm kicking butt at Mario Kart."

Clary pushed her hood back, shaking hair out of her eyes, and rummaged in her pocket for her keys. "Where have you been? I've been calling you all morning."

Simon got to his feet, shoving the blinking rectangle into his messenger bag. "I was at Eric's. Band practice."

Clary stopped jiggling the key in the lock—it always stuck—long enough to frown at him. "*Band* practice? You mean you're still—"

"In the band? Why wouldn't I be?" He reached around her. "Here, let me do it."

Clary stood still while Simon expertly twisted the key with just the right amount of pressure, making the stubborn old lock spring open. His hand brushed hers; his skin was cool, the temperature of the air outside. She shivered a little. They'd only called off their attempt at a romantic relationship last week, and she still felt confused whenever she saw him.

"Thanks." She took the key back without looking at him.

It was hot in the living room. Clary hung her jacket up on the peg inside the front hall and headed to the spare bedroom, Simon trailing in her wake. She frowned. Her suitcase was open like a clamshell on the bed, her clothes and sketchbooks strewn everywhere.

"I thought you were just going to be in Idris a couple of days," Simon said, taking in the mess with a look of faint dismay.

"I am, but I can't figure out what to pack. I hardly own any dresses or skirts, but what if I can't wear pants there?"

"Why wouldn't you be able to wear pants there? It's another country, not another century."

"But the Shadowhunters are so old-fashioned, and Isabelle

always wears dresses—" Clary broke off and sighed. "It's nothing. I'm just projecting all my anxiety about my mom onto my wardrobe. Let's talk about something else. How was practice? Still no band name?"

"It was fine." Simon hopped onto the desk, legs dangling over the side. "We're considering a new motto. Something ironic, like 'We've seen a million faces and rocked about eighty percent of them.'"

"Have you told Eric and the rest of them that—"

"That I'm a vampire? No. It isn't the sort of thing you just drop into casual conversation."

"Maybe not, but they're your *friends*. They should know. And besides, they'll just think it makes you more of a rock god, like that vampire Lester."

"Lestat," Simon said. "That would be the vampire Lestat. And he's fictional. Anyway, I don't see you running to tell all your friends that you're a Shadowhunter."

"What friends? You're my friend." She threw herself down onto the bed and looked up at Simon. "And I told you, didn't I?"

"Because you had no choice." Simon put his head to the side, studying her; the bedside light reflected off his eyes, turning them silver. "I'll miss you while you're gone."

"I'll miss you, too," Clary said, although her skin was prickling all over with a nervous anticipation that made it hard to concentrate. *I'm going to Idris!* her mind sang. *I'll see the Shadowhunter home country, the City of Glass. I'll save my mother.*

And I'll be with Jace.

Simon's eyes flashed as if he could hear her thoughts, but his voice was soft. "Tell me again—why do *you* have to go to Idris? Why can't Madeleine and Luke take care of this without you?"

"My mom got the spell that put her in this state from a warlock—Ragnor Fell. Madeleine says we need to track him down if we want to know how to reverse the spell. But he doesn't know Madeleine. He knew my mom, and Madeleine thinks he'll trust me because I look so much like her. And Luke can't come with me. He could come to Idris, but apparently he can't get into Alicante without permission from the Clave, and they won't give it. And don't say anything about it to him, *please*—he's really not happy about not going with me. If he hadn't known Madeleine before, I don't think he'd let me go at all."

"But the Lightwoods will be there too. And Jace. They'll be helping you. I mean, Jace did say he'd help you, didn't he? He doesn't mind you coming along?"

"Sure, he'll help me," Clary said. "And of course he doesn't mind. He's fine with it."

But that, she knew, was a lie.

Clary had gone straight to the Institute after she'd talked to Madeleine at the hospital. Jace had been the first one she'd told her mother's secret to, before even Luke. And he'd stood there and stared at her, getting paler and paler as she spoke, as if she weren't so much telling him how she could save her mother as draining the blood out of him with cruel slowness.

"You're not going," he said as soon as she'd finished. "If I have to tie you up and sit on you until this insane whim of yours passes, you are not going to Idris."

Clary felt as if he'd slapped her. She had thought he'd be *pleased*. She'd run all the way from the hospital to the Institute to tell him, and here he was standing in the entryway glaring at her with a look of grim death. "But you're going."

"Yes, we're going. We *have* to go. The Clave's called every active Clave member who can be spared back to Idris for a massive Council meeting. They're going to vote on what to do about Valentine, and since we're the last people who've seen him—"

Clary brushed this aside. "So if you're going, why can't I go with you?"

The straightforwardness of the question seemed to make him even angrier. "Because it isn't safe for you there."

"Oh, and it's so safe here? I've nearly been killed a dozen times in the past month, and every time it's been right here in New York."

"That's because Valentine's been concentrating on the two Mortal Instruments that were here." Jace spoke through gritted teeth. "He's going to shift his focus to Idris now, we all know it—"

"We're hardly as certain of anything as all that," said Maryse Lightwood. She had been standing in the shadow of the corridor doorway, unseen by either of them; she moved forward now, into the harsh entryway lights. They illuminated the lines of exhaustion that seemed to draw her face down. Her husband, Robert Lightwood, had been injured by demon poison during the battle last week and had needed constant nursing since; Clary could only imagine how tired she must be. "And the Clave wants to meet Clarissa. You know that, Jace."

"The Clave can screw itself."

"Jace," Maryse said, sounding genuinely parental for a change. "Language."

"The Clave wants a lot of things," Jace amended. "It shouldn't necessarily get them all."

Maryse shot him a look, as if she knew exactly what he was talking about and didn't appreciate it. "The Clave is often right, Jace. It's not unreasonable for them to want to talk to Clary, after what she's been through. What she could tell them—"

"I'll tell them whatever they want to know," Jace said.

Maryse sighed and turned her blue eyes on Clary. "So you want to go to Idris, I take it?"

"Just for a few days. I won't be any trouble," Clary said, gazing entreatingly past Jace's white-hot glare at Maryse. "I swear."

"The question isn't whether you'll be any trouble; the question is whether you'll be willing to meet with the Clave while you're there. They want to talk to you. If you say no, I doubt we can get the authorization to bring you with us."

"No—," Jace began.

"I'll meet with the Clave," Clary interrupted, though the thought sent a ripple of cold down her spine. The only emissary of the Clave she'd known so far was the Inquisitor, who hadn't exactly been pleasant to be around.

Maryse rubbed at her temples with her fingertips. "Then it's settled." She didn't sound settled, though; she sounded as tense and fragile as an overtightened violin string. "Jace, show Clary out and then come see me in the library. I need to talk to you."

She disappeared back into the shadows without even a word of farewell. Clary stared after her, feeling as if she'd just been drenched with ice water. Alec and Isabelle seemed genuinely fond of their mother, and she was sure Maryse wasn't a bad person, really, but she wasn't exactly *warm*.

Jace's mouth was a hard line. "Now look what you've done."

"I need to go to Idris, even if you can't understand why," Clary said. "I need to do this for my mother."

"Maryse trusts the Clave too much," said Jace. "She has to believe they're perfect, and I can't tell her they aren't, because—" He stopped abruptly.

"Because that's something Valentine would say."

She expected an explosion, but "No one is perfect" was all he said. He reached out and stabbed at the elevator button with his index finger. "Not even the Clave."

Clary crossed her arms over her chest. "Is that really why you don't want me to come? Because it isn't safe?"

A flicker of surprise crossed his face. "What do you mean? Why else wouldn't I want you to come?"

She swallowed. "Because—" *Because you told me you don't have feelings for me anymore, and you see, that's very awkward, because I still have them for you. And I bet you know it.*

"Because I don't want my little sister following me everywhere?" There was a sharp note in his voice, half mockery, half something else.

The elevator arrived with a clatter. Pushing the gate aside, Clary stepped into it and turned to face Jace. "I'm not going because you'll be there. I'm going because I want to help my mother. *Our* mother. I have to help her. Don't you get it? If I don't do this, she might never wake up. You could at least pretend you care a little bit."

Jace put his hands on her shoulders, his fingertips brushing the bare skin at the edge of her collar, sending pointless, helpless shivers through her nerves. There were shadows below his eyes, Clary noticed without wanting to, and dark hollows under his cheekbones. The black sweater he was wearing only made his bruise-marked skin stand out more, and the dark lashes, too; he was a study in contrasts, something to be painted in shades of black, white, and gray, with splashes of gold here and there, like his eyes, for an accent color—

"Let me do it." His voice was soft, urgent. "I can help her for you. Tell me where to go, who to ask. I'll get what you need."

"Madeleine told the warlock I'd be the one coming. He'll be expecting Jocelyn's daughter, not Jocelyn's son."

Jace's hands tightened on her shoulders. "So tell her there was a change of plans. I'll be going, not you. *Not you.*"

"Jace—"

"I'll do whatever," he said. "Whatever you want, if you promise to stay here."

"I can't."

He let go of her, as if she'd pushed him away. "*Why not?*"

"Because," she said, "she's my mother, Jace."

"And mine." His voice was cold. "In fact, why didn't Madeleine approach both of us about this? Why just you?"

"You know why."

"Because," he said, and this time he sounded even colder, "to her you're Jocelyn's daughter. But I'll always be Valentine's son."

He slammed the gate shut between them. For a moment she stared at him through it—the mesh of the gate divided up his face into a series of diamond shapes, outlined in metal. A single golden eye stared at her through one diamond, furious anger flickering in its depths.

"Jace—," she began.

But with a jerk and a clatter, the elevator was already moving, carrying her down into the dark silence of the cathedral.

***

"Earth to Clary." Simon waved his hands at her. "You awake?"

"Yeah, sorry." She sat up, shaking her head to clear it of cobwebs. That had been the last time she'd seen Jace. He hadn't picked up the phone when she'd called him afterward, so she'd made all her plans to travel to Idris with the Lightwoods using Alec as reluctant and embarrassed point person. Poor Alec, stuck between Jace and his mother, always trying to do the right thing. "Did you say something?"

"Just that I think Luke is back," Simon said, and jumped off the desk just as the bedroom door opened. "And he is."

"Hey, Simon." Luke sounded calm, maybe a little tired—he was wearing a battered denim jacket, a flannel shirt, and old cords tucked into boots that looked like they'd seen their best days ten years ago. His glasses were pushed up into his brown hair, which seemed flecked with more gray now than Clary remembered. There was a square package under his arm, tied with a length of green ribbon. He held it out to Clary. "I got you something for your trip."

"You didn't have to do that!" Clary protested. "You've done so much. . . ." She thought of the clothes he'd bought her after everything she owned had been destroyed. He'd given her a new phone, new art supplies, without ever having to be asked. Almost everything she owned now was a gift from Luke. *And you don't even approve of the fact that I'm going.* That last thought hung unspoken between them.

"I know. But I saw it, and I thought of you." He handed over the box.

The object inside was swathed in layers of tissue paper. Clary tore through it, her hand seizing on something soft as kitten's fur. She gave a little gasp. It was a bottle-green velvet coat, old-fashioned, with a gold silk lining, brass buttons, and a wide hood. She drew it onto her lap, smoothing her hands lovingly down the soft material. "It looks like something Isabelle would wear," she exclaimed. "Like a Shadowhunter traveling cloak."

"Exactly. Now you'll be dressed more like one of them," Luke said. "When you're in Idris."

She looked up at him. "Do you want me to look like one of them?"

"Clary, you are one of them." His smile was tinged with sadness. "Besides, you know how they treat outsiders. Anything you can do to fit in . . ."

Simon made an odd noise, and Clary looked guiltily at him—she'd almost forgotten he was there. He was looking studiously at his watch. "I should go."

"But you just got here!" Clary protested. "I thought we could hang out, watch a movie or something—"

"*You* need to pack." Simon smiled, bright as sunshine after rain. She could almost believe there was nothing bothering him. "I'll come by later to say good-bye before you go."

"Oh, come on," Clary protested. "Stay—"

"I can't." His tone was final. "I'm meeting Maia."

"Oh. Great," Clary said. Maia, she told herself, was nice. She was smart. She was pretty. She was also a werewolf. A werewolf with a crush on Simon. But maybe that was as it should be. Maybe his new friend *should* be a Downworlder. After all, he was a Downworlder himself now. Technically, he shouldn't even be spending time with Shadowhunters like Clary. "I guess you'd better go, then."

"I guess I'd better." Simon's dark eyes were unreadable. This was new—she'd always been able to read Simon before. She wondered if it was a side effect of the vampirism, or something else entirely. "Good-bye," he said, and bent as if to kiss her on the cheek, sweeping her hair back with one of his hands. Then he paused and drew back, his expression uncertain. She frowned in surprise, but he was already gone, brushing past Luke in the doorway. She heard the front door bang in the distance.

"He's acting so *weird*," she exclaimed, hugging the velvet coat against herself for reassurance. "Do you think it's the whole vampire thing?"

"Probably not." Luke looked faintly amused. "Becoming a Downworlder doesn't change the way you feel about things. Or people. Give him time. You *did* break up with him."

"I did not. He broke up with me."

"Because you weren't in love with him. That's an iffy proposition, and I think he's handling it with grace. A lot of teenage boys would sulk, or lurk around under your window with a boom box."

"No one has a boom box anymore. That was the eighties." Clary scrambled off the bed, pulling the coat on. She buttoned it up to the neck, luxuriating in the soft feel of the velvet. "I just want Simon to go back to normal." She glanced at herself in the mirror and was pleasantly surprised—the green made her red hair stand out and brightened the color of her eyes. She turned to Luke. "What do you think?"

He was leaning in the doorway with his hands in his pockets; a shadow passed over his face as he looked at her. "Your mother had a coat just like that when she was your age," was all he said.

Clary clutched the cuffs of the coat, digging her fingers into the soft pile. The mention of her mother, mixed with the sadness in his expression, was making her want to cry. "We're going to see her later today, right?" she asked. "I want to say good-bye before I go, and tell her—tell her what I'm doing. That she's going to be okay."

Luke nodded. "We'll visit the hospital later today. And, Clary?"

"What?" She almost didn't want to look at him, but to her relief, when she did, the sadness was gone from his eyes.

He smiled. "Normal isn't all it's cracked up to be."

Simon glanced down at the paper in his hand and then at the cathedral, his eyes slitted against the afternoon sun. The Institute rose up against the high blue sky, a slab of granite windowed with pointed arches and surrounded by a high stone wall. Gargoyle faces leered down from its cornices, as if daring him to approach the front door. It didn't look anything like it had the first time he had ever seen it, disguised as a run-down ruin, but then glamours didn't work on Downworlders.

You don't belong here. The words were harsh, sharp as acid; Simon wasn't sure if it was the gargoyle speaking or the voice in his own mind. *This is a church, and you are damned.*

"Shut up," he muttered halfheartedly. "Besides, I don't care about churches. I'm Jewish."

There was a filigreed iron gate set into the stone wall. Simon put his hand to the latch, half-expecting his skin to sear with pain, but nothing happened. Apparently the gate itself wasn't particularly holy. He pushed it open and was halfway up the cracked stonework path to the front door when he heard voices—several of them, and familiar—nearby.

Or maybe not that nearby. He had nearly forgotten how much his hearing, like his sight, had sharpened since he'd been Turned. It sounded as if the voices were just over his shoulder, but as he followed a narrow path around the side of the Institute, he saw that the people were standing quite a distance away, at the far end of the grounds. The grass grew wild here, half-covering the branching paths that led among what had probably once been neatly arranged rosebushes. There was even a stone bench, webbed with green weeds; this had been a real church once, before the Shadowhunters had taken it over.

He saw Magnus first, leaning against a mossy stone wall. It was hard to miss Magnus—he was wearing a splash-painted white T-shirt over rainbow leather trousers. He stood out like a hothouse orchid, surrounded by the black-clad Shadowhunters: Alec, looking pale and uncomfortable; Isabelle, her long black hair twisted into braids tied with silver ribbons, standing beside a little boy who had to be Max, the youngest. Nearby was their mother, looking like a taller, bonier version of her daughter, with the same long black hair. Beside her was a woman Simon didn't know. At first Simon thought she was old, since her hair was nearly white, but then she turned to speak to Maryse and he saw that she probably wasn't more than thirty-five or forty.

And then there was Jace, standing off at a little distance, as if he didn't quite belong. He was all in Shadowhunter black like the others. When Simon wore all black, he looked like he was on his way to a funeral, but Jace just looked tough and dangerous. And *blonder*. Simon felt his shoulders tighten and wondered if anything—time, or forgetfulness—would ever dilute his resentment of Jace. He didn't *want* to feel it, but there it was, a stone weighting down his unbeating heart.

Something seemed odd about the gathering—but then Jace turned toward him, as if sensing he was there, and Simon saw, even from this distance, the thin white scar on his throat, just above his collar. The resentment in his chest faded into something else. Jace dropped a small nod in his direction. "I'll be right back," he said to Maryse, in the sort of voice Simon would never have used with his own mother. He sounded like an adult talking to another adult.

Maryse indicated her permission with a distracted wave. "I don't see why it's taking so long," she was saying to Magnus. "Is that normal?"

"What's not normal is the discount I'm giving you." Magnus tapped the heel of his boot against the wall. "Normally I charge twice this much."

"It's only a *temporary* Portal. It just has to get us to Idris. And then I expect you to close it back up again. That *is* our agreement." She turned to the woman at her side. "And you'll remain here to witness that he does it, Madeleine?"

Madeleine. So this was Jocelyn's friend. There was no time to stare, though—Jace already had Simon by the arm and was dragging him around the side of the church, out of view of the others. It was even more weedy and overgrown back here, the path snaked with ropes of undergrowth. Jace pushed Simon behind a large oak tree and let go of him, darting his eyes around as if to make sure they hadn't been followed. "It's okay. We can talk here."

It was quieter back here certainly, the rush of traffic from

York Avenue muffled behind the bulk of the Institute. "You're the one who asked me here," Simon pointed out. "I got your message stuck to my window when I woke up this morning. Don't you ever use the phone like normal people?"

"Not if I can avoid it, vampire," said Jace. He was studying Simon thoughtfully, as if he were reading the pages of a book. Mingled in his expression were two conflicting emotions: a faint amazement and what looked to Simon like disappointment. "So it's still true. You can walk in the sunlight. Even midday sun doesn't burn you."

"Yes," Simon said. "But you knew that—you were there." He didn't have to elaborate on what "there" meant; he could see in the other boy's face that he remembered the river, the back of the truck, the sun rising over the water, Clary crying out. He remembered it just as well as Simon did.

"I thought perhaps it might have worn off," Jace said, but he didn't sound as if he meant it.

"If I feel the urge to burst into flames, I'll let you know." Simon never had much patience with Jace. "Look, did you ask me to come all the way uptown just so you could stare at me like I was something in a petri dish? Next time I'll send you a photo."

"And I'll frame it and put it on my nightstand," said Jace, but he didn't sound as if his heart were in the sarcasm. "Look, I asked you here for a reason. Much as I hate to admit it, vampire, we have something in common."

"Totally awesome hair?" Simon suggested, but his heart wasn't really in it either. Something about the look on Jace's face was making him increasingly uneasy.

"Clary," Jace said.

Simon was caught off guard. "Clary?"

"Clary," Jace said again. "You know: short, redheaded, bad temper."

"I don't see how Clary is something we have in common," Simon said, although he did. Nevertheless, this wasn't a conversation he particularly wanted to have with Jace now, or, in fact, ever. Wasn't there some sort of manly code that precluded discussions like this—discussions about *feelings*?

Apparently not. "We both care about her," Jace stated, giving him a measured look. "She's important to both of us. Right?"

"You're asking me if I *care* about her?" "Caring" seemed like a pretty insufficient word for it. He wondered if Jace was making fun of him—which seemed unusually cruel, even for Jace. Had Jace brought him over here just to mock him because it hadn't worked out romantically between Clary and himself? Though Simon still had hope, at least a little, that things might change, that Jace and Clary would start to feel about each other the way they were supposed to, the way siblings were *meant* to feel about each other—

He met Jace's gaze and felt that little hope shrivel. The look on the other boy's face wasn't the look brothers got when they talked about their sisters. On the other hand, it was obvious Jace hadn't brought him over here to mock him for his feelings; the misery Simon knew must be plainly written across his own features was mirrored in Jace's eyes.

"Don't think I like asking you these questions," Jace snapped. "I need to know what you'd do for Clary. Would you lie for her?"

"Lie about what? What's going on, anyway?" Simon realized what it was that had bothered him about the tableau of Shadowhunters in the garden. "Wait a second," he said. "You're leaving for Idris *right now*? Clary thinks you're going tonight."

"I know," Jace said. "And I need you to tell the others that Clary sent you here to say she wasn't coming. Tell them she doesn't want to go to Idris anymore." There was an edge to his voice—something Simon barely recognized, or perhaps it was simply so strange coming from Jace that he couldn't process it. Jace was *pleading* with him. "They'll believe you. They know how . . . how close you two are."

Simon shook his head. "I can't believe you. You act like you want me to do something for Clary, but actually you just want me to do something for *you*." He started to turn away. "No deal."

Jace caught his arm, spinning him back around. "This *is* for Clary. I'm trying to protect her. I thought you'd be at least a little interested in helping me do that."

Simon looked pointedly at Jace's hand where it clamped his upper arm. "How can I protect her if you don't tell me what I'm protecting her from?"

Jace didn't let go. "Can't you just trust me that this is important?"

"You don't understand how badly she wants to go to Idris," Simon said. "If I'm going to keep that from happening, there had better be a damn good reason."

Jace exhaled slowly, reluctantly—and let go his grip on Simon's arm. "What Clary did on Valentine's ship," he said, his voice low. "With the rune on the wall—the Rune of Opening—well, you saw what happened."

"She destroyed the ship," said Simon. "Saved all our lives."

"Keep your voice down." Jace glanced around anxiously.

"You're not saying no one else knows about that, are you?" Simon demanded in disbelief.

"I know. You know. Luke knows and Magnus knows. No one else."

"What do they all think happened? The ship just opportunely came apart?"

"I told them Valentine's Ritual of Conversion must have gone wrong."

"You lied to the Clave?" Simon wasn't sure whether to be impressed or dismayed.

"Yes, I lied to the Clave. Isabelle and Alec know Clary has some ability to create new runes, so I doubt I'll be able to keep that from the Clave or the new Inquisitor. But if they knew she could do what she does—amplify ordinary runes so they have incredible destructive power—they'd want her as a fighter, a weapon. And she's not equipped for that. She wasn't brought up for it—" He broke off, as Simon shook his head. "What?"

"You're Nephilim," Simon said slowly. "Shouldn't you want what's best for the Clave? If that's using Clary . . ."

"You want them to have her? To put her in the front lines, up against Valentine and whatever army he's raising?"

"No," said Simon. "I don't want that. But I'm not one of you. I don't have to ask myself who to put first, Clary or my family."

Jace flushed a slow, dark red. "It's not like that. If I thought it would help the Clave—but it won't. She'll just get hurt—"

"Even if you thought it would help the Clave," Simon said, "you'd never let them have her."

"What makes you say that, vampire?"

"Because no one can have her but you," said Simon.

The color left Jace's face. "So you won't help me," he said in disbelief. "You won't help *her*?"

Simon hesitated—and before he could respond, a noise split the silence between them. A high, shrieking cry, terrible in its desperation, and worse for the abruptness with which it was cut off. Jace whirled around. "What was that?"

The single shriek was joined by other cries, and a harsh clanging that scraped Simon's eardrums. "Something's happened—the others—"

But Jace was already gone, running along the path, dodging the undergrowth. After a moment's hesitation Simon followed. He had forgotten how fast he could run now—he was hard on Jace's heels as they rounded the corner of the church and burst out into the garden.

Before them was chaos. A white mist blanketed the garden, and there was a heavy smell in the air—the sharp tang of ozone and something else under it, sweet and unpleasant. Figures darted back and forth—Simon could see them only in fragments, as they appeared and disappeared through gaps in the fog. He glimpsed Isabelle, her hair snapping around her in black ropes as she swung her whip. It made a deadly fork of golden lightning through the shadows. She was fending off the advance of something lumbering and huge—a demon, Simon thought—but it was full daylight; that was impossible. As he stumbled forward, he saw that the creature was humanoid in shape, but humped and twisted, somehow *wrong*. It carried a thick wooden plank in one hand and was swinging at Isabelle almost blindly.

Only a short distance away, through a gap in the stone wall,

Simon could see the traffic on York Avenue rumbling placidly by. The sky beyond the Institute was clear.

"Forsaken," Jace whispered. His face was blazing as he drew one of his seraph blades from his belt. "Dozens of them." He pushed Simon to the side, almost roughly. "Stay here, do you understand? Stay here."

Simon stood frozen for a moment as Jace plunged forward into the mist. The light of the blade in his hand lit the fog around him to silver; dark figures dashed back and forth inside it, and Simon felt as if he were gazing through a pane of frosted glass, desperately trying to make out what was happening on the other side. Isabelle had vanished; he saw Alec, his arm bleeding, as he sliced through the chest of a Forsaken warrior and watched it crumple to the ground. Another reared up behind him, but Jace was there, now with a blade in each hand; he leaped into the air and brought them up and then down with a vicious scissoring movement—and the Forsaken's head tumbled free of its neck, black blood spurting. Simon's stomach wrenched—the blood smelled bitter, poisonous.

He could hear the Shadowhunters calling to one another out of the mist, though the Forsaken were utterly silent. Suddenly the mist cleared, and Simon saw Magnus, standing wild-eyed by the wall of the Institute. His hands were raised, blue lightning sparking between them, and against the wall where he stood, a square black hole seemed to be opening in the stone. It wasn't empty, or dark precisely, but shone like a mirror with whirling fire trapped within its glass. "The Portal!" he was shouting. "Go through the Portal!"

Several things happened at once. Maryse Lightwood appeared out of the mist, carrying the boy, Max, in her arms.

She paused to call something over her shoulder and then plunged toward the Portal and *through* it, vanishing into the wall. Alec followed, dragging Isabelle after him, her blood-spattered whip trailing on the ground. As he pulled her toward the Portal, something surged up out of the mist behind them—a Forsaken warrior, swinging a double-bladed knife.

Simon unfroze. Darting forward, he called out Isabelle's name—then stumbled and pitched forward, hitting the ground hard enough to knock the breath out of him, if he'd *had* any breath. He scrambled into a sitting position, turning to see what he'd tripped over.

It was a body. The body of a woman, her throat slit, her eyes wide and blue in death. Blood stained her pale hair. Madeleine.

"Simon, *move*!" It was Jace, shouting; Simon looked and saw the other boy running toward him out of the fog, bloody seraph blades in his hands. Then he looked up. The Forsaken warrior he'd seen chasing Isabelle loomed over him, its scarred face twisted into a rictus grin. Simon twisted away as the double-bladed knife swung down toward him, but even with his improved reflexes, he wasn't fast enough. A searing pain shot through him as everything went black.

2

The Demon Towers of Alicante

There was no amount of magic, Clary thought as she and Luke circled the block for the third time, that could create new parking spaces on a New York City street. There was nowhere for the truck to pull in, and half the street was double-parked. Finally Luke pulled up at a hydrant and shifted the pickup into neutral with a sigh. "Go on," he said. "Let them know you're here. I'll bring your suitcase."

Clary nodded, but hesitated before reaching for the door handle. Her stomach was tight with anxiety, and she wished, not for the first time, that Luke were going with her. "I always thought that the first time I went overseas, I'd have a passport with me at least."

Luke didn't smile. "I know you're nervous," he said. "But

it'll be all right. The Lightwoods will take good care of you."

I've only told you that a million times, Clary thought. She patted Luke's shoulder lightly before jumping down from the truck. "See you in a few."

She made her way down the cracked stone path, the sound of traffic fading as she neared the church doors. It took her several moments to peel the glamour off the Institute this time. It felt as if another layer of disguise had been added to the old cathedral, like a new coat of paint. Scraping it off with her mind felt hard, even painful. Finally it was gone and she could see the church as it was. The high wooden doors gleamed as if they'd just been polished.

There was a strange smell in the air, like ozone and burning. With a frown she put her hand to the knob. *I am Clary Morgenstern, one of the Nephilim, and I ask entrance to the Institute—*

The door swung open. Clary stepped inside. She looked around, blinking, trying to identify what it was that felt somehow different about the cathedral's interior.

She realized it as the door swung shut behind her, trapping her in a blackness relieved only by the dim glow of the rose window far overhead. She had never been inside the entrance to the Institute when there had not been dozens of flames lit in the elaborate candelabras lining the aisle between the pews.

She took her witchlight stone out of her pocket and held it up. Light blazed from it, sending shining spokes of illumination flaring out between her fingers. It lit the dusty corners of the cathedral's interior as she made her way to the elevator near the bare altar and jabbed impatiently at the call button.

Nothing happened. After half a minute she pressed the button again—and again. She laid her ear against the elevator door and listened. Not a sound. The Institute had gone dark and silent, like a mechanical doll whose clockwork heart had run down.

Her heart pounding now, Clary hurried back down the aisle and pushed the heavy doors open. She stood on the front steps of the church, glancing about frantically. The sky was darkening to cobalt overhead, and the air smelled even more strongly of burning. Had there been a fire? Had the Shadowhunters evacuated? But the place looked untouched. . . .

"It wasn't a fire." The voice was soft, velvety and familiar. A tall figure materialized out of the shadows, hair sticking up in a corona of ungainly spikes. He wore a black silk suit over a shimmering emerald green shirt, and brightly jeweled rings on his narrow fingers. There were fancy boots involved as well, and a good deal of glitter.

"Magnus?" Clary whispered.

"I know what you were thinking," Magnus said. "But there was no fire. That smell is hellmist—it's a sort of enchanted demonic smoke. It mutes the effects of certain kinds of magic."

"*Demonic* mist? Then there was—"

"An attack on the Institute. Yes. Earlier this afternoon. Forsaken—probably a few dozen of them."

"Jace," Clary whispered. "The Lightwoods—"

"The hellsmoke muted my ability to fight the Forsaken effectively. Theirs, too. I had to send them through the Portal into Idris."

"But none of them were hurt?"

"Madeleine," said Magnus. "Madeleine was killed. I'm sorry, Clary."

Clary sank down onto the steps. She hadn't known the

older woman well, but Madeleine had been a tenuous connection to her mother—her *real* mother, the tough, fighting Shadowhunter that Clary had never known.

"Clary?" Luke was coming up the path through the gathering dark. He had Clary's suitcase in one hand. "What's going on?"

Clary sat hugging her knees while Magnus explained. Underneath her pain for Madeleine she was full of a guilty relief. Jace was all right. The Lightwoods were all right. She said it over and over to herself, silently. Jace was all right.

"The Forsaken," Luke said. "They were all killed?"

"Not all of them." Magnus shook his head. "After I sent the Lightwoods through the Portal, the Forsaken dispersed; they didn't seem interested in me. By the time I shut the Portal, they were all gone."

Clary raised her head. "The Portal's closed? But—you can still send me to Idris, right?" she asked. "I mean, I can go through the Portal and join the Lightwoods there, can't I?"

Luke and Magnus exchanged a look. Luke set the suitcase down by his feet.

"Magnus?" Clary's voice rose, shrill in her own ears. "I *have* to go."

"The Portal is closed, Clary—"

"Then open another one!"

"It's not that easy," the warlock said. "The Clave guards any magical entry into Alicante very carefully. Their capital is a holy place to them—it's like their Vatican, their Forbidden City. No Downworlders can come there without permission, and no mundanes."

"But I'm a Shadowhunter!"

"Only barely," said Magnus. "Besides, the towers prevent direct Portaling to the city. To open a Portal that went through to Alicante, I'd have to have them standing by on the other side expecting you. If I tried to send you through on my own, it would be in direct contravention of the Law, and I'm not willing to risk that for you, biscuit, no matter how much I might like you personally."

Clary looked from Magnus's regretful face to Luke's wary one. "But I *need* to get to Idris," she said. "I need to help my mother. There must be some other way to get there, some way that doesn't involve a Portal."

"The nearest airport is a country over," Luke said. "If we could get across the border—and that's a big 'if'—there would be a long and dangerous overland journey after that, through all sorts of Downworlder territory. It could take us days to get there."

Clary's eyes were burning. *I will* not *cry*, she told herself. *I will* not.

"Clary." Luke's voice was gentle. "We'll get in touch with the Lightwoods. We'll make sure they have all the information they need to get the antidote for Jocelyn. They can contact Fell—"

But Clary was on her feet, shaking her head. "It has to be *me*," she said. "Madeleine said Fell wouldn't talk to anyone else."

"Fell? Ragnor Fell?" Magnus echoed. "I can try to get a message to him. Let him know to expect Jace."

Some of the worry cleared from Luke's face. "Clary, do you hear that? With Magnus's help—"

But Clary didn't want to hear any more about Magnus's help. She didn't want to hear anything. She had thought she was going to save her mother, and now there was going to be nothing for her to do but sit by her mother's bedside, hold her limp hand, and hope someone else, somewhere else, would be able to do what she couldn't.

She scrambled down the steps, pushing past Luke when he tried to reach out for her. "I just need to be alone for a second."

"Clary—" She heard Luke call out to her, but she pulled away from him, darting around the side of the cathedral. She found herself following the stone path where it forked, making her way toward the small garden on the Institute's east side, toward the smell of char and ashes—and a thick, sharp smell under that. The smell of demonic magic. There was mist in the garden still, scattered bits of it like trails of cloud caught here and there on the edge of a rosebush or hiding under a stone. She could see where the earth had been churned up earlier by the fighting—and there was a dark red stain there, by one of the stone benches, that she didn't want to look at long.

Clary turned her head away. And paused. There, against the wall of the cathedral, were the unmistakable marks of rune-magic, glowing a hot, fading blue against the gray stone. They formed a squarish outline, like the outline of light around a half-open door. . . .

The Portal.

Something inside her seemed to twist. She remembered other symbols, shining dangerously against the smooth metal hull of a ship. She remembered the shudder the ship had given as it had wrenched itself apart, the black water of the East River pouring in. *They're just runes*, she thought. *Symbols. I can draw them. If my mother can trap the essence of the Mortal Cup inside a piece of paper, then I can make a Portal.*

She found her feet carrying her to the cathedral wall, her hand reaching into her pocket for her stele. Willing her hand not to shake, she set the tip of the stele to the stone.

She squeezed her eyelids shut and, against the darkness behind them, began to draw with her mind in curving lines of light. Lines that spoke to her of doorways, of being carried on whirling air, of travel and faraway places. The lines came together in a rune as graceful as a bird in flight. She didn't know if it was a rune that had existed before or one she had invented, but it existed now as if it always had.

Portal.

She began to draw, the marks leaping out from the stele's tip in charcoaled black lines. The stone sizzled, filling her nose with the acidic smell of burning. Hot blue light grew against her closed eyelids. She felt heat on her face, as if she stood in front of a fire. With a gasp she lowered her hand, opening her eyes.

The rune she had drawn was a dark flower blossoming on the stone wall. As she watched, the lines of it seemed to melt and change, flowing gently down, unfurling, reshaping themselves. Within moments the shape of the rune had changed. It was now the outline of a glowing doorway, several feet taller than Clary herself.

She couldn't tear her eyes from the doorway. It shone with the same dark light as the Portal behind the curtain at Madame Dorothea's. She reached out for it—

And recoiled. To use a Portal, she remembered with a sinking feeling, you had to imagine where you wanted to go, where you wanted the Portal to take you. But she had never been to Idris. It had been described to her, of course. A place of green valleys, of dark woods and bright water, of lakes and mountains, and Alicante, the city of glass towers. She could imagine what it might look like, but imagination wasn't enough, not with this magic. If only . . .

She took a sudden sharp breath. But she *had* seen Idris. She'd seen it in a dream, and she knew, without knowing how she knew, that it had been a true dream. After all, what had Jace said to her in the dream about Simon? That he couldn't stay because "this place is for the living"? And not long after that, Simon had died. . . .

She cast her memory back to the dream. She had been dancing in a ballroom in Alicante. The walls had been gold and white, with a clear, diamondlike roof overhead. There had been a fountain—a silver dish with a mermaid statue at the center—and lights strung in the trees outside the windows, and Clary had been wearing green velvet, just as she was now.

As if she were still in the dream, she reached for the Portal. A bright light spread under the touch of her fingers, a door opening onto a lighted place beyond. She found herself staring into a whirling golden maelstrom that slowly began to coalesce into discernible shapes—she thought she could see the outline of mountains, a piece of sky—

"*Clary!*" It was Luke, racing up the path, his face a mask of anger and dismay. Behind him strode Magnus, his cat eyes shining like metal in the hot Portal light that bathed the garden. "Clary, *stop*! The wards are dangerous! You'll get yourself killed!"

But there was no stopping now. Beyond the Portal the golden light was growing. She thought of the gold walls of the Hall in her dream, the golden light refracting off the cut glass everywhere. Luke was wrong; he didn't understand her gift, how it worked—

what did wards matter when you could create your own reality just by drawing it? "I have to go," she cried, moving forward, her fingertips outstretched. "Luke, I'm sorry—"

She stepped forward—and with a last, swift leap, he was at her side, catching at her wrist, just as the Portal seemed to explode all around them. Like a tornado snatching a tree up by the roots, the force yanked them both off their feet. Clary caught a last glimpse of the cars and buildings of Manhattan spinning away from her, vanishing as a whiplash-hard current of wind caught her, sending her hurtling, her wrist still in Luke's iron grip, into a whirling golden chaos.

Simon awoke to the rhythmic slap of water. He sat up, sudden terror freezing his chest—the last time he'd woken up to the sound of waves, he'd been a prisoner on Valentine's ship, and the soft liquid noise brought him back to that terrible time with an immediacy that was like a dash of ice water in the face.

But no—a quick look around told him that he was somewhere else entirely. For one thing, he was lying under soft blankets on a comfortable wooden bed in a small, clean room whose walls were painted a pale blue. Dark curtains were drawn over the window, but the faint light around their edges was enough for his vampire's eyes to see clearly. There was a bright rug on the floor and a mirrored cupboard on one wall.

There was also an armchair pulled up to the side of the bed. Simon sat up, the blankets falling away, and realized two things: one, that he was still wearing the same jeans and T-shirt he'd been wearing when he'd headed to the Institute to meet Jace; and two, that the person in the chair was dozing, her head propped on her hand, her long black hair spilling down like a fringed shawl.

"Isabelle?" Simon said.

Her head popped up like a startled jack-in-the-box's, her eyes flying open. "Oooh! You're awake!" She sat up straight, flicking her hair back. "Jace'll be so relieved. We were almost totally sure you were going to die."

"Die?" Simon echoed. He felt dizzy and a little sick. "From what?" He glanced around the room, blinking. "Am I in the Institute?" he asked, and realized the moment the words were out of his mouth that, of course, that was impossible. "I mean—where are we?"

An uneasy flicker passed across Isabelle's face. "Well . . . you mean, you don't remember what happened in the garden?" She tugged nervously at the crochet trim that bordered the chair's upholstery. "The Forsaken attacked us. There were a lot of them, and the hellmist made it hard to fight them. Magnus opened up the Portal, and we were all running into it when I saw you coming toward us. You tripped over—over Madeleine. And there was a Forsaken just behind you; you must not have seen him, but Jace did. He tried to get to you, but it was too late. The Forsaken stuck his knife into you. You bled—a lot. And Jace killed the Forsaken and picked you up and dragged you through the Portal with him," she finished, speaking so rapidly that her words blurred together and Simon had to strain to catch them. "And we were already on the other side, and let me tell you, everyone was pretty surprised when Jace came through with you bleeding all over him. The Consul wasn't at all pleased."

Simon's mouth was dry. "The Forsaken *stuck his knife into me?*" It seemed impossible. But then, he had healed before, after Valentine had cut his throat. Still, he at least ought to *remember.*

Shaking his head, he looked down at himself. "Where?"

"I'll show you." Much to his surprise, a moment later Isabelle was seated on the bed beside him, her cool hands on his midriff. She pushed his T-shirt up, baring a strip of pale stomach, bisected by a thin red line. It was barely a scar. "Here," she said, her fingers gliding over it. "Is there any pain?"

"N-no." The first time Simon had ever seen Isabelle, he'd found her so striking, so alight with life and vitality and energy, he'd thought he'd finally found a girl who burned bright enough to blot out the image of Clary that always seemed to be printed on the inside of his eyelids. It was right around the time she'd gotten him turned into a rat at Magnus Bane's loft party that he'd realized maybe Isabelle burned a little too bright for an ordinary guy like him. "It doesn't hurt."

"But my eyes do," said a coolly amused voice from the doorway. Jace. He had come in so quietly that even Simon hadn't heard him; closing the door behind him, he grinned as Isabelle pulled Simon's shirt down. "Molesting the vampire while he's too weak to fight back, Iz?" he asked. "I'm pretty sure that violates at least one of the Accords."

"I'm just showing him where he got stabbed," Isabelle protested, but she scooted back to her chair with a certain amount of haste. "What's going on downstairs?" she asked. "Is everyone still freaking out?"

The smile left Jace's face. "Maryse has gone up to the Gard with Patrick," he said. "The Clave's in session and Malachi thought it would be better if she . . . explained . . . in person."

Malachi. Patrick. Gard. The unfamiliar names whirled through Simon's head. "Explained what?"

Isabelle and Jace exchanged a look. "Explained *you*," Jace

said finally. "Explained why we brought a vampire with us to Alicante, which is, by the way, expressly against the Law."

"To Alicante? We're in Alicante?" A wave of blank panic washed over Simon, quickly replaced by a pain that shot through his midsection. He doubled over, gasping.

"Simon!" Isabelle reached out her hand, alarm in her dark eyes. "Are you all right?"

"Go away, Isabelle." Simon, his hands fisted against his stomach, looked up at Jace, pleading in his voice. "Make her go."

Isabelle recoiled, a hurt look on her face. "Fine. I'll go. You don't have to tell me twice." She flounced to her feet and out of the room, banging the door behind her.

Jace turned to Simon, his amber eyes expressionless. "What's going on? I thought you were healing."

Simon threw up a hand to ward the other boy off. A metallic taste burned in the back of his throat. "It's not Isabelle," he ground out. "I'm not hurt—I'm just . . . hungry." He felt his cheeks burn. "I lost blood, so—I need to replace it."

"Of course," Jace said, in the tone of someone who's just been enlightened by an interesting, if not particularly necessary, scientific fact. The faint concern left his expression, to be replaced by something that looked to Simon like amused contempt. It struck a chord of fury inside him, and if he hadn't been so debilitated by pain, he would have flung himself off the bed and onto the other boy in a rage. As it was, all he could do was gasp, "Screw you, Wayland."

"Wayland, is it?" The amused look didn't leave Jace's face, but his hands went to his throat and began to unzip his jacket.

"No!" Simon shrank back on the bed. "I don't care how hungry I am. I'm not—drinking your blood—again."

Jace's mouth twisted. "Like I'd let you." He reached into the inside pocket of his jacket and drew out a glass flask. It was half-full of a thin red-brown liquid. "I thought you might need this," he said. "I squeezed the juice out of a few pounds of raw meat in the kitchen. It was the best I could do."

Simon took the flask from Jace with hands that were shaking so badly that the other boy had to unscrew the top for him. The liquid inside was foul—too thin and salty to be proper blood, and with that faint unpleasant taste that Simon knew meant the meat had been a few days old.

"Ugh," he said, after a few swallows. "Dead blood."

Jace's eyebrows went up. "Isn't all blood dead?"

"The longer the animal whose blood I'm drinking has been dead, the worse the blood tastes," Simon explained. "Fresh is better."

"But you've never drunk fresh blood. Have you?"

Simon raised his own eyebrows in response.

"Well, aside from mine, of course," Jace said. "And I'm sure my blood is fan-*tastic*."

Simon set the empty flask down on the arm of the chair by the bed. "There's something very wrong with you," he said. "Mentally, I mean." His mouth still tasted of spoiled blood, but the pain was gone. He felt better, stronger, as if the blood were a medicine that worked instantly, a drug he had to have to live. He wondered if this was what it was like for heroin addicts. "So I'm in Idris."

"Alicante, to be specific," said Jace. "The capital city. The *only* city, really." He went to the window and drew back the curtains. "The Penhallows didn't really believe us," he said. "That the sun wouldn't bother you. They put these blackout curtains up. But you should look."

Rising from the bed, Simon joined Jace at the window. And stared.

A few years ago his mother had taken him and his sister on a trip to Tuscany—a week of heavy, unfamiliar pasta dishes, unsalted bread, hardy brown countryside, and his mother speeding down narrow, twisting roads, barely avoiding crashing their Fiat into the beautiful old buildings they'd ostensibly come to see. He remembered stopping on a hillside just opposite a town called San Gimignano, a collection of rust-colored buildings dotted here and there with high towers whose tops soared upward as if reaching for the sky. If what he was looking at now reminded him of anything, it was that; but it was also so alien that it was genuinely unlike anything he'd ever seen before.

He was looking out of an upper window in what must have been a fairly tall house. If he glanced up, he could see stone eaves and sky beyond. Across the way was another house, not quite as tall as this one, and between them ran a narrow, dark canal, crossed here and there by bridges—the source of the water he'd heard before. The house seemed to be built partway up a hill—below it honey-colored stone houses, clustered along narrow streets, fell away to the edge of a green circle: woods, surrounded by hills that were very far away; from here they resembled long green and brown strips dotted with bursts of autumn colors. Behind the hills rose jagged mountains frosted with snow.

But none of that was what was strange; what was strange

was that here and there in the city, placed seemingly at random, rose soaring towers crowned with spires of reflective whitish-silvery material. They seemed to pierce the sky like shining daggers, and Simon realized where he had seen that material before: in the hard, glasslike weapons the Shadowhunters carried, the ones they called seraph blades.

"Those are the demon towers," Jace said, in response to Simon's unasked question. "They control the wards that protect the city. Because of them, no demon can enter Alicante."

The air that came in through the window was cold and clean, the sort of air you never breathed in New York City: It tasted of nothing, not dirt or smoke or metal or other people. Just air. Simon took a deep, unnecessary breath of it before he turned to look at Jace; some human habits died hard. "Tell me," he said, "that bringing me here was an accident. Tell me this wasn't somehow all part of you wanting to stop Clary from coming with you."

Jace didn't look at him, but his chest rose and fell once, quickly, in a sort of suppressed gasp. "That's right," he said. "I created a bunch of Forsaken warriors, had them attack the Institute and kill Madeleine and nearly kill the rest of us, just so that I could keep Clary at home. And lo and behold, my diabolical plan is working."

"Well, it is working," Simon said quietly. "Isn't it?"

"Listen, vampire," Jace said. "Keeping Clary from Idris was the plan. Bringing you here was not the plan. I brought you through the Portal because if I'd left you behind, bleeding and unconscious, the Forsaken would have killed you."

"You could have stayed behind with me—"

"They would have killed us both. I couldn't even tell how

many of them there were, not with the hellmist. Even I can't fight off a hundred Forsaken."

"And yet," Simon said, "I bet it pains you to admit that."

"You're an ass," Jace said, without inflection, "even for a Downworlder. I saved your life and I broke the Law to do it. Not for the first time, I might add. You could show a little gratitude."

"*Gratitude?*" Simon felt his fingers curl in against his palms. "If you hadn't dragged me to the Institute, I wouldn't be here. I never agreed to this."

"You did," said Jace, "when you said you'd do anything for Clary. *This* is anything."

Before Simon could snap back an angry retort, there was a knock on the door. "Hello?" Isabelle called from the other side. "Simon, is your diva moment over? I need to talk to Jace."

"Come in, Izzy." Jace didn't take his eyes off Simon; there was an electric anger in his gaze, and a sort of challenge that made Simon long to hit him with something heavy. Like a pickup truck.

Isabelle entered the room in a swirl of black hair and tiered silvery skirts. The ivory corset top she wore left her arms and shoulders, twined with inky runes, bare. Simon supposed it was a nice change of pace for her to be able to show her Marks off in a place where no one would think them out of the ordinary.

"Alec's going up to the Gard," Isabelle said without preamble. "He wants to talk to you about Simon before he leaves. Can you come downstairs?"

"Sure." Jace headed for the door; halfway there, he realized Simon was following him and turned with a glower. "You stay here."

"No," Simon said. "If you're going to be discussing me, I want to be there for it."

For a moment it looked as if Jace's icy calm were about to snap; he flushed and opened his mouth, his eyes flashing. Just as quickly, the anger vanished, tamped down by an obvious act of will. He gritted his teeth and smiled. "Fine," he said. "Come on downstairs, vampire. You can meet the whole happy family."

The first time Clary had gone through a Portal, there had been a sense of flying, of weightless tumbling. This time it was like being thrust into the heart of a tornado. Howling winds tore at her, ripped her hand from Luke's and the scream from her mouth. She fell whirling through the heart of a black and gold maelstrom.

Something flat and hard and silvery like the surface of a mirror rose up in front of her. She plunged toward it, shrieking, throwing her hands up to cover her face. She struck the surface and broke through, into a world of brutal cold and gasping suffocation. She was sinking through a thick blue darkness, trying to breathe, but she couldn't draw air into her lungs, only more of the freezing coldness—

Suddenly she was seized by the back of her coat and hauled upward. She kicked feebly but was too weak to break the hold on her. It drew her up, and the indigo darkness around her turned to pale blue and then to gold as she broke the surface of the water—it *was* water—and sucked in a gasp of air. Or tried to. Instead she choked and gagged, black spots dotting her vision. She was being dragged through the water, fast, weeds catching and tugging at her legs and arms—she twisted around in the grip that held her and caught a terrifying glimpse of something, not quite wolf and not quite human, ears as pointed as daggers and lips drawn back from sharp white teeth. She tried to scream, but only water came up.

A moment later she was out of the water and being flung onto damp hard-packed earth. There were hands on her shoulders, slamming her facedown against the ground. The hands struck her back, over and over, until her chest spasmed and she coughed up a bitter stream of water.

She was still choking when the hands rolled her onto her back. She was looking up at Luke, a black shadow against a high blue sky touched with white clouds. The gentleness she was used to seeing in his expression was gone; he was no longer wolflike, but he looked furious. He hauled her into a sitting position, shaking her hard, over and over, until she gasped and struck out at him weakly. "Luke! Stop it! You're hurting me—"

His hands left her shoulders. He grabbed her chin in one hand instead, forcing her head up, his eyes searching her face. "The water," he said. "Did you cough up all the water?"

"I think so," she whispered. Her voice came faintly from her swollen throat.

"Where's your stele?" he demanded, and when she hesitated, his voice sharpened. "Clary. Your stele. Find it."

She pulled away from his grasp and rummaged in her wet pockets, her heart sinking as her fingers scrabbled against nothing but damp material. She turned a miserable face up to Luke. "I think I must have dropped it in the lake." She sniffled. "My . . . my mother's stele . . ."

"Jesus, Clary." Luke stood up, clasping his hands distractedly behind his head. He was soaking wet too, water running off his jeans and heavy flannel coat in thick rivulets. The spectacles he usually wore halfway down his nose were gone. He looked down at her somberly. "You're all right," he said. It wasn't really a question. "I mean, right now. You feel all right?"

She nodded. "Luke, what's wrong? Why do we need my stele?"

Luke said nothing. He was looking around as if hoping to glean some assistance from their surroundings. Clary followed his gaze. They were on the wide dirt bank of a good-size lake. The water was pale blue, sparked here and there with reflected sunlight. She wondered if it was the source of the gold light she'd seen through the half-open Portal. There was nothing sinister about the lake now that she was next to it instead of in it. It was surrounded by green hills dotted with trees just beginning to turn russet and gold. Beyond the hills rose high mountains, their peaks capped in snow.

Clary shivered. "Luke, when we were in the water—did you go part wolf? I thought I saw—"

"My wolf self can swim better than my human self," Luke said shortly. "And it's stronger. I had to drag you through the water, and you weren't offering much help."

"I know," she said. "I'm sorry. You weren't—you weren't supposed to come with me."

"If I hadn't, you'd be dead now," he pointed out. "Magnus told you, Clary. You can't use a Portal to get into the Glass City unless you have someone waiting for you on the other side."

"He said it was against the Law. He didn't say if I tried to get there I'd *bounce off.*"

"He told you there are wards up around the city that prevent Portaling into it. It's not his fault you decided to play around with magic you just barely understand. Just because you have power doesn't mean you know how to use it." He scowled.

"I'm sorry," Clary said in a small voice. "It's just—where are we now?"

"Lake Lyn," said Luke. "I think the Portal took us as close to the city as it could and then dumped us. We're on the outskirts of Alicante." He looked around, shaking his head half in amazement and half in weariness. "You did it, Clary. We're in Idris."

"Idris?" Clary said, and stood staring stupidly out across the lake. It twinkled back at her, blue and undisturbed. "But—you said we were on the outskirts of Alicante. I don't see the city anywhere."

"We're miles away." Luke pointed. "You see those hills in the distance? We have to cross over those; the city is on the other side. If we had a car, we could get there in an hour, but we're going to have to walk, which will probably take all afternoon." He squinted up at the sky. "We'd better get going."

Clary looked down at herself in dismay. The prospect of a daylong hike in soaking-wet clothes did not appeal. "Isn't there anything else . . . ?"

"Anything else we can do?" Luke said, and there was a sudden sharp edge of anger to his voice. "Do you have any suggestions, Clary, since you're the one who brought us here?" He pointed away from the lake. "That way lie mountains. Passable on foot only in high summer. We'd freeze to death on the peaks." He turned, stabbed his finger in another direction. "That way lie miles of woods. They run all the way to the border. They're uninhabited, at least by human beings. Past Alicante there's farmland and country houses. Maybe we could get out of Idris, but we'd still have to pass through the city. A city, I may add, where Downworlders like myself are hardly welcome."

Clary looked at him with her mouth open. "Luke, I didn't know—"

"Of course you didn't know. You don't know anything about Idris. You don't even care about Idris. You were just upset about being left behind, like a child, and you had a tantrum. And now we're here. Lost and freezing and—" He broke off, his face tight. "Come on. Let's start walking."

Clary followed Luke along the edge of Lake Lyn in a miserable silence. As they walked, the sun dried her hair and skin, but the velvet coat held water like a sponge. It hung on her like a lead curtain as she tripped hastily over rocks and mud, trying to keep up with Luke's long-legged stride. She made a few further attempts at conversation, but Luke remained stubbornly silent. She'd never done anything so bad before that an apology hadn't softened Luke's anger. This time, it seemed, was different.

The cliffs rose higher around the lake as they progressed, pocked with spots of darkness, like splashes of black paint. As Clary looked more closely, she realized they were caves in the rock. Some looked like they went very deep, twisting away into darkness. She imagined bats and creepy-crawling things hiding in the blackness, and shivered.

At last a narrow path cutting through the cliffs led them to a wide road lined with crushed stones. The lake curved away behind them, indigo in the late afternoon sunlight. The road cut through a flat grassy plain that rose to rolling hills in the distance. Clary's heart sank; the city was nowhere in sight.

Luke was staring toward the hills with a look of intense

dismay on his face. "We're farther than I thought. It's been such a long time. . . ."

"Maybe if we found a bigger road," Clary suggested, "we could hitchhike, or get a ride to the city, or—"

"*Clary*. There are no cars in Idris." Seeing her shocked expression, Luke laughed without much amusement. "The wards foul up the machinery. Most technology doesn't work here—mobile phones, computers, the like. Alicante itself is lit—and powered—mostly by witchlight."

"Oh," Clary said in a small voice. "Well—about how far from the city *are* we?"

"Far enough." Without looking at her, Luke raked both his hands back through his short hair. "There's something I'd better tell you."

Clary tensed. All she'd wanted before was for Luke to talk to her; now she didn't want it anymore. "It's all right—"

"Did you notice," Luke said, "that there weren't any boats on Lake Lyn—no docks—nothing that might suggest the lake is used in any way by the people of Idris?"

"I just thought that was because it was so remote."

"It's not that remote. A few hours from Alicante on foot. The fact is, the lake—" Luke broke off and sighed. "Did you ever notice the pattern on the library floor at the Institute in New York?"

Clary blinked. "I did, but I couldn't figure out what it was."

"It was an angel rising out of a lake, holding a cup and a sword. It's a repeating motif in Nephilim decorations. The legend is that the angel Raziel rose out of Lake Lyn when he first appeared to Jonathan Shadowhunter, the first of the Nephilim, and gave him the Mortal Instruments. Ever since then the lake has been—"

"Sacred?" Clary suggested.

"Cursed," Luke said. "The water of the lake is in some way poisonous to Shadowhunters. It won't hurt Downworlders—the Fair Folk call it the Mirror of Dreams, and they drink its water because they claim it gives them true visions. But for a Shadowhunter to drink the water is very dangerous. It causes hallucinations, fever—it can drive a person to madness."

Clary felt cold all over. "That's why you tried to make me spit the water out."

Luke nodded. "And why I wanted you to find your stele. With a healing rune, we could stave off the water's effects. Without it, we need to get you to Alicante as quickly as possible. There are medicines, herbs, that will help, and I know someone who will almost certainly have them."

"The Lightwoods?"

"Not the Lightwoods." Luke's voice was firm. "Someone else. Someone I know."

"Who?"

He shook his head. "Let's just pray this person hasn't moved away in the last fifteen years."

"But I thought you said it was against the Law for Downworlders to come into Alicante without permission."

His answering smile was a reminder of the Luke who had caught her when she'd fallen off the jungle gym as a child, the Luke who had always protected her. "Some Laws were meant to be broken."

The Penhallows' house reminded Simon of the Institute—it had that same sense of belonging somehow to another era. The halls and stairways were narrow, made of stone and dark wood, and the windows were tall and thin, giving out onto views of the city. There was a distinctly Asian feel to the decorations: a shoji screen stood on the first-floor landing, and there were lacquer-flowered tall Chinese vases on the windowsills. There were also a number of silkscreen prints on the walls, showing what must have been scenes from Shadowhunter mythology, but with an Eastern feel to them—warlords wielding glowing seraph blades were prominently featured, alongside colorful dragonlike creatures and slithering, pop-eyed demons.

"Mrs. Penhallow—Jia—used to run the Beijing Institute. She splits her time between here and the Forbidden City," Isabelle said as Simon paused to examine a print. "And the Penhallows are an old family. Wealthy."

"I can tell," Simon muttered, looking up at the chandeliers, dripping cut-glass crystals like teardrops.

Jace, on the step behind them, grunted. "Move it along. We're not taking a historical tour here."

Simon weighed a rude retort and decided it wasn't worth bothering. He took the rest of the stairs at a rapid pace; they opened out at the bottom into a large room. It was an odd mixture of the old and the new: A glass picture window looked out onto the canal, and there was music playing from a stereo that Simon couldn't see. But there was no television, no stack of DVDs or CDs, the sort of detritus Simon associated with modern living rooms. Instead there were a number of overstuffed couches grouped around a large fireplace, in which flames were crackling.

Alec stood by the fireplace, in dark Shadowhunter gear, drawing on a pair of gloves. He looked up as Simon entered the room and scowled his habitual scowl, but said nothing.

Seated on the couches were two teenagers Simon had

never seen before, a boy and a girl. The girl was slender, with glossy dark hair pulled back from her face, and a mischievous expression. Her delicate chin narrowed into a point. She wasn't exactly pretty, but she was very striking.

The black-haired boy beside her was more than striking. He was probably Jace's height, but seemed taller, even sitting down; he was slender and muscular, with a pale, elegant, restless face, all cheekbones and dark eyes. There was something strangely familiar about him, as if Simon had met him before.

The girl spoke first. "Is that the vampire?" She looked Simon up and down as if she were taking his measurements. "I've never really been this close to a vampire before—not one I wasn't planning to kill, at least." She cocked her head to the side. "He's cute, for a Downworlder."

"You'll have to forgive her; she has the face of an angel and the manners of a Moloch demon," said the boy with a smile, getting to his feet. He held his hand out to Simon. "I'm Sebastian. Sebastian Verlac. And this is my cousin, Aline Penhallow. Aline—"

"I don't shake hands with Downworlders," Aline said, shrinking back against the couch cushions. "They don't have souls, you know. Vampires."

Sebastian's smile disappeared. "Aline—"

"It's true. That's why they can't see themselves in mirrors, or go in the sun."

Very deliberately, Simon stepped backward, into the patch of sunlight in front of the window. He felt the sun hot on his back, his hair. His shadow was cast, long and dark, across the floor, almost reaching Jace's feet.

Aline took a sharp breath but said nothing. It was Sebastian who spoke, looking at Simon with curious black eyes. "So it's true. The Lightwoods said, but I didn't think—"

"That we were telling the truth?" Jace said, speaking for the first time since they'd come downstairs. "We wouldn't lie about something like this. Simon's . . . unique."

"I kissed him once," Isabelle said, to no one in particular.

Aline's eyebrows shot up. "They really do let you do whatever you want in New York, don't they?" she said, sounding half-horrified and half-envious. "The last time I saw you, Izzy, you wouldn't even have considered—"

"The last time we all saw each other, Izzy was eight," Alec said. "Things change. Now, Mom had to leave here in a hurry, so someone has to take her notes and records up to the Gard for her. I'm the only one who's eighteen, so I'm the only one who *can* go while the Clave's in session."

"We know," Isabelle said, flopping down onto a couch. "You've already told us that, like, five times."

Alec, who was looking important, ignored this. "Jace, you brought the vampire here, so you're in charge of him. Don't let him go outside."

The vampire, Simon thought. It wasn't like Alec didn't know his name. He'd saved Alec's life once. Now he was "the vampire." Even for Alec, who was prone to the occasional fit of inexplicable sullenness, this was obnoxious. Maybe it had something to do with being in Idris. Maybe Alec felt a greater need to assert his Shadowhunter-ness here.

"*That's* what you brought me down here to tell me? Don't let the vampire go outside? I wouldn't have done that anyway." Jace slid onto the couch beside Aline, who looked pleased.

"You'd better hurry up to the Gard and back. God knows what depravity we might get up to here without your guidance."

Alec gazed at Jace with calm superiority. "Try to hold it together. I'll be back in half an hour." He vanished through an archway that led to a long corridor; somewhere in the distance, a door clicked shut.

"You shouldn't bait him," Isabelle said, shooting Jace a severe look. "They *did* leave him in charge."

Aline, Simon couldn't help but notice, was sitting very close to Jace, their shoulders touching, even though there was plenty of room around them on the couch. "Did you ever think that in a past life Alec was an old woman with ninety cats who was always yelling at the neighborhood kids to get off her lawn? Because I do," he said, and Aline giggled. "Just because he's the only one who can go to the Gard—"

"What's the Gard?" Simon asked, tired of having no idea what anyone was talking about.

Jace looked at him. His expression was cool, unfriendly; his hand was atop Aline's where it rested on her thigh. "Sit down," he said, jerking his head toward an armchair. "Or did you plan to hover in the corner like a bat?"

Great. Bat jokes. Simon settled himself uncomfortably in the chair.

"The Gard is the official meeting place of the Clave," Sebastian said, apparently taking pity on Simon. "It's where the Law is made, and where the Consul and Inquisitor reside. Only adult Shadowhunters are allowed onto its grounds when the Clave is in session."

"In session?" Simon asked, remembering what Jace had said earlier, upstairs. "You mean—not because of *me*?"

Sebastian laughed. "No. Because of Valentine and the Mortal Instruments. That's why everyone's here. To discuss what Valentine's going to do next."

Jace said nothing, but at the sound of Valentine's name, his face tightened.

"Well, he'll go after the Mirror," Simon said. "The third of the Mortal Instruments, right? Is it here in Idris? Is that why everyone's here?"

There was a short silence before Isabelle answered. "The thing about the Mirror is that no one knows where it is. In fact, no one knows *what* it is."

"It's a mirror," Simon said. "You know—reflective, glass. I'm just assuming."

"What Isabelle means," said Sebastian kindly, "is that nobody knows anything about the Mirror. There are multiple mentions of it in Shadowhunter histories, but no specifics about where it is, what it looks like, or, most important, what it does."

"We assume Valentine wants it," said Isabelle, "but that doesn't help much, since no one's got a clue where it is. None of the surviving Silent Brothers know."

"There are others who weren't in New York?" Simon demanded in surprise.

"The Bone City isn't really in New York," Isabelle said. "It's like—remember the entrance to the Seelie Court, in Central Park? Just because the entrance was there doesn't mean the Court itself is under the park. It's the same with the Bone City. There are various entrances, but the City itself—" Isabelle broke off as Aline shushed her with a quick gesture. Simon looked from her face to Jace's to Sebastian's. They all had the same guarded expression, as if they'd just realized what they'd been doing: telling Nephilim secrets to a Downworlder. A vampire. Not the enemy, precisely, but certainly someone who couldn't be trusted.

Aline was the first one to break the silence. Fixing her pretty, dark gaze on Simon, she said, "So—what's it like, being a vampire?"

"Aline!" Isabelle looked appalled. "You can't just go around asking people what it's like to be a vampire."

"I don't see why," Aline said. "He hasn't been a vampire that long, has he? So he must remember what it was like being a person." She turned back to Simon. "Does blood still taste like blood to you? Or does it taste like something else now, like orange juice or something? Because I would think the taste of blood would—"

"It tastes like chicken," Simon said, just to shut her up.

"Really?" Aline looked astonished.

"He's making fun of you, Aline," said Sebastian, "as well he should. I apologize for my cousin again, Simon. Those of us who were brought up outside Idris tend to have a little more familiarity with Downworlders."

"But weren't you brought up in Idris?" Isabelle asked. "I thought your parents—"

"Isabelle," Jace interrupted, but it was already too late; Sebastian's expression darkened.

"My parents are dead," he said. "A demon nest near Calais—it's all right, it was a long time ago." He waved away Isabelle's protestation of sympathy. "My aunt—my father's sister—brought me up at the Institute in Paris."

"So you speak French?" Isabelle sighed. "I wish *I* spoke another language. But Hodge never thought we needed to learn anything but ancient Greek and Latin, and nobody speaks those."

"I also speak Russian and Italian. And some Romanian," Sebastian said with a modest smile. "I could teach you some phrases—"

"Romanian? That's impressive," said Jace. "Not many people speak it."

"Do you?" Sebastian asked with interest.

"Not really," Jace said with a smile so disarming Simon knew he was lying. "My Romanian is pretty much limited to useful phrases like, 'Are these snakes poisonous?' and 'But you look much too young to be a police officer.'"

Sebastian didn't smile. There was something about his expression, Simon thought. It was mild—everything about him was calm—but Simon had the sense that the mildness hid something beneath it that belied his outward tranquility. "I do like traveling," he said, his eyes on Jace. "But it's good to be back, isn't it?"

Jace paused in the act of playing with Aline's fingers. "What do you mean?"

"Just that there's nowhere else quite like Idris, however much we Nephilim might make homes for ourselves elsewhere. Don't you agree?"

"Why are you asking me?" Jace's look was icy.

Sebastian shrugged. "Well, you lived here as a child, didn't you? And it's been years since you've been back. Or did I get that wrong?"

"You didn't get it wrong," Isabelle said impatiently. "Jace likes to pretend that everyone isn't talking about him, even when he knows they are."

"They certainly are." Though Jace was glaring at him, Sebastian seemed unruffled. Simon felt a sort of half-reluctant liking for the dark-haired Shadowhunter boy. It was rare to find someone who didn't react to Jace's taunts. "These days in Idris it's all anyone talks about. You, the Mortal Instruments, your father, your sister—"

"Clarissa was supposed to come with you, wasn't she?" Aline said. "I was looking forward to meeting her. What happened?"

Though Jace's expression didn't change, he drew his hand back from Aline's, curling it into a fist. "She didn't want to leave New York. Her mother's ill in the hospital." *He never says* our *mother*, Simon thought. *It's always* her *mother.*

"It's weird," Isabelle said. "I really thought she *wanted* to come."

"She did," said Simon. "In fact—"

Jace was on his feet, so fast that Simon didn't even see him move. "Come to think of it, I have something I need to discuss with Simon. In private." He jerked his head toward the double doors at the far end of the room, his eyes glittering a challenge. "Come on, vampire," he said, in a tone that left Simon with the distinct feeling that a refusal would probably end in some kind of violence. "Let's talk."

3

Amatis

By late afternoon Luke and Clary had left the lake far behind and were pacing over seemingly endless broad, flat swatches of high grass. Here and there a gentle rise reared up into a high hill topped with black rocks. Clary was exhausted from staggering up and down the hills, one after another, her boots slipping on the damp grass as if it were greased marble. By the time they left the fields behind for a narrow dirt road, her hands were bleeding and grass-stained.

Luke stalked ahead of her with determined strides. Occasionally he would point out items of interest in a somber voice, like the world's most depressed tour guide. "We just crossed Brocelind Plain," he said as they climbed a rise and saw a tangled expanse of dark trees stretching away toward the west, where the sun hung low in the sky. "This is the forest. The woods used to cover most of the lowland of the country. Much of it was cut down to make way for the city—and to clear out the wolf packs and vampire nests that tended to crop up there. Brocelind Forest has always been a hiding place for Downworlders."

They trudged along in silence as the road curved alongside the forest for several miles before taking an abrupt turn. The trees seemed to lift away as a ridge rose above them, and Clary blinked when they turned the corner of a high hill—unless her eyes were deceiving her, there were *houses* down there. Small, white rows of houses, orderly as a Munchkin village. "We're here!" she exclaimed, and darted forward, only stopping when she realized that Luke was no longer beside her.

She turned and saw him standing in the middle of the dusty road, shaking his head. "No," he said, moving to catch up with her. "That's not the city."

"Then is it a town? You said there weren't any towns near here—"

"It's a graveyard. It's Alicante's City of Bones. Did you think the City of Bones was the only resting place we had?" He sounded sad. "This is the necropolis, the place we bury those who die in Idris. You'll see. We have to walk through it to get to Alicante."

Clary hadn't been to a graveyard since the night Simon had died, and the memory gave her a bone-deep shiver as she passed along the narrow lanes that threaded among the mausoleums like white ribbon. Someone took care of this place: The marble gleamed as if freshly scrubbed, and the grass was evenly cut. There were bunches of white flowers laid here and there on the graves; she thought at first they were lilies, but they had a spicy, unfamiliar scent that made her wonder if they were native to Idris. Each tomb looked like a little house; some even had metal or wire gates, and the names of Shadowhunter families were carved over the doors. CARTWRIGHT. MERRYWEATHER. HIGHTOWER. BLACKWELL. MIDWINTER. She stopped at one: HERONDALE.

She turned to look at Luke. "That was the Inquisitor's name."

"This is her family tomb. Look." He pointed. Beside the door were white letters cut into the gray marble. They were names. MARCUS HERONDALE. STEPHEN HERONDALE. They had both died in the same year. Much as Clary had hated the Inquisitor, she felt something twist inside her, a pity she couldn't help. To lose your husband and your son, so close together . . . Three words in Latin ran under Stephen's name: AVE ATQUE VALE.

"What does that mean?" she asked, turning to Luke.

"It means 'Hail and farewell.' It's from a poem by Catullus. At some point it became what the Nephilim say during funerals, or when someone dies in battle. Now come on—it's better not to dwell on this stuff, Clary." Luke took her shoulder and moved her gently away from the tomb.

Maybe he was right, Clary thought. Maybe it was better not to think too much about death and dying right now. She kept her eyes averted as they made their way out of the necropolis. They were almost through the iron gates at the far end when she spotted a smaller mausoleum, growing like a white toadstool in the shadow of a leafy oak tree. The name above the door leaped out at her as if it had been written in lights.

FAIRCHILD.

"Clary—" Luke reached for her, but she was already gone. With a sigh he followed her into the tree's shadow, where she stood transfixed, reading the names of the grandparents and great-grandparents she had never even known she had. ALOYSIUS FAIRCHILD. ADELE FAIRCHILD, B. NIGHTSHADE. GRANVILLE FAIRCHILD. And below all those names: JOCELYN MORGENSTERN, B. FAIRCHILD.

A wave of cold went over Clary. Seeing her mother's name there was like revisiting the nightmares she had sometimes where she was at her mother's funeral and no one would tell her what had happened or how her mother had died.

"But she's not dead," she said, looking up at Luke. "She's not—"

"The Clave didn't know that," he told her gently.

Clary gasped. She could no longer hear Luke's voice or see him standing in front of her. Before her rose a jagged hillside, gravestones protruding from the dirt like snapped-off bones. A black headstone loomed up in front of her, letters cut unevenly into its face: CLARISSA MORGENSTERN, B. 1991 D. 2007. Under the words was a crudely drawn child's sketch of a skull with gaping eye sockets. Clary staggered backward with a scream.

Luke caught her by the shoulders. "Clary, what is it? What's wrong?"

She pointed. "There—look—"

But it was gone. The grass stretched out ahead of her, green and even, the white mausoleums neat and plain in their orderly rows.

She twisted to look up at him. "I saw my own gravestone," she said. "It said I was going to die—now—this year." She shuddered.

Luke looked grim. "It's the lake water," he said. "You're starting to hallucinate. Come on—we haven't got much time left."

Jace marched Simon upstairs and down a short hallway lined with doors; he paused only to straight-arm one of them open, a scowl on his face. "In here," he said, half-shoving Simon through the doorway. Simon saw what looked like a library inside: rows of bookshelves, long couches, and armchairs. "We should have some privacy—"

He broke off as a figure rose nervously from one of the armchairs. It was a little boy with brown hair and glasses. He had a small, serious face, and there was a book clutched in one of his hands. Simon was familiar enough with Clary's reading habits to recognize it as a manga volume even at a distance.

Jace frowned. "Sorry, Max. We need the room. Grown-up talk."

"But Izzy and Alec already kicked me out of the living room so they could have grown-up talk," Max complained. "Where am I supposed to go?"

Jace shrugged. "Your room?" He jerked a thumb toward the door. "Time to do your duty for your country, kiddo. Scram."

Looking aggrieved, Max stalked past them both, his book clutched to his chest. Simon felt a twinge of sympathy—it sucked to be old enough to want to know what was going on, but so young you were always dismissed. The boy shot him a look as he went past—a scared, suspicious glance. *That's the vampire*, his eyes said.

"Come on." Jace hustled Simon into the room, shutting and locking the door behind them. With the door closed the room was so dimly lit even Simon found it dark. It smelled like dust. Jace walked across the floor and threw open the curtains at the far end of the room, revealing a tall, single-paned picture window that gave out onto a view of the canal just outside. Water splashed against the side of the house below them, under stone railings carved with a weather-beaten design of runes and stars.

Jace turned to Simon with a scowl. "What the hell is your problem, vampire?"

"*My* problem? You're the one who practically dragged me out of there by my hair."

"Because you were about to tell them that Clary never canceled her plans to come to Idris. You know what would happen then? They'd contact her and arrange for her to come. And I already told you why that can't happen."

Simon shook his head. "I don't get you," he said. "Sometimes you act like all you care about is Clary, and then you act like—"

Jace stared at him. The air was full of dancing dust motes; they made a shimmering curtain between the two boys. "Act like what?"

"You were flirting with Aline," Simon said. "It didn't seem like all you cared about was Clary then."

"That is so not your business," Jace said. "And besides, Clary is my sister. You *do* know that."

"I was there in the faerie court too," Simon replied. "I remember what the Seelie Queen said. *The kiss that will free the girl is the kiss that she most desires.*"

"I bet you remember that. Burned into your brain, is it, vampire?"

Simon made a noise in the back of his throat that he hadn't even realized he was capable of making. "Oh, no you don't. I'm not having this argument. I'm not fighting over Clary with you. It's ridiculous."

"Then why did you bring all this up?"

"Because," Simon said. "If you want me to lie—not to Clary, but to all your Shadowhunter friends—if you want me to pretend that it was Clary's own decision not to come here, and if you want me to pretend that I don't know about her powers, or what she can really do, then *you* have to do something for me."

"Fine," Jace said. "What is it you want?"

Simon was silent for a moment, looking past Jace at the line of stone houses fronting the sparkling canal. Past their crenellated roofs he could see the gleaming tops of the demon towers. "I want you to do whatever you need to do to convince Clary that you don't have feelings for her. And don't—don't tell me you're her brother; I already know that. Stop stringing her along when you know that whatever you two have has no future. And I'm not saying this because I want her for myself. I'm saying it because I'm her friend and I don't want her hurt."

Jace looked down at his hands for a long moment without answering. They were thin hands, the fingers and knuckles scuffed with old calluses. The backs of them were laced with the thin white lines of old Marks. They were a soldier's hands, not a teenage boy's. "I've already done that," he said. "I told her I was only interested in being her brother."

"Oh." Simon had expected Jace to fight him on this, to argue, not to just *give up*. A Jace who just gave up was new—and left Simon feeling almost ashamed for having asked. *Clary never mentioned it to me*, he wanted to say, but then why would she have? Come to think of it, she had seemed unusually quiet and withdrawn lately whenever Jace's name had come up. "Well, that takes care of that, I guess. There's one last thing."

"Oh?" Jace spoke without much apparent interest. "And what's that?"

"What was it Valentine said when Clary drew that rune on the ship? It sounded like a foreign language. *Meme* something—?"

"*Mene mene tekel upharsin,*" Jace said with a faint smile. "You don't recognize it? It's from the Bible, vampire. The old one. That's your book, isn't it?"

"Just because I'm Jewish doesn't mean I've memorized the Old Testament."

"It's the Writing on the Wall. 'God hath numbered thy kingdom, and brought it to an end; thou art weighed in the balance and found wanting.' It's a portent of doom—it means the end of an empire."

"But what does that have to do with Valentine?"

"Not just Valentine," said Jace. "All of us. The Clave and the Law—what Clary can do overturns everything they know to be true. No human being can create new runes, or draw the sort of runes Clary can. Only angels have that power. And since Clary can do that—well, it seems like a portent. Things are changing. The Laws are changing. The old ways may never be the right ways again. Just as the rebellion of the angels ended the world as it was—it split heaven in half and created hell—this could mean the end of the Nephilim as they currently exist. This is our war in heaven, vampire, and only one side can win it. And my father means it to be his."

***

Though the air was still cold, Clary was boiling hot in her wet clothes. Sweat ran down her face in rivulets, dampening the collar of her coat as Luke, his hand on her arm, hurried her along the road under a rapidly darkening sky. They were within sight of Alicante now. The city was in a shallow valley, bisected by a silvery river that flowed into one end of the city, seemed to vanish, and flowed again out the other. A tumble of honey-colored buildings with red slate roofs and a tangle of steeply winding dark streets backed up against the side of a steep hill. On the crown of the hill rose a dark stone edifice, pillared and soaring, with a glittering tower at each cardinal direction point: four in all. Scattered among the other buildings were the same tall, thin, glasslike towers, each one shimmering like quartz. They were like glass needles piercing the sky. The fading sunlight struck dull rainbows from their surfaces like a match striking sparks. It was a beautiful sight, and very strange.

You have never seen a city till you have seen Alicante of the glass towers.

"What was that?" Luke said, overhearing. "What did you say?"

Clary hadn't realized she'd spoken out loud. Embarrassed, she repeated her words, and Luke looked at her in surprise. "Where did you hear that?"

"Hodge," Clary said. "It was something Hodge said to me."

Luke peered at her more closely. "You're flushed," he said. "How are you feeling?"

Clary's neck was aching, her whole body on fire, her mouth dry. "I'm fine," she said. "Let's just get there, okay?"

"Okay." Luke pointed; at the edge of the city, where the

buildings ended, Clary could see an archway, two sides curving to a pointed top. A Shadowhunter in black gear stood watch inside the shadow of the archway. "That's the North Gate—it's where Downworlders can legally enter the city, provided they've got the paperwork. Guards are posted there night and day. Now, if we were on official business, or had permission to be here, we'd go in through it."

"But there aren't any walls around the city," Clary pointed out. "It doesn't seem like much of a gate."

"The wards are invisible, but they're there. The demon towers control them. They have for a thousand years. You'll feel it when you pass through them." He glanced one more time at her flushed face, concern crinkling the corners of his eyes. "Are you ready?"

She nodded. They moved away from the gate, along the east side of the city, where buildings were more thickly clustered. With a gesture to be quiet, Luke drew her toward a narrow opening between two houses. Clary shut her eyes as they approached, almost as if she expected to be smacked in the face with an invisible wall as soon as they stepped onto the streets of Alicante. It wasn't like that. She felt a sudden pressure, as if she were in an airplane that was dropping. Her ears popped—and then the feeling was gone, and she was standing in the alley between the buildings.

Just like an alley in New York—like every alley in the world, apparently—it smelled like cat pee.

Clary peered around the corner of one of the buildings. A larger street stretched away up the hill, lined with small shops and houses. "There's no one around," she observed, with some surprise.

In the fading light Luke looked gray. "There must be a meeting going on up at the Gard. It's the only thing that could get everyone off the streets at once."

"But isn't that good? There's no one around to see us."

"It's good and bad. The streets are mostly deserted, which is good. But anyone who does happen by will be much more likely to notice and remark on us."

"I thought you said everyone was in the Gard."

Luke smiled faintly. "Don't be so literal, Clary. I meant most of the city. Children, teenagers, anyone exempted from the meeting, they won't be there."

Teenagers. Clary thought of Jace, and despite herself, her pulse leaped forward like a horse charging out of the starting gate at a race.

Luke frowned, almost as if he could read her thoughts. "As of now, I'm breaking the Law by being in Alicante without declaring myself to the Clave at the gate. If anyone recognizes me, we could be in real trouble." He glanced up at the narrow strip of russet sky visible between the rooftops. "We have to get off the streets."

"I thought we were going to your friend's house."

"We are. And she's not a friend, precisely."

"Then who—?"

"Just follow me." Luke ducked into a passage between two houses, so narrow that Clary could reach out and touch the walls of both houses with her fingers as they made their way down it and onto a cobblestoned winding street lined with shops. The buildings themselves looked like a cross between a Gothic dreamscape and a children's fairy tale. The stone facings were carved with all manner of creatures out of myth and legend—the heads of monsters were a prominent feature, interspersed with winged horses, something that looked like a house on chicken legs, mermaids, and, of course, angels. Gargoyles jutted from every corner, their snarling faces contorted. And everywhere there were runes: splashed across doors, hidden in the design of an abstract carving, dangling from thin metal chains like wind chimes that twisted in the breeze. Runes for protection, for good luck, even for good business; staring at them all, Clary began to feel a little dizzy.

They walked in silence, keeping to the shadows. The cobblestone street was deserted, shop doors shut and barred. Clary cast furtive glances into the windows as they passed. It was strange to see a display of expensive decorated chocolates in one window and in the next an equally lavish display of deadly-looking weapons—cutlasses, maces, nail-studded cudgels, and an array of seraph blades in different sizes. "No guns," she said. Her own voice sounded very far away.

Luke blinked at her. "What?"

"Shadowhunters," she said. "They never seem to use guns."

"Runes keep gunpowder from igniting," he said. "No one knows why. Still, Nephilim have been known to use the occasional rifle on lycanthropes. It doesn't take a rune to kill us—just silver bullets." His voice was grim. Suddently his head went up. In the dim light it was easy to imagine his ears pricking forward like a wolf's. "Voices," he said. "They must be finished at the Gard."

He took her arm and pulled her sideways off the main street. They emerged into a small square with a well at its center. A masonry bridge arched over a narrow canal just ahead of them. In the fading light the water in the canal looked almost black. Clary could hear the voices herself now, coming from the streets nearby. They were raised, angry-sounding. Clary's dizziness increased—she felt as if the ground were tilting under her, threatening to send her sprawling. She leaned back against the wall of the alley, gasping for air.

"Clary," Luke said. "Clary, are you all right?"

His voice sounded thick, strange. She looked at him, and the breath died in her throat. His ears had grown long and pointed, his teeth razor-sharp, his eyes a fierce yellow—

"Luke," she whispered. "What's happening to you?"

"Clary." He reached for her, his hands oddly elongated, the nails sharp and rust-colored. "Is something wrong?"

She screamed, twisting away from him. She wasn't sure why she felt so terrified—she'd seen Luke Change before, and he'd never harmed her. But the terror was a live thing inside her, uncontrollable. Luke caught at her shoulders and she cringed away from him, away from his yellow, animal eyes, even as he hushed her, begging her to be quiet in his ordinary, human voice. "Clary, please—"

"Let me go! Let me *go*!"

But he didn't. "It's the water—you're hallucinating—Clary, try to keep it together." He drew her toward the bridge, half-dragging her. She could feel tears running down her face, cooling her burning cheeks. "It's not real. Try to hold on, please," he said, helping her onto the bridge. She could smell the water below it, green and stale. *Things* moved below the surface of it. As she watched, a black tentacle emerged from the water, its spongy tip lined with needle teeth. She cringed away from the water, unable to scream, a low moaning coming from her throat.

Luke caught her as her knees buckled, swinging her up into his arms. He hadn't carried her since she was five or six years old. "Clary," he said, but the rest of his words melded and blurred into a nonsensical roar as they stepped down off the bridge. They raced past a series of tall, thin houses that almost reminded Clary of Brooklyn row houses—or maybe she was just hallucinating her own neighborhood? The air around them seemed to warp as they went on, the lights of the houses blazing up around them like torches, the canal shimmering with an evil phosphorescent glow. Clary's bones felt as if they were dissolving inside her body.

"Here." Luke jerked to a halt in front of a tall canal house. He kicked hard at the door, shouting; it was painted a bright, almost garish, red, a single rune splashed across it in gold. The rune melted and ran as Clary stared at it, taking the shape of a hideous grinning skull. *It's not real,* she told herself fiercely, stifling her scream with her fist, biting down until she tasted blood in her mouth.

The pain cleared her head momentarily. The door flew open, revealing a woman in a dark dress, her face creased with a mixture of anger and surprise. Her hair was long, a tangled gray-brown cloud escaping from two braids; her blue eyes were familiar. A witchlight rune-stone gleamed in her hand. "Who is it?" she demanded. "What do you want?"

"Amatis." Luke moved into the pool of witchlight, Clary in his arms. "It's me."

The woman blanched and tottered, putting out a hand to brace herself against the doorway. *"Lucian?"* Luke tried to take a step forward, but the woman—Amatis—blocked his path. She was shaking her head so hard that her braids whipped back and forth. "How can you come here, Lucian? How *dare* you come here?"

"I had very little choice." Luke tightened his hold on Clary. She bit back a cry. Her whole body felt as if it were on fire, every nerve ending burning with pain.

"You have to go, then," Amatis said. "If you leave immediately—"

"I'm not here for me. I'm here for the girl. She's dying." As the woman stared at him, he said, "Amatis, please. She's *Jocelyn's daughter.*"

There was a long silence, during which Amatis stood like a statue, unmoving, in the doorway. She seemed frozen, whether from surprise or horror Clary couldn't guess. Clary clenched her fist—her palm was sticky with blood where the nails dug in—but even the pain wasn't helping now; the world was coming apart in soft colors, like a jigsaw puzzle drifting on the surface of water. She barely heard Amatis's voice as the older woman stepped back from the doorway and said, "Very well, Lucian. You can bring her inside."

By the time Simon and Jace came back into the living room, Aline had laid food out on the low table between the couches. There was bread and cheese, slices of cake, apples, and even a bottle of wine, which Max was not allowed to touch. He sat in the corner with a plate of cake, his book open on his lap. Simon sympathized with him. He felt just as alone in the laughing, chatting group as Max probably did.

He watched Aline touch Jace's wrist with her fingers as she reached for a piece of apple, and felt himself tense. *But this is what you want him to do,* he told himself, and yet somehow he couldn't get rid of the sense that Clary was being disregarded.

Jace met his eyes over Aline's head and smiled. Somehow, even though he wasn't a vampire, he was able to manage a smile that seemed to be all pointed teeth. Simon looked away, glancing around the room. He noticed that the music he'd heard earlier wasn't coming from a stereo at all but from a complicated-looking mechanical contraption.

He thought about striking up a conversation with Isabelle, but she was chatting with Sebastian, whose elegant face was bent attentively down to hers. Jace had laughed at Simon's crush on Isabelle once, but Sebastian could doubtless handle her. Shadowhunters were brought up to handle anything, weren't they? Although the look on Jace's face when he'd said that he planned to be only Clary's brother made Simon wonder.

"We're out of wine," Isabelle declared, setting the bottle down on the table with a thump. "I'm going to get some more." With a wink at Sebastian, she disappeared into the kitchen.

"If you don't mind my saying so, you seem a little quiet." It was Sebastian, leaning over the back of Simon's chair with a disarming smile. For someone with such dark hair, Simon thought, Sebastian's skin was very fair, as if he didn't go out in the sun much. "Everything all right?"

Simon shrugged. "There aren't a lot of openings for me in the conversation. It seems to be either about Shadowhunter politics or people I've never heard of, or both."

The smile disappeared. "We can be something of a closed circle, we Nephilim. It's the way of those who are shut out from the rest of the world."

"Don't you think you shut yourselves out? You despise ordinary humans—"

"'Despise' is a little strong," said Sebastian. "And do you really think the world of humans would want anything to do with us? All we are is a living reminder that whenever they comfort themselves that there are no *real* vampires, no real demons or monsters under the bed—they're lying." He turned his head to look at Jace, who, Simon realized, had been staring at them both in silence for several minutes. "Don't you agree?"

Jace smiled. *"De ce crezi ca va ascultam conversatia?"*

Sebastian met his glance with a look of pleasant interest. *"M-ai urmărit de când ai ajuns aici,"* he replied. *"Nu-mi dau seama dacă nu mă placi ori daca eşti atât de bănuitor cu toată lumea."* He got to his feet. "I appreciate the Romanian practice, but if you don't mind, I'm going to see what's taking Isabelle so long in the kitchen." He disappeared through the doorway, leaving Jace staring after him with a puzzled expression.

"What's wrong? Does he not speak Romanian after all?" Simon asked.

"No," said Jace. A small frown line had appeared between his eyes. "No, he speaks it all right."

Before Simon could ask him what he meant by that, Alec entered the room. He was frowning, just as he had been when he'd left. His gaze lingered momentarily on Simon, a look almost of confusion in his blue eyes.

Jace glanced up. "Back so soon?"

"Not for long." Alec reached down to pluck an apple off the table with a gloved hand. "I just came back to get—him," he said, gesturing toward Simon with the apple. "He's wanted at the Gard."

Aline looked surprised. "Really?" she said, but Jace was already rising from the couch, disentangling his hand from hers.

"Wanted for what?" he said, with a dangerous calm. "I hope you found that out before you promised to deliver him, at least."

"Of course I *asked*," Alec snapped. "I'm not stupid."

"Oh, come on," said Isabelle. She had reappeared in the doorway with Sebastian, who was holding a bottle. "Sometimes you are a bit stupid, you know. Just a *bit*," she repeated as Alec shot her a murderous glare.

"They're sending Simon back to New York," he said. "Through the Portal."

"But he just *got* here!" Isabelle protested with a pout. "That's no fun."

"It's not supposed to be fun, Izzy. Simon coming here was an accident, so the Clave thinks the best thing is for him to go home."

"Great," Simon said. "Maybe I'll even make it back before my mother notices I'm gone. What's the time difference between here and Manhattan?"

"You have a *mother*?" Aline looked amazed.

Simon chose to ignore this. "Seriously," he said, as Alec and Jace exchanged glances. "It's fine. All I want is to get out of this place."

"You'll go with him?" Jace said to Alec. "And make sure everything's all right?"

They were looking at each other in a way that was familiar to Simon. It was the way he and Clary sometimes looked at each other, exchanging coded glances when they didn't want their parents to know what they were planning.

"What?" he said, looking from one to the other. "What's wrong?"

They broke their stare; Alec glanced away, and Jace turned a bland and smiling look on Simon. "Nothing," he said. "Everything's fine. Congratulations, vampire—you get to go home."

4

Daylighter

Night had fallen over Alicante when Simon and Alec left the Penhallows' house and headed uphill toward the Gard. The streets of the city were narrow and twisting, wending upward like pale stone ribbons in the moonlight. The air was cold, though Simon felt it only distantly.

Alec walked along in silence, striding ahead of Simon as if pretending that he were alone. In his previous life Simon would have had to hurry, panting, to keep up; now he discovered he could pace Alec just by speeding up his stride. "Must suck," Simon said finally, as Alec stared morosely ahead. "Getting stuck with escorting me, I mean."

Alec shrugged. "I'm eighteen. I'm an adult, so I have to be the responsible one. I'm the only one who can go in and out of the Gard when the Clave's in session, and besides, the Consul knows me."

"What's a Consul?"

"He's like a very high officer of the Clave. He counts the votes of the Council, interprets the Law for the Clave, and advises them and the Inquisitor. If you head up an Institute and you run into a problem you don't know how to deal with, you call the Consul."

"He advises the Inquisitor? I thought—isn't the Inquisitor dead?"

Alec snorted. "That's like saying, 'Isn't the president dead?' Yeah, the Inquisitor died; now there's a new one. Inquisitor Aldertree."

Simon glanced down the hill toward the dark water of the canals far below. They'd left the city behind them and were treading a narrow road between shadowy trees. "I'll tell you, inquisitions haven't worked out well for my people in the past." Alec looked blank. "Never mind. Just a mundane history joke. You wouldn't be interested."

"You're not a mundane," Alec pointed out. "That's why Aline and Sebastian were so excited to get a look at you. Not that you can tell with Sebastian; he always acts like he's seen everything already."

Simon spoke without thinking. "Are he and Isabelle . . . Is there something going on there?"

That startled a laugh out of Alec. "Isabelle and *Sebastian*? Hardly. Sebastian's a nice guy—Isabelle only likes dating thoroughly inappropriate boys our parents will hate. Mundanes, Downworlders, petty crooks . . ."

"Thanks," Simon said. "I'm glad to be classed with the criminal element."

"I think she does it for attention," Alec said. "She's the only girl in the family too, so she has to keep proving how tough she is. Or at least, that's what she thinks."

"Or maybe she's trying to take the attention off you," Simon said, almost absently. "You know, since your parents don't know you're gay and all."

Alec stopped in the middle of the road so suddenly that Simon almost crashed into him. "No," he said, "but apparently everyone *else* does."

"Except Jace," Simon said. "He doesn't know, does he?"

Alec took a deep breath. He was pale, Simon thought, or it could have just been the moonlight, washing the color out of everything. His eyes looked black in the darkness. "I really don't see what business it is of yours. Unless you're trying to threaten me."

"Trying to *threaten* you?" Simon was taken aback. "I'm not—"

"Then why?" said Alec, and there was a sudden, sharp vulnerability in his voice that took Simon aback. "Why bring it up?"

"Because," Simon said. "You seem to hate me most of the time. I don't take it that personally, even if I did save your life. You seem to kind of hate the whole world. And besides, we have practically nothing in common. But I see you looking at Jace, and I see myself looking at Clary, and I figure—maybe we have that one thing in common. And maybe it might make you dislike me a little less."

"So you're not going to tell Jace?" Alec said. "I mean—you told Clary how you felt, and . . ."

"And it wasn't the best idea," said Simon. "Now I wonder all the time how you go back after something like that. Whether we can ever be friends again, or if what we had is broken into pieces. Not because of her, but because of me. Maybe if I found someone else . . ."

"Someone else," Alec repeated. He had started walking again, very quickly, staring at the road ahead of him.

Simon hurried to keep up. "You know what I mean. For instance, I think Magnus Bane really likes you. And he's pretty cool. He throws great parties, anyway. Even if I did get turned into a rat that time."

"Thanks for the advice." Alec's voice was dry. "But I don't think he likes me all that much. He barely spoke to me when he came to open the Portal at the Institute."

"Maybe you should call him," Simon suggested, trying not to think too hard about how weird it was to be giving a demon hunter advice about possibly dating a warlock.

"Can't," Alec said. "No phones in Idris. It doesn't matter, anyway." His tone was abrupt. "We're here. This is the Gard."

A high wall rose in front of them, set with a pair of enormous gates. The gates were carved with the swirling, angular patterns of runes, and though Simon couldn't read them as Clary could, there was something dazzling in their complexity and the sense of power that emanated from them. The gates were guarded by stone angel statues on either side, their faces fierce and beautiful. Each held a carved sword in its hand, and a writhing creature—a mixture of rat, bat, and lizard, with nasty pointed teeth—lay dying at its feet. Simon stood looking at them for a long moment. Demons, he figured—but they could just as easily be vampires.

Alec pushed the gate open and gestured for Simon to pass through. Once inside, he blinked around in confusion. Since he'd become a vampire, his night vision had sharpened to a laserlike clarity, but the dozens of torches lining the path to the doors of the Gard were made of witchlight, and the harsh white glow seemed to bleach the detail out of everything. He was vaguely aware of Alec guiding him forward down a narrow stone pathway that shone with reflected illumination, and then there was someone standing on the path in front of him, blocking his way with an upraised arm.

"So this is the vampire?" The voice that spoke was deep enough to nearly be a growl. Simon looked up, the light making his eyes tear. *Witchlight*, he thought, *angel light, burns me. I suppose it's no surprise.*

The man standing in front of them was very tall, with sallow skin stretched over prominent cheekbones. Under a close-cropped dome of black hair, his forehead was high, his nose beaked and Roman. His expression as he looked down at Simon was the look of a subway commuter watching a large rat run back and forth on the rails, half-hoping a train will come along and squish it.

"This is Simon," said Alec, a little uncertainly. "Simon, this is Consul Malachi Dieudonné. Is the Portal ready, sir?"

"Yes," Malachi said. His voice was harsh and carried a faint accent. "Everything is in readiness. Come, Downworlder." He beckoned to Simon. "The sooner this is all over, the better."

Simon moved to go to the chief officer, but Alec stopped him with a hand on his arm. "Just a moment," he said, addressing the Consul. "He'll be sent directly back to Manhattan? And there will be someone waiting there on the other side for him?"

"Indeed," said Malachi. "The warlock Magnus Bane. Since

he unwisely allowed the vampire into Idris in the first place, he's taken responsibility for his return."

"If Magnus hadn't let Simon through the Portal, he would have died," Alec said, a little sharply.

"Perhaps," said Malachi. "That's what your parents say, and the Clave has chosen to believe them. Against my advice, in fact. Still, one does not lightly bring Downworlders into the City of Glass."

"There was nothing light about it." Anger surged in Simon's chest. "We were under attack—"

Malachi turned his gaze on Simon. "You will speak when you are spoken to, Downworlder, not before."

Alec's hand tightened on Simon's arm. There was a look on his face—half hesitation, half suspicion, as if he were doubting his wisdom in bringing Simon here after all.

"Now, Consul, *really*!" The voice carrying through the courtyard was high, a little breathless, and Simon saw with some surprise that it belonged to a man—a small, round man hurrying along the path toward them. He was wearing a loose gray cloak over his Shadowhunter gear, and his bald head glistened in the witchlight. "There's no need to alarm our guest."

"Guest?" Malachi looked outraged.

The small man came to a halt before Alec and Simon and beamed at them both. "We're so glad—pleased, really—that you decided to cooperate with our request that you return to New York. It does make everything so much easier." He twinkled at Simon, who stared back at him in confusion. He didn't think he'd ever met a Shadowhunter who seemed pleased to see him—not when he was a mundane, and definitely not now that he was a vampire. "Oh, I almost forgot!" The little man slapped himself on the forehead in remorse. "I should have introduced myself. I'm the Inquisitor—the *new* Inquisitor. Inquisitor Aldertree is my name."

Aldertree held his hand out to Simon, and in a welter of confusion Simon took it. "And you. Your name is Simon?"

"Yes," Simon said, drawing his hand back as soon as he could. Aldertree's grip was unpleasantly moist and clammy. "There's no need to thank me for cooperating. All I want is to go home."

"I'm sure you do, I'm sure you do!" Though Aldertree's tone was jovial, something flashed across his face as he spoke—an expression Simon couldn't pin down. It was gone in a moment, as Aldertree smiled and gestured toward a narrow path that wound alongside the Gard. "This way, Simon, if you please."

Simon moved forward, and Alec made as if to follow him. The Inquisitor held up a hand. "That's all we'll be needing from you, Alexander. Thank you for your help."

"But Simon—," Alec began.

"Will be just fine," the Inquisitor assured him. "Malachi, please show Alexander out. And give him a witchlight runestone to get him back home if he hasn't brought one. The path can be tricky at night."

And with another beatific smile, he whisked Simon away, leaving Alec staring after them both.

The world flared up around Clary in an almost tangible blur as Luke carried her over the threshold of the house and down a long hallway, Amatis hurrying ahead of them with her witchlight. More than half-delirious, she stared as the corridor unfolded before her, growing longer and longer like a corridor in a nightmare.

The world turned on its side. Suddenly she was lying on a cold surface, and hands were smoothing a blanket over her. Blue eyes gazed down at her. "She seems so ill, Lucian," Amatis said, in a voice that was warped and distorted like an old recording. "What happened to her?"

"She drank about half of Lake Lyn." The sound of Luke's voice faded, and for a moment Clary's vision cleared: She was lying on the cold tiled floor of a kitchen, and somewhere above her head Luke was rummaging in a cabinet. The kitchen had peeling yellow walls and an old-fashioned black cast-iron stove against one wall; flames leaped behind the stove grating, making her eyes hurt. "Anise, belladonna, hellebore . . ." Luke turned away from the cabinet with an armful of glass canisters. "Can you boil these together, Amatis? I'm going to move her closer to the stove. She's shivering."

Clary tried to speak, to say that she didn't need to be warmed, that she was burning up, but the sounds that came out of her mouth weren't the ones she'd intended. She heard herself whimper as Luke lifted her, and then there was heat, thawing her left side—she hadn't even realized she was cold. Her teeth clicked together hard, and she tasted blood in her mouth. The world began to tremble around her like water shaken in a glass.

"The Lake of Dreams?" Amatis's voice was full of disbelief. Clary couldn't see her clearly, but she seemed to be standing near the stove, a long-handled wooden spoon in her hand. "What were you doing there? Does Jocelyn know where—"

And the world was gone, or at least the real world, the

kitchen with the yellow walls and the comforting fire behind the grate. Instead she saw the waters of Lake Lyn, with fire reflected in them as if in the surface of a piece of polished glass. Angels were walking on the glass—angels with white wings that hung bloodied and broken from their backs, and each of them had Jace's face. And then there were other angels, with wings of black shadow, and they touched their hands to the fire and laughed. . . .

"She keeps calling out for her brother." Amatis's voice sounded hollow, as if filtering down from impossibly high overhead. "He's with the Lightwoods, isn't he? They're staying with the Penhallows on Princewater Street. I could—"

"No," Luke said sharply. "No. It's better Jace doesn't know about this."

Was I calling out for Jace? Why would I do that? Clary wondered, but the thought was short-lived; the darkness came back, and the hallucinations claimed her again. This time she dreamed of Alec and of Isabelle; both looked as if they'd been through a fierce battle, their faces streaked with grime and tears. Then they were gone, and she dreamed of a faceless man with black wings sprouting from his back like a bat's. Blood ran from his mouth when he smiled. Praying that the visions would vanish, Clary squeezed her eyes shut. . . .

It was a long time before she surfaced again to the sound of voices above her. "Drink this," Luke said. "Clary, you have to drink this," and then there were hands on her back and fluid was being dripped into her mouth from a soaked rag. It tasted bitter and awful and she choked and gagged on it, but the hands on her back were firm. She swallowed, past the pain in her swollen throat. "There," said Luke. "There, that should be better."

Clary opened her eyes slowly. Kneeling beside her were Luke and Amatis, their nearly identically blue eyes filled with matching concern. She glanced behind them and saw nothing—no angels or devils with bat wings, only yellow walls and a pale pink teakettle balanced precariously on a windowsill.

"Am I going to die?" she whispered.

Luke smiled haggardly. "No. It'll be a little while before you're back on form, but—you'll survive."

"Okay." She was too exhausted to feel much of anything, even relief. It felt as if all her bones had been removed, leaving a limp suit of skin behind. Looking up drowsily through her eyelashes, she said, almost without thinking, "Your eyes are the same."

Luke blinked. "The same as what?"

"As hers," Clary said, moving her sleepy gaze to Amatis, who looked perplexed. "The same blue."

The ghost of a smile passed over Luke's face. "Well, it's not that surprising, considering," he said. "I didn't get a chance to introduce you properly before. Clary, this is Amatis Herondale. My sister."

The Inquisitor fell silent the moment Alec and the chief officer were out of earshot. Simon followed him up the narrow witchlit path, trying not to squint into the light. He was aware of the Gard rising up around him like the side of a ship rising up out of the ocean; lights blazed from its windows, staining the sky with a silvery light. There were low windows too, set at ground level. Several were barred, and there was only darkness within.

At length they reached a wooden door set into an archway at the side of the building. Aldertree moved to free the lock, and Simon's stomach tightened. People, he'd noticed since he'd become a vampire, had a scent around them that changed with their moods. The Inquisitor stank of something bitter and strong as coffee, but much more unpleasant. Simon felt the prickling pain in his jaw that meant that his fang teeth wanted to come out, and shrank back from the Inquisitor as he passed through the door.

The hallway beyond was long and white, almost tunnel-like, as if it had been carved out of white rock. The Inquisitor hurried along, his witchlight bouncing brightly off the walls. For such a short-legged man he moved remarkably fast, turning his head from side to side as he went, his nose wrinkling as if he were smelling the air. Simon had to hurry to keep pace as they passed a set of huge double doors, thrown wide open like wings. In the room beyond, Simon could see an amphitheater with row upon row of chairs in it, each one occupied by a black-clad Shadowhunter. Voices echoed off the walls, many raised in anger, and Simon caught snatches of the conversation as he passed, the words blurring as the speakers overlapped each other.

"But we have no proof of what Valentine wants. He has communicated his wishes to no one—"

"What does it matter what he wants? He's a renegade and a liar; do you really think any attempt to appease him would benefit us in the end?"

"You know a patrol found the dead body of a werewolf child on the outskirts of Brocelind? Drained of blood. It looks like Valentine's completed the Ritual here in Idris."

"With two of the Mortal Instruments in his possession, he's more powerful than any one Nephilim has a right to be. We may have no choice—"

"My cousin died on that ship in New York! There's no way we're letting Valentine get away with what he's already done! There must be retribution!"

Simon hesitated, curious to hear more, but the Inquisitor was buzzing around him like a fat, irritable bee. "Come along, come along," he said, swinging his witchlight in front of him. "We don't have a lot of time to waste. I should get back to the meeting before it ends."

Reluctantly, Simon allowed the Inquisitor to push him along the corridor, the word "retribution" still ringing in his ears. The reminder of that night on the ship was cold, unpleasant. When they reached a door carved with a single stark black rune, the Inquisitor produced a key and unlocked it, ushering Simon inside with a broad gesture of welcome.

The room beyond was bare, decorated with a single tapestry that showed an angel rising out of a lake, clutching a sword in one hand and a cup in the other. The fact that he'd seen both the Cup and the Sword before momentarily distracted Simon. It wasn't until he heard the click of a lock sliding home that he realized the Inquisitor had bolted the door behind him, locking them both in.

Simon glanced around. There was no furniture in the room besides a bench with a low table beside it. A decorative silver bell rested on the table. "The Portal . . . It's in here?" he asked uncertainly.

"Simon, Simon." Aldertree rubbed his hands together as if anticipating a birthday party or some other delightful event. "Are you really in such a hurry to leave? There are a few questions I had so hoped to ask you first. . . ."

"Okay." Simon shrugged uncomfortably. "Ask me whatever you want, I guess."

"How very cooperative of you! How delightful!" Aldertree beamed. "So, how long is it exactly that you've been a vampire?"

"About two weeks."

"And how did it happen? Were you attacked on the street, or perhaps in your bed at night? Do you know who it was who Turned you?"

"Well—not exactly."

"But, my boy!" Aldertree cried. "How could you not know something like that?" The look he bent on Simon was open and curious. He seemed so harmless, Simon thought. Like someone's grandfather or funny old uncle. Simon must have imagined the bitter smell.

"It really wasn't that simple," said Simon, and went on to explain about his two trips to the Dumort, one as a rat and the second under a compulsion so strong it had felt like a giant set of pincers holding him in their grasp and marching him exactly where they wanted him to go. "And so you see," he finished, "the moment I walked in the door of the hotel, I was attacked—I don't know which of them it was who Turned me, or if it was all of them somehow."

The Inquisitor clucked. "Oh dear, oh dear. That's not good at all. That's very upsetting."

"I certainly thought so," Simon agreed.

"The Clave won't be pleased."

"What?" Simon was baffled. "What does the Clave care how I became a vampire?"

"Well, it would be one thing if you were attacked," Aldertree said apologetically. "But you just walked out there and, well, gave yourself up to the vampires, you see? It looks a bit as if you *wanted* to be one."

"I didn't want to be one! That's not why I went to the hotel!"

"Of course, of course." Aldertree's voice was soothing. "Let's move to another topic, shall we?" Without waiting for a response, he went on. "How is it that the vampires let you survive to rise again, young Simon? Considering that you trespassed on their territory, their normal procedure would have been to feed until you died, and then burn your body to prevent you from rising."

Simon opened his mouth to reply, to tell the Inquisitor how Raphael had taken him to the Institute, and how Clary and Jace and Isabelle had brought him to the cemetery and watched over him as he'd dug his way out of his own grave. Then he hesitated. He had only the vaguest idea how the Law worked, but he doubted somehow that it was standard Shadowhunter procedure to watch over vampires as they rose, or to provide them with blood for their first feeding. "I don't know," he said. "I have no idea why they Turned me instead of killing me."

"But one of them must have let you drink his blood, or you wouldn't be . . . well, what you are today. Are you saying you don't know who your vampire sire was?"

My vampire sire? Simon had never thought of it that way—he'd gotten Raphael's blood in his mouth almost by accident. And it was hard to think of the vampire boy as a sire of any sort. Raphael looked younger than Simon did. "I'm afraid not."

"Oh, dear." The Inquisitor sighed. "Most unfortunate."

"What's unfortunate?"

"Well, that you're lying to me, my boy." Aldertree shook his head. "And I had *so* hoped you'd cooperate. This is terrible, just terrible. You wouldn't *consider* telling me the truth? Just as a favor?"

"I *am* telling you the truth!"

The Inquisitor drooped like an unwatered flower. "Such a shame." He sighed again. "Such a shame." He crossed the room then and rapped sharply on the door, still shaking his head.

"What's going on?" Alarm and confusion tinged Simon's voice. "What about the Portal?"

"The Portal?" Aldertree giggled. "You didn't really think I was just going to let you *go*, did you?"

Before Simon could say a word in reply, the door burst open and Shadowhunters in black gear poured into the room, seizing hold of him. He struggled as strong hands clamped themselves around each of his arms. A hood was tugged down over his head, blinding him. He kicked out at the darkness; his foot connected, and he heard someone swear.

He was jerked backward viciously; a hot voice snarled in his ear. "Do that again, vampire, and I'll pour holy water down your throat and watch you die puking blood."

"That's enough!" The Inquisitor's thin, worried voice rose like a balloon. "There will be no more threats! I'm just trying to teach our guest a lesson." He must have moved forward, because Simon smelled the strange, bitter smell again, muffled through the hood. "Simon, Simon," Aldertree said. "I did so enjoy meeting you. I hope a night in the cells of the Gard will have the desired effect and in the morning you'll be a bit more cooperative. I do still see such a bright future for us, once we get over this little hiccup." His hand came down on Simon's shoulder. "Take him downstairs, Nephilim."

Simon yelled aloud, but his cries were muffled by the hood. The Shadowhunters dragged him from the room and propelled him down what felt like an endless series of mazelike corridors, twisting and turning. Eventually they reached a set of stairs and he was shoved down it by main force, his feet slipping on the steps. He couldn't tell anything about where they were—except that there was a close, dark smell around them, like wet stone, and that the air was growing wetter and colder as they descended.

At last they paused. There was a scraping sound, like iron dragging over stone, and Simon was thrown forward to land on his hands and knees on hard ground. There was a loud, metallic clang, as of a door being slammed shut, and the sound of retreating footsteps, the echo of boots on stone growing fainter as Simon staggered to his feet. He dragged the hood from his head and threw it to the ground. The close, hot, suffocating feeling around his face vanished, and he fought the urge to gasp for breath—breath he didn't need. He knew it was just a reflex, but his chest ached as if he'd really been deprived of air.

He was in a square barren stone room, with just a single barred window set into the wall above the small, hard-looking bed. Through a low door Simon could see a tiny bathroom with a sink and toilet. The west wall of the room was also barred—thick, iron-looking bars running from floor to ceiling, sunk deeply into the floor. A hinged iron door, made of bars itself, was set into the wall; it was fitted with a brass knob, which was carved across its face with a dense black rune. In fact, all the bars were carved with runes; even the window bars were wrapped with spidery lines of them.

Though he knew the cell door must be locked, Simon couldn't help himself; he strode across the floor and seized the knob. A searing pain shot through his hand. He yelled and jerked his arm back, staring. Thin wisps of smoke rose from his burned palm; an intricate design had been charred into the skin. It looked a little like a Star of David inside a circle, with delicate runes drawn in each of the hollow spaces between the lines.

The pain felt like white heat. Simon curled his hand in on itself as a gasp rose to his lips. "What *is* this?" he whispered, knowing no one could hear him.

"It's the Seal of Solomon," said a voice. "It contains, they claim, one of the True Names of God. It repels demons—and your kind as well, being an article of your faith."

Simon jerked upright, half-forgetting the pain in his hand. "Who's there? Who said that?"

There was a pause. Then, "I'm in the cell next to yours, Daylighter," said the voice. It was male, adult, slightly hoarse. "The guards were here half the day talking about how to keep you penned in. So I wouldn't bother trying to get it open. You're better off saving your strength till you find out what the Clave wants from you."

"They can't hold me here," Simon protested. "I don't belong to this world. My family will notice I'm missing—my teachers—"

"They've taken care of that. There are simple enough spells—a beginning warlock could use them—that will supply your parents with the illusion that there's a perfectly legitimate reason for your absence. A school trip. A visit to family. It can be done." There was no threat in the voice, and no sorrow; it was matter-of-fact. "Do you really think they've never made a Downworlder disappear before?"

"Who are you?" Simon's voice cracked. "Are you a Downworlder too? Is this where they keep us?"

This time there was no answer. Simon called out again, but

his neighbor had evidently decided that he'd said all he wanted to say. Nothing answered Simon's cries but silence.

The pain in his hand had faded. Looking down, Simon saw that the skin no longer looked burned, but the mark of the Seal was printed on his palm as if it had been drawn there in ink. He looked back at the cell bars. He realized now that not all the runes were runes at all: Carved between them were Stars of David and lines from the Torah in Hebrew. The carvings looked new.

The guards were here half the day talking about how to keep you penned in, the voice had said.

But it hadn't just been because he was a vampire, laughably; it had partly been because he was Jewish. They had spent half the day carving the Seal of Solomon into that doorknob so it would burn him when he touched it. It had taken them this long to turn the articles of his faith against him.

For some reason the realization stripped away the last of Simon's self-possession. He sank down onto the bed and put his head in his hands.

Princewater Street was dark when Alec returned from the Gard, the windows of the houses shuttered and shaded, only the occasional witchlight streetlamp casting a pool of white illumination onto the cobblestones. The Penhallows' house was the brightest on the block—candles glowed in the windows, and the front door was slightly ajar, letting a slice of yellow light out to curve along the walkway.

Jace was sitting on the low stone wall that bordered the Penhallows' front garden, his hair very bright under the light of the nearest streetlamp. He looked up as Alec approached, and shivered a little. He was wearing only a light jacket, Alec saw, and it had grown cold since the sun had gone down. The smell of late roses hung in the chilly air like thin perfume.

Alec sank down onto the wall beside Jace. "Have you been out here waiting for me all this time?"

"Who says I'm waiting for you?"

"It went fine, if that's what you were worried about. I left Simon with the Inquisitor."

"You *left* him? You didn't stay to make sure everything went all right?"

"It was fine," Alec repeated. "The Inquisitor said he'd take him inside personally and send him back to—"

"The Inquisitor said, the Inquisitor said," Jace interrupted. "The last Inquisitor we met completely exceeded her command—if she hadn't died, the Clave would have relieved her of her position, maybe even cursed her. What's to say this Inquisitor isn't a nut job too?"

"He seemed all right," said Alec. "Nice, even. He was perfectly polite to Simon. Look, Jace—this is how the Clave works. We don't get to control everything that happens. But you have to trust them, because otherwise everything turns into chaos."

"But they've screwed up a lot recently—you have to admit that."

"Maybe," Alec said, "but if you start thinking you know better than the Clave and better than the Law, what makes *you* any better than the Inquisitor? Or Valentine?"

Jace flinched. He looked as if Alec had hit him, or worse.

Alec's stomach dropped. "I'm sorry." He reached out a hand. "I didn't mean that—"

A beam of bright yellow light cut across the garden suddenly. Alec looked up to see Isabelle framed in the open front door, light pouring out around her. She was only a silhouette, but he could tell from the hands on her hips that she was annoyed. "What are you two *doing* out here?" she called. "Everyone's wondering where you are."

Alec turned back to his friend. "Jace—"

But Jace, getting to his feet, ignored Alec's outstretched hand. "You'd better be right about the Clave," was all he said.

Alec watched as Jace stalked back to the house. Unbidden, Simon's voice came into his mind. *Now I wonder all the time how you go back after something like that. Whether we can ever be friends again, or if what we had is broken into pieces. Not because of her, but because of me.*

The front door shut, leaving Alec sitting in the half-lit garden, alone. He closed his eyes for a moment, the image of a face hovering behind his lids. Not Jace's face, for a change. The eyes set in the face were green, slit-pupiled. Cat eyes.

Opening his eyes, he reached into his satchel and drew out a pen and a piece of paper, torn from the spiral-bound notebook he used as a journal. He wrote a few words on it and then, with his stele, traced the rune for fire at the bottom of the page. It went up faster than he'd thought it would; he let go of the paper as it burned, floating in midair like a firefly. Soon all that was left was a fine drift of ash, sifting like white powder across the rosebushes.

5

A Problem of Memory

Afternoon light woke Clary, a beam of pale brightness that laid itself directly over her face, lighting the insides of her eyelids to hot pink. She stirred restlessly and warily opened her eyes.

The fever was gone, and so was the sense that her bones were melting and breaking inside her. She sat up and glanced around with curious eyes. She was in what had to be Amatis's spare room—it was small, white-painted, the bed covered with a brightly woven rag blanket. Lace curtains were drawn back over the windows, letting in shafts of light. She sat up slowly, waiting for dizziness to wash over her. Nothing happened. She felt entirely healthy, even well rested. Getting out of bed, she looked down at herself. Someone had put her in a pair of starched white pajamas, though they were wrinkled now and too big for her; the sleeves hung down comically past her fingers.

She went to one of the circular windows and peered out. Stacked houses of old-gold stone rose up the side of a hill, and the roofs looked as if they had been shingled in bronze. This side of the house faced away from the canal, onto a narrow side garden turning brown and gold with autumn. A trellis crawled up the side of the house; a single last rose hung on it, drooping browning petals.

The doorknob rattled, and Clary climbed hastily back into bed just before Amatis entered, holding a tray in her hands. She raised her eyebrows when she saw Clary was awake, but said nothing.

"Where's Luke?" Clary demanded, drawing the blanket close around herself for comfort.

Amatis set the tray down on the table beside the bed. There was a mug of something hot on it, and some slices of buttered bread. "You should eat something," she said. "You'll feel better."

"I feel fine," Clary said. "Where's Luke?"

There was a high-backed chair beside the table; Amatis sat in it, folded her hands in her lap, and regarded Clary calmly. In the daylight Clary could see more clearly the lines in her face—she looked older than Clary's mother by many years, though they couldn't be that far apart in age. Her brown hair was stippled with gray, her eyes rimmed with dark pink, as if she had been crying. "He's not here."

"Not here like he just popped around the corner to the bodega for a six-pack of Diet Coke and a box of Krispy Kremes, or not here like . . ."

"He left this morning, around dawn, after sitting up with you all night. As to his destination, he wasn't specific." Amatis's tone was dry, and if Clary hadn't felt so wretched, she might have been amused to note that it made her sound much more like Luke. "When he lived here, before he left Idris, after he was . . . Changed . . . he led a wolf pack that made its home in Brocelind Forest. He said he was going back to them, but he wouldn't say why or for how long—only that he'd be back in a few days."

"He just . . . left me here? Am I supposed to sit around and wait for him?"

"Well, he couldn't very well take you with him, could he?" Amatis asked. "And it won't be easy for you to get home. You broke the Law in coming here like you did, and the Clave won't overlook that, or be generous about letting you leave."

"I don't want to go home." Clary tried to collect herself. "I came here to . . . to meet someone. I have something to do."

"Luke told me," said Amatis. "Let me give you a piece of advice—you'll only find Ragnor Fell if he wants to be found."

"But—"

"Clarissa." Amatis looked at her speculatively. "We're expecting an attack by Valentine at any moment. Almost every Shadowhunter in Idris is here in the city, inside the wards. Staying in Alicante is the safest thing for you."

Clary sat frozen. Rationally, Amatis's words made sense, but it didn't do much to quiet the voice inside her screaming that she couldn't wait. She had to find Ragnor Fell *now*; she had to save her mother *now*, she had to go *now*. She bit down on her panic and tried to speak casually. "Luke never told me he had a sister."

"No," Amatis said. "He wouldn't have. We weren't—close."

"Luke said your last name was Herondale," Clary said. "But that's the Inquisitor's last name. Isn't it?"

"It was," said Amatis, and her face tightened as if the words pained her. "She was my mother-in-law."

What was it Luke had told Clary about the Inquisitor? That she'd had a son, who'd married a woman with "undesirable family connections." "You were married to Stephen Herondale?"

Amatis looked surprised. "You know his name?"

"I do—Luke told me—but I thought his wife died. I thought that's why the Inquisitor was so—" *Horrible*, she wanted to say, but it seemed cruel to say it. "Bitter," she said at last.

Amatis reached for the mug she'd brought; her hand shook a little as she lifted it. "Yes, she did die. Killed herself. That was Céline—Stephen's second wife. I was the first."

"And you got divorced?"

"Something like that." Amatis thrust the mug at Clary. "Look, drink this. You have to put something in your stomach."

Distracted, Clary took the mug and swallowed a hot mouthful. The liquid inside was rich and salty—not tea, as she'd thought, but soup. "Okay," she said. "So what happened?"

Amatis was gazing into the distance. "When Luke was—when what happened to Luke happened, Valentine needed a new lieutenant. He chose Stephen—we had both recently joined the Circle. And when he chose Stephen, he decided that perhaps it wouldn't be fitting for the wife of his closest friend and adviser to be someone whose brother was . . ."

"A werewolf."

"He used another word." Amatis sounded bitter. "He convinced Stephen to annul our marriage and to find himself another wife, one that Valentine had picked for him. Céline was so young—so completely obedient."

"That's horrible."

Amatis shook her head with a brittle laugh. "It was a long time ago. Stephen was kind, I suppose—he gave me this house and moved back into the Herondale manor with his parents and Céline. I never saw him again after that. I left the Circle, of course. They wouldn't have wanted me anymore. The only one of them who still visited me was Jocelyn. She even told me when she went to see Luke. . . ." She pushed her graying hair back behind her ears. "I heard about Stephen's death days after it happened. And Céline—I'd hated her, but I felt sorry for her then. She cut her wrists, they say—blood everywhere—" She took a deep breath. "I saw Imogen later at Stephen's funeral, when they put his body into the Herondale mausoleum. She didn't even seem to recognize me. They made her the Inquisitor not long after that. The Clave felt there was no one else who would have hunted down the former members of the Circle more ruthlessly than she did—and they were right. If she could have washed away her memories of Stephen in their blood, she would have."

Clary thought of the cold eyes of the Inquisitor, her narrow, hard stare, and tried to feel pity for her. "I think it made her crazy," she said. "Really crazy. She was horrible to me—but mostly to Jace. It was like she wanted him dead."

"That makes sense," said Amatis. "You look like your mother, and your mother brought you up, but your brother—" She cocked her head to the side. "Does he look as much like Valentine as you look like Jocelyn?"

"No," Clary said. "Jace just looks like himself." A shiver went through her at the thought of Jace. "He's here in Alicante," she said, thinking out loud. "If I could see him—"

"No." Amatis spoke with asperity. "You can't leave the house. Not to see anyone. And definitely not to see your brother."

"Not leave the house?" Clary was horrified. "You mean I'm stuck here? Like a prisoner?"

"It's only for a day or two," Amatis admonished her, "and besides, you're not well. You need to recover. The lake water nearly killed you."

"But Jace—"

"Is one of the Lightwoods. You can't go over there. The moment they see you, they'll tell the Clave you're here. And then you won't be the only one in trouble with the Law. Luke will be too."

But the Lightwoods won't betray me to the Clave. They wouldn't do that—

The words died on her lips. There was no way she was going to be able to convince Amatis that the Lightwoods she'd known fifteen years ago no longer existed, that Robert and Maryse weren't blindly loyal fanatics anymore. This woman might be Luke's sister, but she was still a stranger to Clary. She was almost a stranger to Luke. He hadn't seen her in sixteen years—had never even mentioned she existed. Clary leaned back against the pillows, feigning weariness. "You're right," she said. "I don't feel well. I think I'd better sleep."

"Good idea." Amatis leaned over and plucked the empty mug out of her hand. "If you want to take a shower, the bathroom's across the hall. And there's a trunk of my old clothes at the foot of the bed. You look like you're about the size I was when I was your age, so they might fit you. Unlike those pajamas," she added, and smiled, a weak smile that Clary didn't return. She was too busy fighting the urge to pound her fists against the mattress in frustration.

The moment Amatis's footsteps faded away, Clary scrambled out of bed and headed for the bathroom, hoping that standing in hot water would help clear her head. To her relief, for all their old-fashionedness, the Shadowhunters seemed to believe in modern plumbing and hot and cold running water. There was even sharply scented citrus soap to rinse the lingering smell of Lake Lyn out of her hair. By the time she emerged, wrapped in two towels, she was feeling much better.

In the bedroom she rummaged through Amatis's trunk. Her clothes were packed away neatly between layers of crisp paper. There were what looked like school clothes—merino wool sweaters with an insignia that looked like four *C*s back to back sewed over the breast pocket, pleated skirts, and button-down shirts with narrow cuffs. There was a white dress swathed in layers of tissue paper—a wedding dress, Clary thought, and laid it aside carefully. Below it was another dress, this one made of silvery silk, with slender bejeweled straps holding up its gossamer weight. Clary couldn't imagine Amatis in it, but—*This is the sort of thing my mother might have worn when she went dancing with Valentine*, she couldn't help thinking, and let the dress slide back into the trunk, its texture soft and cool against her fingers.

And then there was the Shadowhunter gear, packed away at the very bottom.

Clary drew out those clothes and spread them curiously

across her lap. The first time she had seen Jace and the Lightwoods, they had been wearing their fighting gear: close-fitting tops and pants of tough, dark material. Up close she could see that the material was not stretchy but stiff, a thin leather pounded very flat until it became flexible. There was a jacket-type top that zipped up and pants that had complicated belt loops. Shadowhunter belts were big, sturdy things, meant for hanging weapons on.

She ought, of course, to put on one of the sweaters and maybe a skirt. That was what Amatis had probably meant her to do. But something about the fighting gear called to her; she had *always* been curious, always wondered what it would be like. . . .

A few minutes later the towels were hanging over the bar at the foot of the bed and Clary was regarding herself in the mirror with surprise and not a little amusement. The gear fit—it was tight but not too tight, and hugged the curves of her legs and chest. In fact, it made her look as if she *had* curves, which was sort of novel. It couldn't make her look formidable—she doubted anything could do that—but at least she looked taller, and her hair against the black material was extraordinarily bright. In fact—*I look like my mother*, Clary thought with a jolt.

And she did. Jocelyn had always had a steely core of toughness under her doll-like looks. Clary had often wondered what had happened in her mother's past to make her the way she was—strong and unbending, stubborn and unafraid. *Does your brother look as much like Valentine as you look like Jocelyn?* Amatis had asked, and Clary had wanted to reply that she didn't look at all like her mother, that her mother was beautiful and she wasn't. But the Jocelyn that Amatis had known was the girl who'd plotted to bring down Valentine, who'd secretly forged an alliance of Nephilim and Downworlders that had broken the Circle and saved the Accords. *That* Jocelyn would never have agreed to stay quietly inside this house and wait while everything in her world fell apart.

Without pausing to think, Clary crossed the room and shot home the bolt on the door, locking it. Then she went to the window and pushed it open. The trellis was there, clinging to the side of the stone wall like—*Like a ladder*, Clary told herself. *Just like a ladder—and ladders are perfectly safe.*

Taking a deep breath, she crawled out onto the window ledge.

The guards came back for Simon the next morning, shaking him awake out of an already fitful sleep plagued with strange dreams. This time they didn't blindfold him as they led him back upstairs, and he snuck a quick glance through the barred door of the cell next to his. If he'd hoped to get a look at the owner of the hoarse voice that had spoken to him the night before, he was disappointed. The only thing visible through the bars was what looked like a pile of discarded rags.

The guards hurried Simon along a series of gray corridors, quick to shake him if he looked too long in any direction. Finally they came to a halt in a richly wallpapered room. There were portraits on the walls of different men and women in Shadowhunter gear, the frames decorated with patterns of runes. Below one of the largest portraits was a red couch on which the Inquisitor was seated, holding what looked like a silver cup in his hand. He held it out to Simon. "Blood?" he inquired. "You must be hungry by now."

He tipped the cup toward Simon, and the view of the red

liquid inside it hit him just as the smell did. His veins strained toward the blood, like strings under the control of a master puppeteer. The feeling was unpleasant, almost painful. "Is it . . . human?"

Aldertree chuckled. "My boy! Don't be ridiculous. It's deer blood. Perfectly fresh."

Simon said nothing. His lower lip stung where his fangs had slid from their sheaths, and he tasted his own blood in his mouth. It filled him with nausea.

Aldertree's face screwed up like a dried plum. "Oh, dear." He turned to the guards. "Leave us now, gentlemen," he said, and they turned to go. Only the Consul paused at the door, glancing back at Simon with a look of unmistakable disgust.

"No, thank you," Simon said through the thickness in his mouth. "I don't want the blood."

"Your fangs say otherwise, young Simon," Aldertree replied genially. "Here. Take it." He held out the cup, and the smell of blood seemed to waft through the room like the scent of roses through a garden.

Simon's incisors stabbed downward, fully extended now, slicing into his lip. The pain was like a slap; he moved forward, almost without volition, and grabbed the cup out of the Inquisitor's hand. He drained it in three swallows, then, realizing what he had done, set it down on the arm of the couch. His hand was shaking. *Inquisitor one*, he thought. *Me zero*.

"I trust your night in the cells wasn't too unpleasant? They're not meant to be torture chambers, my boy, more along the lines of a space for enforced reflection. I find reflection absolutely centers the mind, don't you? Essential to clear thinking. I do hope you got some thinking in. You seem like a thoughtful young man." The Inquisitor cocked his head to the side. "I brought that blanket down for you with my own hands, you know. I wouldn't have wanted you to be cold."

"I'm a vampire," Simon said. "We don't get cold."

"Oh." The Inquisitor looked disappointed.

"I appreciated the Stars of David and the Seal of Solomon," Simon added dryly. "It's always nice to see someone taking an interest in my religion."

"Oh, yes, of course, of course!" Aldertree brightened. "Wonderful, aren't they, the carvings? Absolutely charming, and of course foolproof. I'd imagine any attempt to touch the cell door would melt the skin right off your hand!" He chuckled, clearly amused by the thought. "In any case. Could you take a step backward for me, my man? Just as a favor, a pure favor, you understand."

Simon took a step back.

Nothing happened, but the Inquisitor's eyes widened, the puffy skin around them looking stretched and shiny. "I see," he breathed.

"You see what?"

"Look where you are, young Simon. Look all about you."

Simon glanced around—nothing had changed about the room, and it took a moment for him to realize what Aldertree meant. He was standing in a bright patch of sun that angled through a window high overhead.

Aldertree was almost squirming with excitement. "You're standing in direct sunlight, and it's having no effect on you at all. I almost wouldn't have believed it—I mean, I was told, of course, but I've never seen anything like it before."

Simon said nothing. There seemed to be nothing to say.

"The question for you, of course," Aldertree went on, "is whether you know why you're like this."

"Maybe I'm just nicer than the other vampires." Simon was immediately sorry he'd spoken. Aldertree's eyes narrowed, and a vein bulged at his temple like a fat worm. Clearly, he didn't like jokes unless he was the one making them.

"Very amusing, very amusing," he said. "Let me ask you this: Have you been a Daylighter since the moment you rose from the grave?"

"No." Simon spoke with care. "No. At first the sun burned me. Even just a patch of sunlight would scorch my skin."

"Indeed." Aldertree gave a vigorous nod, as if to say that that was the way things ought to be. "So when was it you first noticed that you could walk in the daylight without pain?"

"It was the morning after the big battle on Valentine's ship—"

"During which Valentine captured you, is that correct? He had captured you and kept you prisoner on his ship, meaning to use your blood to complete the Ritual of Infernal Conversion."

"I guess you know everything already," Simon said. "You hardly need me."

"Oh, no, not at all!" Aldertree cried, throwing up his hands. He had very small hands, Simon noticed, so small that they looked a little out of place at the ends of his plump arms. "You have so much to contribute, my dear boy! For instance, I can't help wondering if there was something that happened on the ship, something that *changed* you. Is there anything you can think of?"

I drank Jace's blood, Simon thought, half-inclined to repeat this to the Inquisitor just to be nasty—and then, with a jolt, realized, *I drank Jace's blood.* Could that have been what changed him? Was it possible? And whether it was possible or not, could he tell the Inquisitor what Jace had done? Protecting Clary was one thing; protecting Jace was another. He didn't owe Jace anything.

Except that wasn't strictly true. Jace had offered him his blood to drink, had saved his life with it. Would another Shadowhunter have done that, for a vampire? And even if he'd only done it for Clary's sake, did it matter? He thought of himself saying, *I could have killed you.* And Jace: *I would have let you.* There was no telling what kind of trouble Jace would get into if the Clave knew he had saved Simon's life, and how.

"I don't remember anything from the boat," Simon said. "I think Valentine must have drugged me or something."

Aldertree's face fell. "That's terrible news. Terrible. I'm so sorry to hear it."

"I'm sorry too," Simon said, although he wasn't.

"So there isn't a single thing you remember? Not one colorful detail?"

"I just remember passing out when Valentine attacked me, and then I woke up later on . . . on Luke's truck, headed home. I don't remember anything else."

"Oh dear, oh dear." Aldertree drew his cloak around him. "I see the Lightwoods seem to have become rather fond of you, but the other members of the Clave are not so . . . understanding. You were captured by Valentine, you emerged from this confrontation with a peculiar new power you hadn't had before, and now you've found your way to the heart of Idris. You do see how it *looks?*"

If Simon's heart had still been able to beat, it would have been racing. "You think I'm a spy for Valentine."

Aldertree looked shocked. "My boy, my boy—I trust you, of course. I trust you implicitly! But the Clave, oh, the Clave, I'm afraid they can be very suspicious. We had so hoped you'd be able to help us. You see—and I shouldn't be telling you this, but I feel I can confide in you, dear boy—the Clave is in dreadful trouble."

"The Clave?" Simon felt dazed. "But what does that have to do with—"

"You see," Aldertree went on, "the Clave is split down the middle—at war with itself, you might say, in a time of war. Mistakes were made, by the previous Inquisitor and others—perhaps it's better not to dwell. But you see, the very authority of the Clave, of the Consul and the Inquisitor, is under question. Valentine always seems to be a step ahead of us, as if he knows our plans in advance. The Council will not listen to my advice or Malachi's, not after what happened in New York."

"I thought that was the Inquisitor—"

"And Malachi was the one who appointed her. Now, of course, he had no idea she would go as mad as she did—"

"But," Simon said, a little sourly, "there is the question of how it *looks*."

The vein bulged in Aldertree's forehead again. "Clever," he said. "And you're correct. Appearances are significant, and never more than in politics. You can always sway the crowd, provided you have *a good story*." He leaned forward, his eyes locked on Simon. "Now let me tell *you* a story. It goes like this. The Lightwoods were once in the Circle. At some point they recanted and were granted mercy on the grounds that they stayed out of Idris, went to New York, and ran the Institute there. Their blameless record began to win them back the trust of the Clave. But all along they knew Valentine was alive. All along they were *his* loyal servants. They took in his son—"

"But they didn't know—"

"Be *quiet*," the Inquisitor snarled, and Simon shut his mouth. "They helped him find the Mortal Instruments and assisted him with the Ritual of Infernal Conversion. When the Inquisitor discovered what they were secretly up to, they arranged to have her killed during the battle on the ship. And now they have come here, to the heart of the Clave, to spy on our plans and reveal them to Valentine as they are made, so that he can defeat us and ultimately bend all Nephilim to his will. And they have brought you with them—you, a vampire who can withstand sunlight—to distract us from their true plans: to return the Circle to its former glory and destroy the Law." The Inquisitor leaned forward, his piggy eyes gleaming. "What do you think of that story, vampire?"

"I think it's insane," said Simon. "And it's got more giant holes in it than Kent Avenue in Brooklyn—which, incidentally, hasn't been resurfaced in years. I don't know what you're hoping to accomplish with this—"

"*Hoping?*" echoed Aldertree. "I don't hope, Downworlder. I know in my heart. I know it is my sacred duty to save the Clave."

"With a lie?" said Simon.

"With a story," said Aldertree. "Great politicians weave tales to inspire their people."

"There's nothing inspirational about blaming the Lightwoods for everything—"

"Some must be sacrificed," said Aldertree. His face shone with a sweaty light. "Once the Council has a common enemy, and a reason to trust the Clave again, they will come together. What is the cost of one family, weighed against all that? In fact, I doubt anything much will happen to the Lightwood children. They won't be blamed. Well, perhaps the eldest boy. But the others—"

"You can't do this," Simon said. "Nobody will believe this story."

"People believe what they want to believe," Aldertree said, "and the Clave wants someone to blame. I can give them that. All I need is you."

"Me? What does this have to do with me?"

"Confess." The Inquisitor's face was scarlet with excitement now. "Confess that you're a servant of the Lightwoods, that you're all in league with Valentine. Confess and I'll show you leniency. I'll send you back to your own people. I swear to it. But I need your confession to make the Clave believe."

"You want me to confess to a lie," Simon said. He knew he was just repeating what the Inquisitor had already said, but his mind was whirling; he couldn't seem to catch hold of a single thought. The faces of the Lightwoods spun through his mind—Alec, catching his breath on the path up to the Gard; Isabelle's dark eyes turned up to his; Max bent over a book.

And Jace. Jace was one of them as much as if he shared their Lightwood blood. The Inquisitor hadn't said his name, but Simon knew Jace would pay along with the rest of them. And whatever he suffered, Clary would suffer. How had it happened,

Simon thought, that he was bound to these people—to people who thought of him as nothing more than a Downworlder, half human at best?

He raised his eyes to the Inquisitor's. Aldertree's were an odd charcoal black; looking into them was like looking into darkness. "No," Simon said. "No, I won't do it."

"That blood I gave you," Aldertree said, "is all the blood you'll see until you give me a different answer." There was no kindness in his voice, not even false kindness. "You'd be surprised how thirsty you can get."

Simon said nothing.

"Another night in the cells, then," the Inquisitor said, rising to his feet and reaching for a bell to summon the guards. "It's quite peaceful down there, isn't it? I do find that a peaceful atmosphere can help with a little problem of memory—don't you?"

Though Clary had told herself she remembered the way she'd come with Luke the night before, this turned out not to be entirely true. Heading toward the city center seemed like the best bet for getting directions, but once she found the stone courtyard with the disused well, she couldn't remember whether to turn left or right from it. She turned left, which plunged her into a warren of twisting streets, each one much like the next and each turn getting her more hopelessly lost than before.

Finally she emerged into a wider street lined with shops. Pedestrians hurried by on either side, none of them giving her a second glance. A few of them were also dressed in fighting gear, although most weren't: It was cool out, and long, old-fashioned coats were the order of the day. The wind was brisk, and with a pang Clary thought of her green velvet coat, hanging up in Amatis's spare bedroom.

Luke hadn't been lying when he'd said that Shadowhunters had come from all over the world for the summit. Clary passed an Indian woman in a gorgeous gold sari, a pair of curved blades hanging from a chain around her waist. A tall, dark-skinned man with an angular Aztec face was gazing into a shop window full of weaponry; bracelets made of the same hard, shining material as the demon towers laddered his wrists. Farther down the street a man in a white nomadic robe consulted what looked like a street map. The sight of him gave Clary the nerve to approach a passing woman in a heavy brocade coat and ask her the way to Princewater Street. If there was ever going to be a time when the city's inhabitants wouldn't necessarily be suspicious of someone who didn't seem to know where they were going, this would be it.

Her instinct was right; without a trace of hesitation the woman gave her a hurried series of directions. "And then right at the end of Oldcastle Canal, and over the stone bridge, and that's where you'll find Princewater." She gave Clary a smile. "Visiting anyone in particular?"

"The Penhallows."

"Oh, that's the blue house, gold trim, backs up onto the canal. It's a big place—you can't miss it."

She was half-right. It was a big place, but Clary walked right by it before realizing her mistake and swerving back around to look at it again. It was really more indigo than blue, she thought, but then again not everyone noticed colors that way. Most people couldn't tell the difference between lemon yellow and saffron. As if they were even close to each other! And the trim on the house wasn't gold; it was bronze. A nice darkish bronze, as if the house had been there for many years, and it probably had. Everything in this place was so ancient—

Enough, Clary told herself. She always did this when she was nervous, let her mind wander off in all sorts of random directions. She rubbed her hands down the sides of her trousers; her palms were sweaty and damp. The material felt rough and dry against her skin, like snake scales.

She mounted the steps and took hold of the heavy door knocker. It was shaped like a pair of angel's wings, and when she let it fall, she could hear the sound echoing like the tolling of a huge bell. A moment later the door was yanked open, and Isabelle Lightwood stood on the threshold, her eyes wide with shock.

"Clary?"

Clary smiled weakly. "Hi, Isabelle."

Isabelle leaned against the doorjamb, her expression dismal. "Oh, *crap*."

Back in the cell Simon collapsed on the bed, listening to the footsteps of the guards recede as they marched away from his door. Another night. Another night down here in prison, while the Inquisitor waited for him to "remember." *You do see how it looks*. In all his worst fears, his worst nightmares, it had never occurred to Simon that anyone might think he was in league with *Valentine*. Valentine hated Downworlders, famously. Valentine had stabbed him and drained his blood and left him to die. Although, admittedly, the Inquisitor didn't know that.

There was a rustle from the other side of the cell wall. "I have to admit, I wondered if you'd be coming back," said the hoarse voice Simon remembered from the night before. "I take it you didn't give the Inquisitor what he wants?"

"I don't think so," Simon said, approaching the wall. He ran his fingers over the stone as if looking for a crack in it, something he could see through, but there was nothing. "Who are you?"

"He's a stubborn man, Aldertree," said the voice, as if Simon hadn't spoken. "He'll keep trying."

Simon leaned against the damp wall. "Then I guess I'll be down here for a while."

"I don't suppose you'd be willing to tell me what it is he wants from you?"

"Why do you want to know?"

The chuckle that answered Simon sounded like metal scraping against stone. "I've been in this cell longer than you have, Daylighter, and as you can see, there's not a lot to keep the mind occupied. Any distraction helps."

Simon laced his hands over his stomach. The deer blood had taken the edge off his hunger, but it hadn't been quite enough. His body still ached with thirst. "You keep calling me that," he said. "*Daylighter.*"

"I heard the guards talking about you. A vampire who can walk around in the sunlight. No one's ever seen anything like it before."

"And yet you have a word for it. Convenient."

"It's a Downworlder word, not a Clave one. They have legends about creatures like you. I'm surprised you don't know that."

"I haven't exactly been a Downworlder for very long," Simon said. "And you seem to know a lot about me."

"The guards like to gossip," said the voice. "And the Lightwoods appearing through the Portal with a bleeding, dying vampire—that's a good piece of gossip. Though I have to say I wasn't expecting you to show up here—not until they started fixing up the cell for you. I'm surprised the Lightwoods stood for it."

"Why wouldn't they?" Simon said bitterly. "I'm nothing. I'm a Downworlder."

"Maybe to the Consul," said the voice. "But the Lightwoods—"

"What about them?"

There was a short pause. "Those Shadowhunters who live outside Idris—especially those who run Institutes—tend to be more tolerant. The local Clave, on the other hand, is a good deal more . . . hidebound."

"And what about you?" Simon said. "Are you a Downworlder?"

"A *Downworlder?*" Simon couldn't be sure, but there was an edge of anger in the stranger's voice, as if he resented the question. "My name is Samuel. Samuel Blackburn. I am Nephilim. Years ago I was in the Circle, with Valentine. I slaughtered Downworlders at the Uprising. I am *not* one of them."

"Oh." Simon swallowed. His mouth tasted of salt. The members of Valentine's Circle had been caught and punished by the Clave, he remembered—except for those like the Lightwoods, who'd managed to make deals or accept exile in exchange for forgiveness. "Have you been down here ever since?"

"No. After the Uprising, I slipped out of Idris before I could be caught. I stayed away for years—*years*—until like a fool, thinking I'd been forgotten, I came back. Of course they caught me the moment I returned. The Clave has its ways of tracking its enemies. They dragged me in front of the Inquisitor, and I was interrogated for days. When they were done, they tossed me in here." Samuel sighed. "In French this sort of prison is called an *oubliette*. It means 'a forgetting place.' It's where you toss the garbage you don't want to remember, so it can rot away without bothering you with its stench."

"Fine. I'm a Downworlder, so I'm garbage. But you're not. You're Nephilim."

"I'm Nephilim who was in league with Valentine. That makes me no better than you. Worse, even. I'm a turncoat."

"But there are plenty of other Shadowhunters who used to be Circle members—the Lightwoods and the Penhallows—"

"They all recanted. Turned their backs on Valentine. I didn't."

"You didn't? But why not?"

"Because I'm more afraid of Valentine than I am of the Clave," said Samuel, "and if you were sensible, Daylighter, you would be too."

"But you're supposed to be in New York!" Isabelle exclaimed. "Jace said you'd changed your mind about coming. He said you wanted to stay with your mother!"

"Jace lied," Clary said flatly. "*He* didn't want me here, so he lied to me about when you were leaving, and then lied to you about me changing my mind. Remember when you told me he never lies? That is *so* not true."

"He normally never does," said Isabelle, who had gone pale. "Look, did you come here—I mean, does this have something to do with Simon?"

"With *Simon*? No. Simon's safe in New York, thank God.

Although he's going to be really pissed that he never got to say good-bye to me." Isabelle's blank expression was starting to annoy Clary. "Come on, Isabelle. Let me in. I need to see Jace."

"So . . . you just came here on your own? Did you have permission from the Clave? Please tell me you had permission from the Clave."

"Not as such—"

"You broke the *Law?*" Isabelle's voice rose, and then dropped. She went on, almost in a whisper, "If Jace finds out, he'll freak. Clary, you've *got* to go home."

"No. I'm supposed to be here," Clary said, not even sure herself quite where her stubbornness was coming from. "And I need to talk to Jace."

"Now isn't a good time." Isabelle looked around anxiously, as if hoping there was someone she could appeal to for help in removing Clary from the premises. "Please, just go back to New York. Please?"

"I thought you *liked* me, Izzy." Clary went for the guilt.

Isabelle bit her lip. She was wearing a white dress and had her hair pinned up and looked younger than she usually did. Behind her Clary could see a high-ceilinged entryway hung with antique-looking oil paintings. "I *do* like you. It's just that Jace—oh my God, what are you *wearing*? Where did you get fighting gear?"

Clary looked down at herself. "It's a long story."

"You *can't* come in here like that. If Jace sees you—"

"Oh, so what if he sees me. Isabelle, I came here because of my mother—*for* my mother. Jace may not want me here, but he can't make me stay home. I'm supposed to be here. My mother expected me to do this for her. You'd do it for your mother, wouldn't you?"

"Of course I would," Isabelle said. "But, Clary, Jace has his reasons—"

"Then I'd love to hear what they are." Clary ducked under Isabelle's arm and into the entryway of the house.

"Clary!" Isabelle yelped, and darted after her, but Clary was already halfway down the hall. She saw, with the half of her mind that wasn't concentrating on dodging Isabelle, that the house was built like Amatis's, tall and thin, but considerably larger and more richly decorated. The hallway opened into a room with high windows that looked out over a wide canal. White boats plied the water, their sails drifting by like dandelion clocks tossed on the wind. A dark-haired boy sat on a couch by one of the windows, apparently reading a book.

"Sebastian!" Isabelle called. "Don't let her go upstairs!"

The boy looked up, startled—and a moment later was in front of Clary, blocking her path to the stairs. Clary skidded to a halt—she'd never seen anyone move that fast before, except Jace. The boy wasn't even out of breath; in fact, he was smiling at her.

"So this is the famous Clary." His smile lit up his face, and Clary felt her breath catch. For years she'd drawn her own ongoing graphic story—the tale of a king's son who was under a curse that meant that everyone he loved would die. She'd put everything she had into dreaming up her dark, romantic, shadowy prince, and here he was, standing in front of her—the same pale skin, the same tumbling hair, and eyes so dark, the pupils seemed to meld with the iris. The same high cheekbones and deep-set, shadowed eyes fringed with long lashes. She knew she'd never set eyes on this boy before, and yet . . .

The boy looked puzzled. "I don't think—have we met before?"

Speechless, Clary shook her head.

"Sebastian!" Isabelle's hair had come out of its pins and hung down over her shoulders, and she was glaring. "Don't be nice to her. She's not supposed to be here. Clary, go home."

With an effort Clary wrenched her gaze away from Sebastian and shot a glare at Isabelle. "What, back to New York? And how am I supposed to get there?"

"How did you get *here*?" Sebastian inquired. "Sneaking into Alicante is quite an accomplishment."

"I came through a Portal," said Clary.

"A Portal?" Isabelle looked astonished. "But there *isn't* a Portal left in New York. Valentine destroyed them both—"

"I don't owe you any explanations," Clary said. "Not until you give me some. For one thing, where's Jace?"

"He's not here," Isabelle answered, at exactly the same time that Sebastian said, "He's upstairs."

Isabelle turned on him. "Sebastian! Shut *up*."

Sebastian looked perplexed. "But she's his sister. Wouldn't he want to see her?"

Isabelle opened her mouth and then closed it again. Clary could see that Isabelle was weighing the advisability of explaining her complicated relationship with Jace to the completely oblivious Sebastian against the advisability of springing an unpleasant surprise on Jace. Finally she threw her hands up in a gesture of despair. "Fine, Clary," she said, with an unusual—for Isabelle—amount of anger in her voice. "Go ahead and do whatever you want, regardless of who it hurts. You always do anyway, don't you?"

Ouch. Clary shot Isabelle a reproachful look before turning back to Sebastian, who stepped silently out of her way. She darted past him and up the stairs, vaguely aware of voices below her as Isabelle shouted at the unfortunate Sebastian. But that was Isabelle—if there was a boy around and blame that needed to be pinned on someone, Isabelle would pin it on him.

The staircase widened into a landing with a bay-windowed alcove that looked out over the city. A boy was sitting in the alcove, reading. He looked up as Clary came up the stairs, and blinked in surprise. "I know you."

"Hi, Max. It's Clary—Jace's sister. Remember?"

Max brightened. "You showed me how to read *Naruto*," he said, holding out his book to her. "Look, I got another one. This one's called—"

"Max, I can't talk now. I promise I'll look at your book later, but do you know where Jace is?"

Max's face fell. "That room," he said, and pointed to the last door down the hall. "I wanted to go in there with him, but he told me he had to do grown-up stuff. Everyone's always telling me that."

"I'm sorry," Clary said, but her mind was no longer on the conversation. It was racing ahead—what would she say to Jace when she saw him, what would he say to *her*? Moving down the hall to the door, she thought, *It would be better to be friendly, not angry; yelling at him will just make him defensive. He has to understand that I belong here, just like he does. I don't need to be protected like a piece of delicate china. I'm strong too—*

She threw the door open. The room seemed to be a sort of

library, the walls lined with books. It was brightly lit, light streaming through a tall picture window. In the middle of the room stood Jace. He wasn't alone, though—not by a long shot. There was a dark-haired girl with him, a girl Clary had never seen before, and the two of them were locked together in a passionate embrace.

6

Bad Blood

Dizziness washed over Clary, as if all the air had been sucked out of the room. She tried to back away but stumbled and hit the door with her shoulder. It shut with a bang, and Jace and the girl broke apart.

Clary froze. They were both staring at her. She noticed that the girl had dark straight hair to her shoulders and was extremely pretty. The top buttons of her shirt were undone, showing a strip of lacy bra. Clary felt as if she were about to throw up.

The girl's hands went to her blouse, quickly doing up the buttons. She didn't look pleased. "Excuse me," she said with a frown. "Who are you?"

Clary didn't answer—she was looking at Jace, who was

staring at her incredulously. His skin was drained of all color, showing the dark rings around his eyes. He looked at Clary as if he were staring down the barrel of a gun.

"Aline." Jace's voice was without warmth or color. "This is my sister, Clary."

"Oh. *Oh.*" Aline's face relaxed into a slightly embarrassed smile. "Sorry! What a way to meet you. Hi, I'm Aline."

She advanced on Clary, still smiling, her hand out. *I don't think I can touch her,* Clary thought with a sinking feeling of horror. She looked at Jace, who seemed to read the expression in her eyes; unsmiling, he took Aline by the shoulders and said something in her ear. She looked surprised, shrugged, and headed for the door without another word.

This left Clary alone with Jace. Alone with someone who was still looking at her as if she were his worst nightmare come to life.

"Jace," she said, and took a step toward him.

He backed away from her as if she were coated in something poisonous. "What," he said, "in the name of the Angel, Clary, are you doing here?"

Despite everything, the harshness of his tone hurt. "You could at least pretend you were glad to see me. Even a little bit."

"I'm not glad to see you," he said. Some of his color had come back, but the shadows under his eyes were still gray smudges against his skin. Clary waited for him to say something else, but he seemed content just to stare at her in undisguised horror. She noticed with a distracted clarity that he was wearing a black sweater that hung off his wrists as if he'd lost weight, and that the nails on his hands were bitten down to the quick. "Not even a little bit."

"This isn't you," she said. "I hate it when you act like this—"

"Oh, you hate it, do you? Well, I'd better stop doing it, then, hadn't I? I mean, you do everything *I* ask you to do."

"You had no right to do what you did!" she snapped at him, suddenly furious. "Lying to me like that. You had no right—"

"I had *every right*!" he shouted. She didn't think he'd ever shouted at her before. "I had every right, you stupid, stupid girl. I'm your brother and I—"

"And you what? You own me? You don't own me, whether you're my brother or not!"

The door behind Clary flew open. It was Alec, soberly dressed in a long, dark blue jacket, his black hair in disarray. He wore muddy boots and an incredulous expression on his usually calm face. "What in all possible dimensions is going on here?" he said, looking from Jace to Clary with amazement. "Are you two trying to kill each other?"

"Not at all," said Jace. As if by magic, Clary saw, it had all been wiped away: his rage and his panic, and he was icy calm again. "Clary was just leaving."

"Good," Alec said, "because I need to talk to you, Jace."

"Doesn't anyone in this house ever say, 'Hi, nice to see you' anymore?" Clary demanded of no one in particular.

It was much easier to guilt Alec than Isabelle. "It *is* good to see you, Clary," he said, "except of course for the fact that you're really not supposed to be here. Isabelle told me you got here on your own somehow, and I'm impressed—"

"Could you *not* encourage her?" Jace inquired.

"But I really, really need to talk to Jace about something. Can you give us a few minutes?"

"I need to talk to him too," she said. "About our mother—"

"I don't feel like talking," said Jace, "to either of you, as a matter of fact."

"Yes, you do," Alec said. "You really want to talk to me about this."

"I doubt that," Jace said. He had turned his gaze back to Clary. "You didn't come here alone, did you?" he said slowly, as if realizing that the situation was even worse than he'd thought. "Who came with you?"

There seemed to be no point in lying about it. "Luke," said Clary. "Luke came with me."

Jace blanched. "But Luke is a Downworlder. Do you know what the Clave does to unregistered Downworlders who come into the Glass City—who cross the wards without permission? Coming to Idris is one thing, but entering Alicante? Without telling anyone?"

"No," Clary said, in a half whisper, "but I know what you're going to say—"

"That if you and Luke don't go back to New York immediately, you'll find out?"

For a moment Jace was silent, meeting her eyes with his own. The desperation in his expression shocked her. He was the one threatening her, after all, not the other way around.

"Jace," Alec said into the silence, a tinge of panic creeping into his voice. "Haven't you wondered where I've been all day?"

"That's a new coat you're wearing," Jace said, without looking at his friend. "I figure you went shopping. Though why you're so eager to bother me about it, I have no idea."

"I didn't go shopping," Alec said furiously. "I went—"

The door opened again. In a flutter of white dress, Isabelle darted in, shutting the door behind her. She looked at Clary and shook her head. "I told you he'd freak out," she said. "Didn't I?"

"Ah, the 'I told you so,'" Jace said. "Always a classy move."

Clary looked at him with horror. "How can you *joke*?" she whispered. "You just threatened Luke. Luke, who likes you and trusts you. Because he's a *Downworlder*. What's wrong with you?"

Isabelle looked horrified. "Luke's here? Oh, Clary—"

"He's *not* here," Clary said. "He left—this morning—and I don't know where he went. But I can certainly see now why he had to go." She could hardly bear to look at Jace. "Fine. You win. We should never have come. I should never have made that Portal—"

"*Made* a Portal?" Isabelle looked bewildered. "Clary, only a warlock can make a Portal. And there aren't very many of them. The only Portal here in Idris is in the Gard."

"Which is what I had to talk to you about," Alec hissed at Jace—who looked, Clary saw with surprise, even worse than he had before; he looked as if he were about to pass out. "About the errand I went on last night—the thing I had to deliver to the Gard—"

"Alec, stop. *Stop*," Jace said, and the harsh desperation in his voice cut the other boy off; Alec shut his mouth and stood staring at Jace, his lip caught between his teeth. But Jace didn't seem to see him; he was looking at Clary, and his eyes were hard as glass. Finally he spoke. "You're right," he said in a choked voice, as if he had to force out the words. "You should never have come. I know I told you it's because it isn't safe for you here, but that wasn't true. The truth is that I don't want you here because you're rash and thoughtless and you'll mess everything up. It's just how you are. You're not careful, Clary."

"Mess . . . everything . . . up?" Clary couldn't get enough air into her lungs for anything but a whisper.

"Oh, *Jace*," Isabelle said sadly, as if *he* were the one who was hurt. He didn't look at her. His gaze was fixed on Clary.

"You always just race ahead without thinking," he said. "You know that, Clary. We'd never have ended up in the Dumort if it wasn't for you."

"And Simon would be *dead*! Doesn't that count for anything? Maybe it was rash, but—"

His voice rose. "*Maybe?*"

"But it's not like every decision I've made was a bad one! You said, after what I did on the boat, you *said* I'd saved everyone's life—"

All the remaining color in Jace's face went. He said, with a sudden and astounding viciousness, "Shut up, Clary, SHUT UP—"

"On the boat?" Alec's gaze danced between them, bewildered. "What about what happened on the boat? Jace—"

"I just told you that to keep you from whining!" Jace shouted, ignoring Alec, ignoring everything but Clary. She could feel the force of his sudden anger like a wave threatening to knock her off her feet. "You're a disaster for us, Clary! You're a mundane, you'll always be one, you'll never be a Shadowhunter. You don't know how to think like we do, think about what's best for everyone—all you ever think about is yourself! But there's a war on now, or there will be, and I don't have the time or the inclination to follow around after you, trying to make sure you don't get one of us killed!"

She just stared at him. She couldn't think of a thing to say; he'd never spoken to her like this. She'd never even imagined him speaking to her like this. However angry she'd managed to make him in the past, he'd never spoken to her as if he hated her before.

"Go home, Clary," he said. He sounded very tired, as if the effort of telling her how he really felt had drained him. "Go home."

All her plans evaporated—her half-formed hopes of rushing after Fell, saving her mother, even finding Luke—nothing mattered, no words came. She crossed to the door. Alec and Isabelle moved to let her pass. Neither of them would look at her; they looked away instead, their expressions shocked and embarrassed. Clary knew she probably ought to feel humiliated as well as angry, but she didn't. She just felt dead inside.

She turned at the door and looked back. Jace was staring after her. The light that streamed through the window behind him left his face in shadow; all she could see was the bright bits of sunshine that dusted his fair hair, like shards of broken glass.

"When you told me the first time that Valentine was your father, I didn't believe it," she said. "Not just because I didn't want it to be true, but because you weren't anything like him. I've never thought you were anything like him. But you are. You *are*."

She went out of the room, shutting the door behind her.

"They're going to starve me," Simon said.

He was lying on the floor of his cell, the stone cold under his back. From this angle, though, he could see the sky through the window. In the days after Simon had first become a vampire, when he had thought he would never see daylight again, he'd found himself thinking incessantly about the sun and the sky. About the ways the color of the sky changed during the day: about the pale sky of morning, the hot blue of midday, and the cobalt darkness of twilight. He'd lain awake in the darkness with a parade of blues marching through his brain. Now, flat on his back in the cell under the Gard, he wondered if he'd had daylight and all its blues restored to him just so that he could spend the short, unpleasant rest of his life in this tiny space with only a patch of sky visible through the single barred window in the wall.

"Did you hear what I said?" He raised his voice. "The Inquisitor's going to starve me to death. No more blood."

There was a rustling noise. An audible sigh. Then Samuel spoke. "I heard you. I just don't know what you want me to do about it." He paused. "I'm sorry for you, Daylighter, if that helps."

"It doesn't really," Simon said. "The Inquisitor wants me to lie. Wants me to tell him that the Lightwoods are in league with Valentine. Then he'll send me home." He rolled over onto his stomach, the stones jabbing into his skin. "Never mind. I don't know why I'm telling you all this. You probably have no idea what I'm talking about."

Samuel made a noise halfway between a chuckle and a cough. "Actually, I do. I knew the Lightwoods. We were in the Circle together. The Lightwoods, the Waylands, the Pangborns, the Herondales, the Penhallows. All the fine families of Alicante."

"And Hodge Starkweather," Simon said, thinking of the Lightwoods' tutor. "He was too, wasn't he?"

"He was," said Samuel. "But his family was hardly a well-respected one. Hodge showed some promise once, but I fear he never lived up to it." He paused. "Aldertree's always hated the Lightwoods, of course, since we were children. He wasn't rich or clever or attractive, and, well, they weren't very kind to him. I don't think he's ever gotten over it."

"Rich?" Simon said. "I thought all Shadowhunters got paid by the Clave. Like . . . I don't know, communism or something."

"In theory all Shadowhunters are fairly and equally paid," said Samuel. "Some, like those with high positions in the Clave, or those with great responsibility—running an Institute, for example—receive a higher salary. Then there are those who live outside Idris and choose to make money in the mundane world; it's not forbidden, as long as they tithe a part of it to the Clave. But"—Samuel hesitated—"you saw the Penhallows' house, didn't you? What did you think of it?"

Simon cast his mind back. "Very fancy."

"It's one of the finest houses in Alicante," said Samuel. "And they have another house, a manor out in the country. Almost all the rich families do. You see, there's another way for Nephilim to gain wealth. They call it 'spoils.' Anything owned by a demon or Downworlder who is killed by a Shadowhunter becomes that Shadowhunter's property. So if a wealthy warlock breaks the Law, and is killed by a Nephilim . . ."

Simon shivered. "So killing Downworlders is a lucrative business?"

"It can be," said Samuel bitterly, "if you're not too choosy about who you kill. You can see why there's so much opposition to the Accords. It cuts into people's pocketbooks, having to be careful about murdering Downworlders. Perhaps that's why I joined the Circle. My family was never a rich one, and to be looked down on for not accepting blood money—" He broke off.

"But the Circle murdered Downworlders too," said Simon.

"Because they thought it was their sacred duty," said Samuel. "Not out of greed. Though I can't imagine now why I ever thought that mattered." He sounded exhausted. "It was Valentine. He had a way about him. He could convince you of anything. I remember standing beside him with my hands covered in blood, looking down at the body of a dead woman, and thinking only that what I was doing had to be right, because Valentine said it was so."

"A dead Downworlder?"

Samuel breathed raggedly on the other side of the wall. At last, he said, "You must understand, I would have done anything he asked. Any of us would have. The Lightwoods as well. The Inquisitor knows that, and that is what he is trying to exploit. But you should know—there's the chance that if you give in to him and throw blame on the Lightwoods, he'll kill you anyway to shut you up. It depends on whether the idea of being merciful makes him feel powerful at the time."

"It doesn't matter," Simon said. "I'm not going to do it. I won't betray the Lightwoods."

"Really?" Samuel sounded unconvinced. "Is there some reason why not? Do you care for the Lightwoods that much?"

"Anything I told him about them would be a lie."

"But it might be the lie he wants to hear. You do want to go home, don't you?"

Simon stared at the wall as if he could somehow see through it to the man on the other side. "Is that what you'd do? Lie to him?"

Samuel coughed—a wheezy sort of cough, as if he weren't very healthy. Then again, it was damp and cold down here, which didn't bother Simon, but would probably bother a normal human being very much. "I wouldn't take moral advice from *me*," he said. "But yes, I probably would. I've always put saving my own skin first."

"I'm sure that's not true."

"Actually," said Samuel, "it is. One thing you'll learn as you get older, Simon, is that when people tell you something unpleasant about themselves, it's usually true."

But I'm not going to get older, Simon thought. Out loud he said, "That's the first time you've called me Simon. Simon and not Daylighter."

"I suppose it is."

"And as for the Lightwoods," Simon said, "it's not that I like them that much. I mean, I like Isabelle, and I sort of like Alec and Jace, too. But there's this girl. And Jace is her brother."

When Samuel replied, he sounded, for the first time, genuinely amused. "Isn't there always a girl."

The moment the door shut behind Clary, Jace slumped back against the wall, as if his legs had been cut out from under him. He looked gray with a mixture of horror, shock, and what looked almost like . . . relief, as if a catastrophe had been narrowly avoided.

"Jace," Alec said, taking a step toward his friend. "Do you really think—"

Jace spoke in a low voice, cutting Alec off. "Get out," he said. "Just get out, both of you."

"So you can do what?" Isabelle demanded. "Wreck your life some more? What the hell was that *about*?"

Jace shook his head. "I sent her home. It was the best thing for her."

"You did a hell of a lot more than send her home. You *destroyed* her. Did you see her face?"

"It was worth it," said Jace. "You wouldn't understand."

"For her, maybe," Isabelle said. "I hope it winds up worth it for you."

Jace turned his face away. "Just . . . leave me alone, Isabelle. Please."

Isabelle cast a startled look toward her brother. Jace *never* said please. Alec put a hand on her shoulder. "Never mind, Jace," he said, as kindly as he could. "I'm sure she'll be fine."

Jace raised his head and looked at Alec without actually *looking* at him—he seemed to be staring off at nothing. "No, she won't," he said. "But I knew that. Speaking of which, you might as well tell me what you came in here to tell me. You seemed to think it was pretty important at the time."

Alec took his hand off Isabelle's shoulder. "I didn't want to tell you in front of Clary—"

Jace's eyes finally focused on Alec. "Didn't want to tell me *what* in front of Clary?"

Alec hesitated. He'd rarely seen Jace so upset, and he could only imagine what effect further unpleasant surprises might have on him. But there was no way to hide this. Jace had to know. "Yesterday," he said, in a low voice, "when I brought Simon up to the Gard, Malachi told me Magnus Bane would be meeting Simon at the other end of the Portal, in New York. So I sent a fire-message to Magnus. I heard back from him this morning.

He never met Simon in New York. In fact, he says there's been no Portal activity in New York since Clary came through."

"Maybe Malachi was wrong," Isabelle suggested, after a quick look at Jace's ashen face. "Maybe someone else met Simon on the other side. And Magnus could be wrong about the Portal activity—"

Alec shook his head. "I went up to the Gard this morning with Mom. I meant to ask Malachi about it myself, but when I saw him—I can't say why—I ducked behind a corner. I couldn't face him. Then I heard him talking to one of the guards. Telling them to go bring the vampire upstairs because the Inquisitor wanted to speak to him again."

"Are you sure they meant Simon?" Isabelle asked, but there was no conviction in her voice. "Maybe . . ."

"They were talking about how stupid the Downworlder had been to believe that they'd just send him back to New York without questioning him. One of them said that he couldn't believe anyone had had the gall to try to sneak him into Alicante to begin with. And Malachi said, 'Well, what do you expect from Valentine's son?'"

"Oh," Isabelle whispered. "Oh my God." She glanced across the room. "Jace . . ."

Jace's hands were clenched at his sides. His eyes looked sunken, as if they were pushing back into his skull. In other circumstances Alec would have put a hand on his shoulder, but not now; something about Jace made him hold back. "If it hadn't been me who brought him through," Jace said in a low, measured voice, as if he were reciting something, "maybe they would have just let him go home. Maybe they would have believed—"

"No," Alec said. "No, Jace, it's not your fault. You saved his life."

"Saved him so the Clave could torture him," said Jace. "Some favor. When Clary finds out . . ." He shook his head blindly. "She'll think I brought him here on purpose, gave him to the Clave *knowing* what they'd do."

"She won't think that. You'd have no reason to do a thing like that."

"Perhaps," Jace said, slowly, "but after how I just treated her . . ."

"No one could ever think you'd do that, Jace," said Isabelle. "No one who knows you. No one—"

But Jace didn't wait to find out what else no one would ever think. Instead he turned around and walked over to the picture window that looked over the canal. He stood there for a moment, the light coming through the window turning the edges of his hair to gold. Then he moved, so quickly Alec didn't have to time to react. By the time he saw what was going to happen and darted forward to prevent it, it was already too late.

There was a crash—the sound of shattering—and a sudden spray of broken glass like a shower of jagged stars. Jace looked down at his left hand, the knuckles streaked with scarlet, with a clinical interest as fat red drops of blood collected and splattered down onto the floor at his feet.

Isabelle stared from Jace to the hole in the glass, lines radiating out from the empty center, a spiderweb of thin silver cracks. "Oh, Jace," she said, her voice as soft as Alec had ever heard it. "How on earth are we going to explain this to the Penhallows?"

***

Somehow Clary made it out of the house. She wasn't sure how—everything was a fast blur of stairs and hallways, and then she was running to the front door and out of it and somehow she was on the Penhallows' front steps, trying to decide whether or not she was going to throw up in their rosebushes.

They were ideally placed for throwing up in, and her stomach was roiling painfully, but the fact that all she'd eaten was some soup was catching up with her. She didn't think there was anything in her stomach *to* throw up. Instead she made her way down the steps and turned blindly out of the front gate—she couldn't remember which direction she'd come from anymore, or how to get back to Amatis's, but it didn't seem to matter much. It wasn't as if she were looking forward to getting back and explaining to Luke that they had to leave Alicante or Jace would turn them in to the Clave.

Maybe Jace was right. Maybe she *was* rash and thoughtless. Maybe she never thought about how what she did impacted the people she loved. Simon's face flashed across her vision, sharp as a photograph, and then Luke's—

She stopped and leaned against a lamppost. The square glass fixture looked like the sort of gas lamp that topped the vintage posts in front of the brownstones in Park Slope. Somehow it seemed reassuring.

"Clary!" It was a boy's voice, anxious. Immediately Clary thought, *Jace*. She spun around.

It wasn't Jace. Sebastian, the dark-haired boy from the Penhallows' living room, stood in front of her, panting a little as if he'd chased her down the street at a run.

She felt a burst of the same feeling she'd had earlier, when she'd first seen him—recognition, mixed with something she couldn't identify. It wasn't like or dislike—it was a sort of pull, as if something drew her toward this boy she didn't know. Maybe it was just the way he looked. He was beautiful, as beautiful as Jace, though where Jace was all gold, this boy was pallor and shadows. Although now that she looked at him more closely, she could see that his resemblance to her imaginary prince was not as exact as she'd thought. Even their coloring was different. It was just something in the shape of his face, the way he held himself, the dark secretiveness of his eyes . . .

"Are you okay?" he said. His voice was soft. "You ran out of the house like . . ." His voice trailed off as he looked at her. She was still gripping the lamppost as if she needed it to hold her up. "What happened?"

"I had a fight with Jace," she said, trying to keep her voice even. "You know how it is."

"I don't, actually." He sounded almost apologetic. "I don't have any sisters or brothers."

"Lucky," she said, and was startled at the bitterness in her own voice.

"You don't mean that." He took a step closer to her, and as he did, the streetlamp flickered on, casting a pool of white witchlight over them both. Sebastian looked up at the light and smiled. "It's a sign."

"A sign of what?"

"A sign that you should let me walk you home."

"But I have no idea where that is," she said, realizing. "I snuck out of the house to come here. I don't remember the way I came."

"Well, who are you staying with?"

She hesitated before replying.

"I won't tell anyone," he said. "I swear on the Angel."

She stared. That was quite an oath, for a Shadowhunter. "All right," she said, before she could overthink her decision. "I'm staying with Amatis Herondale."

"Great. I know exactly where she lives." He offered her his arm. "Shall we?"

She managed a smile. "You're kind of pushy, you know."

He shrugged. "I have a fetish for damsels in distress."

"Don't be sexist."

"Not at all. My services are also available to gentlemen in distress. It's an equal opportunity fetish," he said, and, with a flourish, offered his arm again.

This time, she took it.

Alec shut the door of the small attic room behind him and turned to face Jace. His eyes were normally the color of Lake Lyn, a pale, untroubled blue, but the color tended to change with his moods. At the moment they were the color of the East River during a thunderstorm. His expression was stormy as well. "Sit," he said to Jace, pointing at a low chair near the gabled window. "I'll get the bandages."

Jace sat. The room he shared with Alec at the top of the Penhallows' house was small, with two narrow beds in it, one against each wall. Their clothes hung from a row of pegs on the wall. There was a single window, letting in faint light—it was getting dark now, and the sky outside the glass was indigo blue. Jace watched as Alec knelt to grab the duffel bag from under his bed and yank it open. He rummaged noisily among the contents before getting to his feet with a box in his hands. Jace recognized it as the box of medical supplies they used sometimes when runes weren't an option—antiseptic, bandages, scissors, and gauze.

"Aren't you going to use a healing rune?" Jace asked, more out of curiosity than anything else.

"No. You can just—" Alec broke off, flinging the box onto the bed with an inaudible curse. He went to the small sink against the wall and washed his hands with such force that water splashed upward in a fine spray. Jace watched him with a distant curiosity. His hand had begun to burn with a dull and fiery ache.

Alec retrieved the box, pulled a chair up opposite Jace's, and flung himself down onto it. "Give me your hand."

Jace held his hand out. He had to admit it looked pretty bad. All four knuckles were split open like red starbursts. Dried blood clung to his fingers, a flaking red-brown glove.

Alec made a face. "You're an idiot."

"Thanks," Jace said. He watched patiently as Alec bent over his hand with a pair of tweezers and gently nudged at a bit of glass embedded in his skin. "So, why not?"

"Why not what?"

"Why not use a healing rune? This isn't a demon injury."

"Because." Alec retrieved the blue bottle of antiseptic. "I think it would do you good to feel the pain. You can heal like a mundane. Slow and ugly. Maybe you'll learn something." He splashed the stinging liquid over Jace's cuts. "Although I doubt it."

"I can always do my own healing rune, you know."

Alec began wrapping a strip of bandages around Jace's

hand. "Only if you want me to tell the Penhallows what really happened to their window, instead of letting them think it was an accident." He jerked a knot in the bandages tight, making Jace wince. "You know, if I'd thought you were going to do this to yourself, I would never have told you anything."

"Yes, you would have." Jace cocked his head to the side. "I didn't realize my attack on the picture window would upset you quite so much."

"It's just—" Done with the bandaging, Alec looked down at Jace's hand, the hand he was still holding between his. It was a white club of bandages, spotted with blood where Alec's fingers had touched it. "Why do you do these things to yourself? Not just what you did to the window, but the way you talked to Clary. What are you punishing yourself for? You can't help how you feel."

Jace's voice was even. "How do I feel?"

"I see how you look at her." Alec's eyes were remote, seeing something just past Jace, something that wasn't there. "And you can't have her. Maybe you just never knew what it was like to want something you couldn't have before."

Jace looked at him steadily. "What's between you and Magnus Bane?"

Alec's head jerked back. "I don't—there's nothing—"

"I'm not stupid. You went right to Magnus after you talked to Malachi, before you talked to me or Isabelle or anyone—"

"Because he was the only one who could answer my question, that's why. There isn't anything between us," Alec said—and then, catching the look on Jace's face, added with great reluctance, "anymore. There's nothing between us anymore. Okay?"

"I hope that's not because of me," said Jace.

Alec went white and drew back, as if he were preparing to ward off a blow. "What do you mean?"

"I know how you think you feel about me," Jace said. "You don't, though. You just like me because I'm safe. There's no risk. And then you never have to try to have a real relationship, because you can use me as an excuse." Jace knew he was being cruel, and he barely cared. Hurting people he loved was almost as good as hurting himself when he was in this kind of mood.

"I get it," Alec said tightly. "First Clary, then your hand, now me. To hell with you, Jace."

"You don't believe me?" Jace asked. "Fine. Go ahead. Kiss me right now."

Alec stared at him in horror.

"Exactly. Despite my staggering good looks, you actually don't like me that way. And if you're blowing off Magnus, it's not because of me. It's because you're too scared to tell anyone who you really love. Love makes us liars," said Jace. "The Seelie Queen told me that. So don't judge me for lying about how I feel. You do it too." He stood up. "And now I want you to do it again."

Alec's face was stiff with hurt. "What do you mean?"

"Lie for me," Jace said, taking his jacket down from the wall peg and shrugging it on. "It's sunset. They'll start coming back from the Gard about now. I want you to tell everyone I'm not feeling well and that's why I'm not coming downstairs. Tell them I felt faint and tripped, and that's how the window got broken."

Alec tipped his head back and looked up at Jace squarely.

"Fine," he said. "If you tell me where you're really going."

"Up to the Gard," said Jace. "I'm going to break Simon out of jail."

Clary's mother had always called the time of day between twilight and nightfall "the blue hour." She said the light was strongest and most unusual then, and that it was the best time to paint. Clary had never really understood what she meant, but now, making her way through Alicante at twilight, she did.

The blue hour in New York wasn't really *blue*; it was too washed out by streetlights and neon signs. Jocelyn must have been thinking of Idris. Here the light fell in swatches of pure violet across the golden stonework of the city, and the witchlight lamps cast circular pools of white light so bright Clary expected to feel heat when she walked through them. She wished her mother were with her. Jocelyn could have pointed out the parts of Alicante that were familiar to her, that had a place in her memories.

But she'd never tell you any of those things. She kept them secret from you on purpose. And now you may never know them. A sharp pain—half anger and half regret—caught at Clary's heart.

"You're awfully quiet," Sebastian said. They were passing over a canal bridge, its stonework sides carved with runes.

"Just wondering how much trouble I'll be in when I get back. I had to climb out a window to leave, but Amatis has probably noticed I'm gone by now."

Sebastian frowned. "Why sneak out? Wouldn't you be allowed to go see your brother?"

"I'm not supposed to be in Alicante at all," Clary said. "I'm supposed to be home, watching safely from the sidelines."

"Ah. That explains a lot."

"Does it?" She cast a curious sideways glance at him. Blue shadows were caught in his dark hair.

"Everyone seemed to blanch when your name came up earlier. I gathered there was some bad blood between your brother and you."

"Bad blood? Well, that's one way to put it."

"You don't like him much?"

"*Like* Jace?" She'd given so much thought these past weeks as to whether she loved Jace Wayland and how, that she'd never much paused to consider whether she liked him.

"Sorry. He's family—it's not really about whether you like him or not."

"I do like him," she said, surprising herself. "I do, it's just—he makes me furious. He tells me what I can and can't do—"

"Doesn't seem to work very well," Sebastian observed.

"What do you mean?"

"You seem to do what you want anyway."

"I suppose." The observation startled her, coming from a near stranger. "But it seems to have made him a lot angrier than I thought it had."

"He'll get over it." Sebastian's tone was dismissive.

Clary looked at him curiously. "Do *you* like him?"

"I like him. But I don't think he likes me much." Sebastian sounded rueful. "Everything I say seems to piss him off."

They turned off the street into a wide cobble-paved square ringed with tall, narrow buildings. At the center was the bronze statue of an angel—*the* Angel, the one who'd given his blood to make the race of Shadowhunters. At the northern end of the square was a massive structure of white stone. A waterfall of wide marble steps led up to a pillared arcade, behind which was a pair of huge double doors. The overall effect in the evening light was stunning—and weirdly familiar. Clary wondered if she'd seen a picture of this place before. Maybe her mother had painted one?

"This is Angel Square," Sebastian said, "and that was the Great Hall of the Angel. The Accords were first signed there, since Downworlders aren't allowed into the Gard—now it's called the Accords Hall. It's a central meeting place—celebrations take place there, marriages, dances, that sort of thing. It's the center of the city. They say all roads lead to the Hall."

"It looks a bit like a church—but you don't have churches here, do you?"

"No need," said Sebastian. "The demon towers keep us safe. We need nothing else. That's why I like coming here. It feels . . . peaceful."

Clary looked at him in surprise. "So you don't live here?"

"No. I live in Paris. I'm just visiting Aline—she's my cousin. My mother and her father, my uncle Patrick, were brother and sister. Aline's parents ran the Institute in Beijing for years. They moved back to Alicante about a decade ago."

"Were they—the Penhallows weren't in the Circle, were they?"

A startled look flashed across Sebastian's face. He was silent as they turned and left the square behind them, making their way into a warren of dark streets. "Why would you ask that?" he said finally.

"Well—because the Lightwoods were."

They passed under a streetlight. Clary glanced sideways at Sebastian. In his long dark coat and white shirt, under the pool of white light, he looked like a black-and-white illustration of a gentleman from a Victorian scrapbook. His dark hair curled close against his temples in a way that made her itch to draw him in pen and ink. "You have to understand," he said. "A good half of the young Shadowhunters in Idris were part of the Circle, and plenty of those who weren't in Idris too. Uncle Patrick was in the early days, but he got out of the Circle once he started to realize how serious Valentine was. Neither of Aline's parents was part of the Uprising—my uncle went to Beijing to get away from Valentine and met Aline's mother at the Institute there. When the Lightwoods and the other Circle members were tried for treason against the Clave, the Penhallows voted for leniency. Got them sent away to New York instead of cursed. So the Lightwoods have always been grateful."

"What about your parents?" Clary said. "Were they in it?"

"Not really. My mother was younger than Patrick—he sent her to Paris when he went to Beijing. She met my father there."

"Your mother *was* younger than Patrick?"

"She's dead," said Sebastian. "My father, too. My aunt Élodie brought me up."

"Oh," Clary said, feeling stupid. "I'm sorry."

"I don't remember them," Sebastian said. "Not really. When I was younger, I wished I had an older sister or a brother, someone who could tell me what it was like having them as parents." He looked at her thoughtfully. "Can I ask you something, Clary? Why did you come to Idris at all when you knew how badly your brother would take it?"

Before she could answer him, they emerged from the narrow alley they'd been following into a familiar unlit courtyard, the disused well at its center gleaming in the moonlight. "Cistern Square," Sebastian said, an unmistakable note of disappointment in his voice. "We got here faster than I thought we would."

Clary glanced over the masonry bridge that spanned the nearby canal. She could see Amatis's house in the distance. All the windows were lit. She sighed. "I can get back myself from here, thanks."

"You don't want me to walk you to the—"

"No. Not unless you want to get in trouble too."

"You think *I'd* get in trouble? For being gentlemanly enough to walk you home?"

"No one's supposed to know I'm in Alicante," she said. "It's supposed to be a secret. And no offense, but you're a stranger."

"I'd like to not be," he said. "I'd like to get to know you better." He was looking at her with a mixture of amusement and a certain shyness, as if he weren't sure how what he'd just said would be received.

"Sebastian," she said, with a sudden feeling of overwhelming tiredness. "I'm glad you want to get to know me. But I just don't have the energy to get to know you. Sorry."

"I didn't mean—"

But she was already walking away from him, toward the bridge. Halfway there she turned around and glanced back at Sebastian. He was looking oddly forlorn in a patch of moonlight, his dark hair falling over his face.

"Ragnor Fell," she said.

He stared at her. "What?"

"You asked me why I came here even though I wasn't supposed to," Clary said. "My mother is sick. Really sick. Maybe dying. The only thing that can help her, the only *person* who can help her, is a warlock named Ragnor Fell. Only I have no idea where to find him."

"Clary—"

She turned back toward the house. "Good night, Sebastian."

It was harder climbing *up* the trellis than it had been climbing down. Clary's boots slipped a number of times on the damp stone wall, and she was relieved when she finally hauled herself up over the sill of the window and half-jumped, half-fell into the bedroom.

Her euphoria was short-lived. No sooner had her boots hit the floor than a bright light flared up, a soft explosion that lit the room to a daylight brightness.

Amatis was sitting on the edge of the bed, her back very straight, a witchlight stone in her hand. It burned with a harsh light that did nothing to soften the hard planes of her face or the lines at the corners of her mouth. She stared at Clary in silence for several long moments. Finally she said, "In those clothes, you look just like Jocelyn."

Clary scrambled to her feet. "I—I'm sorry," she said. "About going out like that—"

Amatis closed her hand around the witchlight, snuffing its glow. Clary blinked in the sudden dimness. "Change out of that gear," Amatis said, "and meet me downstairs in the kitchen. And don't even think about sneaking back out through the window," she added, "or the next time you return to this house, you'll find it sealed against you."

Swallowing hard, Clary nodded.

Amatis rose to her feet and left without another word. Quickly Clary shucked off her gear and dressed in her own clothes, which hung over the bedpost, now dry—her jeans were a little stiff, but it was nice to pull on her familiar T-shirt. Shaking her tangled hair back, she headed downstairs.

The last time she'd seen the lower floor of Amatis's house, she'd been delirious and hallucinating. She remembered long corridors stretching out to infinity and a huge grandfather clock whose ticks had sounded like the beats of a dying heart. Now she found herself in a small, homely living room, with plain wooden furniture and a rag rug on the floor. The small size and bright colors reminded her a little of her own living room at home in Brooklyn. She crossed through in silence and entered the kitchen, where a fire burned in the grate and the room was full of warm yellow light. Amatis was sitting at the table. She had a blue shawl wrapped around her shoulders; it made her hair seem more gray.

"Hi." Clary hovered in the doorway. She couldn't tell if Amatis was angry or not.

"I suppose I hardly need to ask where you went," Amatis said, without looking up from the table. "You went to see Jonathan, didn't you? I suppose it was only to be expected. Perhaps if I'd ever had children of my own, I'd know when a child was lying to me. But I had so hoped that, this time at least, I wouldn't *completely* disappoint my brother."

"Disappoint Luke?"

"You know what happened when he was bitten?" Amatis stared straight in front of her. "When *my brother* was bitten by a werewolf—and of course he was, Valentine was always taking stupid risks with himself and his followers, it was just a matter of time—he came and told me what had happened and how scared he was that he might have contracted the lycanthropic disease. And I said . . . I said . . ."

"Amatis, you don't have to tell me this—"

"I told him to get out of my house and not to come back until he was sure he didn't have it. I cringed away from him—I couldn't help it." Her voice shook. "He could *see* how disgusted I was, it was all over my face. He said he was afraid that if he did have it, if he'd become a were-creature, that Valentine would ask him to kill himself, and I said . . . I said that *maybe that would be the best thing.*"

Clary gave a little gasp; she couldn't help it.

Amatis looked up quickly. Self-loathing was written all over her face. "Luke was always so basically *good*, whatever Valentine tried to get him to do—sometimes I thought he and Jocelyn were the only really good people I knew—and I couldn't stand the idea of him being turned into some monster. . . ."

"But he's not like that. He's not a monster."

"I didn't *know*. After he did Change, after he fled from here, Jocelyn worked and worked to convince me that he was still the same person inside, still my brother. If it hadn't been for her, I never would have agreed to see him again. I let him stay here sometimes at the full moon—shut him in the cellar—but I could tell he didn't really trust me, not after I'd turned my back on him. I think he still doesn't."

"He trusted you enough to come to you when I was sick," Clary said. "He trusted you enough to leave me here with you—"

"He had nowhere else to go," said Amatis. "And look how well I've fared with you. I couldn't even keep you in the house for a single day."

Clary flinched. This was worse than being yelled at. "It's not your fault. I *lied* to you and sneaked out. There wasn't anything you could have done about it."

"Oh, Clary," Amatis said. "Don't you see? There's *always* something you can do. It's just people like me who always tell themselves otherwise. I told myself there was nothing I could do about Luke. I told myself there was nothing I could do about Stephen leaving me. And I refuse even to attend the Clave's meetings because I tell myself there's nothing I can do to influence their decisions, even when I hate what they do. But then when I *do* choose to do something—well, I can't even do that one thing right." Her eyes shone, hard and bright in the firelight. "Go to bed, Clary," she finished. "And from now on, you can come and go as you please. I won't do anything to stop you. After all, like you said, there's nothing I *can* do."

"Amatis—"

"Don't." Amatis shook her head. "Just go to bed. Please." Her voice held a note of finality; she turned away, as if Clary were already gone, and stared at the wall, unblinking.

Clary spun on her heel and ran up the stairs. In the spare room she kicked the door shut behind her and flung herself down onto the bed. She'd thought she wanted to cry, but the tears wouldn't come. *Jace hates me,* she thought. *Amatis hates me. I never got to say good-bye to Simon. My mother's dying. And Luke has abandoned me. I'm alone. I've never been so alone, and it's all my own fault.* Maybe that was why she couldn't cry, she realized, staring dry-eyed at the ceiling. Because what was the point in crying when there was no one there to comfort you? And what was worse, when you couldn't even comfort yourself?

7

Where Angels Fear to Tread

Out of a dream of blood and sunlight, Simon woke suddenly to the sound of a voice calling his name.

"*Simon.*" The voice was a hissing whisper. "Simon, *get up*."

Simon was on his feet—sometimes how fast he could move now surprised even him—and spinning around in the darkness of the cell. "Samuel?" he whispered, staring into the shadows. "Samuel, was that you?"

"Turn around, Simon." Now the voice, faintly familiar, held a note of irritability. "And come to the window." Simon knew immediately who it was and looked through the barred window to see Jace kneeling on the grass outside, a witchlight stone in his hand. He was looking at Simon with a strained scowl. "What, did you think you were having a nightmare?"

"Maybe I still am." There was a buzzing in Simon's ears—if he'd had a heartbeat, he would have thought it was the blood rushing through his veins, but it was something else, something less corporeal but more proximate than blood.

The witchlight threw a crazy-quilt pattern of light and shadow across Jace's pale face. "So here's where they put you. I didn't think they even used these cells anymore." He glanced sideways. "I got the wrong window at first. Gave your friend in the next cell something of a shock. Attractive fellow, what with the beard and the rags. Kind of reminds me of the street folk back home."

And Simon realized what the buzzing sound in his ears was. Rage. In some distant corner of his mind he was aware that his lips were drawn back, the tips of his fangs grazing his lower lip. "I'm glad you think all this is funny."

"You're *not* happy to see me, then?" Jace said. "I have to say, I'm surprised. I've always been told my presence brightened up any room. One might think that went doubly for dank underground cells."

"You knew what would happen, didn't you? 'They'll send you right back to New York,' you said. No problem. But they never had any intention of doing that."

"I didn't know." Jace met his eyes through the bars, and his gaze was clear and steady. "I know you won't believe me, but I thought I was telling you the truth."

"You're either lying or stupid—"

"Then I'm stupid."

"—or both," Simon finished. "I'm inclined to think both."

"I don't have a reason to lie to you. Not now." Jace's gaze remained steady. "And quit baring your fangs at me. It's making me nervous."

"Good," Simon said. "If you want to know why, it's because you smell like blood."

"It's my cologne. Eau de Recent Injury." Jace raised his left hand. It was a glove of white bandages, stained across the knuckles where blood had seeped through.

Simon frowned. "I thought your kind didn't get injuries. Not ones that lasted."

"I put it through a window," Jace said, "and Alec's making me heal like a mundane to teach me a lesson. There, I told you the truth. Impressed?"

"No," Simon said. "I have bigger problems than you. The Inquisitor keeps asking me questions I can't answer. He keeps accusing me of getting my Daylighter powers from Valentine. Of being a *spy* for him."

Alarm flickered in Jace's eyes. "Aldertree said that?"

"Aldertree implied the whole Clave thought so."

"That's bad. If they decide you're a spy, then the Accords don't apply. Not if they can convince themselves you've broken the Law." Jace glanced around quickly before returning his gaze to Simon. "We'd better get you out of here."

"And then what?" Simon almost couldn't believe what he was saying. He wanted to get out of this place so badly he could taste it, yet he couldn't stop the words tumbling out of his mouth. "Where do you plan on hiding me?"

"There's a Portal here in the Gard. If we can find it, I can send you back through—"

"And everyone will know you helped me. Jace, it's not just me the Clave is after. In fact, I doubt they care about one Downworlder at all one way or the other. They're trying to prove something about your family—about the Lightwoods. They're trying to prove that they're connected with Valentine somehow. That they never really left the Circle."

Even in the darkness, it was possible to see the color rush into Jace's cheeks. "But that's ridiculous. They fought Valentine—on the ship—Robert nearly died—"

"The Inquisitor wants to believe that they sacrificed the other Nephilim who fought on the boat to preserve the illusion that they were against Valentine. But they still lost the Mortal Sword, and that's what he cares about. Look, you tried to warn the Clave, and they didn't care. Now the Inquisitor is looking for someone to blame everything on. If he can brand your family as traitors, then no one will blame the Clave for what happened, and he'll be able to make whatever policies he wants to without opposition."

Jace put his face in his hands, his long fingers tugging distractedly at his hair. "But I can't just leave you here. If Clary finds out—"

"I should have known that's what you were worried about." Simon laughed harshly. "So don't tell her. She's in New York, anyway, thank—" He broke off, unable to say the word. "You were right," he said instead. "I'm glad she's not here."

Jace lifted his head out of his hands. "What?"

"The Clave is insane. Who knows what they'd do to her if they knew what she could do. You were right," Simon repeated, and when Jace said nothing in reply, added, "And you might as well enjoy that I just said that to you. I probably won't ever say it again."

Jace stared at him, his face blank, and Simon was reminded with an unpleasant jolt of the way Jace had looked on the ship, bloody and dying on the metal floor. Finally, Jace spoke. "So you're telling me you plan to stay here? In prison? Until when?"

"Until we think of a better idea," said Simon. "But there is one thing."

Jace raised his eyebrows. "What's that?"

"Blood," said Simon. "The Inquisitor's trying to starve me into talking. I already feel pretty weak. By tomorrow I'll be—well, I don't know how I'll be. But I don't want to give in to him. And I *won't* drink your blood again, or anyone else's," he added quickly, before Jace could offer. "Animal blood will do."

"Blood I can get you," Jace said. He hesitated. "Did you . . . tell the Inquisitor that I let you drink my blood? That I saved you?"

Simon shook his head.

Jace's eyes shone with reflected light. "Why not?"

"I suppose I didn't want to get you into more trouble."

"Look, vampire," Jace said. "Protect the Lightwoods if you can. But don't protect me."

Simon raised his head. "Why not?"

"I suppose," said Jace—and for a moment, as he looked down through the bars, Simon could almost imagine that he was outside, and Jace was the one inside the cell—"because I don't deserve it."

Clary woke to a sound like hailstones on a metal roof. She sat up in bed, staring around groggily. The sound came again, a sharp rattle-thump emanating from the window. Peeling her blanket back reluctantly, she went to investigate.

Throwing the window open let in a blast of cold air that cut through her pajamas like a knife. She shivered and leaned out over the sill.

Someone was standing in the garden below, and for a moment, with a leap of her heart, all she saw was that the figure was slender and tall, with boyish, rumpled hair. Then he raised his face and she saw that the hair was dark, not fair, and she realized that for the second time, she'd hoped for Jace and gotten Sebastian instead.

He was holding a handful of pebbles in one hand. He smiled when he saw her poke her head out, and gestured at himself and then at the rose trellis. *Climb downstairs.*

She shook her head and pointed toward the front of the house. *Meet me at the front door.* Shutting the window, she hurried downstairs. It was late morning—the light pouring in through the windows was strong and golden, but the lights were all off and the house was quiet. *Amatis must still be asleep,* she thought.

Clary went to the front door, unbolted it, and threw it open. Sebastian was there, standing on the front step, and once again she had that feeling, that strange burst of recognition, though it was fainter this time. She smiled weakly at him. "You threw stones at my window," she said. "I thought people only did that in movies."

He grinned. "Nice pajamas. Did I wake you up?"

"Maybe."

"Sorry," he said, though he didn't seem sorry. "But this couldn't wait. You might want to run upstairs and get dressed, by the way. We'll be spending the day together."

"Wow. Confident, aren't you?" she said, but then boys who looked like Sebastian probably had no reason to be anything but confident. She shook her head. "I'm sorry, but I can't. I can't leave the house. Not today."

A faint line of concern appeared between his eyes. "You left the house yesterday."

"I know, but that was before—" *Before Amatis made me feel about two inches tall.* "I just can't. And please don't try to argue me out of it, okay?"

"Okay," he said. "I won't argue. But at least let me tell you what I came here to tell you. Then, I promise, if you still want me to go, I'll go."

"What is it?"

He raised his face, and she wondered how it was possible that dark eyes could glow just like golden ones. "I know where you can find Ragnor Fell."

It took Clary less than ten minutes to run upstairs, throw on her clothes, scribble a hasty note to Amatis, and rejoin Sebastian, who was waiting for her at the edge of the canal. He grinned as she ran to meet him, breathless, her green coat flung over one arm. "I'm here," she said, skidding to a stop. "Can we go now?"

Sebastian insisted on helping her on with the coat. "I don't think anyone's ever helped me with my coat before," Clary observed, freeing the hair that had gotten trapped under her collar. "Well, maybe waiters. Were you ever a waiter?"

"No, but I was brought up by a Frenchwoman," Sebastian reminded her. "It involves an even more rigorous course of training."

Clary smiled, despite her nervousness. Sebastian was good at making her smile, she realized with a faint sense of surprise. Almost *too* good at it. "Where are we going?" she asked abruptly. "Is Fell's house near here?"

"He lives outside the city, actually," said Sebastian, starting toward the bridge. Clary fell into step beside him.

"Is it a long walk?"

"Too long to walk. We're going to get a ride."

"A ride? From who?" She came to a dead stop. "Sebastian, we have to be careful. We can't trust just anyone with the information about what we're doing—what *I'm* doing. It's a secret."

Sebastian regarded her with thoughtful dark eyes. "I swear on the Angel that the friend we'll be getting a ride from won't breathe a word to anyone about what we're doing."

"You're sure?"

"I'm *very* sure."

Ragnor Fell, Clary thought as they wove through the crowded streets. *I'm going to see Ragnor Fell.* Wild excitement clashed with trepidation—Madeleine had made him sound formidable. What if he had no patience with her, no time? What if she couldn't make him believe she was who she said she was? What if he didn't even *remember* her mother?

It didn't help her nerves that every time she passed a blond man or a girl with long dark hair her insides tensed up as she thought she recognized Jace or Isabelle. But Isabelle would probably just ignore her, she thought glumly, and Jace was doubtless back at the Penhallows', necking with his new girlfriend.

"You worried about being followed?" Sebastian asked as they turned down a side street that led away from the city center, noticing the way she kept glancing around her.

"I keep thinking I see people I know," she admitted. "Jace, or the Lightwoods."

"I don't think Jace has left the Penhallows' since they got

here. He mostly seems to be skulking in his room. He hurt his hand pretty badly yesterday too—"

"Hurt his hand? How?" Clary, forgetting to look where she was going, stumbled over a rock. The road they'd been walking on had somehow turned from cobblestones to gravel without her noticing. "Ouch."

"We're here," Sebastian announced, stopping in front of a high wood-and-wire fence. There were no houses around—they had rather abruptly left the residential district behind, and there was only this fence on one side and a gravelly slope leading away toward the forest on the other.

There was a door in the fence, but it was padlocked. From his pocket Sebastian produced a heavy steel key and opened the gate. "I'll be right back with our ride." He swung the gate shut behind him. Clary put her eye to the slats. Through the gaps she could glimpse what looked like a low-slung red clapboard house. Though it didn't appear to really have a door—or proper windows—

The gate opened, and Sebastian reappeared, grinning from ear to ear. He held a lead in one hand: Pacing docilely behind him was a huge gray and white horse with a blaze like a star on its forehead.

"A *horse*? You have a horse?" Clary stared in amazement. "Who has a horse?"

Sebastian stroked the horse fondly on the shoulder. "A lot of Shadowhunter families keep a horse in the stables here in Alicante. If you've noticed, there are no cars in Idris. They don't work well with all these wards around." He patted the pale leather of the horse's saddle, emblazoned with a crest of arms that depicted a water serpent rising out of a lake in a series of coils. The name *Verlac* was written beneath in delicate script. "Come on up."

Clary backed up. "I've never ridden a horse before."

"I'll be riding Wayfarer," Sebastian reassured her. "You'll just be sitting in front of me."

The horse grunted softly. He had huge teeth, Clary noticed uneasily; each one the size of a Pez dispenser. She imagined those teeth sinking into her leg and thought of all the girls she'd known in middle school who'd wanted ponies of their own. She wondered if they were insane.

Be brave, she told herself. *It's what your mother would do.*

She took a deep breath. "All right. Let's go."

Clary's resolution to be brave lasted as long as it took for Sebastian—after helping her into the saddle—to swing himself up onto the horse behind her and dig in his heels. Wayfarer took off like a shot, pounding over the graveled road with a force that sent jolting shocks up her spine. She clutched at the bit of the saddle that stuck up in front of her, her nails digging into it hard enough to leave marks in the leather.

The road they were on narrowed as they headed out of town, and now there were banks of thick trees on either side of them, walls of green that blocked any wider view. Sebastian drew back on the reins, and the horse ceased its frantic galloping, Clary's heartbeat slowing along with its pace. As her panic receded, she became slowly conscious of Sebastian behind her—he was holding the reins on either side of her, his arms making a sort of cage around her that kept her from feeling like she was about to slide off the horse. She was suddenly very aware of him, not just the hard strength in the arms that held her, but that she was leaning back against his chest and that he smelled of, for some reason, black pepper. Not in a bad way—it was spicy and pleasant, very different from Jace's smell of soap and sunlight. Not that sunlight had a smell, really, but if it did—

She gritted her teeth. She was here with Sebastian, on her way to see a powerful warlock, and mentally she was maundering on about the way Jace smelled. She forced herself to look around. The green banks of trees were thinning out and now she could see a sweep of marbled countryside to either side. It was beautiful in a stark sort of way: a carpet of green broken up here and there by a scar of gray stone road or a crag of black rock rising up out of the grass. Clusters of delicate white flowers, the same ones she'd seen in the necropolis with Luke, starred the hills like occasional snowfall.

"How did you find out where Ragnor Fell is?" she asked as Sebastian skillfully guided the horse around a rut in the road.

"My aunt Élodie. She's got quite a network of informants. She knows everything that's going on in Idris, even though she never comes here herself. She hates to leave the Institute."

"What about you? Do you come to Idris much?"

"Not really. The last time I was here I was about five years old. I haven't seen my aunt and uncle since then either, so I'm glad to be here now. It gives me a chance to catch up. Besides, I miss Idris when I'm not here. There's nowhere else like it. It's in the earth of the place. You'll start to feel it, and then you'll miss it when you're not here."

"I know Jace missed it," she said. "But I thought that was because he lived here for years. He was brought up here."

"In the Wayland manor," Sebastian said. "Not that far from where we're going, in fact."

"You do seem to know everything."

"Not *everything*," Sebastian said with a laugh that Clary felt through her back. "Yeah, Idris works its magic on everyone—even those like Jace who have reason to hate the place."

"Why do you say that?"

"Well, he was brought up by Valentine, wasn't he? And that must have been pretty awful."

"I don't know." Clary hesitated. "The truth is, he has mixed feelings about it. I think Valentine was a horrible father in a way, but in another way the little bits of kindness and love he did show were all the kindness and love Jace ever knew." She felt a wave of sadness as she spoke. "I think he remembered Valentine with a lot of affection, for a long time."

"I can't believe Valentine ever showed Jace kindness or love. Valentine's a monster."

"Well, yes, but Jace is his son. And he was just a little boy. I think Valentine did love him, in his way—"

"No." Sebastian's voice was sharp. "I'm afraid that's impossible."

Clary blinked and almost turned around to see his face, but then thought better of it. All Shadowhunters were sort of crazy on the topic of Valentine—she thought of the Inquisitor and shuddered inwardly—and she could hardly blame them. "You're probably right."

"We're here," Sebastian said abruptly—so abruptly that Clary wondered if she really had offended him somehow—and slid down from the horse's back. But when he looked up at her, he was smiling. "We made good time," he said, tying the reins to the lower branch of a nearby tree. "Better than I thought we would."

He indicated with a gesture that she should dismount, and after a moment's hesitation Clary slid off the horse and into his arms. She clutched him as he caught her, her legs unsteady after the long ride. "Sorry," she said sheepishly. "I didn't mean to grab you."

"I wouldn't apologize for *that*." His breath was warm against her neck, and she shivered. His hands lingered just a moment longer on her back before he reluctantly let her go.

All this wasn't helping Clary's legs feel any steadier. "Thanks," she said, knowing full well she was blushing, and wishing heartily that her fair skin didn't show color so readily. "So—this is it?" She looked around. They were standing in a small valley between low hills. There were a number of gnarled-looking trees ranged around a clearing. Their twisted branches had a sculptural beauty against the steel blue sky. But otherwise . . . "There's nothing here," she said with a frown.

"Clary. *Concentrate.*"

"You mean—a glamour? But I don't usually have to—"

"Glamours in Idris are often stronger than they are elsewhere. You may have to try harder than you usually do." He put his hands on her shoulders and turned her gently. "Look at the clearing."

Clary silently performed the mental trick that allowed her to peel glamour from the thing it disguised. She imagined herself rubbing turpentine on a canvas, peeling away layers of paint to reveal the true image underneath—and there it was, a small stone house with a sharply gabled roof, smoke twisting from the chimney in an elegant curlicue. A winding path lined with stones led up to the front door. As she looked, the smoke puffing from the chimney stopped curling upward and began to take on the shape of a wavering black question mark.

Sebastian laughed. "I think that means, *Who's there?*"

Clary pulled her coat closer around her. The wind blowing across the level grass wasn't that brisk, but there was ice in her bones nevertheless. "It looks like something out of a fairy tale."

"Are you cold?" Sebastian put an arm around her. Immediately the smoke curling from the chimney stopped forming itself into question marks and began puffing out in the shape of lopsided hearts. Clary ducked away from him, feeling both embarrassed and somehow guilty, as if she'd done something wrong. She hurried toward the front walk of the house, Sebastian just behind her. They were halfway up the front path when the door flew open.

Despite having been obsessed with finding Ragnor Fell ever since Madeleine had told her his name, Clary had never stopped to picture what he might look like. A large, bearded man, she would have thought, if she'd thought about it at all. Someone who looked like a Viking, with big broad shoulders.

But the person who stepped out of the front door was tall and thin, with short, spiky dark hair. He was wearing a gold mesh vest and a pair of silk pajama pants. He regarded Clary with mild interest, puffing gently on a fantastically large pipe as he did so. Though he looked nothing at all like a Viking, he was instantly and totally familiar.

Magnus Bane.

"But . . ." Sebastian seemed as astonished as Clary. He was

staring at Magnus with his mouth slightly open, a blank look on his face. Finally he stammered, "Are you—Ragnor Fell? The warlock?"

Magnus took the pipe out of his mouth. "Well, I'm certainly not Ragnor Fell the exotic dancer."

"I . . ." Sebastian seemed at a loss for words. Clary wasn't sure what he'd been expecting, but Magnus was a lot to take in. "We were hoping you could help us. I'm Sebastian Verlac, and this is Clarissa Morgenstern—her mother is Jocelyn Fairchild—"

"I don't care who her mother is," Magnus said. "You can't see me without an appointment. Come back later. Next March would be good."

"March?" Sebastian looked horrified.

"You're right," Magnus said. "Too rainy. How about June?"

Sebastian drew himself upright. "I don't think you understand how important this is—"

"Sebastian, don't bother," Clary said in disgust. "He's just messing with your head. He can't help us, anyway."

Sebastian only looked more confused. "But I don't see why he can't—"

"All right, that's enough," Magnus said, and snapped his fingers once.

Sebastian froze in place, his mouth still open, his hand partially outstretched.

"*Sebastian!*" Clary reached out to touch him, but he was as rigid as a statue. Only the slight rise and fall of his chest showed that he was even still *alive*. "Sebastian?" she said again, but it was hopeless: She knew somehow that he couldn't see or hear her. She turned on Magnus. "I can't believe you just did that. What on *earth* is wrong with you? Has whatever's in that pipe melted your brain? Sebastian's on our side."

"I don't have a side, Clary darling," Magnus said with a wave of his pipe. "And really, it's your own fault I had to freeze him for a short while. You were awfully close to telling him I'm not Ragnor Fell."

"That's because you're *not* Ragnor Fell."

Magnus blew a stream of smoke out of his mouth and regarded her thoughtfully through the haze. "Come on," he said. "Let me show you something."

He held the door of the small house open, gesturing her inside. With a last, disbelieving glance at Sebastian, Clary followed him.

The interior of the cottage was unlit. The faint daylight streaming in through the windows was enough to show Clary that they stood inside a large room crowded with dark shadows. There was an odd smell in the air, as of burning garbage. She made a faint choking noise as Magnus raised his hand and snapped his fingers once again. A bright blue light bloomed from his fingertips.

Clary gasped. The room was a shambles—furniture smashed into splinters, drawers opened and their contents scattered. Pages ripped from books drifted in the air like ash. Even the window glass was shattered.

"I got a message from Fell last night," said Magnus, "asking me to meet him here. I turned up here—and found it like this. Everything destroyed, and the stench of demons all around."

"Demons? But demons can't come into Idris—"

"I didn't say they have. I'm just telling you what happened." Magnus spoke without inflection. "The place stank of something demonic in origin. Ragnor's body was on the floor. He hadn't been dead when they left him, but he was dead when I arrived." He turned to her. "Who knew you were looking for him?"

"Madeleine," Clary whispered. "But she's dead. Sebastian, Jace, and Simon. The Lightwoods—"

"Ah," said Magnus. "If the Lightwoods know, the Clave may well know by now, and Valentine has spies in the Clave."

"I should have kept it a secret instead of asking everyone about him," Clary said in horror. "This is my fault. I should have warned Fell—"

"Might I point out," said Magnus, "that you couldn't *find* Fell, which is in fact why you were asking people about him. Look, Madeleine—and you—just thought of Fell as someone who could help your mother. Not someone Valentine might be interested in beyond that. But there's more to it. Valentine might not have known how to wake up your mother, but he seems to have known that what she did to put herself in that state had a connection to something he wanted very much. A particular spell book."

"How do you know all this?" Clary asked.

"Because Ragnor told me."

"But—"

Magnus cut her off with a gesture. "Warlocks have ways of communicating with each other. They have their own languages." He raised the hand that held the blue flame. "*Logos.*"

Letters of fire, each at least six inches tall, appeared on the walls as if etched into the stone with liquid gold. The letters raced around the walls, spelling out words Clary couldn't read. She turned to Magnus. "What does it say?"

"Ragnor did this when he knew he was dying. It tells whatever warlock comes after him what happened." As Magnus turned, the glow of the burning letters lit his cat eyes to gold. "He was attacked here by servants of Valentine. They demanded the Book of the White. Aside from the Gray Book, it's among the most famous volumes of supernatural work ever written. Both the recipe for the potion Jocelyn took and the recipe for the antidote to it are contained in that book."

Clary's mouth dropped open. "So was it here?"

"No. It belonged to your mother. All Ragnor did was advise her where to hide it from Valentine."

"So it's—"

"It's at the Wayland family manor. The Waylands had their home very close to where Jocelyn and Valentine lived; they were their nearest neighbors. Ragnor suggested that your mother hide the book in their home, where Valentine would never look for it. In the library, as a matter of fact."

"But Valentine lived in the Wayland manor for years after that," Clary protested. "Wouldn't he have found it?"

"It was hidden inside another book. One Valentine was unlikely to ever open." Magnus smiled crookedly. "*Simple Recipes for Housewives*. No one can say your mother didn't have a sense of humor."

"So have you gone to the Wayland manor? Have you looked for the book?"

Magnus shook his head. "Clary, there are misdirection wards on the manor. They don't just keep out the Clave; they keep out everyone. *Especially* Downworlders. Maybe if I had time to work on them, I could crack them, but—"

"Then no one can get into the manor?" Despair clawed at her chest. "It's impossible?"

"I didn't say no one," Magnus said. "I can think of at least one person who could almost certainly get into the manor."

"You mean Valentine?"

"I mean," said Magnus, "Valentine's son."

Clary shook her head. "Jace won't help me, Magnus. He doesn't want me here. In fact, I doubt he's speaking to me at all."

Magnus looked at her meditatively. "I think," he said, "there isn't much that Jace wouldn't do for you, if you asked him."

Clary opened her mouth and then shut it again. She thought of the way Magnus had always seemed to know how Alec felt about Jace, how Simon felt about her. Her feelings for Jace must be written on her face even now, and Magnus was an expert reader. She glanced away. "Say I *can* convince Jace to come to the manor with me and get the book," she said. "Then what? I don't know how to cast a spell, or make an antidote—"

Magnus snorted. "Did you think I was giving you all this advice for free? Once you get hold of the Book of the White, I want you to bring it straight to me."

"The book? *You* want it?"

"It's one of the most powerful spell books in the world. Of course I want it. Besides, it belongs, by right, to Lilith's children, not Raziel's. It's a warlock book and should be in warlock hands."

"But *I* need it—to cure my mother—"

"You need one page out of it, which you can keep. The rest is mine. And in return, when you bring me the book, I'll make up the antidote for you and administer it to Jocelyn. You can't say it's not a fair deal." He held out a hand. "Shake on it?"

After a moment's hesitation Clary shook. "I'd better not regret this."

"I certainly hope not," Magnus said, turning cheerfully back toward the front door. On the walls the fire-letters were already fading. "Regret is such a pointless emotion, don't you agree?"

The sun outside seemed especially bright after the darkness of the cottage. Clary stood blinking as the view swam into focus: the mountains in the distance, Wayfarer contentedly munching grass, and Sebastian immobile as a lawn statue, one hand still outstretched. She turned to Magnus. "Could you unfreeze him now, please?"

Magnus looked amused. "I was surprised to see you in unfamiliar company. How did you wind up meeting him?"

"He's a cousin of some friends of the Lightwoods or something. He's nice, I promise."

"Nice, bah. He's gorgeous." Magnus gazed dreamily in his direction. "You should leave him here. I could hang hats on him and things."

"No. You can't have him."

"Why not? Do you *like* him?" Magnus's eyes gleamed. "He seems to like you. I saw him going for your hand out there like a squirrel diving for a peanut."

"Why don't we talk about *your* love life?" Clary countered. "What about you and Alec?"

"Alec refuses to acknowledge that we have a relationship, and so I refuse to acknowledge him. He sent me a fire message asking for a favor the other day. It was addressed to 'Warlock Bane,' as if I were a perfect stranger. He's still hung up on Jace, I think, though *that* relationship will never go anywhere. A problem I imagine *you* know nothing about . . ."

"Oh, shut up." Clary eyed Magnus with distaste. "Look, if

you don't unfreeze Sebastian, then I can never leave here, and you'll never get the Book of the White."

"Oh, all right, all right. But if I might make a request? Don't tell him any of what I just told you, friend of the Lightwoods or not." Magnus snapped his fingers petulantly.

Sebastian's face came alive, like a video flashing back to action after it had been paused. "—help us," he said. "This isn't just some minor problem. This is life and death."

"You Nephilim think all your problems are life and death," said Magnus. "Now go away. You've begun to bore me."

"But—"

"Go," Magnus said, a dangerous tone to his voice. Blue sparks glittered at the tips of his long fingers, and there was suddenly a sharp smell in the air, like burning. Magnus's cat eyes glowed. Even though she knew it was an act, Clary couldn't help but back away.

"I think we should go, Sebastian," she said.

Sebastian's eyes were narrow. "But, Clary—"

"We're *going*," she insisted, and, grabbing him by the arm, half-dragged him toward Wayfarer. Reluctantly, he followed her, muttering under his breath. With a sigh of relief, Clary glanced back over her shoulder. Magnus was standing at the door to the cottage, his arms folded across his chest. Catching her eye, he grinned and dropped one eyelid in a single, glittering wink.

"I'm sorry, Clary." Sebastian had a hand on Clary's shoulder and another on her waist as he helped her up onto Wayfarer's broad back. She fought down the little voice inside her head that warned her not to get back onto the horse—or any horse—and let him hoist her up. She swung a leg over and settled herself in the saddle, telling herself she was balancing on a large, moving sofa and not on a living creature that might turn around and bite her at any moment.

"Sorry about what?" she asked as he swung up behind her. It was almost annoying how easily he did it—as if he were dancing—but comforting to watch. He clearly knew what he was doing, she thought as he reached around her to take the reins. She supposed it was good that one of them did.

"About Ragnor Fell. I wasn't expecting him to be that unwilling to help. Although, warlocks are capricious. You've met one before, haven't you?"

"I met Magnus Bane." She twisted around momentarily to look past Sebastian at the cottage receding into the distance behind them. The smoke was puffing out of the chimney in the shape of little dancing figures. Dancing Magnuses? She couldn't tell from here. "He's the High Warlock of Brooklyn."

"Is he much like Fell?"

"Shockingly similar. It's all right about Fell. I knew there was a chance he'd refuse to help us."

"But I promised you help." Sebastian sounded genuinely upset. "Well, at least there's something else I can show you, so the day won't have been a complete waste of time."

"What is it?" She twisted around again to look up at him. The sun was high in the sky behind him, firing the strands of his dark hair with an outline of gold.

Sebastian grinned. "You'll see."

As they rode farther away from Alicante, walls of green foliage whipped by on either side, giving way every so often to improbably beautiful vistas: frost blue lakes, green valleys, gray mountains, silver slivers of river and creek flanked by banks of flowers. Clary wondered what it would be like to live in a land like this. She couldn't help but feel nervous, almost exposed, without the comfort of tall buildings closing her in.

Not that there were no buildings at all. Every once in a while the roof of a large stone building would rise into view above the trees. These were manor houses, Sebastian explained (by shouting in her ear): the country houses of wealthy Shadowhunter families. They reminded Clary of the big old mansions along the Hudson River, north of Manhattan, where rich New Yorkers had spent their summers hundreds of years ago.

The road beneath them had turned from gravel to dirt. Clary was jerked out of her reverie as they crested a hill and Sebastian pulled Wayfarer up short. "This is it," he said.

Clary stared. "It" was a tumbled mass of charred, blackened stone, recognizable only by outline as something that had once been a house: There was a hollow chimney, still pointing toward the sky, and a chunk of wall with a glassless window gaping in its center. Weeds grew up through the foundations, green among the black. "I don't understand," she said. "Why are we here?"

"You don't know?" Sebastian asked. "This was where your mother and father lived. Where your brother was born. This was Fairchild manor."

Not for the first time, Clary heard Hodge's voice in her head. *Valentine set a great fire and burned himself to death along with his family, his wife, and his child. Scorched the land black. No one will build there still. They say the land is cursed.*

Without another word she slid from the horse's back. She heard Sebastian call out to her, but she was already half-running, half-sliding down the low hill. The ground evened out where the house had once stood; the blackened stones of what had once been a walkway lay dry and cracked at her feet. In among the weeds she could see a set of stairs that ended abruptly a few feet from the ground.

"Clary—" Sebastian followed her through the weeds, but she was barely aware of his presence. Turning in a slow circle, she took it all in. Burned, half-dead trees. What had probably once been a shady lawn, stretching away down a sloping hill. She could see the roof of what was probably another nearby manor house in the distance, just above the tree line. The sun sparked off broken bits of window glass in the one full wall that was still standing. She stepped into the ruins over a shelf of blackened stones. She could see the outline of rooms, of doorways—even a scorched cabinet, almost intact, flung on its side with smashed bits of china spilling out, mixing with the black earth.

Once this had been a real house, inhabited by living, breathing people. Her mother had lived here, gotten married here, had a baby here. And then Valentine had come and turned it all to dust and ash, leaving Jocelyn thinking her son was dead, leading her to hide the truth about the world from her daughter. . . . A sense of piercing sadness invaded Clary. More than one life had been wrecked in this place. She put her hand to her face and was almost surprised to find it damp: She had been crying without knowing it.

"Clary, I'm sorry. I thought you'd want to see this." It was Sebastian, crunching toward her across the rubble, his boots kicking up puffs of ash. He looked worried.

She turned to him. "Oh, I do. I did. Thank you."

The wind had picked up. It blew strands of his dark hair

across his face. He gave a rueful smile. "It must be hard to think about everything that happened in this place, about Valentine, about your mother—she had incredible courage."

"I know," Clary said. "She did. She does."

He touched her face lightly. "So do you."

"Sebastian, you don't know anything about me."

"That's not true." His other hand came up, and now he was cupping her face. His touch was gentle, almost tentative. "I've heard all about you, Clary. About the way you fought your father for the Mortal Cup, the way you went into that vampire-infested hotel after your friend. Isabelle's told me stories, and I've heard rumors, too. And ever since the first one—the first time I heard your name—I've wanted to meet you. I knew you'd be extraordinary."

She laughed shakily. "I hope you're not too disappointed."

"No," he breathed, sliding his fingertips under her chin. "Not at all." He lifted her face to his. She was too surprised to move, even when he leaned toward her and she realized, belatedly, what he was doing: Reflexively she shut her eyes as his lips brushed gently over hers, sending shivers through her. A sudden fierce longing to be held and kissed in a way that would make her forget everything else surged through her. She put her arms up, twining them around his neck, partly to steady herself and partly to draw him closer.

His hair tickled her fingertips, not silky like Jace's but fine and soft, and *she shouldn't be thinking about Jace.* She pushed back thoughts of him as Sebastian's fingers traced her cheeks and the line of her jaw. His touch was gentle, despite the calluses on his fingertips. Of course, Jace had the same calluses from fighting; probably all Shadowhunters had them—

She clamped down on the thought of Jace, or tried to, but it was no good. She could see him even with her eyes closed—see the sharp angles and planes of a face she could never properly draw, no matter how much the image of it had burned itself into her mind; see the delicate bones of his hands, the scarred skin of his shoulders—

The fierce longing that had surged up in her so swiftly receded with a sharp recoil that was like an elastic band springing back. She went numb, even as Sebastian's lips pressed down on hers and his hands moved to cup the back of her neck—she went numb with an icy shock of wrongness. Something was terribly wrong, something even more than her hopeless longing for someone she could never have. This was something else: a sudden jolt of horror, as if she'd been taking a confident step forward and suddenly plunged into a black void.

She gasped and jerked away from Sebastian with such force that she almost stumbled. If he hadn't been holding her, she would have fallen.

"Clary." His eyes were unfocused, his cheeks flushed with a high bright color. "Clary, what's wrong?"

"Nothing." Her voice sounded thin to her own ears. "Nothing—it's just, I shouldn't have—I'm not really ready—"

"Did we go too fast? We can take it slower—" He reached for her, and before she could stop herself, she flinched away. He looked stricken. "I'm not going to hurt you, Clary."

"I know."

"Did something happen?" His hand came up, stroked her hair back; she bit back the urge to jerk away. "Did Jace—"

"*Jace?*" Did he know she'd been thinking about Jace, had he been able to tell? And at the same time . . . "Jace is my *brother.*

Why would you bring him up like that? What do you mean?"

"I just thought—" He shook his head, pain and confusion chasing each other across his features. "That maybe someone else had hurt you."

His hand was still on her cheek; she reached up and gently but firmly detached it, returning it to his side. "No. Nothing like that. I just—" She hesitated. "It felt wrong."

"*Wrong?*" The hurt on his face vanished, replaced by disbelief. "Clary, we have a connection. You know we do. Since the first second I saw you—"

"Sebastian, *don't*—"

"I felt like you were someone I'd always been waiting for. I saw you feel it too. Don't tell me you didn't."

But that *hadn't* been what she'd felt. She'd felt as if she'd walked around a corner in a strange city and suddenly seen her own brownstone looming up in front of her. A surprising and not entirely pleasant recognition, almost: *How can this be here?*

"I didn't," she said.

The anger that rose in his eyes—sudden, dark, uncontrolled—took her by surprise. He caught her wrists in a painful grasp. "That's not true."

She tried to pull away. "Sebastian—"

"It's *not true.*" The blackness of his eyes seemed to have swallowed up the pupils. His face was like a white mask, stiff and rigid.

"Sebastian," she said as calmly as she could. "You're hurting me."

He let go of her. His chest was rising and falling rapidly. "I'm sorry," he said. "I'm sorry. I thought—"

Well, you thought wrong, Clary wanted to say, but she bit the words back. She didn't want to see that *look* on his face again. "We should go back," she said instead. "It'll be dark soon."

He nodded numbly, seeming as shocked by his outburst as she was. He turned and headed back toward Wayfarer, who was cropping grass in the long shadow of a tree. Clary hesitated a moment, then followed him—there didn't seem to be anything else she *could* do. She glanced down surreptitiously at her wrists as she fell into step behind him—they were ringed with red where his fingers had gripped her, and more strangely, her fingertips were smudged black, as if she had somehow stained them with ink.

Sebastian was silent as he helped her up onto Wayfarer's back. "I'm sorry if I implied anything about Jace," he said finally as she settled herself in the saddle. "He would never do anything to hurt you. I know it's for your sake that he's been visiting that vampire prisoner in the Gard—"

It was as if everything in the world ground to a sudden halt. Clary could hear her own breath whistling in and out of her ears, saw her hands, frozen like the hands of a statue, lying still against the saddle pommel. "Vampire prisoner?" she whispered.

Sebastian turned a surprised face up to hers. "Yes," he said, "Simon, that vampire they brought over with them from New York. I thought—I mean, I was sure you knew all about it. Didn't Jace tell you?"

8

One of the Living

Simon woke to sunlight glinting brightly off an object that had been shoved through the bars of his window. He got to his feet, his body aching with hunger, and saw that it was a metal flask, about the size of a lunchbox thermos. A rolled-up bit of notepaper had been tied around the neck. Plucking it down, Simon unrolled the paper and read:

Simon: This is cow blood, fresh from the butcher's. Hope it's all right. Jace told me what you said, and I want you to know I think it's really brave. Just hang in there and we'll figure out a way to get you out.
XOXOXOXOXOXOX Isabelle

Simon smiled at the scribbled *X*s and *O*s that ran along the bottom of the page. Good to know Isabelle's flamboyant affection hadn't suffered under the current circumstances. He unscrewed the flask's top and had swallowed several mouthfuls before a sharp prickling sensation between his shoulder blades made him turn around.

Raphael stood calmly in the center of the room. He had his hands clasped behind his back, his slight shoulders set. He was wearing a sharply pressed white shirt and a dark jacket. A gold chain glittered at his throat.

Simon almost gagged on the blood he was drinking. He swallowed hard, still staring. "You—you can't be here."

Raphael's smile somehow managed to give the impression that his fangs were showing, even though they weren't. "Don't panic, Daylighter."

"I'm not panicking." This wasn't strictly true. Simon felt as if he'd swallowed something sharp. He hadn't seen Raphael since the night he'd clawed himself, bloody and bruised, out of a hastily dug grave in Queens. He still remembered Raphael throwing packets of animal blood at him, and the way he'd torn into them with his teeth as if he were an animal himself. It wasn't something he liked to remember. He would have been happy never to see the vampire boy again. "The sun's still up. How are you here?"

"I'm not." Raphael's voice was smooth as butter. "I am a Projection. Look." He swung his hand, passing it through the stone wall beside him. "I am like smoke. I cannot hurt you. Of course, neither can you hurt me."

"I don't want to hurt you." Simon set the flask down on the cot. "I *do* want to know what you're doing here."

"You left New York very suddenly, Daylighter. You do realize that you're supposed to inform the head vampire of your local area when you're leaving the city, don't you?"

"Head vampire? You mean you? I thought the head vampire was someone else—"

"Camille has not yet returned to us," Raphael said, without any apparent emotion. "I lead in her stead. You'd know all this if you'd bothered to get acquainted with the laws of your kind."

"My leaving New York wasn't exactly planned in advance. And no offense, but I don't really think of you as my kind."

"*Dios.*" Raphael lowered his eyes, as if hiding amusement. "You are stubborn."

"How can you say that?"

"It seems obvious, doesn't it?"

"I mean—" Simon's throat closed up. "That word. You can say it, and I can't say—" *God.*

Raphael's eyes flashed upward; he did look amused. "Age," he said. "And practice. And faith, or its loss—they are in some ways the same thing. You will learn, over time, little fledgling."

"Don't *call* me that."

"But it is what you are. You're a Child of the Night. Isn't that why Valentine captured you and took your blood? Because of what you are?"

"You seem pretty well-informed," Simon said. "Maybe you should tell me."

Raphael's eyes narrowed. "I have also heard a rumor that you drank the blood of a Shadowhunter and that is what gave you your gift, your ability to walk in sunlight. Is it true?"

Simon's hair prickled. "That's ridiculous. If Shadowhunter

blood could give vampires the ability to walk in daylight, everyone would know it by now. Nephilim blood would be at a premium. And there would *never* be peace between vampires and Shadowhunters after that. So it's a good thing it isn't true."

A faint smile turned up the edges of Raphael's mouth. "True enough. Speaking of premiums, you do realize, don't you, Daylighter, that you are a valuable commodity now? There isn't a Downworlder on this earth who doesn't want to get their hands on you."

"Does that include you?"

"Of course it does."

"And what would you do if you did get your hands on me?"

Raphael shrugged his slight shoulders. "Perhaps I am alone in thinking that the ability to walk in the daylight might not be such a gift as other vampires believe. We are the Children of the Night for a reason. It is possible that I consider you as much of an abomination as humanity considers me."

"Do you?"

"It's possible." Raphael's expression was neutral. "I think you're a danger to us all. A danger to vampirekind, if you will. And you can't stay in this cell forever, Daylighter. Eventually you'll have to leave and face the world again. Face me again. But I can tell you one thing. I will swear to do you no harm, and not try to find you, if you in turn swear to hide yourself away once Aldertree releases you. If you swear to go so far away that no one will ever find you, and to never again contact anyone you knew in your mortal life. I can't be more fair than that."

But Simon was already shaking his head. "I can't leave my family. Or Clary."

Raphael made an irritable noise. "They are no longer part of who you are. You're a vampire now."

"But I don't want to be," said Simon.

"Look at you, complaining," said Raphael. "You will never get sick, never die, and be strong and young forever. You will never age. What have you got to complain about?"

Young forever, Simon thought. It sounded good, but did anyone really want to be sixteen forever? It would have been one thing to be frozen forever at twenty-five, but sixteen? To always be this gangly, to never really grow into himself, his face or his body? Not to mention that, looking like this, he'd never be able to go into a bar and order a drink. Ever. For eternity.

"And," Raphael added, "you do not even have to give up the sun."

Simon had no desire to go down that road again. "I heard the others talking about you in the Dumort," he said. "I know you put on a cross every Sunday and go to see your family. I bet they don't even know you're a vampire. So don't tell me to leave everyone in my life behind. I won't do it, and I won't lie and say I will."

Raphael's eyes glittered. "What my family believes doesn't matter. It's what *I* believe. What I know. A true vampire knows he is dead. He accepts his death. But you, you think you are still one of the living. It is that which makes you so dangerous. You cannot acknowledge that you are no longer alive."

It was twilight when Clary shut the door of Amatis's house behind her and threw the bolts home. She leaned against the door for a long moment in the shadowy entryway, her eyes half-shut. Exhaustion weighed down every one of her limbs, and her legs ached painfully.

"Clary?" Amatis's insistent voice cut through the silence. "Is that you?"

Clary stayed where she was, adrift in the calming darkness behind her closed eyes. She wanted so badly to be home, she could almost taste the metallic air of the Brooklyn streets. She could see her mother sitting in her chair by the window, dusty, pale yellow light streaming in through the open apartment windows, illuminating her canvas as she painted. Homesickness twisted in her gut like pain.

"Clary." The voice came from much closer this time. Clary's eyes snapped open. Amatis was standing in front of her, her gray hair pulled severely back, her hands on her hips. "Your brother's here to see you. He's waiting in the kitchen."

"*Jace* is here?" Clary fought to keep her rage and astonishment off her face. There was no point showing how angry she was in front of Luke's sister.

Amatis was looking at her curiously. "Should I not have let him in? I thought you'd want to see him."

"No, it's fine," Clary said, maintaining her even tone with some difficulty. "I'm just tired."

"Huh." Amatis looked as if she didn't believe it. "Well, I'll be upstairs if you want me. I need a nap."

Clary couldn't imagine what she'd want Amatis for, but she nodded and limped down the corridor into the kitchen, which was awash with bright light. There was a bowl of fruit on the table—oranges, apples, and pears—and a loaf of thick bread along with butter and cheese, and a plate beside it of what looked like . . . cookies? Had Amatis actually made *cookies*?

At the table sat Jace. He was leaning forward on his elbows, his golden hair tousled, his shirt slightly open at the neck. She could see the thick banding of black Marks tracing his collarbone. He held a cookie in his bandaged hand. So Sebastian was right; he *had* hurt himself. Not that she cared. "Good," he said, "you're back. I was beginning to think you'd fallen into a canal."

Clary just stared at him, wordless. She wondered if he could read the anger in her eyes. He leaned back in the chair, throwing one arm casually over the back of it. If it hadn't been for the rapid pulse at the base of his throat, she might almost have believed his air of unconcern.

"You look exhausted," he added. "Where have you been all day?"

"I was out with Sebastian."

"*Sebastian?*" His look of utter astonishment was momentarily gratifying.

"He walked me home last night," Clary said, and in her mind the words *I'll just be your brother from now on, just your brother* beat like the rhythm of a damaged heart. "And so far, he's the only person in this city who's been remotely nice to me. So yes, I was out with Sebastian."

"I see." Jace set his cookie back down on the plate, his face blank. "Clary, I came here to apologize. I shouldn't have spoken to you the way I did."

"No," Clary said. "You shouldn't have."

"I also came to ask you if you'd reconsider going back to New York."

"God," Clary said. "This again—"

"It's not safe for you here."

"What are you worried about?" she asked tonelessly. "That

they'll throw me in prison like they did with Simon?"

Jace's expression didn't change, but he rocked back in his chair, the front legs lifting off the floor, almost as if she had shoved him. "Simon—?"

"Sebastian told me what happened to him," she went on in the same flat voice. "What you did. How you brought him here and then let him just get thrown in jail. Are you *trying* to get me to hate you?"

"And you trust Sebastian?" Jace asked. "You barely know him, Clary."

She stared at him. "Is it *not* true?"

He met her gaze, but his face had gone still, like Sebastian's face when she'd pushed him away. "It's true."

She seized a plate off the table and flung it at him. He ducked, sending the chair spinning, and the plate hit the wall above the sink and shattered in a starburst of broken porcelain. He leaped out of the chair as she picked up another plate and threw it, her aim going wild: This one bounced off the refrigerator and hit the floor at Jace's feet where it cracked into two even pieces. "How could you? Simon trusted you. Where is he now? What are they going to do to him?"

"Nothing," Jace said. "He's all right. I saw him last night—"

"Before or after I saw you? Before or after you pretended everything was all right and you were just fine?"

"You came away from *that* thinking I was just fine?" Jace choked on something almost like a laugh. "I must be a better actor than I thought." There was a twisted smile on his face. It was a match to the tinder of Clary's rage: How *dare* he laugh at her now? She scrabbled for the fruit bowl, but it suddenly didn't seem like enough. She kicked the chair out of the way and flung herself at him, knowing it would be the last thing he'd expect her to do.

The force of her sudden assault caught him off guard. She slammed into him and he staggered backward, fetching up hard against the edge of the counter. She half-fell against him, heard him gasp, and drew back her arm blindly, not even knowing what she intended to do—

She had forgotten how fast he was. Her fist slammed not into his face, but into his upraised hand; he wrapped his fingers around hers, forcing her arm back down to her side. She was suddenly aware of how close they were standing; she was leaning against him, pressing him back against the counter with the slight weight of her body. "Let go of my hand."

"Are you really going to hit me if I do?" His voice was rough and soft, his eyes blazing.

"Don't you think you deserve it?"

She felt the rise and fall of his chest against her as he laughed without amusement. "Do you think I planned all this? Do you really think I'd do that?"

"Well, you don't like Simon, do you? Maybe you never have."

Jace made a harsh, incredulous sound and let go of her hand. When Clary stepped back, he held out his right arm, palm up. It took her a moment to realize what he was showing her: the ragged scar along his wrist. "This," he said, his voice as taut as a wire, "is where I cut my wrist to let your vampire friend drink my blood. It nearly killed me. And now you think, what, that I just abandoned him without a thought?"

She stared at the scar on Jace's wrist—one of so many all over his body, scars of all shapes and sizes. "Sebastian told me that you brought Simon here, and then Alec marched him up to the

Gard. Let the Clave have him. You must have known—"

"I brought him here by *accident*. I asked him to come to the Institute so I could talk to him. About *you*, actually. I thought maybe he could convince you to drop the idea of coming to Idris. If it's any consolation, he wouldn't even consider it. While he was there, we were attacked by Forsaken. I *had* to drag him through the Portal with me. It was that or leave him there to die."

"But why bring him to the Clave? You must have known—"

"The reason we sent him there was because the only Portal in Idris is in the Gard. They told us they were sending him back to New York."

"And you *believed* them? After what happened with the Inquisitor?"

"Clary, the Inquisitor was an anomaly. That might have been your first experience with the Clave, but it wasn't mine—the Clave is *us*. The Nephilim. They abide by the Law."

"Except they didn't."

"No," Jace said. "They didn't." He sounded very tired. "And the worst part about all this," he added, "is remembering Valentine ranting about the Clave, how it's corrupt, how it needs to be cleansed. And by the Angel if I don't agree with him."

Clary was silent, first because she could think of nothing to say, and then in startlement as Jace reached out—almost as if he weren't thinking about what he was doing—and drew her toward him. To her surprise, she let him. Through the white material of his shirt she could see the outlines of his Marks, black and curling, stroking across his skin like licks of flame. She wanted to lean her head against him, wanted to feel his arms around her the way she'd wanted air when she was drowning in Lake Lyn.

"He might be right that things need fixing," she said finally. "But he's not right about the way they should be fixed. You can see that, can't you?"

He half-closed his eyes. There were crescents of gray shadow under them, she saw, the remnants of sleepless nights. "I'm not sure I can see anything. You're right to be angry, Clary. I shouldn't have trusted the Clave. I wanted so badly to think that the Inquisitor was an abnormality, that she was acting without their authority, that there was still some part of being a Shadowhunter I could trust."

"Jace," she whispered.

He opened his eyes and looked down at her. She and Jace were pressed so close together, even their knees were touching, and she could feel his heartbeat. *Move away from him,* she told herself, but her legs wouldn't obey.

"What is it?" he said, his voice very soft.

"I want to see Simon," she said. "Can you take me to see him?"

As abruptly as he had caught hold of her, he let her go. "No. You're not even supposed to be in Idris. You can't go waltzing into the Gard."

"But he'll think everyone's abandoned him. He'll think—"

"I went to see him," Jace said. "I was going to let him out. I was going to tear the bars out of the window with my hands." His voice was matter-of-fact. "But he wouldn't let me."

"He wouldn't *let* you? He wanted to stay in jail?"

"He said the Inquisitor was sniffing around after my family, after me. Aldertree wants to blame what happened in New York on us. He can't grab one of us and torture it out of us—the Clave would frown on *that*—but he's trying to get Simon to tell him some story where we're all in cahoots with Valentine. Simon said if I break him out, then the Inquisitor will know I did it, and it'll be even worse for the Lightwoods."

"That's very noble of him and all, but what's his long-range plan? To stay in jail forever?"

Jace shrugged. "We hadn't exactly worked that out."

Clary blew out an exasperated breath. "*Boys,*" she said. "All right, look. What you need is an alibi. We'll make sure you're somewhere everyone can see you, and the Lightwoods are too, and then we'll get Magnus to break Simon out of prison and get him back to New York."

"I hate to tell you this, Clary, but there's no way Magnus would do that. I don't care how cute he thinks Alec is, he's not going to go directly against the Clave as a favor to us."

"He might," Clary said, "for the Book of the White."

Jace blinked. "The what?"

Quickly Clary told him about Ragnor Fell's death, about Magnus showing up in Fell's place, and about the spell book. Jace listened with stunned attentiveness until she finished.

"Demons?" he said. "Magnus said Fell was killed by demons?"

Clary cast her mind back. "No—he said the place stank of something demonic in origin. And that Fell was killed by 'Valentine's servants.' That's all he said."

"Some dark magic leaves an aura that reeks like demons," Jace said. "If Magnus wasn't specific, it's probably because he's none too pleased that there's a warlock out there practicing dark magic, breaking the Law. But it's hardly the first time Valentine's gotten one of Lilith's children to do his nasty bidding. Remember the warlock kid he killed in New York?"

"Valentine used his blood for the Ritual. I remember." Clary shuddered. "Jace, does Valentine want the Book for the same reason I do? To wake my mother up?"

"He might. Or if it's what Magnus says it is, Valentine might just want it for the power he could gain from it. Either way, we'd better get it before he does."

"Do you think there's any chance it's in the Wayland manor?"

"I know it's there," he said, to her surprise. "That cookbook? *Recipes for Housewives* or whatever? I've seen it before. In the manor's library. It was the only cookbook in there."

Clary felt dizzy. She almost hadn't let herself believe it could be true. "Jace—if you take me to the manor, and we get the book, I'll go home with Simon. Do this for me and I'll go to New York, and I won't come back, I swear."

"Magnus was right—there are misdirection wards on the manor," he said slowly. "I'll take you there, but it's not close. Walking, it might take us five hours."

Clary reached out and drew his stele out of its loop on his belt. She held it up between them, where it glowed with a faint white light not unlike the light of the glass towers. "Who said anything about walking?"

"You get some strange visitors, Daylighter," Samuel said. "First Jonathan Morgenstern, and now the head vampire of New York City. I'm impressed."

Jonathan Morgenstern? It took Simon a moment to realize that this was, of course, Jace. He was sitting on the floor in the center of the room, turning the empty flask in his hands over and over idly. "I guess I'm more important than I realized."

"And Isabelle Lightwood bringing you blood," Samuel said. "That's quite a delivery service."

Simon's head went up. "How do you know Isabelle brought it? I didn't say anything—"

"I saw her through the window. She looks just like her mother," said Samuel, "at least, the way her mother did years ago." There was an awkward pause. "You know the blood is only a stopgap," he added. "Pretty soon the Inquisitor will start wondering if you've starved to death yet. If he finds you perfectly healthy, he'll figure out something's up and kill you anyway."

Simon looked up at the ceiling. The runes carved into the stone overlapped one another like shingled sand on a beach. "I guess I'll just have to believe Jace when he says they'll find a way to get me out," he said. When Samuel said nothing in return, he added, "I'll ask him to get you out too, I promise. I won't leave you down here."

Samuel made a choked noise, like a laugh that couldn't quite make it out of his throat. "Oh, I don't think Jace Morgenstern is going to want to rescue *me*," he said. "Besides, starving down here is the least of your problems, Daylighter. Soon enough Valentine will attack the city, and then we'll likely all be killed."

Simon blinked. "How can you be so sure?"

"I was close to him at one point. I knew his plans. His goals. He intends to destroy Alicante's wards and strike at the Clave from the heart of their power."

"But I thought no demons could get past the wards. I thought they were impenetrable."

"So it's said. It requires demon blood to take the wards down, you see, and it can only be done from inside Alicante. But because no demon can get through the wards—well, it's a perfect paradox, or should be. But Valentine claimed he'd found a way to get around that, a way to break through. And I believe him. He will find a way to take the wards down, and he will come into the city with his demon army, and he will kill us all."

The flat certainty in Samuel's voice sent a chill up Simon's spine. "You sound awfully resigned. Shouldn't you do something? Warn the Clave?"

"I did warn them. When they interrogated me. I told them over and over again that Valentine meant to destroy the wards, but they dismissed me. The Clave thinks the wards will stand forever because they've stood for a thousand years. But so did Rome, till the barbarians came. Everything falls someday." He chuckled: a bitter, angry sound. "Consider it a race to see who kills you first, Daylighter—Valentine, the other Downworlders, or the Clave."

Somewhere between *here* and *there* Clary's hand was torn out of Jace's. When the hurricane spit her out and she hit the floor, she hit it alone, hard, and rolled gasping to a stop.

She sat up slowly and looked around. She was lying in the center of a Persian rug thrown over the floor of a large stone-walled room. There were items of furniture here and there; the white sheets thrown over them turned them into humped, unwieldy ghosts. Velvet curtains sagged across huge glass windows; the velvet was gray-white with dust, and motes of dust danced in the moonlight.

"Clary?" Jace emerged from behind a massive white-sheeted shape; it might have been a grand piano. "Are you all right?"

"Fine." She stood up, wincing a little. Her elbow ached. "Aside from the fact that Amatis will probably kill me when we get back. Considering that I smashed all her plates *and* opened up a Portal in her kitchen."

He reached his hand down to her. "For whatever it's worth,"

he said, helping her to her feet, "I was very impressed."

"Thanks." Clary glanced around. "So this is where you grew up? It's like something out of a fairy tale."

"I was thinking a horror movie," Jace said. "God, it's been years since I've seen this place. It didn't used to be so—"

"So cold?" Clary shivered a little. She buttoned her coat, but the cold in the manor was more than physical cold: The place *felt* cold, as if there had never been warmth or light or laughter inside it.

"No," said Jace. "It was always cold. I was going to say *dusty*." He took a witchlight stone out of his pocket, and it flared to life between his fingers. Its white glow lit his face from beneath, picking out the shadows under his cheekbones, the hollows at his temples. "This is the study, and we need the library. Come on."

He led her from the room and down a long corridor lined with dozens of mirrors that gave back their own reflections. Clary hadn't realized quite how disheveled she looked: her coat streaked with dust, her hair snarled from the wind. She tried to smooth it down discreetly and caught Jace's grin in the next mirror. For some reason, due doubtless to a mysterious Shadowhunter magic she didn't have a hope of understanding, *his* hair looked perfect.

The corridor was lined with doors, some open; through them Clary could glimpse other rooms, as dusty and unused-looking as the study had been. Michael Wayland had had no relatives, Valentine had said, so she supposed no one had inherited this place after his "death"—she had assumed Valentine had carried on living here, but that seemed clearly not to be the case. Everything breathed sorrow and disuse. At Renwick's, Valentine had called this place "home," had showed it to Jace in the Portal mirror, a gilt-edged memory of green fields and mellow stone, but that, Clary thought, had been a lie too. It was clear Valentine hadn't really lived here in years—perhaps he had just left it here to rot, or he had come here only occasionally, to walk the dim corridors like a ghost.

They reached a door at the end of the hallway and Jace shouldered it open, standing back to let Clary pass into the room before him. She had been picturing the library at the Institute, and this room was not entirely unlike it: the same walls filled with row upon row of books, the same ladders on rolling casters so the high shelves could be reached. The ceiling was flat and beamed, though, not conical, and there was no desk. Green velvet curtains, their folds iced with white dust, hung over windows that alternated panes of green and blue glass. In the moonlight they sparkled like colored frost. Beyond the glass, all was black.

"This is the library?" she said to Jace in a whisper, though she wasn't sure why she was whispering. There was something so profoundly still about the big, empty house.

He was looking past her, his eyes dark with memory. "I used to sit in that window seat and read whatever my father had assigned me that day. Different languages on different days—French on Saturday, English on Sunday—but I can't remember now what day Latin was, if it was Monday or Tuesday. . . ."

Clary had a sudden flashing image of Jace as a little boy, book balanced on his knees as he sat in the window embrasure, looking out over—over what? Were there gardens? A view? A high wall of thorns like the wall around Sleeping Beauty's castle? She saw him as he read, the light that came in through the window casting squares of blue and green over his fair hair and the small face more serious than any ten-year-old's should be.

"I can't remember," he said again, staring into the dark.

She touched his shoulder. "It doesn't matter, Jace."

"I suppose not." He shook himself, as if waking out of a dream, and moved across the room, the witchlight lighting his way. He knelt down to inspect a row of books and straightened up with one of them in his hand. "*Simple Recipes for Housewives,*" he said. "Here it is."

She hurried across the room and took it from him. It was a plain-looking book with a blue binding, and dusty, like everything in the house. When she opened it, dust swarmed up from its pages like a gathering of moths.

A large, square hole had been cut out of the center of the book. Fitted into the hole like a jewel in a bezel was a smaller volume, about the size of a small chapbook, bound in white leather with the title printed in gilded Latin letters. Clary recognized the words for "white" and "book," but when she lifted it out and opened it, to her surprise the pages were covered with thin, spidery handwriting in a language she couldn't understand.

"Greek," Jace said, looking over her shoulder. "Of the ancient variety."

"Can you read it?"

"Not easily," he admitted. "It's been years. But Magnus will be able to, I imagine." He closed the book and slipped it into the pocket of her green coat before turning back to the bookshelves, skimming his fingers along the rows of books, his fingertips tracing their spines.

"Are there any of these you want to take with you?" she asked gently. "If you'd like—"

Jace laughed and dropped his hand. "I was only allowed to read what I was assigned," he said. "Some of the shelves had books on them I wasn't even allowed to touch." He indicated a row of books, higher up, bound in matching brown leather. "I read one of them once, when I was about six, just to see what the fuss was about. It turned out to be a journal my father was keeping. About me. Notes about *'my son, Jonathan Christopher.'* He whipped me with a belt when he found out I'd read it. Actually, it was the first time I even knew I had a middle name."

A sudden ache of hatred for her father went through Clary. "Well, Valentine's not here now."

"Clary . . . ," Jace began, a warning note in his voice, but she'd already reached up and yanked one of the books out from the forbidden shelf, knocking it to the ground. It made a satisfying thump. "Clary!"

"Oh, come on." She did it again, knocking another book down, and then another. Dust puffed up from their pages as they hit the floor. "You try."

Jace looked at her for a moment, and then a half smile teased the corner of his mouth. Reaching up, he swept his arm along the shelf, knocking the rest of the books to the ground with a loud crash. He laughed—and then broke off, lifting his head, like a cat pricking up its ears at a distant sound. "Do you hear that?"

Hear what? Clary was about to ask, and stopped herself. There *was* a sound, getting louder now—a high-pitched whirring and grinding, like the sound of machinery coming to life. The sound seemed to be coming from inside the wall. She took an involuntary step back just as the stones in front of them slid back with a groaning, rusty scream. An opening gaped behind the stones—a sort of doorway, roughly hacked out of the wall.

Beyond the doorway was a set of stairs, leading down into darkness.

9
This Guilty Blood

"I didn't remember there even *being* a cellar here," Jace said, staring past Clary at the gaping hole in the wall. He raised the witchlight, and its glow bounced off the downward-leading tunnel. The walls were black and slick, made of a smooth dark stone Clary didn't recognize. The steps gleamed as if they were damp. A strange smell drifted up through the opening: dank, musty, with a weird metallic tinge that set her nerves on edge.

"What do you think could be down there?"

"I don't know." Jace moved toward the stairs; he put a foot on the top step, testing it, and then shrugged as if he'd made up his mind. He began to make his way down the steps, moving carefully. Partway down he turned and looked up at Clary. "Are you coming? You can wait up here for me if you want to."

She glanced around the empty library, then shivered and hurried after him.

The stairs spiraled down in tighter and tighter circles, as if they were making their way through the inside of a huge conch shell. The smell grew stronger as they reached the bottom, and the steps widened out into a large square room whose stone walls were streaked with the marks of damp—and other, darker stains. The floor was scrawled with markings: a jumble of pentagrams and runes, with white stones scattered here and there.

Jace took a step forward and something crunched under his feet. He and Clary looked down at the same time. "Bones," Clary whispered. Not white stones after all, but bones of all shapes and sizes, scattered across the floor. "What was he *doing* down here?"

The witchlight burned in Jace's hand, casting its eerie glow over the room. "Experiments," Jace said in a dry, tense tone. "The Seelie Queen said—"

"What kind of bones are these?" Clary's voice rose. "Are they animal bones?"

"No." Jace kicked a pile of bones with his feet, scattering them. "Not all of them."

Clary's chest felt tight. "I think we should go back."

Instead Jace raised the witchlight in his hand. It blazed out, brightly and then more brightly, lighting the air with a harsh white brilliance. The far corners of the room sprang into focus. Three of them were empty. The fourth was blocked with a hanging cloth. There was something behind the cloth, a humped shape—

"Jace," Clary whispered. "What *is* that?"

He didn't reply. There was a seraph blade in his free hand, suddenly; Clary didn't know when he'd drawn it, but it shone in the witchlight like a blade of ice.

"Jace, *don't*," said Clary, but it was too late—he strode forward and twitched the cloth aside with the tip of the blade, then seized it and jerked it down. It fell in a blossoming cloud of dust.

Jace staggered back, the witchlight falling from his grasp. As the blazing light fell, Clary caught a single glimpse of his face: It was a white mask of horror. Clary snatched the witchlight up before it could go dark and raised it high, desperate to see what could have shocked Jace—unshockable Jace—so badly.

At first all she saw was the shape of a man—a man wrapped in a dirty white rag, crouched on the floor. Manacles circled his wrists and ankles, attached to thick metal staples driven into the stone floor. *How can he be alive?* Clary thought in horror, and bile rose up in her throat. The rune-stone shook in her hand, and light danced in patches over the prisoner: She saw emaciated arms and legs, scarred all over with the marks of countless tortures. The skull of a face turned toward her, black empty sockets where the eyes should have been—and then there was a dry rustle, and she saw that what she had thought was a white rag were *wings*, white wings rising up behind his back in two pure white crescents, the only pure things in this filthy room.

She gave a dry gasp. "*Jace.* Do you see—"

"I see." Jace, standing beside her, spoke in a voice that cracked like broken glass.

"You said there weren't any angels—that no one had ever seen one—"

Jace was whispering something under his breath, a string of what sounded like panicked curses. He stumbled forward, toward the huddled creature on the floor—and recoiled, as if he had bounced off an invisible wall. Looking down, Clary saw that the angel crouched inside a pentagram made of connected runes graven deeply into the floor; they glowed with a faint phosphorescent light. "The runes," she whispered. "We can't get past—"

"But there must be something—," Jace said, his voice nearly breaking, "something we can do."

The angel raised its head. Clary saw with a distracted, terrible pity that it had curling golden hair like Jace's that shone dully in the light. Tendrils clung close to the hollows of its skull. Its eyes were pits, its face slashed with scars, like a beautiful painting destroyed by vandals. As she stared, its mouth opened and a sound poured from its throat—not words but a piercing golden music, a single singing note, held and held and held so high and sweet that the sound was like pain—

A flood of images rose up before Clary's eyes. She was still clutching the rune-stone, but its light was gone; she was gone, no longer there but somewhere else, where the pictures of the past flowed before her in a waking dream—fragments, colors, sounds.

She was in a wine cellar, bare and clean, a single huge rune scrawled on the stone floor. A man stood beside it; he held an open book in one hand and a blazing white torch in the other. When he raised his head, Clary saw that it was Valentine: much younger, his face unlined and handsome, his dark eyes clear and bright. As he chanted, the rune blazed up into fire, and when the flames receded, a crumpled figure lay among the ashes: an angel, wings spread and bloody, like a bird shot out of the sky. . . .

The scene changed. Valentine stood by a window, at his side a young woman with shining red hair. A familiar silver ring gleamed on his hand as he reached to put his arms around her. With a jolt of pain Clary recognized her mother—but she was young, her features soft and vulnerable. She was wearing a white nightgown and was obviously pregnant.

"The Accords," Valentine was saying angrily, "were not just the worst idea the Clave has ever had, but the worst thing that could happen to Nephilim. That we should be *bound* to Downworlders, tied to those creatures—"

"Valentine," Jocelyn said with a smile, "enough about politics, *please*." She reached up and twined her arms around Valentine's neck, her expression full of love—and his was as well, but there was something else in it, something that sent a shiver down Clary's spine. . . .

Valentine knelt in the center of a circle of trees. There was a bright moon overhead, illuminating the black pentagram that had been scrawled into the scraped earth of the clearing. The branches of trees made a thick net overhead; where they extended above the edge of the pentagram, their leaves curled and turned black. In the center of the five-pointed star sat a woman with long, shining hair; her shape was slim and lovely, her face hidden in shadow, her arms bare and white. Her left hand was extended in front of her, and as she opened her fingers, Clary could see that there was a long slash across her palm, dripping a slow stream of blood into a silver cup that rested on the pentagram's edge. The blood looked black in the moonlight, or perhaps it *was* black.

"The child born with this blood in him," she said, and her voice was soft and lovely, "will exceed in power the Greater Demons of the abysses between the worlds. He will be more mighty than the Asmodei, stronger than the *shedim* of the storms. If he is properly trained, there is nothing he will not be able to do. Though I warn you," she added, "it will burn out his humanity, as poison burns the life from the blood."

"My thanks to you, Lady of Edom," said Valentine, and as he reached to take the cup of blood, the woman lifted her face, and Clary saw that though she was otherwise beautiful, her eyes were hollow black holes from which curled waving black tentacles, like feelers probing the air. Clary stifled a scream—

The night, the forest, vanished. Jocelyn stood facing someone Clary couldn't see. She was no longer pregnant, and her bright hair straggled around her stricken, despairing face. "I can't stay with him, Ragnor," she said. "Not for another day. I read his book. Do you know what he did to Jonathan? I didn't think even Valentine could do that." Her shoulders shook. "He used demon blood—Jonathan's not a baby anymore. He isn't even human; he's a monster—"

She vanished. Valentine was pacing restlessly around the circle of runes, a seraph blade shining in his hand. "Why won't you *speak?*" he muttered. "Why won't you *give me what I want?*" He drove down with the knife, and the angel writhed as golden liquid poured from its wound like spilled sunlight. "If you won't give me answers," Valentine hissed, "you can give me your blood. It will do me and mine more good than it will you."

Now they were in the Wayland library. Sunlight shone through the diamond-paned windows, flooding the room with blue and green. Voices came from another room: the sounds of laughter and chatting, a party going on. Jocelyn knelt by the bookshelf, glancing from side to side. She drew a thick book from her pocket and slipped it onto the shelf. . . .

And she was gone. The scene showed a cellar, the same cellar that Clary knew she was standing in right now. The same scrawled pentagram scarred the floor, and within the center of the star lay the angel. Valentine stood by, once again with a burning seraph blade in his hand. He looked years older now, no longer a young man. "Ithuriel," he said. "We are old friends now, aren't we? I could have left you buried alive under those ruins, but no, I brought you here with me. All these years I've kept you close, hoping one day you would tell me what I wanted—needed—to know." He came closer, holding the blade out, its blaze lighting the runic barrier to a shimmer. "When I summoned you, I dreamed that you would tell me *why*. Why Raziel created us, his race of Shadowhunters, yet did not give us the powers Downworlders have—the speed of the wolves, the immortality of the Fair Folk, the magic of warlocks, even the endurance of vampires. He left us naked before the hosts of hell but for these painted lines on our skin. Why should their powers be greater than ours? Why can't we share in what they have? How is that *just?*"

Within its imprisoning star the angel sat silent as a marble statue, unmoving, its wings folded. Its eyes expressed nothing beyond a terrible silent sorrow. Valentine's mouth twisted.

"Very well. Keep your silence. I will have my chance." Valentine lifted the blade. "I have the Mortal Cup, Ithuriel, and soon I shall have the Sword—but without the Mirror I cannot begin the summoning. The Mirror is all I need. Tell me where it is. Tell me where it is, Ithuriel, and I will let you die."

The scene broke apart in fragments, and as her vision faded, Clary caught glimpses of images now familiar to her from her own nightmares—angels with wings both white and black, sheets of mirrored water, gold and blood—and Jace, turning away from her, always turning away. Clary reached out for him, and for the first time the angel's voice spoke in her head in words that she could understand.

These are not the first dreams I have ever showed you.

The image of a rune burst behind her eyes, like fireworks—not a rune she had ever seen before; it was as strong, simple, and straightforward as a tied knot. It was gone in a breath as well, and as it vanished, the angel's singing ceased. Clary was back in her own body, reeling on her feet in the filthy and reeking room. The angel was silent, frozen, wings folded, a grieving effigy.

Clary let out her breath in a sob. "*Ithuriel.*" She reached her hands out to the angel, knowing she couldn't pass the runes, her heart aching. For years the angel had been down here, sitting silent and alone in the blackness, chained and starving but unable to die. . . .

Jace was beside her. She could see from his stricken face that he'd seen everything she had. He looked down at the seraph blade in his hand and then back at the angel. Its blind face was turned toward them in silent supplication.

Jace took a step forward, and then another. His eyes were fixed on the angel, and it was as if, Clary thought, there were some silent communication passing between them, some speech she couldn't hear. Jace's eyes were bright as gold disks, full of reflected light.

"*Ithuriel,*" he whispered.

The blade in his hand blazed up like a torch. Its glow was blinding. The angel raised its face, as if the light were visible to its blind eyes. It reached out its hands, the chains that bound its wrists rattling like harsh music.

Jace turned to her. "Clary," he said. "The runes."

The runes. For a moment she stared at him, puzzled, but his eyes urged her onward. She handed Jace the witchlight, took his stele from her pocket, and knelt down by the scrawled runes. They looked as if they'd been gouged into the stone with something sharp.

She glanced up at Jace. His expression startled her, the blaze in his eyes—they were full of faith in her, of confidence in her abilities. With the tip of the stele she traced several lines into the floor, changing the runes of binding to runes of release, imprisonment to openness. They flared up as she traced them, as if she were dragging a match tip across sulphur.

Done, she rose to her feet. The runes shimmered before her. Abruptly Jace moved to stand beside her. The witchlight stone was gone, the only illumination coming from the seraph blade that he'd named for the angel, blazing in his hand. He stretched it out, and this time his hand passed through the barrier of the runes as if there were nothing there.

The angel reached its hands up and took the blade from him. It shut its blind eyes, and Clary thought for a moment that it smiled. It turned the blade in its grasp until the sharp tip rested just blow its breastbone. Clary gave a little gasp and moved forward, but Jace grabbed her arm, his grip like iron, and yanked her backward—just as the angel drove the blade home.

The angel's head fell back, its hands dropping from the hilt, which protruded from just where its heart would be—if angels had hearts; Clary didn't know. Flames burst from the wound, spreading outward from the blade. The angel's body shimmered into white flame, the chains on its wrist burning scarlet, like iron left too long in a fire. Clary thought of medieval paintings of saints consumed in the blaze of holy ecstasy—and the angel's wings flew wide and white before they, too, caught and blazed up, a lattice of shimmering fire.

Clary could no longer watch. She turned and buried her face in Jace's shoulder. His arm came around her, his grip tight and hard. "It's all right," he said into her hair, "it's all right," but the air was full of smoke and the ground felt like it was rocking under her feet. It was only when Jace stumbled that she realized it wasn't shock: The ground *was* moving. She let go of Jace and staggered; the stones underfoot were grinding together, and a thin rain of dirt was sifting down from the ceiling. The angel was a pillar of smoke; the runes around it glowed painfully bright. Clary stared at them, decoding their meaning, and then looked wildly at Jace: "The manor—it was tied to Ithuriel. If the angel dies, the manor—"

She didn't finish her sentence. He had already seized her hand and was running for the stairs, pulling her along after him. The stairs themselves were surging and buckling; Clary fell, banging her knee painfully on a step, but Jace's grip on her arm didn't loosen. She raced on, ignoring the pain in her leg, her lungs full of choking dust.

They reached the top of the steps and exploded out into the library. Behind them Clary could hear the soft roar as the rest of the stairs collapsed. It wasn't much better here; the room was shuddering, books tumbling from their shelves. A statue lay where it had tipped over, in a pile of jagged shards. Jace let go of Clary's hand, seized up a chair, and, before she could ask him what he meant to do, threw it at the stained-glass window.

It sailed through in a waterfall of broken glass. Jace turned and held his hand out to her. Behind him, through the jagged frame that remained, she could see a moonlight-saturated stretch of grass and a line of treetops in the distance. They seemed a long way down. *I can't jump that far,* she thought, and was about to shake her head at Jace when she saw his eyes widen, his mouth shaping a warning. One of the heavy marble busts that lined the higher shelves had slid free and was falling toward her; she ducked out of its way, and it hit the floor inches from where she'd been standing, leaving a sizable dent in the floor.

A second later Jace's arms were around her and he was lifting her off her feet. She was too surprised to struggle as he carried her over to the broken window and dumped her unceremoniously out of it.

She hit a grassy rise just below the window and tumbled down its steep incline, gaining speed until she fetched up against a hillock with enough force to knock the breath out of her. She sat up, shaking grass out of her hair. A second later Jace came to a stop next to her; unlike her, he rolled immediately into a crouch, staring up the hill at the manor house.

Clary turned to look where he was looking, but he'd already grabbed her, shoving her down into the depression between the two hills. Later she'd find dark bruises on her upper arms where he'd held her; now she just gasped in surprise as he knocked her down and rolled on top of her, shielding her with his body as a huge roar went up. It sounded like the earth shattering apart, like a volcano erupting. A blast of white dust shot into the sky. Clary heard a sharp pattering noise all around her.

For a bewildered moment she thought it had started to rain—then she realized it was rubble and dirt and broken glass: the detritus of the shattered manor being flung down around them like deadly hail.

Jace pressed her harder into the ground, his body flat against hers, his heartbeat nearly as loud in her ears as the sound of the manor's subsiding ruins.

The roar of the collapse faded slowly, like smoke dissipating into the air. It was replaced by the loud chirruping of startled birds; Clary could see them over Jace's shoulder, circling curiously against the dark sky.

"Jace," she said softly. "I think I dropped your stele somewhere."

He drew back slightly, propping himself on his elbows, and looked down at her. Even in the darkness she could see herself reflected in his eyes; his face was streaked with soot and dirt, the collar of his shirt torn. "That's all right. As long as you're not hurt."

"I'm fine." Without thinking, she reached up, her fingers brushing lightly through his hair. She felt him tense, his eyes darkening.

"There was grass in your hair," she said. Her mouth was dry; adrenaline sang through her veins. Everything that had just happened—the angel, the shattering manor—seemed less real than what she saw in Jace's eyes.

"You shouldn't touch me," he said.

Her hand froze where it was, her palm against his cheek. "Why not?"

"You know why," he said, and shifted away from her,

rolling onto his back. "You saw what I saw, didn't you? The past, the angel. Our parents."

It was the first time, she thought, that he'd called them that. *Our parents.* She turned onto her side, wanting to reach out to him but not sure if she should. He was staring blindly up at the sky. "I saw."

"You know what I am." The words breathed out in an anguished whisper. "I'm part demon, Clary. Part *demon.* You understood that much, didn't you?" His eyes bored into her like drills. "You saw what Valentine was trying to do. He used demon blood—used it on me before I was even born. I'm part monster. Part everything I've tried so hard to burn out, to destroy."

Clary pushed away the memory of Valentine's voice saying, *She told me that I had turned her first child into a monster.* "But warlocks are part demon. Like Magnus. It doesn't make them evil—"

"But they were born that way. Having demon blood put into you is different. It's like being exposed to radiation. It changes you."

Clary's voice trembled. "It's not true. It can't be. It doesn't make sense—"

"But it does." There was a furious desperation in Jace's expression. She could see the gleam of the silver chain around his bare throat, lit to a white flare by the starlight. "It explains *everything.*"

"You mean it explains why you're such an amazing Shadowhunter? Why you're loyal and fearless and honest and everything demons *aren't?*"

"It explains," he said, evenly, "why I feel the way I do about you."

"What do you mean?"

He was silent for a long moment, staring at her across the tiny space that separated them. She could feel him, even though he wasn't touching her, as if he still lay with his body against hers. "You're my sister," he said finally. "My sister, my blood, my family. I should want to protect you"—he laughed soundlessly and without any humor—"to protect you from the sort of boys who want to do with you exactly what *I* want to do."

Clary's breath caught. "You said you just wanted to be my brother from now on."

"I lied," he said. "Demons lie, Clary. You know, there are some kinds of wounds you can get when you're a Shadowhunter—internal injuries from demon poison. You don't even know what's wrong with you, but you're bleeding to death slowly inside. That's what it's like, just being your brother."

"But Aline—"

"I had to *try*. And I did." His voice was lifeless. "But God knows, I don't want anyone but you. I don't even *want* to want anyone but you." He reached out, trailed his fingers lightly through her hair, fingertips brushing her cheek. "Now at least I know why."

Clary's voice had sunk to a whisper. "I don't want anyone but you, either."

She was rewarded by the catch in his breathing. Slowly he drew himself up onto his elbows. Now he was looking down at her, and his expression had changed—there was a look on his face she'd never seen before, a sleepy, almost deadly light in his eyes. He let his fingers trail down her cheek to her lips, outlining the shape of her mouth with the tip of a finger. "You should probably," he said, "tell me not to do this."

She said nothing. She didn't want to tell him to stop. She was tired of saying no to Jace—of never letting herself feel what her whole heart *wanted* her to feel. Whatever the cost.

He bent down, his lips against her cheek, brushing it lightly—and still that light touch sent shivers through her nerves, shivers that made her whole body tremble. "If you want me to stop, tell me now," he whispered. When she still said nothing, he brushed his mouth against the hollow of her temple. "Or now." He traced the line of her cheekbone. "Or now." His lips were against hers. "Or—"

But she had reached up and pulled him down to her, and the rest of his words were lost against her mouth. He kissed her gently, carefully, but it wasn't gentleness she wanted, not now, not after all this time, and she knotted her fists in his shirt, pulling him harder against her. He groaned softly, low in his throat, and then his arms circled her, gathering her against him, and they rolled over on the grass, tangled together, still kissing. There were rocks digging into Clary's back, and her shoulder ached where she'd fallen from the window, but she didn't care. All that existed was Jace; all she felt, hoped, breathed, wanted, and saw was Jace. Nothing else mattered.

Despite her coat, she could feel the heat of him burning through his clothes and hers. She tugged his jacket off, and then somehow his shirt was off too. Her fingers explored his body as his mouth explored hers: soft skin over lean muscle, scars like thin wires. She touched the star-shaped scar on his shoulder—it was smooth and flat, as if it were a part of his skin, not raised like his other scars. She supposed they were imperfections, these marks, but they didn't feel that way to her; they were a history, cut into his body: the map of a life of endless war.

He fumbled with the buttons of her coat, his hands shaking. She didn't think she'd ever seen Jace's hands unsteady before. "I'll do it," she said, and reached for the last button herself; as she raised herself up, something cold and metallic struck her collarbone, and she gasped in surprise.

"What is it?" Jace froze. "Did I hurt you?"

"No. It was this." She touched the silver chain around his neck. On its end hung a small silver circle of metal. It had bumped against her when she'd leaned forward. She stared at it now.

That ring—the weather-beaten metal with its pattern of stars—she knew that ring.

The Morgenstern ring. It was the same ring that had gleamed on Valentine's hand in the dream the angel had showed them. It had been his, and he had given it to Jace, as it had always been passed along, father to son.

"I'm sorry," Jace said. He traced the line of her cheek with his fingertip, a dreamlike intensity in his gaze. "I forgot I was wearing the damn thing."

Sudden cold flooded Clary's veins. "Jace," she said, in a low voice. "Jace, don't."

"Don't what? Don't wear the ring?"

"No, don't—don't touch me. Stop for a second."

His face went still. Questions had chased away the dreamlike confusion in his eyes, but he said nothing, just withdrew his hand.

"Jace," she said again. "Why? Why now?"

His lips parted in surprise. She could see a dark line where he had bitten his bottom lip, or maybe she had bitten it. "Why *what* now?"

"You said there was nothing between us. That if we—if we let ourselves feel what we might want to feel, we'd be hurting everyone we care about."

"I told you. I was lying." His eyes softened. "You think I don't want to—?"

"No," she said. "No, I'm not stupid, I know that you do. But when you said that now you finally understand why you feel this way about me, what did you mean?"

Not that she didn't know, she thought, but she had to ask, had to hear him say it.

Jace caught her wrists and drew her hands up to his face, lacing his fingers through hers. "You remember what I said to you at the Penhallows' house?" he asked. "That you never think about what you do before you do it, and that's why you wreck everything you touch?"

"No, I'd forgotten that. Thanks for the reminder."

He barely seemed to notice the sarcasm in her voice. "I wasn't talking about you, Clary. I was talking about me. That's what *I'm* like." He turned his face slightly and her fingers slid along his cheek. "At least now I know why. I know what's wrong with me. And maybe—maybe that's why I need you so much. Because if Valentine made me a monster, then I suppose he made you a sort of angel. And Lucifer loved God, didn't he? So says Milton, anyway."

Clary sucked in her breath. "I am *not* an angel. And you don't even know that that's what Valentine used Ithuriel's blood for—maybe Valentine just wanted it for himself—"

"He said the blood was for 'me and mine,'" Jace said quietly. "It explains why you can do what you can do, Clary. The Seelie Queen said we were both experiments. Not just me."

"I'm not an angel, Jace," she repeated. "I don't return library books. I steal illegal music off the Internet. I lie to my mom. I am *completely ordinary*."

"Not to me." He looked down at her. His face hovered against a background of stars. There was nothing of his usual arrogance in his expression—she had never seen him look so unguarded, but even that unguardedness was mixed with a self-hatred that ran as deep as a wound. "Clary, I—"

"Get off me," Clary said.

"*What?*" The desire in his eyes cracked into a thousand pieces like the shards of the Portal mirror at Renwick's, and for a moment his expression was blankly astonished. She could hardly bear to look at him and still say no. Looking at him now—even if she *hadn't* been in love with him, that part of her that was her mother's daughter, that loved every beautiful thing for its beauty alone, would still have wanted him.

But, then, it was precisely because she *was* her mother's daughter that it was impossible.

"You heard me," she said. "And leave my hands alone." She snatched them back, knotting them into tight fists to stop their shaking.

He didn't move. His lip curled back, and for a moment she saw that predatory light in his eyes again, but now it was mixed with anger. "I don't suppose you want to tell me *why*?"

"You think you only want me because you're evil, not human. You just want something else you can hate yourself for. I won't let you use me to prove to yourself how worthless you are."

"I never said that. I never said I was using you."

"Fine," she said. "Tell me now that you're not a monster.

Tell me there's nothing wrong with you. And tell me you would want me even if you didn't have demon blood." *Because I don't have demon blood. And I still want you.*

Their gazes locked, his blindly furious; for a moment neither breathed, and then he flung himself off her, swearing, and rolled to his feet. Snatching his shirt up from the grass, he drew it over his head, still glaring. He yanked the shirt down over his jeans and turned away to look for his jacket.

Clary stood up, staggering a little. The stinging wind raised goose bumps on her arms. Her legs felt like they were made of half-melted wax. She did up the buttons on her coat with numb fingers, fighting the urge to burst into tears. Crying wouldn't help anything now.

The air was still full of dancing dust and ash, the grass all around scattered with debris: shattered bits of furniture; the pages of books blowing mournfully in the wind; splinters of gilded wood; a chunk of almost half a staircase, mysteriously unharmed. Clary turned to look at Jace; he was kicking bits of debris with a savage satisfaction. "Well," he said, "we're screwed."

It wasn't what she'd expected. She blinked. "What?"

"Remember? You lost my stele. There's no chance of you drawing a Portal now." He spoke the words with a bitter pleasure, as if the situation satisfied him in some obscure way. "We've got no other way of getting back. We're going to have to walk."

It wouldn't have been a pleasant walk under normal circumstances. Accustomed to city lights, Clary couldn't believe how dark it was in Idris at night. The thick black shadows that lined the road on either side seemed to be crawling with barely visible *things*, and even with Jace's witchlight she could see only a few feet ahead of them. She missed streetlights, the ambient glow of headlights, the sounds of the city. All she could hear now was the steady crunch of their boots on gravel and, every once in a while, her own breath puffing out in surprise as she tripped over a stray rock.

After a few hours her feet began to ache and her mouth was dry as parchment. The air had grown very cold, and she hunched along shivering, her hands thrust deep into her pockets. But even all that would have been bearable if only Jace had been talking to her. He hadn't spoken a word since they'd left the manor except to snap out directions, telling her which way to turn at a fork in the road, or ordering her to skirt a pothole. Even then she doubted if he would have minded much if she'd fallen *into* the pothole, except that it would have slowed them down.

Eventually the sky in the east began to lighten. Clary, stumbling along half-asleep, raised her head in surprise. "It's early for dawn."

Jace looked at her with bland contempt. "That's Alicante. The sun doesn't come up for another three hours at least. Those are the city lights."

Too relieved that they were nearly home to mind his attitude, Clary picked up her pace. They rounded a corner and found themselves walking along a wide dirt path cut into a hillside. It snaked along the curve of the slope, disappearing around a bend in the distance. Though the city was not yet visible, the air had grown brighter, the sky shot through with a peculiar reddish glow.

"We must be nearly there," Clary said. "Is there a shortcut down the hill?"

Jace was frowning. "Something's wrong," he said abruptly. He took off, half-running down the road, his boots sending up puffs of dust that gleamed ochre in the strange light. Clary ran to keep pace, ignoring the protests of her blistered feet. They rounded the next curve and Jace skidded to a sudden halt, sending Clary crashing into him. In another circumstance it might have been comic. It wasn't now.

The reddish light was stronger now, throwing a scarlet glow up into the night sky, lighting the hill they stood on as if it were daylight. Plumes of smoke curled up from the valley below like the unfurling feathers of a black peacock. Rising from the black vapor were the demon towers of Alicante, their crystalline shells like arrows of fire piercing the smoky air. Through the thick smoke, Clary could glimpse the leaping scarlet of flames, scattered across the city like a handful of glittering jewels across a dark cloth.

It seemed incredible, but there it was: They were standing on a hillside high over Alicante, and below them the city was burning.

Part Two
Stars Shine Darkly

ANTONIO: *Will you stay no longer? Nor will you not that I go with you?*

SEBASTIAN: *By your patience, no. My stars shine darkly over me; the malignancy of my fate might, perhaps, distemper yours; therefore I shall crave of you your leave that I may bear my evils alone. It were a bad recompense for your love to lay any of them on you.*

—William Shakespeare, *Twelfth Night*

10

Fire and Sword

"It's late," Isabelle said, fretfully twitching the lace curtain across the high living room window back into place. "He ought to be back by now."

"Be reasonable, Isabelle," Alec pointed out, in that superior big-brother tone that seemed to imply that while she, Isabelle, might be prone to hysteria, he, Alec, was always perfectly calm. Even his posture—he was lounging in one of the overstuffed armchairs next to the Penhallows' fireplace as if he didn't have a care in the world—seemed designed to show off how unworried he was. "Jace does this when he's upset, goes off and wanders around. He said he was going for a walk. He'll be back."

Isabelle sighed. She almost wished her parents were there, but they were still up at the Gard. Whatever the Clave was discussing, the Council meeting was dragging on brutally late. "But he knows New York. He doesn't know Alicante—"

"He probably knows it better than you do." Aline was sitting on the couch reading a book, its pages bound in dark red leather. Her black hair was pulled behind her head in a French braid, her eyes fastened on the volume spread across her lap. Isabelle, who had never been much of a reader, always envied other people their ability to get lost in a book. There were a lot of things she once would have envied Aline for—being small and delicately pretty, for one thing, not Amazonian and so tall in heels she towered over almost every boy she met. But then again, it was only recently that Isabelle had realized other girls weren't just for envying, avoiding, or disliking. "He lived in Idris until he was ten. You guys have only visited a few times."

Isabelle raised her hand to her throat with a frown. The ruby pendant slung on the chain around her neck had given a sudden, sharp pulse—but it normally only pulsed in the presence of demons, and they were in Alicante. There was no way there were demons nearby. Maybe the pendant was malfunctioning. "I don't think he's wandering around, anyway. I think it's pretty obvious where he went," Isabelle responded.

Alec raised his eyes. "You think he went to see Clary?"

"Is she still here? I thought she was supposed to be going back to New York." Aline let her book fall closed. "Where is Jace's sister staying, anyway?"

Isabelle shrugged. "Ask *him*," she said, cutting her eyes toward Sebastian.

Sebastian was sprawled on the couch opposite Aline's. He had a book in his hand too, and his dark head was bent over it. He raised his eyes as if he could feel Isabelle's gaze on him.

"Were you talking about me?" he asked mildly. Everything about Sebastian was mild, Isabelle thought with a twinge of annoyance. She'd been impressed by his looks at first—those sharply planed cheekbones and those black, fathomless eyes—but his affable, sympathetic personality grated on her now. She didn't like boys who looked as if they never got mad about anything. In Isabelle's world, rage equaled passion equaled a good time.

"What are you reading?" she asked, more sharply than she'd meant to. "Is that one of Max's comic books?"

"Yep." Sebastian looked down at the copy of *Angel Sanctuary* balanced on the sofa's arm. "I like the pictures."

Isabelle blew out an exasperated breath. Shooting her a look, Alec said, "Sebastian, earlier today . . . Does Jace know where you went?"

"You mean that I was out with Clary?" Sebastian looked amused. "Look, it's not a secret. I would have told Jace if I'd seen him since."

"I don't see why he would care." Aline put her book aside, an edge to her voice. "It's not like Sebastian did anything wrong. So what if he wants to show Clarissa some of Idris before she goes home? Jace ought to be pleased his sister isn't sitting around bored and annoyed."

"He can be very . . . protective," Alec said after a slight hesitation.

Aline frowned. "He should back off. It can't be good for her, being so overprotected. The look on her face when she walked in on us, it was like she'd never seen anyone *kissing* before. I mean, who knows, maybe she hasn't."

"She has," Isabelle said, thinking of the way Jace had kissed Clary in the Seelie Court. It wasn't something she liked to think about—Isabelle didn't enjoy wallowing in her own sorrows, much less other people's. "It's not that."

"Then what is it?" Sebastian straightened up, pushing a lock of dark hair out of his eyes. Isabelle caught a flash of something—a red line across his palm, like a scar. "Is it just that he hates me personally? Because I don't know what it is I ever—"

"That's my book." A small voice interrupted Sebastian's speech. It was Max, standing in the living room doorway. He was wearing gray pajamas and his brown hair was disarrayed as if he'd just woken up. He was glaring at the manga novel sitting next to Sebastian.

"What, this?" Sebastian held out the copy of *Angel Sanctuary*. "Here you go, kid."

Max stalked across the room and snatched the book back. He scowled at Sebastian. "Don't call me kid."

Sebastian laughed and stood up. "I'm getting some coffee," he said, and headed for the kitchen. He paused and turned in the doorway. "Does anyone want anything?"

There was a chorus of refusals. With a shrug Sebastian disappeared into the kitchen, letting the door swing shut behind him.

"Max," Isabelle said sharply. "Don't be rude."

"I don't like it when people take my stuff." Max hugged the comic book to his chest.

"Grow up, Max. He was just borrowing it." Isabelle's voice came out more irritably than she'd intended; she was still worried about Jace, she knew, and was taking it out on her little brother. "You should be in bed anyway. It's late."

"There were noises up on the hill. They woke me up." Max blinked; without his glasses, everything was pretty much a blur to him. "Isabelle . . ."

The questioning note in his voice got her attention. Isabelle turned away from the window. "What?"

"Do people ever climb the demon towers? Like, for any reason?"

Aline looked up. "Climb the demon towers?" She laughed. "No, no one ever does that. It's totally illegal, for one thing, and besides, why would you want to?"

Aline, Isabelle thought, did not have much imagination. She herself could think of lots of reasons why someone might want to climb the demon towers, if only to spit gum down on passersby below.

Max was frowning. "But someone did. I know I saw—"

"Whatever you think you saw, you probably dreamed it," Isabelle told him.

Max's face creased. Sensing a potential meltdown, Alec stood up and held out a hand. "Come on, Max," he said, not without affection. "Let's get you back to bed."

"We should *all* get to bed," Aline said, standing up. She came over to the window beside Isabelle and drew the curtains firmly shut. "It's already almost midnight; who knows when they'll get back from the Council? There no point staying—"

The pendant at Isabelle's throat pulsed again, sharply—and then the window Aline was standing in front of shattered inward. Aline screamed as hands reached through the gaping hole—not hands, really, Isabelle saw with the clarity of shock, but huge, scaled claws, streaked with blood and blackish fluid. They seized Aline and yanked her through the smashed window before she could utter a second scream.

Isabelle's whip was lying on the table by the fireplace. She dashed for it now, ducking around Sebastian, who had come racing out of the kitchen. "Get weapons," she snapped as he stared around the room in astonishment. *"Go!"* she shrieked, and ran for the window.

By the fireplace Alec was holding Max as the younger boy squirmed and yelled, trying to wriggle out of his brother's grip. Alec dragged him toward the door. *Good*, Isabelle thought. *Get Max out of here.*

Cold air blew through the shattered window. Isabelle pulled her skirt up and kicked out the rest of the broken glass, thankful for the thick soles of her boots. When the glass was gone, she ducked her head and jumped out through the gaping hole in the frame, landing with a jolt on the stone walkway below.

At first glance the walkway looked empty. There were no streetlights along the canal; the main illumination here came from the windows of nearby houses. Isabelle moved forward cautiously, her electrum whip coiled at her side. She had owned the whip for so long—it had been a twelfth birthday present from her father—that it felt like part of her now, like a fluid extension of her right arm.

The shadows thickened as she moved away from the house and toward Oldcastle Bridge, which arched over the Princewater canal at an odd angle to the walkway. The shadows at its base were clustered as thickly as black flies—and then, as Isabelle stared, something moved within the shadow, something white and darting.

Isabelle ran, crashing through a low border of hedges at the end of someone's garden and hopping down onto the narrow brick causeway that ran below the bridge. Her whip had begun to glow with a harsh silvery light, and in its faint illumination she could see Aline lying limply at the edge of the canal.

A massive scaled demon was sprawled on top of her, pressing her down with the weight of its thick lizardlike body, its face buried in her neck—

But it couldn't be a demon. There had never been demons in Alicante. Never. As Isabelle stared in shock, the thing raised its head and sniffed the air, as if sensing her there. It was blind, she saw, a thick line of serrated teeth running like a zipper across its forehead where eyes should be. It had another mouth on the lower half of its face as well, fanged with dripping tusks. The sides of its narrow tail glittered as it whipped back and forth, and Isabelle saw, drawing closer, that the tail was edged with razor-sharp lines of bone.

Aline twitched and made a noise, a gasping whimper. Relief spilled over Isabelle—she'd been half-sure Aline was dead—but it was short-lived. As Aline moved, Isabelle saw that her blouse had been sliced open down the front. There were claw marks on her chest, and the thing had another claw hooked into the waistband of her jeans.

A wave of nausea rolled over Isabelle. The demon wasn't trying to *kill* Aline—not yet. Isabelle's whip came alive in her hand like the flaming sword of an avenging angel; she launched herself forward, her whip slashing down across the demon's back.

The demon screeched and rolled off Aline. It advanced on Isabelle, its two mouths gaping, talons slashing toward her face. Dancing backward, she threw the whip forward again; it slashed across the demon's face, its chest, its legs. A myriad of crisscrossing lash marks sprang up across the demon's scaled skin, dripping blood and ichor. A long forked tongue shot from its upper mouth, probing for Isabelle's face. There was a bulb on the end of it, she saw, a sort of stinger, like a scorpion's. She flicked her wrist to the side and the whip curled around the demon's tongue, roping it with bands of flexible electrum. The demon screamed and screamed as she pulled the knot tight and jerked. The demon's tongue fell with a wet, sickening thump to the bricks of the causeway.

Isabelle jerked the whip back. The demon turned and fled, moving with quick, darting motions like a snake. Isabelle darted after it. The demon was halfway to the path that led up from the causeway when a dark shape rose up in front of it. Something flashed in the darkness, and the demon fell twitching to the ground.

Isabelle came to an abrupt stop. Aline stood over the fallen demon, a slender dagger in her hand—she must have been wearing it on her belt. The runes on the blade shone like flashing lightning as she drove the dagger down, plunging it over and over into the demon's twitching body until the thing stopped moving entirely and vanished.

Aline looked up. Her face was blank. She made no move to hold her blouse closed, despite its torn buttons. Blood oozed from the deep scratch marks on her chest.

Isabelle let out a low whistle. "Aline—are you all right?"

Aline let the dagger fall to the ground with a clatter. Without another word she turned and ran, disappearing into the darkness under the bridge.

Caught by surprise, Isabelle swore and dashed after Aline. She wished she'd worn something more practical than a velvet dress tonight, although at least she'd put her boots on. She doubted she could have caught up to Aline wearing heels.

There were metal stairs on the other side of the causeway, leading back up to Princewater Street. Aline was a blur at the top of the stairway. Hiking up the heavy hem of her dress, Isabelle followed, her boots clattering on the steps. When she reached the top, she looked around for Aline.

And stared. She was standing at the foot of the broad road on which the Penhallows' house fronted. She could no longer see Aline—the other girl had disappeared into the churning throng of people crowding the street. And not just people, either. There were *things* in the street—demons—dozens of them, maybe more, like the taloned lizard-creature Aline had dispatched under the bridge. Two or three bodies lay in the street already, one only a few feet from Isabelle—a man, half his rib cage torn away. Isabelle could see from his gray hair that he'd been elderly. *But of course he was,* she thought, her brain ticking over slowly, the speed of her thoughts dulled by panic. *All the adults were in the Gard. Down in the city were only children, the old, and the sick. . . .*

The red-tinged air was full of the smell of burning, the night split by shrieks and screams. Doors were open all up and down the rows of houses—people were darting out of them, then stopping dead as they saw the street filled with monsters.

It was impossible, unimaginable. Never in history had a single demon crossed the wards of the demon towers. And now there were dozens. Hundreds. Maybe more, flooding the streets like a poisonous tide. Isabelle felt as if she were trapped behind a glass wall, able to see everything but unable to move—watching, frozen, as a demon seized a fleeing boy and lifted him bodily off the ground, sinking its serrated teeth into his shoulder.

The boy screamed, but his screams were lost in the clamor that was tearing the night apart. The sound rose and rose in volume: the howling of demons, people calling one another's names, the sounds of running feet and shattering glass. Someone down the street was shouting words she could barely understand—something about the demon towers. Isabelle looked up. The tall spires stood sentry over the city as they always had, but instead of reflecting the silver light of the stars, or even the red light of the burning city, they were as dead white as the skin of a corpse. Their luminescence had vanished. A chill ran through her. No wonder the streets were full of monsters—somehow, impossibly, the demon towers had lost their magic. The wards that had protected Alicante for a thousand years were gone.

Samuel had fallen silent hours ago, but Simon was still awake, staring sleeplessly into the darkness, when he heard the screaming.

His head jerked up. Silence. He looked around uneasily—had he dreamed the noise? He strained his ears, but even with his newly sensitive hearing, nothing was audible. He was about to lie back down when the screams came again, driving into his ears like needles. It sounded as if they were coming from outside the Gard.

Rising, he stood on the bed and looked out the window. He saw the green lawn stretching away, the faraway light of the city a faint glow in the distance. He narrowed his eyes. There was something wrong about the city light, something . . . off. It was dimmer than he remembered it—and there were moving points here and there in the darkness, like needles of fire, weaving through the streets. A pale cloud rose above the towers, and the air was full of the stench of smoke.

"Samuel." Simon could hear the alarm in his own voice. "There's something wrong."

He heard doors slamming open and running feet. Hoarse voices shouted. Simon pressed his face close to the bars as pairs of boots hurtled by outside, kicking up stones as they ran, the Shadowhunters calling to one another as they raced away from the Gard, down toward the city.

"The wards are down! The wards are down!"

"We can't abandon the Gard!"

"The Gard doesn't matter! Our children are down there!"

Their voices were already growing fainter. Simon jerked back from the window, gasping. "Samuel! The wards—"

"I know. I heard." Samuel's voice came strongly through the wall. He didn't sound frightened but resigned, and even perhaps a little triumphant at being proved right. "Valentine has attacked while the Clave is in session. Clever."

"But the Gard—it's fortified—why don't they stay up here?"

"You heard them. Because all the children are in the city. Children—aged parents—they can't just leave them down there."

The Lightwoods. Simon thought of Jace, and then, with terrible clarity, of Isabelle's small, pale face under her crown of dark hair, of her determination in a fight, of the little-girl *X*s and *O*s on the note she'd written him. "But you told them—you told the Clave what would happen. Why didn't they believe you?"

"Because the wards are their religion. Not to believe in the power of the wards is not to believe that they are special, chosen, and protected by the Angel. They might as well believe they're just ordinary mundanes."

Simon swung back to stare out the window again, but the smoke had thickened, filling the air with a grayish pallor. He could no longer hear voices shouting outside; there were cries in the distance, but they were very faint. "I think the city is on fire."

"No." Samuel's voice was very quiet. "I think it's the Gard that's burning. Probably demon fire. Valentine would go after the Gard, if he could."

"But—" Simon's words stumbled over one another. "But someone will come and let us out, won't they? The Consul, or—or Aldertree. They can't just leave us down here to die."

"You're a Downworlder," said Samuel. "And I'm a traitor. Do you really think they're likely to do anything else?"

"Isabelle! *Isabelle!*"

Alec had his hands on her shoulders and was shaking her. Isabelle raised her head slowly; her brother's white face floated against the darkness behind him. A curved piece of wood stuck up behind his right shoulder: He had his bow strapped across his back, the same bow that Simon had used to kill Greater Demon Abbadon. She couldn't remember Alec walking toward her, couldn't remember seeing him in the street at all; it was as if he'd materialized in front of her all at once, like a ghost.

"Alec." Her voice came out slow and uneven. "Alec, stop it. I'm all right."

She pulled away from him.

"You didn't look all right." Alec glanced up and cursed under his breath. "We have to get off the street. Where's Aline?"

Isabelle blinked. There were no demons in view; someone was sitting on the front steps of the house opposite them and crying in a loud and grating series of shrieks. The old man's body was still in the street, and the smell of demons was everywhere. "Aline—one of the demons tried to—it tried to—" She caught her breath, held it. She was Isabelle Lightwood. She did not get hysterical, no matter what the provocation. "We killed it, but then she ran off. I tried to follow her, but she was too fast." She looked up at her brother. "Demons in the city," she said. "How is it possible?"

"I don't know." Alec shook his head. "The wards must be down. There were four or five Oni demons out here when I came out of the house. I got one lurking by the bushes. The others ran off, but they could come back. Come on. Let's get back to the house."

The person on the stairs was still sobbing. The sound followed them as they hurried back to the Penhallows' house. The street stayed empty of demons, but they could hear explosions, cries, and running feet echoing from the shadows of other darkened streets. As they climbed the Penhallows' front steps, Isabelle glanced back just in time to see a long snaking tentacle whip out from the darkness between the two houses and snatch the sobbing woman off the front steps. Her sobs turned to shrieks. Isabelle tried to turn back, but Alec had already grabbed her and shoved her ahead of him into the house, slamming and locking the front door behind them. The house was dark. "I doused the lights. I didn't want to attract any more of them," Alec explained, pushing Isabelle ahead of him into the living room.

Max was sitting on the floor by the stairs, his arms hugging his knees. Sebastian was by the window, nailing logs of wood he'd taken from the fireplace across the gaping hole in the glass. "There," he said, standing back and letting the hammer drop onto the bookshelf. "That should hold for a while."

Isabelle dropped down by Max and stroked his hair. "Are you all right?"

"No." His eyes were huge and scared. "I tried to see out the window, but Sebastian told me to get down."

"Sebastian was right," Alec said. "There were demons out in the street."

"Are they still there?"

"No, but there are some still in the city. We have to think about what we're going to do next."

Sebastian was frowning. "Where's Aline?"

"She ran off," Isabelle explained. "It was my fault. I should have been—"

"It was *not* your fault. Without you she'd be dead." Alec spoke in a clipped voice. "Look, we don't have time for self-recriminations. I'm going to go after Aline. I want you three to stay here. Isabelle, look after Max. Sebastian, finish securing the house."

Isabelle spoke up indignantly. "I don't want you going out there alone! Take me with you."

"I'm the adult here. What I say goes." Alec's tone was even. "There's every chance our parents will be coming back any minute from the Gard. The more of us here, the better. It'll be too easy for us to get separated out there. I'm not risking it, Isabelle." His glance moved to Sebastian. "Do you understand?"

Sebastian had already taken out his stele. "I'll work on warding the house with Marks."

"Thanks." Alec was already halfway to the door; he turned and looked back at Isabelle. She met his eyes for a split second. Then he was gone.

"Isabelle." It was Max, his small voice low. "Your wrist is bleeding."

Isabelle glanced down. She had no memory of having hurt her wrist, but Max was right: Blood had already stained the sleeve of her white jacket. She got to her feet. "I'm going to get my stele. I'll be right back and help you with the runes, Sebastian."

He nodded. "I could use some help. These aren't my specialty."

Isabelle went upstairs without asking him what his specialty might actually be. She felt bone-tired, in dire need of an energy Mark. She could do one herself if necessary, though Alec and Jace had always been better at those sorts of runes than she was.

Once inside her room, she rummaged through her things for her stele and a few extra weapons. As she shoved seraph blades into the tops of her boots, her mind was on Alec and the look they'd shared as he'd gone out the door. It wasn't the first time she'd watched her brother leave, knowing she might never see him again. It was something she accepted, had always accepted, as part of her life; it wasn't until she'd gotten to know Clary and Simon that she'd realized that for most people, of course, it was never like that. They didn't live with death as a constant companion, a cold breath down the back of their neck on even the most ordinary days. She'd always had such contempt for mundanes, the way all Shadowhunters did—she'd believed that they were soft, stupid, sheeplike in their complacency. Now she wondered if all that hatred didn't just stem from the fact that she was jealous. It must be nice not worrying that every time one of your family members walked out the door, they'd never come back.

She was halfway down the stairs, her stele in hand, when she sensed that something was wrong. The living room was empty. Max and Sebastian were nowhere to be seen. There was a half-finished protection Mark on one of the logs Sebastian had nailed over the broken window. The hammer he'd used was gone.

Her stomach tightened. "Max!" she shouted, turning in a circle. "Sebastian! Where are you?"

Sebastian's voice answered her from the kitchen. "Isabelle—in here."

Relief washed over her, leaving her light-headed. "Sebastian, that's not funny," she said, marching into the kitchen. "I thought you were—"

She let the door fall shut behind her. It was dark in the kitchen, darker than it had been in the living room. She strained her eyes to see Sebastian and Max and saw nothing but shadows.

"Sebastian?" Uncertainty crept into her voice. "Sebastian, what are you doing in here? Where's Max?"

"Isabelle." She thought she saw something move, a shadow dark against lighter shadows. His voice was soft, kind, almost lovely. She hadn't realized before now what a beautiful voice he had. "Isabelle, I'm sorry."

"Sebastian, you're acting weird. Stop it."

"I'm sorry it's you," he said. "See, out of all of them, I liked you the best."

"Sebastian—"

"Out of all of them," he said again, in the same low voice, "I thought you were the most like me."

He brought his fist down then, with the hammer in it.

Alec raced through the dark and burning streets, calling out over and over for Aline. As he left the Princewater district and entered the heart of the city, his pulse quickened. The streets were like a Bosch painting come to life: full of grotesque and macabre creatures and scenes of sudden, hideous violence.

Panicked strangers shoved Alec aside without looking and ran screaming past without any apparent destination. The air stank of smoke and demons. Some of the houses were in flames; others had their windows knocked out. The cobblestones sparkled with broken glass. As he drew close to one building, he saw that what he'd thought was a discolored patch of paint was a huge swath of fresh blood splattered across the plaster. He spun in place, glancing in every direction, but saw nothing that explained it; nevertheless, he hurried away as quickly as he could.

Alec, alone of all the Lightwood children, remembered Alicante. He'd been a toddler when they'd left, yet he still carried recollections of the shimmering towers, the streets full of snow in winter, chains of witchlight wreathing the shops and houses, water splashing in the mermaid fountain in the Hall. He had always felt an odd tug at his heart at the thought of Alicante, the half-painful hope that his family would return one day to the place where they belonged. To see the city like this was like the death of all joy. Turning onto a wider boulevard, one of the streets that led down to the Accords Hall, he saw a pack of Belial demons ducking through an archway, hissing and howling. They dragged something behind them—something that twitched and spasmed as it slid over the cobbled street. He darted down the street, but the demons were already gone. Crumpled against the base of a pillar was a limp shape leaking a spidery trail of blood. Broken glass crunched like pebbles under Alec's boots as he knelt to turn the body over. After a single glance at the purple, distorted face, he shuddered and drew away, grateful that it was no one he knew.

A noise made him scramble to his feet. He smelled the stench before he saw it: the shadow of something humped and huge slithering toward him from the far end of the street. A Greater Demon? Alec didn't wait to find out. He darted across the street toward one of the taller houses, leaping up onto a sill whose window glass had been smashed in. A few minutes later he was pulling himself onto the roof, his hands aching, his knees scraped. He got to his feet, brushing grit from his hands, and looked out over Alicante.

The ruined demon towers cast their dull, dead light down onto the moving streets of the city, where *things* loped and crawled and slunk in the shadows between buildings, like roaches skittering through a dark apartment. The air carried cries and shouts, the sound of screaming, names called on the wind—and there were the cries of demons as well, howls of mayhem and delight, shrieks that pierced the human ear like pain. Smoke rose above the honey-colored stone houses in a haze, wreathing the spires of the Hall of Accords. Glancing up toward the Gard, Alec saw a flood of Shadowhunters racing down the path from the hill, illuminated by the witchlights they carried. The Clave were coming down to battle.

He moved to the edge of the roof. The buildings here were very close together, their eaves almost touching. It was easy to jump from this roof to the next, and then to the one after that. He found himself running lightly along the rooftops, jumping the slight distances between houses. It was good to have the cold wind in his face, overpowering the stench of demons.

He'd been running for a few minutes before he realized two things: One, he was running toward the white spires of the Accords Hall. And two, there was something up ahead, in a square between two alleys, something that looked like a shower of rising sparks—except that they were blue, a dark gas-flame blue. Alec had seen blue sparks like that before. He stared for a moment before he began to run.

The roof closest to the square was steeply pitched. Alec skidded down the side of it, his boots knocking against loose shingles. Poised precariously at the edge, he looked down.

Cistern Square was below him, and his view was partly blocked by a massive metal pole that jutted out midway down the face of the building he was standing on. A wooden shop sign dangled from it, swaying in the breeze. The square beneath was full of Iblis demons—human-shaped but formed of a substance like coiling black smoke, each with a pair of burning yellow eyes. They had formed a line and were moving slowly toward the lone figure of a man in a sweeping gray coat, forcing him to retreat against a wall. Alec could only stare. Everything about the man was familiar—the lean curve of his back, the wild tangle of his dark hair, and the way that blue fire sprang from his fingertips like darting cyanotic fireflies.

Magnus. The warlock was hurling spears of blue fire at the Iblis demons; one spear struck an advancing demon in the chest. With a sound like a pail of water poured onto flames, it shuddered and vanished in a burst of ash. The others moved to fill his place—Iblis demons weren't very bright—and Magnus hurled another spate of fiery spears. Several Iblis fell, but now another demon, more cunning than the others, had drifted *around* Magnus and was coalescing behind him, ready to strike—

Alec didn't stop to think. Instead he jumped, catching the edge of the roof as he fell, and then dropped straight down to seize the metal pole and swing himself up and around it, slowing his fall. He released it and dropped lightly to the ground. The demon, startled, began to turn, its yellow eyes like flaming jewels; Alec had time only to reflect that if he were Jace, he would have had something clever to say before he snatched the seraph blade from his belt and ran it through the demon. With a dusty shriek the demon vanished, the violence of its exit from this dimension splattering Alec with a fine rain of ash.

"*Alec?*" Magnus was staring at him. He had dispatched the remaining Iblis demons, and the square was empty but for the two of them. "Did you just—did you just save my life?"

Alec knew he ought to say something like, *Of course, because I'm a Shadowhunter and that's what we do,* or *That's my job.* Jace would have said something like that. Jace always knew the right thing to say. But the words that actually came out of Alec's mouth were quite different—and sounded petulant, even to his own ears. "You never called me back," he said. "I called you so many times and you never called me back."

Magnus looked at Alec as if he'd lost his mind. "Your city is under attack," he said. "The wards have broken, and the streets are full of demons. And you want to know why I haven't *called you?*"

Alec set his jaw in a stubborn line. "I want to know why you haven't called me *back*."

Magnus threw his hands up in the air in a gesture of utter exasperation. Alec noted with interest that when he did it, a few sparks escaped from his fingertips, like fireflies escaping from a jar. "You're an idiot."

"Is *that* why you didn't call me? Because I'm an idiot?"

"No." Magnus strode toward him. "I didn't call you because I'm tired of you only wanting me around when you need something. I'm tired of watching you be in love with someone else—someone, incidentally, who will never love you back. Not the way I do."

"You *love* me?"

"You stupid Nephilim," Magnus said patiently. "Why else am I here? Why else would I have spent the past few weeks patching up all your moronic friends every time they got hurt? And getting you out of every ridiculous situation you found yourself in? Not to mention helping you win a battle against Valentine. And all completely free of charge!"

"I hadn't looked at it that way," Alec admitted.

"Of course not. You never looked at it in any way." Magnus's cat eyes shone with anger. "I'm four hundred years old, Alexander. I know when something isn't going to work. You won't even admit I exist to your parents."

Alec stared at him. "I thought you were three hundred! You're *four hundred years old?*"

"Well," Magnus amended, "five hundred. But I don't look it. Anyway, you're missing the point. The point is—"

But Alec never found out what the point was because at that moment a dozen more Iblis demons flooded into the square. He felt his jaw drop. "Damn it."

Magnus followed his gaze. The demons were already fanning out into a half circle around them, their yellow eyes glowing. "Way to change the subject, Lightwood."

“Tell you what.” Alec reached for a second seraph blade. “We live through this, and I promise I’ll introduce you to my whole family.”

Magnus raised his hands, his fingers shining with individual azure flames. They lit his grin with a fiery blue glow. “It’s a deal.”

11

All the Host of Hell

"Valentine," Jace breathed. His face was white as he stared down at the city. Through the layers of smoke, Clary thought she could almost glimpse the narrow warren of city streets, choked with running figures, tiny black ants darting desperately to and fro—but she looked again and there was nothing, nothing but the thick clouds of black vapor and the stench of flame and smoke.

"You think Valentine did this?" The smoke was bitter in Clary's throat. "It looks like a fire. Maybe it started on its own—"

"The North Gate is open." Jace pointed toward something Clary could barely make out, given the distance and the distorting smoke. "It's never left open. And the demon towers have lost their light. The wards must be down." He drew a seraph blade from his belt, clutching it so tightly his knuckles turned the color of ivory. "I have to get over there."

A knot of dread tightened Clary's throat. "Simon—"

"They'll have evacuated him from the Gard. Don't worry, Clary. He's probably better off than most down there. The demons aren't likely to bother him. They tend to leave Downworlders alone."

"I'm sorry," Clary whispered. "The Lightwoods—Alec—Isabelle—"

"Jahoel," Jace said, and the angel blade flared up, bright as daylight in his bandaged left hand. "Clary, I want you to stay here. I'll come back for you." The anger that had been in his eyes since they'd left the manor had evaporated. He was all soldier now.

She shook her head. "No. I want to go with you."

"Clary—" He broke off, stiffening all over. A moment later Clary heard it too—a heavy, rhythmic pounding, and laid over that, a sound like the crackling of an enormous bonfire. It took Clary several long moments to deconstruct the sound in her mind, to break it down as one might break down a piece of music into its component notes. "It's—"

"Werewolves." Jace was staring past her. Following his gaze, she saw them, streaming over the nearest hill like a spreading shadow, illuminated here and there with fierce bright eyes. A pack of wolves—more than a pack; there must have been hundreds of them, even a thousand. Their barking and baying had been the sound she'd thought was a fire, and it rose up into the night, brittle and harsh.

Clary's stomach turned over. She knew werewolves. She had

fought beside werewolves. But these were not Luke's wolves, not wolves who'd been instructed to look after her and not to harm her. She thought of the terrible killing power of Luke's pack when it was unleashed, and suddenly she was afraid.

Beside her Jace swore once, fiercely. There was no time to reach for another weapon; he pulled her tightly against him, his free arm wrapped around her, and with his other hand he raised Jahoel high over their heads. The light of the blade was blinding. Clary gritted her teeth—

And the wolves were on them. It was like a wave crashing—a sudden blast of deafening noise, and a rush of air as the first wolves in the pack broke forward and *leaped*—there were burning eyes and gaping jaws—Jace dug his fingers into Clary's side—

And the wolves sailed by on either side of them, clearing the space where they stood by a good two feet. Clary whipped her head around in disbelief as two wolves—one sleek and brindled, the other huge and steely gray—hit the ground softly behind them, paused, and kept running, without even a backward glance. There were wolves all around them, and yet not a single wolf touched them. They raced past, a flood of shadows, their coats reflecting moonlight in flashes of silver so that they almost seemed to be a single, moving river of shapes thundering toward Jace and Clary—and then parting around them like water around a stone. The two Shadowhunters might as well have been statues for all the attention the lycanthropes paid them as they hurtled by, their jaws gaping, their eyes fixed on the road ahead of them.

And then they were gone. Jace turned to watch the last of the wolves pass by and race to catch up with its companions.

There was silence again now, only the very faint sounds of the city in the distance.

Jace let go of Clary, lowering Jahoel as he did so. "Are you all right?"

"What happened?" she whispered. "Those werewolves—they just went right by us—"

"They're going to the city. To Alicante." He took a second seraph blade from his belt and held it out to her. "You'll need this."

"You're not leaving me here, then?"

"No point. It's not safe anywhere. But—" He hesitated. "You'll be careful?"

"I'll be careful," Clary said. "What do we do now?"

Jace looked down at Alicante, burning below them. "Now we run."

It was never easy to keep up with Jace, and now, when he was running nearly flat out, it was almost impossible. Clary sensed that he was in fact restraining himself, cutting back his speed to let her catch up, and that it cost him something to do it.

The road flattened out at the base of the hill and curved through a stand of high, thickly branched trees, creating the illusion of a tunnel. When Clary came out the other side, she found herself standing before the North Gate. Through the arch Clary could see a confusion of smoke and leaping flames. Jace stood in the gateway, waiting for her. He was holding Jahoel in one hand and another seraph blade in the other, but even their combined light was lost against the greater brightness of the burning city behind him.

"The guards," she panted, racing up to him. "Why aren't they here?"

"At least one of them is over in that stand of trees." Jace jerked his chin in the direction they'd come from. "In pieces. No, don't look." He glanced down. "You're holding your seraph blade wrong. Hold it like this." He showed her. "And you need to name it. Cassiel would be a good one."

"*Cassiel,*" Clary repeated, and the light of the blade flared up.

Jace looked at her soberly. "I wish I'd had time to train you for this. Of course, by all rights, no one with as little training as you should be able to use a seraph blade at all. It surprised me before, but now that we know what Valentine did—"

Clary very much did not want to talk about what Valentine had done. "Or maybe you were just worried that if you did train me properly, I'd turn out to be better than you," she said.

The ghost of a smile touched the corner of his mouth. "Whatever happens, Clary," he said, looking at her through Jahoel's light, "stay with me. You understand?" He held her gaze, his eyes demanding a promise from her.

For some reason the memory of kissing him in the grass at the Wayland manor rose up in her mind. It seemed like a million years ago. Like something that had happened to someone else. "I'll stay with you."

"Good." He looked away, releasing her. "Let's go."

They moved slowly through the gate, side by side. As they entered the city, she became aware of the noise of battle as if for the first time—a wall of sound made up of human screams and nonhuman howls, the sounds of smashing glass and the crackle of fire. It made the blood sing in her ears.

The courtyard just past the gate was empty. There were huddled shapes scattered here and there on the cobblestones; Clary tried not to look at them too hard. She wondered how it was that you could tell someone was dead even from a distance, without looking too closely. Dead bodies didn't resemble unconscious ones; it was as if you could sense that something had fled from them, that some essential spark was now missing.

Jace hurried them across the courtyard—Clary could tell he didn't like the open, unprotected space much—and down one of the streets that led off it. There was more wreckage here. Shop windows had been smashed and their contents looted and strewn around the street. There was a smell in the air too—a rancid, thick, garbage smell. Clary knew that smell. It meant demons.

"This way," Jace hissed. They ducked down another, narrower street. A fire was burning in an upper floor of one of the houses lining the road, though neither of the buildings on either side of it seemed to have been touched. Clary was oddly reminded of photos she'd seen of the Blitz in London, where destruction had rained down haphazardly from the sky.

Looking up, she saw that the fortress above the city was wreathed in a funnel of black smoke. "The Gard."

"I told you, they'll have evacuated—" Jace broke off as they came out from the narrow street into a larger thoroughfare. There were bodies in the road here, several of them. Some were small bodies. Children. Jace ran forward, Clary following more hesitantly. There were three, she saw as they got closer—none of them, she thought with guilty relief, old enough to be Max. Beside them was the corpse of an older man, his arms still thrown wide as if he'd been protecting the children with his own body.

Jace's expression was hard. "Clary—turn around. Slowly."

Clary turned. Just behind her was a broken shop window. There had been cakes in the display at some point—a tower of them covered in bright icing. They were scattered on the ground now among the smashed glass, and there was blood on the cobblestones too, mixing with the icing in long pinkish streaks. But that wasn't what had put the note of warning into Jace's voice. Something was crawling out of the window—something formless and huge and slimy. Something equipped with a double row of teeth running the length of its oblong body, which was smeared with icing and dusted with broken glass like a layer of glittering sugar.

The demon flopped down out of the window onto the cobblestones and began to slither toward them. Something about its oozing, boneless motion made bile rise up in the back of Clary's throat. She backed up, almost knocking into Jace.

"It's a Behemoth demon," he said, staring at the slithering thing in front of them. "They eat *everything*."

"Do they eat . . . ?"

"People? Yes," Jace said. "Get behind me."

She took a few steps back to stand behind him, her eyes on the Behemoth. There was something about it that repulsed her even more than the demons she'd encountered before. It looked like a blind slug with teeth, and the way it *oozed* . . . But at least it didn't move fast. Jace shouldn't have much trouble killing it.

As if spurred on by her thought, Jace darted forward, slashing down with his blazing seraph blade. It sank into the

Behemoth's back with a sound like overripe fruit being stepped on. The demon seemed to spasm, then shudder and reform, suddenly several feet away from where it had been before.

Jace drew Jahoel back. "I was afraid of that," he muttered. "It's only semi-corporeal. Hard to kill."

"Then don't." Clary tugged at his sleeve. "At least it doesn't move fast. Let's get out of here."

Jace let her pull him back reluctantly. They turned to run in the direction they'd come from—

And the demon was there again, in front of them, blocking the street. It seemed to have grown bigger, and a low noise was coming from it, a sort of angry insectile chittering.

"I don't think it wants us to leave," Jace said.

"Jace—"

But he was already running at the thing, sweeping Jahoel down in a long arc meant to decapitate, but the thing just shuddered again and reformed, this time behind him. It reared up, showing a ridged underside like a cockroach's. Jace whirled and brought Jahoel down, slicing into the creature's midsection. Green fluid, thick as mucus, spurted over the blade.

Jace stepped back, his face twisting in disgust. The Behemoth was still making the same chittering noise. More fluid was spurting from it, but it didn't seem hurt. It was moving forward purposefully.

"Jace!" Clary called. "Your blade—"

He looked down. The Behemoth demon's mucus had coated Jahoel's blade, dulling its flame. As he stared, the seraph blade spluttered and went out like a fire doused by sand. He dropped the weapon with a curse before any of the demon's slime could touch him.

The Behemoth reared back again, ready to strike. Jace ducked back—and then Clary was there, darting between him and the demon, her seraph blade swinging. She jabbed the creature just below its row of teeth, the blade sinking into its mass with a wet, ugly sound.

She jerked back, gasping, as the demon went into another spasm. It seemed to take the creature a certain amount of energy to reform each time it was wounded. If they could just wound it enough times—

Something moved at the edge of Clary's vision. A flicker of gray and brown, moving fast. They weren't alone in the street. Jace turned, his eyes widening. "Clary!" he shouted. "Behind you!"

Clary whirled, Cassiel blazing in her grip, just as the wolf launched itself at her, its lips drawn back in a fierce snarl, its jaws gaping wide.

Jace shouted something; Clary didn't know what, but she saw the wild look in his eyes, even as she threw herself sideways, out of the path of the wolf. It sailed by her, claws outstretched, body arced—and struck its target, the Behemoth, knocking it flat to the ground before tearing at it with bared teeth.

The demon screamed, or as close as it could come to screaming—a high-pitched whining sound, like air being let out of a balloon. The wolf was on top of it, pinning it, its muzzle buried deep in the demon's slimy hide. The Behemoth shuddered and thrashed in a desperate effort to reform and heal its injuries, but the wolf wasn't giving it a chance. Its claws sunk deeply into demon flesh, the wolf tore chunks of jellylike flesh out of the Behemoth's body with its teeth, ignoring the spurting green fluid that fountained around it. The Behemoth began a last, desperate series of convulsive spasms, its serrated jaws clacking together as it thrashed—and then it was gone, only a viscous puddle of green fluid steaming on the cobblestones where it had been.

The wolf made a noise—a sort of satisfied grunt—and turned to regard Jace and Clary with eyes turned silver by the moonlight. Jace pulled another blade from his belt and held it high, drawing a fiery line on the air between themselves and the werewolf.

The wolf snarled, the hair rising stiffly along its spine.

Clary caught at his arm. "No—don't."

"It's a *werewolf*, Clary—"

"It killed the demon for us! It's on our side!" She broke away from Jace before he could hold her back, approaching the wolf slowly, her hands out, palms flat. She spoke in a low, calm voice: "I'm sorry. We're sorry. We know you don't want to hurt us." She paused, hands still outstretched, as the wolf regarded her with blank eyes. "Who—who are you?" she asked. She looked back over her shoulder at Jace and frowned. "Can you put that thing away?"

Jace looked as if he were about to tell her in no uncertain terms that you didn't just *put away* a seraph blade that was blazing in the presence of danger, but before he could say anything, the wolf gave another low growl and began to rise. Its legs elongated, its spine straightening, its jaw retracting. In a few seconds a girl stood in front of them—a girl wearing a stained white shift dress, her curling hair tied back in multiple braids, a scar banding her throat.

"'Who are you?'" the girl mimicked in disgust. "I can't

believe you didn't recognize me. It's not like all wolves look exactly alike. *Humans*."

Clary let out a breath of relief. "Maia!"

"It's me. Saving your butts, as usual." She grinned. She was spattered with blood and ichor—it hadn't been that visible against her wolf's coat, but the black and red streaks stood out startlingly against her brown skin. She put her hand against her stomach. "And *gross*, by the way. I can't believe I munched all that demon. I hope I'm not allergic."

"But what are you *doing* here?" Clary demanded. "I mean, not that we're not glad to see you, but—"

"Don't you know?" Maia looked from Jace to Clary in puzzlement. "Luke brought us here."

"Luke?" Clary stared. "Luke is . . . here?"

Maia nodded. "He got in touch with his pack, and a bunch of others, everyone he could think of, and told us all we had to come to Idris. We flew to the border and traveled from there. Some of the other packs, they Portaled into the forest and met us there. Luke said the Nephilim were going to need our help. . . ." Her voice trailed off. "Did you not know about this?"

"No," said Jace, "and I doubt the Clave did either. They're not big on taking help from Downworlders."

Maia straightened up, her eyes sparking with anger. "If it hadn't been for us, you all would have been *slaughtered*. There was no one protecting the city when we got here—"

"Don't," Clary said, shooting an angry look at Jace. "I'm really, really grateful to you for saving us, Maia, and Jace is too, even though he's so stubborn that he'd rather jam a seraph blade through his eyeball than say so. And don't say you hope he does," she added hastily, seeing the look on the other girl's face, "because that's really not helpful. Right now we need to get to the Lightwoods' house, and then I have to find Luke—"

"The Lightwoods? I think they're in the Accords Hall. That's where we've been bringing everyone. I saw Alec there, at least," Maia said, "and that warlock, too, the one with the spiky hair. Magnus."

"If Alec is there, the others must be too." The look of relief on Jace's face made Clary want to put her hand on his shoulder. She didn't. "Clever to bring everyone to the Hall; it's warded." He slid the glowing seraph blade into his belt. "Come on—let's go."

Clary recognized the inside of the Hall of Accords the moment she entered it. It was the place she had dreamed about, where she had been dancing with Simon and then Jace.

This was where I was trying to send myself when I went through the Portal, she thought, looking around at the pale white walls and the high ceiling with its enormous glass skylight through which she could see the night sky. The room, though very large, seemed somehow smaller and dingier than it had in her dream. The mermaid fountain was still there in the center of the room, spurting water, but it looked tarnished, and the steps that led up to it were crowded with people, many sporting bandages. The space was full of Shadowhunters, people hurrying here and there, sometimes stopping to peer into the faces of other passersby as if hoping to find a friend or a relative. The floor was filthy with dirt, tracked with smeared mud and blood.

What struck Clary more than anything else was the silence. If this had been the aftermath of some disaster in the mundane world, there would have been people shouting, screaming, calling out to one another. But the room was almost soundless. People sat quietly, some with their heads in their hands, some staring into space. Children huddled close to their parents, but none of them were crying.

She noticed something else, too, as she made her way into the room, Jace and Maia on either side of her. There was a group of scruffy-looking people standing by the fountain in a ragged circle. They stood somehow apart from the rest of the crowd, and when Maia caught sight of them and smiled, Clary realized why.

"My pack!" Maia exclaimed. She darted toward them, pausing only to glance back over her shoulder at Clary as she went. "I'm sure Luke's around here somewhere," she called, and vanished into the group, which closed around her. Clary wondered, for a moment, what would happen if she followed the werewolf girl into the circle. Would they welcome her as Luke's friend, or just be suspicious of her as another Shadowhunter?

"Don't," Jace said, as if reading her mind. "It's not a good—"

But Clary never found out what it wasn't, because there was a cry of "*Jace!*" and Alec appeared, breathless from pushing his way through the crowd to get to them. His dark hair was a mess and there was blood on his clothes, but his eyes were bright with a mixture of relief and anger. He grabbed Jace by the front of his jacket. "What *happened* to you?"

Jace looked affronted. "What happened to *me*?"

Alec shook him, not lightly. "You said you were going for a *walk*! What kind of walk takes six hours?"

"A long one?" Jace suggested.

"I could kill you," Alec said, releasing his grip on Jace's clothes. "I'm seriously thinking about it."

"That would kind of defeat the point, though, wouldn't it?" said Jace. He glanced around. "Where is everyone? Isabelle, and—"

"Isabelle and Max are back at the Penhallows', with Sebastian," said Alec. "Mom and Dad are on their way there to get them. And Aline's here, with her parents, but she's not talking much. She had a pretty bad time with a Rahab demon down by one of the canals. But Izzy saved her."

"And Simon?" Clary said anxiously. "Have you seen Simon? He should have come down with the others from the Gard."

Alec shook his head. "No, I haven't—but I haven't seen the Inquisitor, either, or the Consul. He'd probably be with one of them. Maybe they stopped somewhere else, or—" He broke off, as a murmur swept the room; Clary saw the group of lycanthropes look up, alert as a group of hunting dogs scenting game. She turned—

And saw Luke, tired and bloodstained, coming through the double doors of the Hall.

She ran toward him. Forgetting how upset she'd been when he'd left, and forgetting how angry he'd been with her for bringing them here, forgetting everything but how glad she was to see him. He looked surprised for a moment as she barreled toward him—then he smiled, and put his arms out, and picked her up as he hugged her, the way he'd done when she'd been very small. He smelled like blood and flannel and smoke, and for a moment she closed her eyes, thinking of the way Alec had grabbed onto Jace the moment he'd seen him in the Hall, because that was what you did with family when you'd been worried about them, you grabbed them and held on to them and told them how much they'd pissed you off, and it was okay, because no matter how angry you got, they still belonged to you. And what she had said to Valentine was true. Luke was her family.

He set her back down on her feet, wincing a little as he did so. "Careful," he said. "A Croucher demon got me in the shoulder down by Merryweather Bridge." He put his hands on her shoulders, studying her face. "But you're all right, aren't you?"

"Well, this is a touching scene," said a cold voice. "Isn't it?"

Clary turned, Luke's hand still on her shoulder. Behind her stood a tall man in a blue cloak that swirled around his feet as he moved toward them. His face under the hood of his cloak was the face of a carved statue: high-cheekboned with eagle-sharp features and heavy-lidded eyes. "Lucian," he said, without looking at Clary. "I might have expected you'd be the one behind this—this invasion."

"*Invasion?*" Luke echoed, and suddenly, there was his pack of lyncanthropes, standing behind him. They had moved into place so quickly and silently it was as if they'd appeared from out of nowhere. "We're not the ones who invaded your city, Consul. That was Valentine. We're just trying to help."

"The Clave doesn't need help," the Consul snapped. "Not from the likes of you. You're breaking the Law just by entering the Glass City, wards or no wards. You must know that."

"I think it's fairly clear that the Clave *does* need help. If we hadn't come when we did, many more of you would now be dead." Luke glanced around the room; several groups of Shadowhunters had moved toward them, drawn to see what was going on. Some of them met Luke's gaze head-on; others dropped their eyes, as if ashamed. But none of them, Clary thought with a sudden surge of surprise, looked angry. "I did it to prove a point, Malachi."

Malachi's voice was cold. "And what point might that be?"

"That you need us," Luke said. "To defeat Valentine, you need our help. Not just the help of lycanthropes, but of all Downworlders."

"What can Downworlders do against Valentine?" Malachi asked scornfully. "Lucian, you know better than that. You were one of us once. We have always stood alone against all perils and guarded the world from evil. We will meet Valentine's power now with a power of our own. The Downworlders would do well to stay out of our way. We are Nephilim; we fight our own battles."

"That's not *precisely* true, is it?" said a velvety voice. It was Magnus Bane, wearing a long and glittering coat, multiple hoops in his ears, and a roguish expression. Clary had no idea where he'd come from. "You lot have used the help of warlocks on more than one occasion in the past, and paid handsomely for it too."

Malachi scowled. "I don't remember the Clave inviting you into the Glass City, Magnus Bane."

"They didn't," Magnus said. "Your wards are down."

"Really?" the Consul's voice dripped sarcasm. "I hadn't noticed."

Magnus looked concerned. "That's terrible. Someone should have told you." He glanced at Luke. "Tell him the wards are down."

Luke looked exasperated. "Malachi, for God's sake, the

Downworlders are strong; we have numbers. I told you, we can help."

The Consul's voice rose. "And I told *you*, we don't need or want your help!"

"Magnus," Clary slipped silently to his side and whispered. A small crowd had gathered, watching Luke and the Consul fight; she was fairly sure no one was paying attention to her. "Come talk to me. While they're all too busy squabbling to notice."

Magnus gave her a quick questioning look, nodded, and drew her away, cutting through the crowd like a can opener. None of the assembled Shadowhunters or werewolves seemed to want to stand in the way of a six-foot-tall warlock with cat eyes and a manic grin. He hustled her into a quieter corner. "What is it?"

"I got the book." Clary drew it from the pocket of her bedraggled coat, leaving smeared fingerprints on the ivory cover. "I went to Valentine's manor. It was in the library like you said. And—" She broke off, thinking of the imprisoned angel. "Never mind." She offered him the Book of the White. "Here. Take it."

Magnus plucked the book from her grasp with a long-fingered hand. He flipped through the pages, his eyes widening. "This is even better than I'd heard it was," he announced gleefully. "I can't wait to get started on these spells."

"Magnus!" Clary's sharp voice brought him back down to earth. "My mom first. You promised."

"And I abide by my promises." The warlock nodded gravely.

"There's something else, too," she added, thinking of Simon. "Before you go—"

"Clary!" A voice spoke, breathless, at her shoulder. She

turned in surprise to see Sebastian standing beside her. He was wearing gear, and it looked right on him somehow, she thought, as if he were born to wear it. Where everyone else looked bloodstained and disheveled, he was unmarked—except for a double line of scratches that ran the length of his left cheek, as if something had clawed at him with a taloned hand. "I was worried about you. I went by Amatis's house on the way here, but you weren't there, and she said she hadn't seen you—"

"Well, I'm fine." Clary glanced from Sebastian to Magnus, who was holding the Book of the White against his chest. Sebastian's angular eyebrows were raised. "Are you? Your face—" She reached up to touch his injuries. The scratches were still oozing a trace amount of blood.

Sebastian shrugged, brushing her hand away gently. "A she-demon got me near the Penhallows'. I'm fine, though. What's going on?"

"Nothing. I was just talking to Ma—Ragnor," Clary said hastily, realizing with a sudden horror that Sebastian had no idea who Magnus actually was.

"Maragnor?" Sebastian arched his eyebrows. "Okay, then." He glanced curiously at the Book of the White. Clary wished Magnus would put it away—the way he was holding it, its gilded lettering was clearly visible. "What's that?"

Magnus studied him for a moment, his cat eyes considering. "A spell book," he said finally. "Nothing that would be of interest to a Shadowhunter."

"Actually, my aunt collects spell books. Can I see?" Sebastian held his hand out, but before Magnus could refuse, Clary heard someone call her name, and Jace and Alec descended on them, clearly none too pleased to see Sebastian.

"I thought I told you to stay with Max and Isabelle!" Alec snapped at him. "Did you leave them alone?"

Slowly Sebastian's eyes moved from Magnus to Alec. "Your parents came home, just like you said they would." His voice was cold. "They sent me ahead to tell you they were all right, and so are Izzy and Max. They're on their way."

"Well," said Jace, his voice heavy with sarcasm, "thanks for passing on *that* news the second you got here."

"I didn't see you the second I got here," said Sebastian. "I saw Clary."

"Because you were looking for her."

"Because I needed to talk to her. Alone." He caught Clary's eyes again, and the intensity in them gave her pause. She wanted to tell him not to look at her like that when Jace was there, but that would sound unreasonable and crazy, and besides, maybe he actually had something important to tell her. "Clary?"

She nodded. "All right. Just for a second," she said, and saw Jace's expression change: He didn't scowl, but his face went very still. "I'll be right back," she added, but Jace didn't look at her. He was looking at Sebastian.

Sebastian took her by the wrist and drew her away from the others, pulling her toward the thickest part of the crowd. She glanced back over her shoulder. They were all watching her, even Magnus. She saw him shake his head once, very slightly.

She dug her heels in. "Sebastian. *Stop*. What is it? What do you have to tell me?"

He turned to face her, still holding her wrist. "I thought we could go outside," he said. "Talk in private—"

"No. I want to stay here," she said, and heard her own voice waver slightly, as if she weren't sure. But she *was* sure. She yanked her wrist back, pulling it out of his grasp. "What is going on with you?"

"That book," he said. "That Fell was holding—the Book of the White—do you know where he got it?"

"*That's* what you wanted to talk to me about?"

"It's an extraordinarily powerful spell book," explained Sebastian. "And one that—well, that a lot of people have been looking for for a long time."

She blew out an exasperated breath. "All right, Sebastian, look," she said. "That's not Ragnor Fell. That's Magnus Bane."

"*That's* Magnus Bane?" Sebastian spun around and stared before turning back to Clary with an accusatory look in his eyes. "And you knew all along, right? You know Bane."

"Yes, and I'm sorry. But he didn't want me to tell you. And he was the only one who could help me save my mother. That's why I gave him the Book of the White. There's a spell in there that might help her."

Something flashed behind Sebastian's eyes, and Clary had the same feeling she'd had after he'd kissed her: a sudden wrench of wrongness, as if she'd taken a step forward expecting to find solid ground under her feet and instead plunged into empty space. His hand shot out and grabbed her wrist. "You gave the book—the Book of the White—to a *warlock*? A filthy Downworlder?"

Clary went very still. "I can't believe you just said that." She looked down at the place where Sebastian's hand encircled her wrist. "Magnus is my friend."

Sebastian loosened his grip on her wrist, just a fraction. "I'm sorry," he said. "I shouldn't have said that. It's just—how well do you know Magnus Bane?"

"Better than I know you," Clary said coldly. She glanced back toward the place she'd left Magnus standing with Jace and Alec—and a shock of surprise went through her. Magnus was gone. Jace and Alec stood by themselves, watching her and Sebastian. She could sense the heat of Jace's disapproval like an open oven.

Sebastian followed her gaze, his eyes darkening. "Well enough to know where he went with your book?"

"It's not my book. I gave it to him," Clary snapped. "And I don't see what business it is of yours, either. Look, I appreciate that you offered to help me find Ragnor Fell yesterday, but you're really freaking me out now. I'm going back to my friends."

She started to turn away, but he moved to block her. "I'm sorry. I shouldn't have said what I did. It's just—there's more to all this than you know."

"So tell me."

"Come outside with me. I'll tell you everything." His tone was anxious, worried. "Clary, please."

She shook her head. "I have to stay here. I have to wait for Simon." It was partly true, and partly an excuse. "Alec told me they'd be bringing the prisoners here—"

Sebastian was shaking his head. "Clary, didn't anyone tell you? They left the prisoners behind. I heard Malachi say so. The city was attacked, and they evacuated the Gard, but they didn't get the prisoners out. Malachi said they were both in league with Valentine anyway. That there was no way letting them out wouldn't be too much of a risk."

Clary's head seemed to be full of fog; she felt dizzy, and a little sick. "That can't be true."

"It is true," Sebastian said. "I swear it is." His grip on Clary's wrist tightened again, and she swayed on her feet. "I can take you up there. Up to the Gard. I can help you get him out. But you have to promise me that you'll—"

"She doesn't have to promise you anything," Jace said. "Let her go, Sebastian."

Sebastian, startled, loosened his grip on Clary's wrist. She pulled it free, turning to see Jace and Alec, both scowling. Jace's hand was resting lightly on the hilt of the seraph blade at his waist.

"Clary can do what she wants," Sebastian said. He wasn't scowling, but there was an odd, fixed look about his face that was somehow worse. "And right now she wants to come with me to save her friend. The friend *you* got thrown in prison."

Alec blanched at that, but Jace only shook his head. "I don't like you," he said thoughtfully. "I know everyone else likes you, Sebastian, but I don't. Maybe it's that you work so hard to *make* people like you. Maybe I'm just a contrary bastard. But I don't like you, and I don't like the way you were grabbing at my sister. If she wants to go up to the Gard and look for Simon, fine. She'll go with us. Not you."

Sebastian's fixed expression didn't change. "I think that should be her choice," he said. "Don't you?"

They both looked at Clary. She looked past them, toward Luke, still arguing with Malachi.

"I want to go with my brother," she said.

Something flickered behind Sebastian's eyes—something that was there and gone too quickly for Clary to identify it, though she felt a chill at the base of her neck, as if a cold hand had touched her there. "Of course you do," he said, and stepped aside.

It was Alec who moved first, pushing Jace ahead of him, making him walk. They were partway to the doors when she realized that her wrist was hurting—stinging as if it had been burned. Looking down, she expected to see a mark on her wrist, where Sebastian had gripped her, but there was nothing there. Just a smear of blood on her sleeve where she had touched the cut on his face. Frowning, with her wrist still stinging, she drew her sleeve down and hurried to catch up with the others.

12

De Profundis

Simon's hands were black with blood.

He had tried yanking the bars out of the window and the cell door, but touching any of them for very long seared bleeding score marks into his palms. Eventually he collapsed, gasping, on the floor, and stared numbly at his hands as the injuries swiftly healed, the lesions closing up and the blackened skin flaking away like in a video on fast-forward.

On the other side of the cell wall, Samuel was praying. "*If, when evil cometh upon us, as the sword, judgment, or pestilence, or famine, we stand before this house, and in thy presence, and cry unto thee in our affliction, then thou wilt hear and help—*"

Simon knew he couldn't pray. He'd tried it before, and the name of God burned his mouth and choked his throat. He wondered why he could think the words but not say them. And why he could stand in the noonday sun and not die but he couldn't say his last prayers.

Smoke had begun to drift down the corridor like a purposeful ghost. He could smell burning and hear the crackle of fire spreading out of control, but he felt oddly detached, far from everything. It was strange to become a vampire, to be presented with what could only be described as an eternal life, and then to die anyway when you were sixteen.

"Simon!" The voice was faint, but his hearing caught it over the pop and crackle of growing flames. The smoke in the corridor had presaged heat; the heat was here now, pressing against him like an oppressive wall. "Simon!"

The voice was Clary's. He would know it anywhere. He wondered if his mind was conjuring it up now, a sense memory of what he'd most loved during life to carry him through the process of death.

"Simon, you stupid idiot! I'm over here! At the window!"

Simon jumped to his feet. He doubted his mind would conjure *that* up. Through the thickening smoke he saw something white moving against the bars of the window. As he came closer, the white objects evolved into hands gripping the bars. He leaped onto the cot, yelling over the sound of the fire. "Clary?"

"Oh, thank God." One of the hands reached out, squeezed his shoulder. "We're going to get you out of here."

"How?" Simon demanded, not unreasonably, but there was the sound of a scuffle and Clary's hands vanished, replaced a moment later by another pair. These were bigger hands, unquestionably masculine, with scarred knuckles and thin pianist's fingers.

"Hang on." Jace's voice was calm, confident, for all the world as if they were chatting at a party instead of through the bars of a rapidly burning dungeon. "You might want to stand back."

Startled into obedience, Simon moved aside. Jace's hands tightened on the bars, his knuckles whitening alarmingly. There was a groaning crack, and the square of bars jerked free of the stone that held it and clattered to the ground beside the bed. Stone dust rained down in a choking white cloud.

Jace's face appeared at the empty square of window. "Simon. Come ON." He reached down.

Simon reached up and caught Jace's hands. He felt himself hauled up, and then he was grabbing at the edge of the window, lifting himself through the narrow square like a snake wriggling through a tunnel. A second later he was sprawled out on damp grass, staring up at a circle of worried faces above his. Jace, Clary, and Alec. They were all looking down at him in concern.

"You look like crap, vampire," Jace said. "What happened to your hands?"

Simon sat up. The injuries to his hands had healed, but they were still black where he'd grabbed at the bars of his cell. Before he could reply, Clary caught him in a sudden, fierce hug.

"Simon," she breathed. "I can't believe it. I didn't even know you were here. I thought you were in New York until last night—"

"Yeah, well," Simon said, "I didn't know you were here either." He glared at Jace over her shoulder. "In fact, I think I was specifically told that you weren't."

"I never said that," Jace pointed out. "I just didn't correct you when you were, you know, wrong. Anyway, I just saved you from being burned to death, so I figure you're not allowed to be mad."

Burned to death. Simon pulled away from Clary and stared around. They were in a square garden, surrounded on two sides by the walls of the fortress and on the other two sides by a heavy growth of trees. The trees had been cleared where a gravel path led down the hill to the city—it was lined with witchlight torches, but only a few were burning, their light dim and erratic. He looked up at the Gard. Seen from this angle, you could barely even tell there was a fire—black smoke stained the sky overhead, and the light in a few windows seemed unnaturally bright, but the stone walls hid their secret well.

"Samuel," he said. "We have to get Samuel out."

Clary looked baffled. "Who?"

"I wasn't the only person down there. Samuel—he was in the next cell."

"The heap of rags I saw through the window?" Jace recalled.

"Yeah. He's kind of weird, but he's a good guy. We can't leave him down there." Simon scrambled to his feet. "Samuel? Samuel!"

There was no answer. Simon ran to the low, barred window beside the one he'd just crawled through. Through the bars he could see only swirling smoke. "Samuel! Are you in there?"

Something moved inside the smoke—something hunched and dark. Samuel's voice, roughened by smoke, rose hoarsely. "Leave me alone! Go away!"

"Samuel! You'll die down there." Simon yanked at the bars. Nothing happened.

"No! Leave me alone! I want to stay!"

Simon looked desperately around to see Jace beside him. "Move," Jace said, and when Simon leaned to the side, he kicked out with a booted foot. It connected with the bars, which tore free violently from their mooring and tumbled into Samuel's cell. Samuel gave a hoarse shout.

"Samuel! Are you all right?" A vision of Samuel being brained by the falling bars rose up before Simon's eyes.

Samuel's voice rose to a scream. "GO AWAY!"

Simon looked sideways at Jace. "I think he means it."

Jace shook his blond head in exasperation. "You had to make a crazy jail friend, didn't you? You couldn't just count ceiling tiles or tame a pet mouse like normal prisoners do?" Without waiting for an answer, Jace got down on the ground and crawled through the window.

"Jace!" Clary yelped, and she and Alec hurried over, but Jace was already through the window, dropping into the cell below. Clary shot Simon an angry look. "How could you let him do that?"

"Well, he couldn't leave that guy down there to die," Alec said unexpectedly, though he looked a little anxious himself. "It's Jace we're talking about here—"

He broke off as two hands rose up out of the smoke. Alec grabbed one and Simon the other, and together they hauled Samuel like a limp sack of potatoes out of the cell and deposited him on the lawn. A moment later Simon and Clary were grabbing Jace's hands and pulling him out, though he was considerably less limp and swore when they accidentally banged his head on the ledge. He shook them off, crawling the rest of the way onto the grass himself and then collapsing onto his back. "Ouch," he said, staring up at the sky. "I think

I pulled something." He sat up and glanced over at Samuel. "Is he okay?"

Samuel sat hunched on the ground, his hands splayed over his face. He was rocking back and forth soundlessly.

"I think there's something wrong with him," said Alec. He reached down to touch Samuel's shoulder. Samuel jerked away, almost toppling over. "Leave me alone," he said, his voice cracking. "Please. Leave me alone, Alec."

Alec went still all over. "What did you say?"

"He said to leave him alone," said Simon, but Alec wasn't looking at him, didn't even appear to notice he had spoken. He was looking at Jace—who, suddenly very pale, had already begun to rise to his feet.

"Samuel," Alec said. His tone was strangely harsh. "Take your hands away from your face."

"No." Samuel tucked his chin down, his shoulders shaking. "No, please. No."

"Alec!" Simon protested. "Can't you see he isn't well?"

Clary caught at Simon's sleeve. "Simon, there's something wrong."

Her eyes were on Jace—when weren't they?—as he moved to stare down at the crouched figure of Samuel. The tips of Jace's fingers were bleeding where he'd scraped them on the window ledge, and when he moved to push his hair back from his eyes, they left bloody tracks across his cheek. He didn't seem to notice. His eyes were wide, his mouth a flat, angry line. "Shadowhunter," he said. His voice was deathly clear. "Show us your face."

Samuel hesitated, then dropped his hands. Simon had never seen his face before, and he hadn't realized how gaunt

Samuel was, or how old he looked. His face was half-covered by a thatch of thick gray beard, the eyes swimming in dark hollows, his cheeks grooved with lines. But for all that, he was still—somehow—strangely familiar.

Alec's lips moved, but no sound came out. It was Jace who spoke.

"Hodge," he said.

"Hodge?" Simon echoed in confusion."But it can't be. Hodge was . . . and Samuel, he can't be . . ."

"Well, that's just what Hodge does, apparently," Alec said bitterly. "He makes you think he's someone he's not."

"But he said—," Simon began. Clary's grip tightened on his sleeve, and the words died on his lips. The expression on Hodge's face was enough. Not guilt, really, or even horror at being discovered, but a terrible grief that was hard to look at for long.

"Jace," Hodge said very quietly. "Alec . . . I'm so sorry."

Jace moved then the way he moved when he was fighting, like sunlight across water. He was standing in front of Hodge with a knife out, the sharp tip of it aimed at his old tutor's throat. The reflected glow of the fire slid off the blade. "I don't want your apologies. I want a reason why I shouldn't kill you right now, right here."

"Jace." Alec looked alarmed. "Jace, wait."

There was a sudden roar as part of the Gard roof went up in orange tongues of flame. Heat shimmered in the air and lit the night. Clary could see every blade of grass on the ground, every line on Hodge's thin and dirty face.

"No," Jace said. His blank expression as he gazed down at Hodge reminded Clary of another masklike face. Valentine's.

"You knew what my father did to me, didn't you? You knew all his dirty secrets."

Alec was looking uncomprehendingly from Jace to his old tutor. "What are you talking about? What's going on?"

Hodge's face creased. "Jonathan . . ."

"You've always known, and you never said anything. All those years in the Institute, and you never said anything."

Hodge's mouth sagged. "I—I wasn't sure," he whispered. "When you haven't seen a child since he was a baby—I wasn't sure who you were, much less *what* you were."

"Jace?" Alec was looking from his best friend to his tutor, his blue eyes dismayed, but neither of the two was paying attention to anything but the other. Hodge looked like a man trapped in a tightening vise, his hands jerking at his sides as if with pain, his eyes darting. Clary thought of the neatly dressed man in his book-lined library who had offered her tea and kindly advice. It seemed like a thousand years ago.

"I don't believe you," Jace said. "You knew Valentine wasn't dead. He must have told you—"

"He told me nothing," Hodge gasped. "When the Lightwoods informed me they were taking in Michael Wayland's son, I hadn't heard a word from Valentine since the Uprising. I had thought he had forgotten me. I'd even prayed he was dead, but I never knew. And then, the night before you arrived, Hugo came with a message for me from Valentine. 'The boy is my son.' That's all it said." He took a ragged breath. "I had no idea whether to believe him. I thought I'd know—I thought I'd know, just looking at you, but there was nothing, *nothing*, to make me sure. And I thought that this was a trick of Valentine's, but what trick? What was he trying to do? You had no idea, that was clear enough to me, but as for Valentine's purpose—"

"*You should have told me what I was,*" Jace said, all in one breath, as if the words were being punched out of him. "I could have done something about it, then. Killed myself, maybe."

Hodge raised his head, looking up at Jace through his matted, filthy hair. "I wasn't sure," he said again, half to himself, "and in the times that I wondered—I thought, perhaps, that upbringing might matter more than blood—that you could be taught—"

"Taught what? Not to be a monster?" Jace's voice shook, but the knife in his hand was steady. "You should know better. He made a crawling coward out of you, didn't he? And you weren't a helpless little kid when he did it. You could have fought back."

Hodge's eyes fell. "I tried to do my best by you," he said, but even to Clary's ears his words sounded weak.

"Until Valentine came back," Jace said, "and then you did everything he asked of you—you gave me to him like I was a dog that had belonged to him once, that he'd asked you to look after for a few years—"

"And then you left," said Alec. "You left us all. Did you really think you could hide here, in Alicante?"

"I didn't come here to hide," said Hodge, his voice lifeless. "I came here to stop Valentine."

"You can't expect us to believe that." Alec sounded angry again now. "You've always been on Valentine's side. You could have chosen to turn your back on him—"

"I could never have chosen that!" Hodge's voice rose. "Your parents were given their chance for a new life—I was never given that! I was trapped in the Institute for fifteen years—"

"The Institute was our home!" Alec said. "Was it really so bad living with us—being part of our family?"

"Not because of you." Hodge's voice was ragged. "I loved you children. But you were *children.* And no place that you are never allowed to leave can be a home. I went weeks sometimes without speaking to another adult. No other Shadowhunter would trust me. Not even your parents truly liked me; they tolerated me because they had no choice. I could never marry. Never have children of my own. Never have a life. And eventually you children would have been grown and gone, and then I wouldn't even have had that. I lived in fear, as much as I lived at all."

"You can't make us feel sorry for you," Jace said. "Not after what you did. And what the hell were you afraid of, spending all your time in the library? Dust mites? We were the ones who went out and fought demons!"

"He was afraid of Valentine," Simon said. "Don't you get it—"

Jace shot him a venomous look. "Shut up, vampire. This isn't in any way about you."

"Not Valentine exactly," Hodge said, looking at Simon for almost the first time since he'd been dragged from the cell. There was something in that look that surprised Clary—a tired almost-affection. "My own weakness where Valentine was concerned. I knew he would return someday. I knew he would make a bid for power again, a bid to rule the Clave. And I knew what he could offer me. Freedom from my curse. A life. A place in the world. I could have been a Shadowhunter again, in his world. I could never be one again in this one." There was a naked longing in his voice that was painful to hear. "And I knew I would be too weak to refuse him if he offered it."

"And look at the life you got," Jace spat. "Rotting in the cells of the Gard. Was it worth it, betraying us?"

"You know the answer to that." Hodge sounded exhausted. "Valentine took the curse off me. He'd sworn he would, and he did. I thought he'd bring me back to the Circle, or what remained of it then. He didn't. Even he didn't want me. I knew there would be no place for me in his new world. And I knew I'd sold out everything I did have for a lie." He looked down at his clenched, filthy hands. "There was only one thing I had left—one chance to make something other than an utter waste out of my life. After I heard that Valentine had attacked the Silent City—that he had the Mortal Sword—I knew he would go after the Mortal Glass next. I knew he needed all three of the Instruments. And I knew the Mortal Glass was here in Idris."

"Wait." Alec held up a hand. "The Mortal Glass? You mean, you know where it is? And who has it?"

"No one has it," said Hodge. "No one could own the Mortal Glass. No Nephilim, and no Downworlder."

"You really did go crazy down there," Jace said, jerking his chin toward the burned-out windows of the dungeons, "didn't you?"

"Jace." Clary was looking anxiously up at the Gard, its roof crowned with a thorny net of red-gold flames. "The fire is spreading. We should get out of here. We can talk down in the city—"

"I was locked in the Institute for fifteen years," Hodge went on, as if Clary hadn't spoken. "I couldn't put so much as a hand or a foot outside. I spent all my time in the library, researching ways to remove the curse the Clave had put on me. I learned that only a Mortal Instrument could reverse it. I read book after book telling the story of the mythology of the Angel, how he rose from the lake bearing the Mortal Instruments and gave them to Jonathan Shadowhunter, the first Nephilim, and how there were three of them: Cup, Sword, and Mirror—"

"We know all this," Jace interrupted, exasperated. "You taught it to us."

"You think you know all of it, but you don't. As I went over and over the various versions of the histories, I happened again and again on the same illustration, the same image—we've all seen it—the Angel rising out of the lake with the Sword in one hand and the Cup in the other. I could never understand why the Mirror wasn't pictured. Then I realized. The Mirror is the lake. The lake is the Mirror. They are one and the same."

Slowly Jace lowered the knife. "Lake Lyn?"

Clary thought of the lake, like a mirror rising to meet her, the water shattering apart on impact. "I fell in the lake when I first got here. There *is* something about it. Luke said it has strange properties and that the Fair Folk call it the Mirror of Dreams."

"Exactly," Hodge began eagerly. "And I realized the Clave wasn't aware of this, that the knowledge had been lost to time. Even Valentine didn't know—"

He was interrupted by a crashing roar, the sound of a tower at the far end of the Gard collapsing. It sent up a fireworks display of red and glittering sparks.

"Jace," Alec said, raising his head in alarm. "Jace, we have to get out of here. Get up," he said to Hodge, yanking him upright by the arm. "You can tell the Clave what you just told us."

Hodge got shakily to his feet. What must it be like, Clary thought with a pang of unwelcome pity, to live your life ashamed not just of what you'd done but of what you were doing and of what you knew you'd do again? Hodge had given up a long time ago trying to live a better life or a different one; all he wanted was not to be afraid, and so he was afraid all the time.

"Come on." Alec, still gripping Hodge's arm, propelled him forward. But Jace stepped in front of them both, blocking their way.

"If Valentine gets the Mortal Glass," he said, "what then?"

"Jace," Alec said, still holding Hodge's arm, "not now—"

"If he tells it to the Clave, we'll never hear it from them," Jace said. "To them we're just children. But Hodge *owes us this.*" He turned on his old tutor. "You said you realized you had to stop Valentine. Stop him doing what? What does the Mirror give him the power to do?"

Hodge shook his head. "I can't—"

"And no lies." The knife gleamed at Jace's side; his hand was tight on the hilt. "Because maybe for every lie you tell me, I'll cut off a finger. Or two."

Hodge cringed back, real fear in his eyes. Alec looked stricken. "Jace. No. This is what your father's like. It's not what you're like."

"Alec," said Jace. He didn't look at his friend, but his tone was like the touch of a regretful hand. "You don't really know what I'm like."

Alec's eyes met Clary's across the grass. *He can't imagine why Jace is acting like this,* she thought. *He doesn't know.* She took a step foward. "Jace, Alec is right—we can take Hodge down to the Hall and he can tell the Clave what he's just told us—"

"If he'd been willing to tell the Clave, he would have done it already," Jace snapped without looking at her. "The fact that he didn't proves he's a liar."

"The Clave isn't to be trusted!" Hodge protested desperately. "There are spies in it—Valentine's men—I couldn't tell them where the Mirror is. If Valentine found the Mirror, he would be—"

He never finished his sentence. Something bright silver gleamed out in the moonlight, a nail head of light in the darkness. Alec cried out. Hodge's eyes flew wide as he staggered, clawing at his chest. As he sank backward, Clary saw why: The hilt of a long dagger protruded from his rib cage, like the haft of an arrow bristling from its target.

Alec, leaping forward, caught his old tutor as he fell, and lowered him gently to the ground. He looked up helplessly, his face spattered with Hodge's blood. "Jace, why—"

"I didn't—" Jace's face was white, and Clary saw that he still held his knife, gripped tightly at his side. "I . . ."

Simon spun around, and Clary turned with him, staring into the darkness. The fire lit the grass with a hellish orange glow, but it was black between the trees of the hillside—and then something emerged from the blackness, a shadowy figure, with familiar dark, tumbled hair. He moved toward them, the light catching his face and reflecting off his dark eyes; they looked as if they were burning.

"*Sebastian?*" Clary said.

Jace looked wildly from Hodge to Sebastian standing uncertainly at the edge of the garden; Jace looked almost dazed. "You," he said. "You—did this?"

"I had to do it," Sebastian said. "He would have killed you."

"With *what?*" Jace's voice rose and cracked. "He didn't even have a weapon—"

"Jace." Alec cut through Jace's shouting. "Come here. Help me with Hodge."

"He would have killed you," Sebastian said again. "He would have—"

But Jace had gone to kneel beside Alec, sheathing his knife at his belt. Alec was holding Hodge in his arms, blood on his own shirtfront now. "Take the stele from my pocket," he said to Jace. "Try an *iratze*—"

Clary, stiff with horror, felt Simon stir beside her. She turned to look at him and was shocked—he was white as paper except for a hectic red flush on both cheekbones. She could see the veins snaking under his skin, like the growth of some delicate, branching coral. "The blood," he whispered, not looking at her. "I have to get away from it."

Clary reached to catch his sleeve, but he lurched back, jerking his arm out of her grasp.

"No, Clary, please. Let me go. I'll be okay; I'll be back. I just—" She started after him, but he was too quick for her to hold him back. He vanished into the darkness between the trees.

"Hodge—" Alec sounded panicked. "Hodge, hold still—"

But his tutor was struggling feebly, trying to pull away from him, away from the stele in Jace's hand. "No." Hodge's face was the color of putty. His eyes darted from Jace to Sebastian, who was still hanging back in the shadows. "Jonathan—"

"Jace," Jace said, almost in a whisper. "Call me Jace."

Hodge's eyes rested on him. Clary could not decipher the look in them. Pleading, yes, but something more than that, filled with dread, or something like it, and with need. He lifted a warding hand. "Not you," he whispered, and blood spilled from his mouth with the words.

A look of hurt flashed across Jace's face. "Alec, do the *iratze*—I don't think he wants me to touch him."

Hodge's hand tightened into a claw; he clutched at Jace's sleeve. The rattle of his breath was audible. "You were . . . never . . ."

And he died. Clary could tell the moment the life left him. It was not a quiet, instant thing, like in a movie; his voice choked off in a gurgle and his eyes rolled back and he went limp and heavy, his arm bent awkwardly under him.

Alec closed Hodge's eyes with his fingertips. "*Vale*, Hodge Starkweather."

"He doesn't deserve that." Sebastian's voice was sharp. "He wasn't a Shadowhunter; he was a traitor. He doesn't deserve the last words."

Alec's head jerked up. He lowered Hodge to the ground and rose to his feet, his blue eyes like ice. Blood streaked his clothes. "You know nothing about it. You killed an unarmed man, a Nephilim. You're a murderer."

Sebastian's lip curled. "You think I don't know who that was?" He gestured at Hodge. "Starkweather was in the Circle. He betrayed the Clave then and was cursed for it. He should have died for what he did, but the Clave was lenient—and where did it get them? He betrayed us all again when he sold the Mortal Cup to Valentine just to get his curse lifted—a curse he deserved." He paused, breathing hard. "I shouldn't have done it, but you can't say he didn't deserve it."

"How do you know so much about Hodge?" Clary demanded. "And what are you doing here? You should be back at the Hall."

Sebastian hesitated. "You were taking so long," he said finally. "I got worried. I thought you might need my help."

"So you decided to help us by *killing the guy we were talking to?*" Clary demanded. "Because you thought he had a shady past? Who—who *does* that? It doesn't make any sense."

"That's because he's lying," Jace said. He was looking at Sebastian—a cold, considering look. "And not well. I thought you'd be a little faster on your feet there, Verlac."

Sebastian met his look evenly. "I don't know what you mean, Morgenstern."

"He means," said Alec, stepping forward, "that if you really think what you just did was justified, you won't mind coming with us to the Accords Hall and explaining yourself to the Council. Will you?"

A beat passed before Sebastian smiled—the smile that had charmed Clary before, but now there was something a little off-kilter about it, like a picture hanging slightly crookedly on a wall. "Of course not." He moved toward them slowly, almost strolling, as if he didn't have a worry in the world. As if he hadn't just committed murder. "Of course," he said, "it is a little odd that you're so upset that I killed a man when Jace was planning on cutting his fingers off one by one."

Alec's mouth tightened. "He wouldn't have done it."

"*You*—" Jace looked at Sebastian with loathing. "You have no idea what you're talking about."

"Or maybe," Sebastian said, "you're really just angry because I kissed your sister. Because she wanted me."

"I did *not*," Clary said, but neither of them was looking at her. "Want you, I mean."

"She has this little habit, you know—the way she gasps when you kiss her, like she's surprised?" Sebastian had come to a stop now, just in front of Jace, and was smiling like an angel. "It's rather endearing; you must have noticed it."

Jace looked as if he wanted to throw up. "My sister—"

"*Your sister,*" Sebastian said. "Is she? Because you two don't act like it. You think other people can't see the way you look at each other? You think you're hiding the way you feel? You think everyone doesn't think it's sick and unnatural? Because it is."

"That's enough." The look on Jace's face was murderous.

"Why are you doing this?" Clary said. "Sebastian, why are you saying all these things?"

"Because I finally can," Sebastian said. "You've no idea what it's been like, being around the lot of you these past few days, having to pretend I could stand you. That the sight of you didn't make me sick. You," he said to Jace, "every second you're not panting after your own sister, you're whining on and on about how your daddy didn't love you. Well, who could blame him? And you, you stupid bitch"—he turned to Clary—"giving that priceless book away to a half-breed warlock; have you got a single brain cell in that tiny head of yours? And you—" He directed his next sneer at Alec. "I think we all know what's wrong with *you*. They shouldn't let your kind in the Clave. You're disgusting."

Alec paled, though he looked more astonished than anything else. Clary couldn't blame him—it was hard to look at Sebastian, at his angelic smile, and imagine he could say these things. "*Pretend* you could stand us?" she echoed. "But why would you have to pretend that unless you were . . . unless you were spying on us," she finished, realizing the truth even as she spoke it. "Unless you were a spy for Valentine."

Sebastian's handsome face twisted, the full mouth

flattening, his long, elegant eyes narrowing to slits. "And finally they get it," he said. "I swear, there are utterly lightless demon dimensions out there that are less dim than the bunch of you."

"We may not be all that bright," Jace said, "but at least we're alive."

Sebastian looked at him in disgust. "I'm alive," he pointed out.

"Not for long," said Jace. Moonlight exploded off the blade of his knife as he flung himself at Sebastian, his motion so fast that it seemed blurred, faster than any human movement Clary had ever seen.

Until now.

Sebastian darted aside, missing the blow, and caught Jace's knife arm as it descended. The knife clattered to the ground, and then Sebastian had Jace by the back of his jacket. He lifted him and flung him with incredible strength. Jace flew through the air, hit the wall of the Gard with bone-cracking force, and crumpled to the ground.

"Jace!" Clary's vision went white. She ran at Sebastian to choke the life out of him. But he sidestepped her and brought his hand down as casually as if he were swatting an insect aside. The blow caught her hard on the side of the head, sending her spinning to the ground. She rolled over, blinking a red mist of pain out of her eyes.

Alec had taken his bow from his back; it was drawn, an arrow notched at the ready. His hands didn't waver as he aimed at Sebastian. "Stay where you are," he said, "and put your hands behind your back."

Sebastian laughed. "You wouldn't really shoot me," he said.

He moved toward Alec with an easy, careless step, as if he were striding up the stairs to his own front door.

Alec's eyes narrowed. His hands went up in a graceful, even series of movements; he drew the arrow back and loosed it. It flew toward Sebastian—

And missed. Sebastian had ducked or moved somehow, Clary couldn't tell, and the arrow had gone past him, lodging in the trunk of a tree. Alec had time only for a momentary look of surprise before Sebastian was on him, wrenching the bow out of his grasp. Sebastian snapped it in his hands—cracked it in half, and the crack of the splintering made Clary wince as if she were hearing bones splinter. She tried to drag herself into a sitting position, ignoring the searing pain in her head. Jace was lying a few feet away from her, utterly still. She tried to get up, but her legs didn't seem to be working properly.

Sebastian tossed the shattered halves of the bow aside and closed in on Alec. Alec already had a seraph blade out, glittering in his hand, but Sebastian swept it aside as Alec came at him—swept it aside and caught Alec by the throat, almost lifting him off his feet. He squeezed mercilessly, viciously, grinning as Alec choked and struggled. "Lightwood," he breathed. "I've taken care of one of you already today. I hadn't expected I'd be lucky enough to get to do it twice."

He jerked backward, like a puppet whose strings had been yanked. Released, Alec slumped to the ground, his hands at his throat. Clary could hear his rattling, desperate breath—but her eyes were on Sebastian. A dark shadow had affixed itself to his back and was clinging to him like a leech. He clawed at his throat, gagging and choking as he spun in place, clawing at the thing that had hold of his throat. As he turned, the moonlight fell on him, and Clary saw what it was.

It was Simon. His arms were wrapped around Sebastian's neck, his white incisors glittering like bone needles. It was the first time Clary had seen him actually look fully like a vampire since the night he'd risen from his grave, and she stared in horrified amazement, unable to look away. His lips were curled back in a snarl, his fangs fully extended and sharp as daggers. He sank them into Sebastian's forearm, opening up a long red tear in the skin.

Sebastian yelled out loud and flung himself backward, landing hard on the ground. He rolled, Simon half on top of him, the two of them clawing at each other, tearing and snarling like dogs in a pit. Sebastian was bleeding in several places when he finally staggered to his feet and delivered two hard kicks to Simon's rib cage. Simon doubled over, clutching his midsection. "You foul little tick," Sebastian snarled, drawing his foot back for another blow.

"I wouldn't," said a quiet voice.

Clary's head jerked up, sending another starburst of pain shooting behind her eyes. Jace stood a few feet from Sebastian. His face was bloody, one eye swollen nearly shut, but in one hand was a blazing seraph blade, and the hand that held it was steady. "I've never killed a human being with one of these before," said Jace. "But I'm willing to try."

Sebastian's face twisted. He glanced down once at Simon, and then raised his head and spat. The words he said after that were in a language Clary didn't recognize—and then he turned with the same terrifying swiftness with which he'd moved when he'd attacked Jace, and vanished into the darkness.

"No!" Clary cried. She tried to raise herself to her feet, but the pain was like an arrow searing its way through her brain. She crumpled to the damp grass. A moment later Jace was leaning over her, his face pale and anxious. She looked up at him, her vision blurring—it had to be blurred, didn't it, or she could never have imagined that whiteness around him, a sort of light—

She heard Simon's voice and then Alec's, and something was handed down to Jace—a stele. Her arm burned, and a moment later the pain began to recede, and her head cleared. She blinked up at the three faces hovering over hers. "My head . . ."

"You have a concussion," Jace said. "The *iratze* should help, but we ought to get you to the Basilias. It's our hospital. Head injuries can be tricky." He handed the stele back to Alec. "Do you think you can stand up?"

She nodded. It was a mistake. Pain shot through her again as hands reached down and helped her to her feet. Simon. She leaned against him gratefully, waiting for her balance to return. She still felt as if she might fall over at any minute.

Jace was scowling. "You shouldn't have attacked Sebastian like that. You didn't even have a weapon. What were you thinking?"

"What we were all thinking." Alec, unexpectedly, came to her defense. "That he'd just thrown you through the air like a softball. Jace, I've never seen anyone get the better of you like that."

"I—he surprised me," Jace said a little reluctantly. "He must have had some kind of special training. I wasn't expecting it."

"Yeah, well." Simon touched his rib cage, wincing. "I think he kicked in a couple of my ribs. It's okay," he added at

Clary's worried look. "They're healing. But Sebastian's definitely strong. Really strong." He looked at Jace. "How long do you think he was standing there in the shadows?"

Jace looked grim. He glanced among the trees in the direction Sebastian had gone. "Well, the Clave will catch him—and curse him, probably. I'd like to see them put the same curse on him they put on Hodge. That would be poetic justice."

Simon turned aside and spat into the bushes. He wiped his mouth with the back of his hand, his face twisted into a grimace. "His blood tastes foul—like poison."

"I suppose we can add that to his list of charming qualities," said Jace. "I wonder what else he was up to tonight."

"We need to get back to the Hall." The look on Alec's face was strained, and Clary remembered that Sebastian had said something to him, something about the other Lightwoods. . . . "Can you walk, Clary?"

She drew away from Simon. "I can walk. What about Hodge? We can't just leave him."

"We have to," said Alec. "There'll be time to come back for him if we all survive the night."

As they left the garden, Jace paused, drew off his jacket, and laid it over Hodge's slack, upturned face. Clary wanted to go to Jace, put a hand on his shoulder even, but something in the way he held himself told her not to. Even Alec didn't go near him or offer a healing rune, despite the fact that Jace was limping as he walked down the hill.

They moved together down the zigzag path, weapons drawn and at the ready, the sky lit red by the burning Gard behind them. But they saw no demons. The stillness and eerie light made Clary's head throb; she felt as if she were in a dream.

Exhaustion gripped her like a vise. Just putting one foot in front of the other was like lifting a block of cement and slamming it down, over and over. She could hear Jace and Alec talking up ahead on the path, their voices faintly blurred despite their proximity.

Alec was speaking softly, almost pleading: "Jace, the way you were talking up there, to Hodge. You can't think like that. Being Valentine's son, it doesn't make you a monster. Whatever he did to you when you were a kid, whatever he taught you, you have to see it's not your fault—"

"I don't want to talk about this, Alec. Not now, not ever. Don't ask me about it again." Jace's tone was savage, and Alec fell silent. Clary could almost feel his hurt. What a night, Clary thought. A night of so much pain for everyone.

She tried not to think of Hodge, of the pleading, pitiful look on his face before he'd died. She hadn't liked Hodge, but he hadn't deserved what Sebastian had done to him. No one did. She thought of Sebastian, of the way he'd moved, like sparks flying. She'd never seen anyone but Jace move like that. She wanted to puzzle it out—what had happened to Sebastian? How had a cousin of the Penhallows managed to go so wrong, and how had they never noticed? She'd thought he'd wanted to help her save her mother, but he'd only wanted to get the Book of the White for Valentine. Magnus had been wrong—it hadn't been because of the Lightwoods that Valentine had found out about Ragnor Fell. It had been because she'd told Sebastian. How could she have been so stupid?

Appalled, she barely noticed as the path turned into an avenue, leading them into the city. The streets were deserted, the houses dark, many of the witchlight streetlamps smashed, their glass scattered across the cobblestones. Voices were audible, echoing as if at a distance, and the gleam of torches was visible here and there among the shadows between buildings, but—

"It's awfully quiet," Alec said, looking around in surprise. "And—"

"It doesn't stink like demons." Jace frowned. "Strange. Come on. Let's get to the Hall."

Though Clary was half-braced for an attack, they didn't see a single demon as they moved through the streets. Not a live one, at least—though as they passed a narrow alley, she saw a group of three or four Shadowhunters gathered in a circle around something that pulsed and twitched on the ground. They were taking turns stabbing it with long, sharpened poles. With a shudder she looked away.

The Hall of Accords was lit like a bonfire, witchlight pouring out of its doors and windows. They hurried up the stairs, Clary steadying herself when she stumbled. Her dizziness was getting worse. The world seemed to be swinging around her, as if she stood inside a great spinning globe. Above her the stars were white-painted streaks across the sky. "You should lie down," Simon said, and then, when she said nothing, "Clary?"

With an enormous effort, she forced herself to smile at him. "I'm all right."

Jace, standing at the entrance to the Hall, looked back at her in silence. In the harsh glare of the witchlight, the blood on his face and his swollen eye looked ugly, streaked and black.

There was a dull roar inside the Hall, the low murmur of hundreds of voices. To Clary it sounded like the beating of an enormous heart. The lights of the bracketed torches, coupled with the glow of witchlights carried everywhere, seared her eyes and fragmented her vision; she could see only vague shapes now, vague shapes and colors. White, gold, and then the night sky above, fading from dark to paler blue. How late was it?

"I don't see them." Alec, casting anxiously around the room for his family, sounded as if he were a hundred miles off, or deep under water. "They should be here by now—"

His voice faded as Clary's dizziness worsened. She put a hand against a nearby pillar to steady herself. A hand brushed across her back—Simon. He was saying something to Jace, sounding anxious. His voice faded into the pattern of dozens of others, rising and falling around her like waves breaking.

"Never seen anything like it. The demons just turned around and left, just vanished."

"Sunrise, probably. They're afraid of sunrise, and it's not far off."

"No, it was more than that."

"You just don't want to think they'll be back the next night, or the next."

"Don't say that; there's no reason to say that. They'll get the wards back up."

"And Valentine will just take them down again."

"Maybe it's no better than we deserve. Maybe Valentine was right—maybe allying ourselves with Downworlders means we've lost the Angel's blessing."

"Hush. Have some respect. They're tallying the dead out in Angel Square."

"There they are," Alec said. "Over there, by the dais. It looks like . . ." His voice trailed off, and then he was gone, pushing his way through the crowd. Clary squinted, trying to sharpen her vision. All she could see were blurs—

She heard Jace catch his breath, and then, without another word, he was shoving through the crowd after Alec. Clary let go of the pillar, meaning to follow them, but stumbled. Simon caught her.

"You need to lie down, Clary," he said.

"No," she whispered. "I want to see what happened—"

She broke off. He was staring past her, after Jace, and he looked stricken. Bracing herself against the pillar, she raised herself up on her toes, struggling to see over the crowd—

There they were, the Lightwoods: Maryse with her arms around Isabelle, who was sobbing, and Robert Lightwood sitting on the ground and holding something—no, *someone*, and Clary thought of the first time she had seen Max, at the Institute, lying limp and asleep on a couch, his glasses knocked askew and his hand trailing along the floor. *He can sleep anywhere,* Jace had said, and he almost looked as if he were sleeping now, in his father's lap, but Clary knew he wasn't.

Alec was on his knees, holding one of Max's hands, but Jace was just standing where he was, not moving, and more than anything else he looked lost, as if he had no idea where he was or what he was doing there. All Clary wanted was to run to him and put her arms around him, but the look on Simon's face told her no, no, and so did her memory of the manor house and Jace's arms around her there. She was the last person on earth who could ever give him any comfort.

"Clary," Simon said, but she was pulling away from him, despite her dizziness and the pain in her head. She ran for the door of the Hall and pushed it open, ran out onto the steps and stood there, gulping down breaths of cold air. In the distance the horizon was streaked with red fire, the stars fading, bleached out of the lightening sky. The night was over. Dawn had come.

13

Where There Is Sorrow

Clary woke gasping out of a dream of bleeding angels, her sheets twisted around her in a tight spiral. It was pitch-black and close in Amatis's spare bedroom, like being locked in a coffin. She reached out and twitched the curtains open. Daylight poured in. She frowned and pulled them shut again.

Shadowhunters burned their dead, and ever since the demon attack, the sky to the west of the city had been stained with smoke. Looking at it out the window made Clary feel sick, so she kept the curtains closed. In the darkness of the room she closed her eyes, trying to remember her dream. There had been angels in it, and the image of the rune Ithuriel had showed her, flashing over and over against the inside of her eyelids like a blinking WALK sign. It was a simple rune, as simple as a tied knot, but no matter how hard she concentrated, she couldn't read it, couldn't figure out what it meant. All she knew was that it seemed somehow incomplete to her, as if whoever had created the pattern hadn't quite finished it.

These are not the first dreams I have ever showed you, Ithuriel had said. She thought of her other dreams: of Simon with crosses burned into his hands, Jace with wings, lakes of cracking ice that shone like mirror glass. Had the angel sent her those, too?

With a sigh she sat up. The dreams might be bad, but the waking images that marched across her brain weren't much better. Isabelle, weeping on the floor of the Hall of Accords, tugging with such force on the black hair threaded through her fingers that Clary worried she would rip it out. Maryse shrieking at Jia Penhallow that the boy they'd brought into their house had done this, their nephew, and if he was so closely allied with Valentine, what did that say about them? Alec trying to calm his mother down, asking Jace to help him, but Jace just standing there as the sun rose over Alicante and blazed down through the ceiling of the Hall. "It's dawn," Luke had said, looking more tired than Clary had ever seen him. "Time to bring the bodies inside." And he'd sent out patrols to gather up the dead Shadowhunters and lycanthropes lying in the streets and bring them to the plaza outside the Hall, the plaza Clary had crossed with Sebastian when she'd commented that the Hall looked like a church. It had seemed like a pretty place to her then, lined with flower boxes and brightly painted shops. And now it was full of corpses.

Including Max. Thinking of the little boy who'd so gravely talked about manga with her made her stomach knot. She'd promised once that she'd take him to Forbidden Planet, but that would never happen now. *I would have bought him books,* she thought. *Whatever books he wanted.* Not that it mattered.

Don't think about it. Clary kicked her sheets back and got up. After a quick shower she changed into the jeans and sweater she'd worn the day she'd come from New York. She pressed her face to the material before she put the sweater on, hoping to catch a whiff of Brooklyn, or the smell of laundry detergent—something to remind her of home—but it had been washed and smelled like lemon soap. With another sigh she headed downstairs.

The house was empty except for Simon, sitting on the couch in the living room. The open windows behind him streamed daylight. He'd become like a cat, Clary thought, always seeking out available patches of sunlight to curl up in. No matter how much sun he got, though, his skin stayed the same ivory white.

She picked an apple out of the bowl on the table and sank down next to him, curling her legs up under her. "Did you get any sleep?"

"Some." He looked at her. "I ought to ask you that. You're the one with the shadows under your eyes. More nightmares?"

She shrugged. "Same stuff. Death, destruction, bad angels."

"So a lot like real life, then."

"Yeah, but at least when I wake up, it's over." She took a bite out of her apple. "Let me guess. Luke and Amatis are at the Accords Hall, having another meeting."

"Yeah. I think they're having the meeting where they get together and decide what other meetings they need to have." Simon picked idly at the fringe edging a throw pillow. "Have you heard anything from Magnus?"

"No." Clary was trying not to think about the fact that it had been three days since she'd seen Magnus, and he'd sent no word at all. Or the fact that there was really nothing stopping him from taking the Book of the White and disappearing into the ether, never to be heard from again. She wondered why she'd ever thought trusting someone who wore that much eyeliner was a good idea.

She touched Simon's wrist lightly. "And you? What about you? You're still okay here?" She'd wanted Simon to go home the moment the battle was over—home, where it was safe. But he'd been strangely resistant. For whatever reason, he seemed to want to stay. She hoped it wasn't because he thought he had to take care of her—she'd nearly come out and told him she didn't need his protection—but she hadn't, because part of her couldn't bear to see him go. So he stayed, and Clary was secretly, guiltily glad. "You're getting—you know—what you need?"

"You mean blood? Yeah, Maia's still bringing me bottles every day. Don't ask me where she gets it, though." The first morning Simon had been at Amatis's house, a grinning lycanthrope had showed up on the doorstep with a live cat for him. "Blood," he'd said, in a heavily accented voice. "For you. Fresh!" Simon had thanked the werewolf, waited for him to leave, and let the cat go, his expression faintly green.

"Well, you're going to have to get your blood from *somewhere*," said Luke, looking amused.

"I have a pet cat," Simon replied. "There's no way."

"I'll tell Maia," Luke promised, and from then on the blood had come in discreet glass milk bottles. Clary had no idea how Maia was arranging it and, like Simon, didn't want to ask. She hadn't seen the werewolf girl since the night of the battle—the lycanthropes were camped somewhere in the nearby forest, with only Luke remaining in the city.

"What's up?" Simon leaned his head back, looking at her through his lowered eyelashes. "You look like you want to ask me something."

There were several things Clary wanted to ask him, but she decided to go for one of the safer options. "Hodge," she said, and hesitated. "When you were in the cell—you really didn't know it was him?"

"I couldn't *see* him. I could just hear him through the wall. We talked—a lot."

"And you liked him? I mean, he was nice?"

"Nice? I don't know. Tortured, sad, intelligent, compassionate in brief flashes—yeah, I liked him. I think I sort of reminded him of himself, in a way—"

"Don't *say* that!" Clary sat up straight, almost dropping her apple. "You're nothing like Hodge was."

"You don't think I'm tortured and intelligent?"

"Hodge was evil. You're not." Clary spoke decidedly. "That's all there is to it."

Simon sighed. "People aren't born good or bad. Maybe they're born with tendencies either way, but it's the way you live your life that matters. And the people you know. Valentine was Hodge's friend, and I don't think Hodge really had anyone else in his life to challenge him or make him be a better person. If I'd had that life, I don't know how I would have turned out. But I didn't. I have my family. And I have you."

Clary smiled at him, but his words rang painfully in her ears. *People aren't born good or bad.* She'd always thought that was true, but in the images the angel had showed her, she'd seen her mother call her own child evil, a monster. She wished she could tell Simon about it, tell him everything the angel had showed her, but she couldn't. It would have meant telling what they'd discovered about Jace, and that she couldn't do. It was his secret to tell, not hers. Simon had asked her once what Jace had meant when he'd spoken to Hodge, why he'd called himself a monster, but she'd only answered that it was hard to understand what Jace meant by anything at the best of times. She wasn't sure Simon had believed her, but he hadn't asked again.

She was saved from saying anything at all by a loud knock on the door. With a frown Clary set her apple core down on the table. "I'll get it."

The open door let in a wave of cold, fresh air. Aline Penhallow stood on the front steps, wearing a dark pink silk jacket that almost matched the circles under her eyes. "I need to talk to you," she said without preamble.

Surprised, Clary could only nod and hold the door open. "All right. Come on in."

"Thanks." Aline pushed past her brusquely and went into the living room. She froze when she saw Simon sitting on the couch, her lips parting in astonishment. "Isn't that . . ."

"The vampire?" Simon grinned. The slight but inhuman acuity of his incisors was just visible against his lower lip when he grinned like that. Clary wished he wouldn't.

Aline turned to Clary. "Can I talk to you alone?"

"No," Clary said, and sat down on the couch next to Simon. "Anything you have to say, you can say to both of us."

Aline bit her lip. "Fine. Look, I have something I want to tell Alec and Jace and Isabelle, but I have no idea where to find them right now."

Clary sighed. "They pulled some strings and got into an empty house. The family in it left for the country."

Aline nodded. A lot of people had left Idris since the attacks. Most had stayed—more than Clary would have expected—but quite a few had packed up and departed, leaving their houses standing empty.

"They're okay, if that's what you want to know. Look, I haven't seen them either. Not since the battle. I could pass on a message through Luke if you want—"

"I don't know." Aline was chewing her lower lip. "My parents had to tell Sebastian's aunt in Paris what he did. She was really upset."

"As one would be if one's nephew turned out to be an evil mastermind," said Simon.

Aline shot him a dark look. "She said it was completely unlike him, that there must be some mistake. So she sent me some photos of him." Aline reached into her pocket and drew out several slightly bent photographs, which she handed to Clary. "Look."

Clary looked. The photographs showed a laughing dark-haired boy, handsome in an off-kilter sort of way, with a crooked grin and a slightly-too-big nose. He looked like the sort of boy it would be fun to hang out with. He also looked nothing at all like Sebastian. "*This* is your cousin?"

"That's Sebastian Verlac. Which means—"

"That the boy who was here, who was calling himself Sebastian, is someone else entirely?" Clary rifled through the photos with increasing agitation.

"I thought—" Aline was worrying her lip again. "I thought that if the Lightwoods knew Sebastian—or whoever that boy was—wasn't really our cousin, maybe they'd forgive me. Forgive *us*."

"I'm sure they will." Clary made her voice as kind as she could. "But this is bigger than that. The Clave will want to know that Sebastian wasn't just some misguided Shadowhunter kid. Valentine sent him here deliberately as a spy."

"He was just so convincing," Aline said. "He knew things only my family knows. He knew things from our childhood—"

"It kind of makes you wonder," said Simon, "what happened to the real Sebastian. Your cousin. It sounds like he left Paris, headed to Idris, and never actually got here. So what happened to him on the way?"

Clary answered. "Valentine happened. He must have planned it all and known where Sebastian would be and how to intercept him on the way. And if he did that with Sebastian—"

"Then there may be others," said Aline. "You should tell the Clave. Tell Lucian Graymark." She caught Clary's surprised look. "People listen to him. My parents said so."

"Maybe you should come to the Hall with us," Simon suggested. "Tell him yourself."

Aline shook her head. "I can't face the Lightwoods. Especially Isabelle. She saved my life, and I—I just ran away. I couldn't stop myself. I just ran."

"You were in shock. It's not your fault."

Aline looked unconvinced. "And now her brother—" She broke off, biting her lip again. "Anyway. Look, there's something I've been meaning to tell you, Clary."

"To tell *me*?" Clary was baffled.

"Yes." Aline took a deep breath. "Look, what you walked in

on, with me and Jace, it wasn't anything. *I* kissed *him*. It was—an experiment. And it didn't really work."

Clary felt herself blushing what she thought must be a truly spectacular red. *Why is she telling me this?* "Look, it's okay. It's Jace's business, not mine."

"Well, you seemed pretty upset at the time." A small smile played around the corners of Aline's mouth. "And I think I know why."

Clary swallowed against the acid taste in her mouth. "You do?"

"Look, your brother gets around. Everyone knows that; he's dated lots of girls. You were worried that if he messed around with me, he'd get in trouble. After all, our families are—*were*—friends. You don't need to worry, though. He's not my type."

"I don't think I've ever heard a girl say that before," said Simon. "I thought Jace was the kind of guy who was everyone's type."

"I thought so too," Aline said slowly, "which is why I kissed him. I was trying to figure out if any guy is my type."

She kissed Jace, Clary thought. *He didn't kiss her. She kissed him.* She met Simon's eyes over Aline's head. Simon was looking amused. "Well, what'd you decide?"

Aline shrugged. "Not sure yet. But, hey, at least you don't have Jace to worry about."

If only. "I always have Jace to worry about."

The space inside the Hall of Accords had been swiftly reconfigured since the night of the battle. With the Gard gone it now served as a Council chamber, a gathering place for people looking for missing family members, and a place to learn the latest news. The central fountain was dry, and on either side of it long benches were drawn up in rows facing a raised dais at the far end of the room. While some Nephilim were seated on the benches in what looked like a Council session, in the aisles and beneath the arcades that ringed the great room dozens of other Shadowhunters were milling anxiously. The Hall no longer looked like a place where anyone would consider dancing. There was a peculiar atmosphere in the air, a mixture of tension and anticipation.

Despite the gathering of the Clave in the center, murmured conversations were everywhere. Clary caught snippets of chatter as she and Simon moved through the room. The rumors all seemed to conflict with each other: The demon towers were working again. The wards were back up, but weaker than before. The wards were back up, but stronger than before. Demons had been sighted on the hills south of the city. The country houses were abandoned, more families had left the city, and some had left the Clave altogether.

On the raised dais, surrounded by hanging maps of the city, stood the Consul, glowering like a bodyguard beside a short, plump man in gray. The plump man was gesticulating angrily as he spoke, but no one seemed to be paying any attention.

"Oh, crap, that's the Inquisitor," Simon muttered in Clary's ear, pointing. "Aldertree."

"And there's Luke," Clary said, picking him out from the crowd. He stood near the dry fountain, deep in conversation with a man in heavily scuffed gear and a bandage covering the left half of his face. Clary looked around for Amatis and finally saw her, sitting silently at the end of a bench, as far away from the other Shadowhunters as she could get. She caught sight of Clary and made a startled face, beginning to rise to her feet.

Luke saw Clary, frowned, and spoke to the bandaged man in a low voice, excusing himself. He crossed the room to where Clary and Simon stood by one of the pillars, his frown deepening as he approached. "What are you doing here? You know the Clave doesn't allow children into its meetings, and as for *you*—" He glared at Simon. "It's probably not the best idea for you to show your face in front of the Inquisitor, even if there isn't really anything he can do about it." A smile twitched the corner of his mouth. "Not without jeopardizing any alliance the Clave might want to have with Downworlders in the future, anyway."

"That's right." Simon wiggled his fingers in a wave at the Inquisitor, which Aldertree ignored.

"Simon, stop it. We're here for a reason." Clary thrust the photographs of Sebastian at Luke. "This is Sebastian Verlac. The *real* Sebastian Verlac."

Luke's expression darkened. He shuffled through the photos without saying anything as Clary repeated the story Aline had told her. Simon, meanwhile, stood uneasily, glowering across the room at Aldertree, who was studiously ignoring him.

"So does the real Sebastian look much like the imposter version?" Luke asked finally.

"Not really," Clary said. "The fake Sebastian was taller. And I think he was probably blond, because he was definitely dyeing his hair. No one has hair *that* black." *And the dye came off on my fingers when I touched it,* she thought, but kept the thought to herself. "Anyway, Aline wanted us to show these to you and to the Lightwoods. She thought maybe if they knew he wasn't really related to the Penhallows, then—"

"She hasn't told her parents about these, has she?" Luke indicated the photos.

"Not yet, I think," Clary said. "I think she came straight to me. She wanted me to tell you. She said people listen to you."

"Maybe some of them do." Luke glanced back at the man with the bandaged face. "I was just talking to Patrick Penhallow, actually. Valentine was a good friend of his back in the day and may have kept tabs on the Penhallow family in one way or another in the years since. You said Hodge told you he had spies here." He handed the photos back to Clary. "Unfortunately, the Lightwoods aren't going to be part of the Council today. This morning was Max's funeral. They're most likely in the cemetery." Seeing the look on Clary's face, he added, "It was a very small ceremony, Clary. Just the family."

But I am Jace's family, said a small, protesting voice inside her head. But there was another voice, a louder one, surprising her with its bitterness. *And he told you that being around you was like bleeding to death slowly. Do you really think he needs that when he's already at Max's funeral?*

"Then you can tell them tonight, maybe," Clary said. "I mean—I think it'll be good news. Whoever Sebastian really is, he isn't related to their friends."

"It'd be better news if we knew where he was," Luke muttered. "Or what other spies Valentine has here. There must have been several of them, at least, involved in taking down the wards. It could only have been done from inside the city."

"Hodge said Valentine had figured out how to do it," said Simon. "He said that you need demon blood to take the wards down, but that there was no way to get demon blood into the city. Except that Valentine had figured out a way."

"Someone painted a rune in demon blood on the apex of one of the towers," Luke said with a sigh, "so, clearly, Hodge was right. Unfortunately, the Clave has always trusted too much in their wards. But even the cleverest puzzle has a solution."

"It seems to me like the sort of clever that gets your butt kicked in gaming," Simon said. "The second you protect your fortress with a Spell of Total Invincibility, someone comes along and figures out how to trash the place."

"Simon," Clary said. "Shut up."

"He's not so far off," said Luke. "We just don't know how they got demon blood into the city without setting the wards off in the first place." He shrugged. "It's the least of our problems at the moment. The wards are back up, but we already know they're not foolproof. Valentine could return at any moment with an even bigger force of arms, and I doubt we could fight him off. There aren't enough Nephilim, and those who are here are utterly demoralized."

"But what about the Downworlders?" Clary said. "You *told* the Consul that the Clave had to fight with the Downworlders."

"I can tell Malachi and Aldertree that until I'm blue in the face, but it doesn't mean they'll listen," Luke said wearily. "The only reason they're even letting me stay here is because the Clave voted to keep me on as an adviser. And they only did *that* because quite a few of them had their lives saved by my pack. But that doesn't mean they want more Downworlders in Idris—"

Someone screamed.

Amatis was on her feet, her hand over her mouth, staring toward the front of the Hall. A man stood in the doorway, framed in the glow of the sunlight outside. He was only a silhouette, until he took a step forward, into the Hall, and Clary could see his face for the first time.

Valentine.

For some reason the first thing Clary noticed was that he was clean shaven. It made him look younger, more like the angry boy in the memories Ithuriel had showed her. Instead of battle dress, he wore an elegantly cut pin-striped suit and a tie. He was unarmed. He could have been any man walking down the streets of Manhattan. He could have been anyone's father.

He didn't look toward Clary, didn't acknowledge her presence at all. His eyes were on Luke as he walked up the narrow aisle between the benches.

How could he come in here like this without any weapons? Clary wondered, and had her question answered a moment later: Inquisitor Aldertree made a noise like a wounded bear; tore himself away from Malachi, who was trying to hold him back; staggered down the dais steps; and hurled himself at Valentine.

He passed through Valentine's body like a knife tearing through paper. Valentine turned to watch Aldertree with an expression of bland interest as the Inquisitor staggered, collided with a pillar, and sprawled awkwardly to the ground. The Consul, following, bent to help him to his feet—there was a look of barely concealed disgust on his face as he did it, and Clary wondered if the disgust was directed at Valentine or at Aldertree for acting such a fool.

Another faint murmur carried around the room. The Inquisitor squeaked and struggled like a rat in a trap, Malachi holding him firmly by the arms as Valentine proceeded into the room without another glance at either of them. The Shadowhunters who had been clustered around the benches drew back, like the waves of the Red Sea parting for Moses, leaving a clear path down the center of the room. Clary shivered as he drew closer to where she stood with Luke and Simon. *He's only a Projection,* she told herself. *Not really here. He can't hurt you.*

Beside her Simon shuddered. Clary took his hand just as Valentine paused at the steps of the dais and turned to look directly at her. His eyes raked her once, casually, as if taking her measure; passed over Simon entirely; and came to rest on Luke.

"Lucian," he said.

Luke returned his gaze, steady and level, saying nothing. It was the first time they had been together in the same room since Renwick's, Clary thought, and then Luke had been half-dead from fighting and covered in blood. It was easier now to mark both the differences and the similarities between the two men—Luke in his ragged flannel and jeans, and Valentine in his beautiful and expensive-looking suit; Luke with a day's worth of stubble and gray in his hair, and Valentine looking much as he had when he was twenty-five—only colder, somehow, and harder, as if the passing years were in the process of turning him slowly to stone.

"I hear the Clave has brought you onto the Council now," Valentine said. "It would only be fitting for a Clave diluted by corruption and pandering to find itself infiltrated by half-breed degenerates." His voice was placid, even cheerful—so much so that it was hard to feel the poison in his words, or to really believe that he meant them. His gaze moved back to Clary. "Clarissa," he said, "here with the vampire, I see. When things have settled a bit, we really must discuss your choice of pets."

A low growling noise came from Simon's throat. Clary gripped his hand, hard—hard enough that there would have been a time he'd have jerked away in pain. Now he didn't seem to feel it. "Don't," she whispered. "Just don't."

Valentine had already turned his attention away from them. He climbed the dais steps and turned to gaze down at the crowd. "So many familiar faces," he observed. "Patrick. Malachi. Amatis."

Amatis stood rigid, her eyes bright with hatred.

The Inquisitor was still struggling in Malachi's grasp. Valentine's gaze flicked over him, half-amused. "Even you, Aldertree. I hear you were indirectly responsible for the death of my old friend Hodge Starkweather. A pity, that."

Luke found his voice. "You admit it, then," he said. "You brought the wards down. You sent the demons."

"I sent them," said Valentine. "I can send more. Surely the Clave—even the Clave, stupid as they are—must have expected this? *You* expected it, didn't you, Lucian?"

Luke's eyes were gravely blue. "I did. But I know you, Valentine. So have you come to bargain, or to gloat?"

"Neither." Valentine regarded the silent crowd. "I have no need to bargain," he said, and though his tone was calm, his voice carried as if amplified. "And no desire to gloat. I don't *enjoy* causing the deaths of Shadowhunters; there are precious few of us already, in a world that needs us desperately. But that's how the Clave likes it, isn't it? It's just another one of their nonsensical rules, the rules they use to grind ordinary Shadowhunters into the dust. I did what I did because I had to. I did what I did because it was the only way to make the Clave listen. Shadowhunters didn't die because of me; they died because the Clave ignored me." He met Aldertree's eyes across the crowd; the Inquisitor's face was white and twitching. "So many of you here were once in my Circle," said Valentine slowly. "I speak to you now, and to those who knew of the Circle but stood outside it. Do you remember what I predicted fifteen years ago? That unless we acted against the Accords, the city of Alicante, our own precious capital, would be overrun by slobbering, slavering crowds of half-breeds, the degenerate races trampling underfoot everything we hold dear? And just as I predicted, all that has come to pass. The Gard burned to the ground, the Portal destroyed, our streets awash with monsters. Half-human scum presuming to lead us. So, my friends, my enemies, my brothers under the Angel, I ask you—do you believe me now?" His voice rose to a shout: "DO YOU BELIEVE ME NOW?"

His gaze swept the room as if he expected an answer. There was none—only a sea of staring faces.

"Valentine." Luke's voice, though soft, broke the silence. "Can't you see what you've done? The Accords you dreaded so much didn't make Downworlders equal to Nephilim. They didn't assure half humans a spot on the Council. All the old hatreds were still in place. You should have trusted to those, but you didn't—you couldn't—and now you've given us the one thing that could possibly have united us all." His eyes sought Valentine's. "A common enemy."

A flush passed over Valentine's pale face. "I am not an enemy. Not of Nephilim. *You* are that. You're the one trying to entice them into a hopeless fight. You think those demons you saw are all I have? They were a fraction of what I can summon."

"There are more of us as well," said Luke. "More Nephilim, and more Downworlders."

"Downworlders," Valentine sneered. "They will run at the first sign of true danger. Nephilim are born to be warriors, to protect this world, but the world hates your kind. There is a reason clean silver burns you, and daylight scorches the Night Children."

"It doesn't scorch me," Simon said in a hard, clear voice, despite the grip of Clary's hand. "Here I am, standing in sunlight—"

But Valentine just laughed. "I've seen you choke on the name of God, vampire," he said. "As for why you can stand in the sunlight—" He broke off and grinned. "You're an anomaly, perhaps. A freak. But still a monster."

A monster. Clary thought of Valentine on the ship, of what he had said there: *Your mother told me that I had turned her first child into a monster. She left before I could do the same to her second.*

Jace. The thought of his name was a sharp pain. *After what Valentine did, he stands here talking about monsters—*

"The only monster here," she said, despite herself and despite her resolution to keep silent, "is you. I saw Ithuriel," she went on when he turned to look at her in surprise. "I know everything—"

"I doubt that," Valentine said. "If you did, you'd keep your mouth shut. For your brother's sake, if not your own."

Don't you even talk about Jace to me! Clary wanted to shout, but another voice came to cut hers off, a cool, unexpected female voice, fearless and bitter.

"And what about *my* brother?" Amatis moved to stand at the foot of the dais, looking up at Valentine. Luke started in surprise and shook his head at her, but she ignored him.

Valentine frowned. "What about Lucian?" Amatis's question, Clary sensed, had unsettled him, or maybe it was just that Amatis was there, asking, confronting him. He had written her off years ago as weak, unlikely to challenge him. Valentine never liked it when people surprised him.

"You told me he wasn't my brother anymore," said Amatis. "You took Stephen away from me. You destroyed my family. You say you aren't an enemy of Nephilim, but you set each of us against each other, family against family, wrecking lives without compunction. You say you hate the Clave, but you're the one who made them what they are now—petty and paranoid. We used to trust one another, we Nephilim. *You* changed that. I will never forgive you for it." Her voice shook. "Or for making me treat Lucian as if he were no longer my brother. I won't forgive you for that, either. Nor will I forgive myself for listening to you."

"Amatis—" Luke took a step forward, but his sister put up a hand to stop him. Her eyes were shining with tears, but her back was straight, her voice firm and unwavering.

"There was a time we were *all* willing to listen to you, Valentine," she said. "And we all have that on our conscience. But no more. *No more.* That time is over. Is there anyone here who disagrees with me?"

Clary jerked her head up and looked out at the gathered Shadowhunters: They looked to her like a rough sketch of a crowd, with white blurs for faces. She saw Patrick Penhallow, his jaw set, and the Inquisitor, who was shaking like a frail tree in a high wind. And Malachi, whose dark, polished face was strangely unreadable.

No one said a word.

If Clary had expected Valentine to be angry at this lack of response from the Nephilim he had hoped to lead, she was disappointed. Other than a twitch in the muscle of his jaw, he was expressionless. As if he had expected this response. As if he had planned for it.

"Very well," he said. "If you will not listen to reason, you will have to listen to force. I have already showed you I can take down the wards around your city. I see that you've put them back up, but that's of no consequence; I can easily do it again. You will either accede to my requirements or face every demon the Mortal Sword can summon. I will tell them not to spare a single one of you, not a man, woman, or child. It's your choice."

A murmur swept around the room; Luke was staring. "You would deliberately destroy *your own kind*, Valentine?"

"Sometimes diseased plants must be culled to preserve the whole garden," said Valentine. "And if *all* are diseased . . ." He turned to face the horrified crowd. "It is your choice," he went on. "I have the Mortal Cup. If I must, I will start over with a new world of Shadowhunters, created and taught by me. But I can give you this one chance. If the Clave will sign over all the powers of the Council to me and accept my unequivocal sovereignty and rule, I will stay my hand. All Shadowhunters will swear an oath of obedience and accept a permanent loyalty rune that binds them to me. These are my terms."

There was silence. Amatis had her hand over her mouth; the rest of the room swung before Clary's eyes in a whirling blur. *They can't give in to him,* she thought. *They can't.* But what choice did they have? What choice did any of them ever have? *They are trapped by Valentine,* she thought dully, *as surely as Jace and I are trapped by what he made us. We are all chained to him by our own blood.*

It was only a moment, though it felt like an hour to Clary, before a thin voice cut through the silence—the high, spidery voice of the Inquisitor. "Sovereignty and rule?" he shrieked. "*Your* rule?"

"Aldertree—" The Consul moved to restrain him, but the Inquisitor was too quick. He wriggled free and darted toward the dais. He was yelping something, the same words over and over, as if he'd lost his mind entirely, his eyes rolled back practically to the whites. He thrust Amatis aside, staggering up the steps of the dais to face Valentine. "I am the Inquisitor, do you understand, the *Inquisitor*!" he shouted. "I am part of the Clave! The *Council*! I make the rules, not you! I rule, not you! I won't let you do this, you upstart, demon-loving slime—"

With a look very close to boredom, Valentine reached out a hand, almost as if he meant to touch the Inquisitor on the shoulder. But Valentine couldn't touch anything—he was just a Projection—and then Clary gasped as Valentine's hand passed *through* the Inquisitor's skin, bones and flesh, vanishing into his rib cage. There was a second—only a second—during which the whole Hall seemed to gape at Valentine's left arm, buried somehow, impossibly, wrist-deep in Aldertree's chest. Then Valentine jerked his wrist hard and suddenly to the left—a twisting motion, as if he were turning a stubbornly rusty doorknob.

The Inquisitor gave a single cry and dropped like a stone.

Valentine drew his hand back. It was slicked with blood, a scarlet glove reaching halfway to his elbow, staining the expensive wool of his suit. Lowering his bloody hand, he gazed out across the horrified crowd, his eyes coming to rest at last on Luke. He spoke slowly. "I will give you until tomorrow at midnight to consider my terms. At that time I will bring my army, in all its force, to Brocelind Plain. If I have not yet received a message of surrender from the Clave, I will march with my army here to Alicante, and this time we will leave nothing living. You have that long to consider my terms. Use the time wisely."

And with that, he vanished.

14

In the Dark Forest

"Well, how about that," said Jace, still without looking at Clary—he hadn't really looked at her since she and Simon had arrived on the front step of the house the Lightwoods were now inhabiting. Instead he was leaning against one of the high windows in the living room, staring out toward the rapidly darkening sky. "A guy attends the funeral of his nine-year-old brother and misses all the fun."

"Jace," Alec said, in a tired sort of voice. "Don't."

Alec was slumped in one of the worn, overstuffed chairs that were the only things to sit on in the room. The house had the odd, alien feel of houses belonging to strangers: It was decorated in floral-printed fabrics, frilly and pastel, and everything in it was slightly worn or tattered. There was a glass bowl filled with chocolates on the small end table near Alec; Clary, starving, had eaten a few and found them crumbly and dry. She wondered what kind of people had lived here. The kind who ran away when things got tough, she thought sourly; they deserved to have their house taken over.

"Don't *what?*" Jace asked; it was dark enough outside now that Clary could see his face reflected in the window glass. His eyes looked black. He was wearing Shadowhunter mourning clothes—they didn't wear black to funerals, since black was the color of gear and fighting. The color of death was white, and the white jacket Jace wore had scarlet runes woven into the material around the collar and wrists. Unlike battle runes, which were all about aggression and protection, these spoke a gentler language of healing and grief. There were bands of hammered metal around his wrists, too, with similar runes on them. Alec was dressed the same way, all in white with the same red-gold runes traced over the material. It made his hair look very black.

Jace, Clary thought, on the other hand, all in white, looked like an angel. Albeit one of the avenging kind.

"You're not mad at Clary. Or Simon," Alec said. "At least," he added, with a faint, worried frown, "I don't *think* you're mad at Simon."

Clary half-expected Jace to snap an angry retort, but all he said was, "Clary knows I'm not angry at her."

Simon, leaning his elbows on the back of the sofa, rolled his eyes but said only, "What I don't get is how Valentine managed to kill the Inquisitor. I thought Projections couldn't actually affect anything."

"They shouldn't be able to," said Alec. "They're just illusions. So much colored air, so to speak."

"Well, not in this case. He reached into the Inquisitor and he *twisted* . . ." Clary shuddered. "There was a lot of blood."

"Like a special bonus for you," Jace said to Simon.

Simon ignored this. "Has there ever been an Inquisitor who didn't die a horrible death?" he wondered aloud. "It's like being the drummer in Spinal Tap."

Alec rubbed a hand across his face. "I can't believe my parents don't know about this yet," he said. "I can't say I'm looking forward to telling them."

"Where are your parents?" asked Clary. "I thought they were upstairs."

Alec shook his head. "They're still at the necropolis. At Max's grave. They sent us back. They wanted to be there alone for a while."

"What about Isabelle?" Simon asked. "Where is she?"

The humor, such as it was, left Jace's expression. "She won't come out of her room," he said. "She thinks what happened to Max was her fault. She wouldn't even come to the funeral."

"Have you tried talking to her?"

"No," Jace said, "we've been punching her repeatedly in the face instead. Why, do you think that won't work?"

"Just thought I'd ask." Simon's tone was mild.

"We'll tell her this stuff about Sebastian not actually being Sebastian," said Alec. "It might make her feel better. She thinks she ought to have been able to tell that there was something off about Sebastian, but if he was a spy . . ." Alec shrugged. "*Nobody* noticed anything off about him. Not even the Penhallows."

"*I* thought he was a knob," Jace pointed out.

"Yes, but that's just because—" Alec sank deeper into his

chair. He looked exhausted, his skin a pale gray color against the stark white of his clothes. "It hardly matters. Once she finds out what Valentine's threatening, nothing's going to cheer her up."

"But would he really do it?" Clary asked. "Send a demon army against Nephilim—I mean, he's still a *Shadowhunter*, isn't he? He couldn't destroy all his own people."

"He didn't care enough about his children not to destroy them," Jace said, meeting her eyes across the room. Their gazes held. "What makes you think he'd care about his people?"

Alec looked from one of them to the other, and Clary could tell from his expression that Jace hadn't told him about Ithuriel yet. He looked baffled, and very sad. "Jace . . ."

"The Clave tried to use tracking runes on the things Sebastian had left in his room, to see if we could locate him that way. They weren't able to get much of a reading on any of it. Just . . . flat."

"What does that mean?"

"They were Sebastian Verlac's things. The fake Sebastian probably took them whenever he intercepted him. And the Clave isn't getting anything from them because the real Sebastian—"

"Is probably dead," finished Alec. "And the Sebastian we know is too smart to leave anything behind that could be used to track him. I mean, you can't track somebody from just anything. It has to be an object that's in some way very connected to that person. A family heirloom, or a stele, or a brush with some hair in it, something like that."

"Which is too bad," said Jace, "because if we could follow him, he'd probably lead us straight to Valentine. I'm sure he's scuttled right back to his master with a full report. Probably told him all about Hodge's crackpot mirror-lake theory."

"It might not have been crackpot," Alec said. "They've stationed guards at the paths that go to the lake, and set up wards that will warn them if anyone Portals there."

"Fantastic. I'm sure we all feel very safe now." Jace leaned back against the wall.

"What I don't get," Simon said, "is why Sebastian stayed around. After what he did to Izzy and Max, he was going to get caught, there was no more pretending. I mean, even if he thought he'd killed Izzy instead of just knocking her out, how was he going to explain that they were both dead and he was still fine? No, he was busted. So why hang around through the fighting? Why come up to the Gard to get *me*? I'm pretty sure he didn't actually care one way or the other whether I lived or died."

"Now you're being too hard on him," Jace said. "I'm sure he'd rather you'd died."

"Actually," Clary said, "I think he stayed because of me."

Jace's gaze flicked up to hers with a flash of gold. "Because of you? Hoping for another hot date, was he?"

Clary felt herself flush. "No. And our date wasn't hot. In fact, it wasn't even a date. Anyway, that's not the point. When he came into the Hall, he kept trying to get me to go outside with him so we could talk. He wanted something from me. I just don't know what."

"Or maybe he just wanted you," Jace said. Seeing Clary's expression, he added, "Not that way. I mean maybe he wanted to bring you to Valentine."

"Valentine doesn't care about me," Clary said. "He's only ever cared about you."

Something flickered in the depths of Jace's eyes. "Is that

what you call it?" His expression was frighteningly bleak. "After what happened on the boat, he's interested in you. Which means you need to be careful. Very careful. In fact, it wouldn't hurt if you just spent the next few days inside. You can lock yourself in your room like Isabelle."

"I'm not going to do that."

"Of course you're not," said Jace, "because you live to torture me, don't you?"

"Not everything, Jace, is *about you*," Clary said furiously.

"Possibly," Jace said, "but you have to admit that the majority of things are."

Clary resisted the urge to scream.

Simon cleared his throat. "Speaking of Isabelle—which we only sort of were, but I thought I ought to mention this before the arguing really got under way—I think maybe I should go talk to her."

"You?" Alec said, and then, looking faintly embarrassed by his own discomfiture, added quickly, "It's just—she won't even come out of her room for her own family. Why would she come out for you?"

"Maybe because I'm *not* family," Simon said. He was standing with his hands in his pockets, his shoulders back. Earlier, when Clary had been sitting close to him, she had seen that there was still a thin white line circling his neck, where Valentine had cut his throat, and scars on his wrists where those had been cut too. His encounters with the Shadowhunters' world had changed him, and not just the surface of him, or even his blood; the change went deeper than that. He stood straight, with his head up, and took whatever Jace and Alec threw at him and didn't seem to care. The Simon who would have been frightened of them, or made uneasy by them, was gone.

She felt a sudden pain in her heart, and realized with a jolt what it was. She was *missing* him—missing Simon. Simon as he had been.

"I think I'll have a try at getting Isabelle to talk to me," said Simon. "It can't hurt."

"But it's almost dark," Clary said. "We told Luke and Amatis we'd be back before the sun went down."

"I'll walk you back," Jace said. "As for Simon, he can manage his own way back in the dark—can't you, Simon?"

"Of course he can," Alec said indignantly, as if eager to make up for his earlier slighting of Simon. "He's a *vampire*—and," he added, "I just now realized you were probably joking. Never mind me."

Simon smiled. Clary opened her mouth to protest again—and closed it. Partly because she was, she knew, being unreasonable. And partly because there was a look on Jace's face as he gazed past her, at Simon, a look that startled her into silence: It was amusement, Clary thought, mixed with gratitude and maybe even—most surprising of all—a little bit of respect.

It was a short walk between the Lightwoods' new house and Amatis's; Clary wished it were longer. She couldn't shake the feeling that every moment she spent with Jace was somehow precious and limited, that they were closing in on some half-invisible deadline that would separate them forever.

She looked sideways at him. He was staring straight ahead, almost as if she weren't there. The line of his profile was sharp and clear-edged in the witchlight that illuminated the streets. His hair curled against his cheek, not quite hiding the white scar on one temple where a Mark had been. She could see a line of metal glittering at his throat, where the Morgenstern ring dangled on its chain. His left hand was bare; his knuckles looked raw. So he really was healing like a mundane, as Alec had asked him to.

She shivered. Jace glanced at her. "Are you cold?"

"I was just thinking," she said. "I'm surprised that Valentine went after the Inquisitor instead of Luke. The Inquisitor's a Shadowhunter, and Luke—Luke's a Downworlder. Plus, Valentine hates him."

"But in a way, he respects him, even if he is a Downworlder," Jace said, and Clary thought of the look Jace had given Simon earlier, and then tried not to think of it. She hated thinking of Jace and Valentine as being in any way alike, even in so trivial a thing as a glance. "Luke is trying to get the Clave to change, to think in a new way. That's exactly what Valentine did, even if his goals were—well, not the same. Luke's an iconoclast. He wants change. To Valentine, the Inquisitor represents the old, hidebound Clave he hates so much."

"And they were friends once," Clary said. "Luke and Valentine."

"'The Marks of that which once hath been,'" Jace said, and Clary could tell he was quoting something, from the half-mocking tone in his voice. "Unfortunately, you never really hate anyone as much as someone you cared about once. I imagine Valentine has something special planned for Luke, down the road, after he takes over."

"But he won't take over," said Clary, and when Jace said

nothing, her voice rose. "He *won't* win—he can't. He doesn't really want war, not against Shadowhunters *and* Downworlders—"

"What makes you think Shadowhunters will fight with Downworlders?" Jace said, and he still wasn't looking at her. They were walking along the canal street, and he was looking out at the water, his jaw set. "Just because Luke says so? Luke's an idealist."

"And why is that a bad thing to be?"

"It's not. I'm just not one," said Jace, and Clary felt a cold pang in her heart at the emptiness in his voice. *Despair, anger, hate. These are demon qualities. He's acting the way he thinks he should act.*

They had reached Amatis's house; Clary stopped at the foot of the steps, turning to face him. "Maybe," she said. "But you're not like *him*, either."

Jace started a little at that, or maybe it was just the firmness in her tone. He turned his head to look at her for what felt like the first time since they'd left the Lightwoods. "Clary—," he began, and broke off, with an intake of breath. "There's blood on your sleeve. Are you hurt?"

He moved toward her, taking her wrist in his hand. Clary glanced down and saw to her surprise that he was right—there was an irregular scarlet stain on the right sleeve of her coat. What was odd was that it was still bright red. Shouldn't dried blood be a darker color? She frowned. "That's not my blood."

He relaxed slightly, his grip on her wrist loosening. "Is it the Inquisitor's?"

She shook her head. "I actually think it's Sebastian's."

"*Sebastian's* blood?"

"Yes—when he came into the Hall the other night, remember, his face was bleeding. I think Isabelle must have clawed him, but anyway—I touched his face and got his blood on me." She looked more closely at it. "I thought Amatis washed the coat, but I guess she didn't."

She expected him to let go of her then, but instead he held her wrist for a long moment, examining the blood, before returning her arm to her, apparently satisfied. "Thanks."

She stared at him for a moment before shaking her head. "You're not going to tell me what that was about, are you?"

"Not a chance."

She threw her arms up in exasperation. "I'm going inside. I'll see you later."

She turned and headed up the steps to Amatis's front door. There was no way she could have known that the moment she turned her back, the smile vanished from Jace's face, or that he stood for a long time in the darkness once the door closed behind her, looking after her, and twisting a small piece of thread over and over between his fingers.

"Isabelle," Simon said. It had taken him a few tries to find her door, but the scream of "Go away!" that had emanated from behind this one convinced him he'd made the right choice. "Isabelle, let me in."

There was a muffled thump and the door reverberated slightly, as if Isabelle had thrown something at it. Possibly a shoe. "I don't want to talk to you and Clary. I don't want to talk to anyone. Leave me alone, Simon."

"Clary's not here," said Simon. "And I'm not going away until you talk to me."

"Alec!" Isabelle yelled. "Jace! Make him go away!"

Simon waited. There was no sound from downstairs. Either Alec had left or he was lying low. "They're not here, Isabelle. It's just me."

There was a silence. Finally Isabelle spoke again. This time her voice came from much nearer, as if she were standing just on the other side of the door. "You're alone?"

"I'm alone," Simon said.

The door cracked open. Isabelle was standing there in a black slip, her hair lying long and tangled over her shoulders. Simon had never seen her like this: barefoot, with her hair unbrushed, and no makeup on. "You can come in."

He stepped past her into the room. In the light from the door he could see that it looked, as his mother would have said, like a tornado had hit it. Clothes were scattered across the floor in piles, a duffel bag open on the floor as if it had exploded. Isabelle's bright silver-gold whip hung from one bedpost, a lacy white bra from another. Simon averted his eyes. The curtains were drawn, the lamps extinguished.

Isabelle flopped down on the edge of the bed and looked at him with bitter amusement. "A blushing vampire. Who would have guessed." She raised her chin. "So, I let you in. What do you want?"

Despite her angry glare, Simon thought she looked younger than usual, her eyes huge and black in her pinched white face. He could see the white scars that traced her light skin, all over her bare arms, her back and collarbones, even her legs. *If Clary remains a Shadowhunter,* he thought, *one day she'll look like this, scarred all over.* The thought didn't upset him as once it might have done. There was something about the way Isabelle wore her scars, as if she were proud of them.

She had something in her hands, something she was turning over and over between her fingers. It was a small something that glinted dully in the half-light. He thought for a moment it might be a piece of jewelry.

"What happened to Max," Simon said. "It wasn't your fault."

She didn't look at him. She was staring down at the object in her hands. "Do you know what this is?" she said, and held it up. It seemed to be a small toy soldier, carved out of wood. A toy Shadowhunter, Simon realized, complete with painted-on black gear. The silver glint he'd noticed was the paint on the little sword it held; it was nearly worn away. "It was Jace's," she said, without waiting for him to answer. "It was the only toy he had when he came from Idris. I don't know, maybe it was part of a bigger set once. I think he made it himself, but he never said much about it. He used to take it everywhere with him when he was little, always in a pocket or whatever. Then one day I noticed Max carrying it around. Jace must have been around thirteen then. He just gave it to Max, I guess, when he got too old for it. Anyway, it was in Max's hand when they found him. It was like he grabbed it to hold on to when Sebastian—when he—" She broke off. The effort she was making not to cry was visible; her mouth was set in a grimace, as if it were twisting itself out of shape. "*I* should have been there protecting him. I should have been there for him to hold on to, not some stupid little wooden toy." She flung it down onto the bed, her eyes shining.

"You were unconscious," Simon protested. "You nearly died, Izzy. There was nothing you could have done."

Isabelle shook her head, her tangled hair bouncing on her

shoulders. She looked fierce and wild. "What do you know about it?" she demanded. "Did you know that Max came to us the night he died and told us he'd seen someone climbing the demon towers, and I told him he was dreaming and sent him away? And he was right. I bet it was that bastard Sebastian, climbing the tower so he could take the wards down. And Sebastian killed him so he couldn't tell anyone what he'd seen. If I'd just listened—just taken one second to listen—it wouldn't have happened."

"There's no way you could have known," Simon said. "And about Sebastian—he wasn't really the Penhallows' cousin. He had everyone fooled."

Isabelle didn't look surprised. "I know," she said. "I heard you talking to Alec and Jace. I was listening from the top of the stairs."

"You were eavesdropping?"

She shrugged. "Up to the part where you said you were going to come and talk to me. Then I came back here. I didn't feel like seeing you." She looked at him sideways. "I'll give you this much, though: You're persistent."

"Look, Isabelle." Simon took a step forward. He was oddly, suddenly conscious of the fact that she wasn't very dressed, so he held back from putting a hand on her shoulder or doing anything else overtly soothing. "When my father died, I knew it wasn't my fault, but I still kept thinking over and over of all the things I should have done, should have said, before he died."

"Yeah, well, this *is* my fault," Isabelle said. "And what I should have done is listened. And what I still can do is track down the bastard who did this and kill him."

"I'm not sure that'll help—"

"How do you know?" Isabelle demanded. "Did you find the person responsible for your father's death and kill him?"

"My father had a heart attack," Simon said. "So, no."

"Then you don't know what you're talking about, do you?" Isabelle raised her chin and looked at him squarely. "Come here."

"What?"

She beckoned imperiously with her index finger. "Come *here*, Simon."

Reluctantly he came toward her. He was barely a foot away when she seized him by the front of his shirt, yanking him toward her. Their faces were inches apart; he could see how the skin below her eyes shone with the marks of recent tears. "You know what I really need right now?" she said, enunciating each word clearly.

"Um," Simon said. "No?"

"To be distracted," she said, and with a half turn yanked him bodily onto the bed beside her.

He landed on his back amid a tangled pile of clothes. "Isabelle," Simon protested weakly, "do you really think this is going to make you feel any better?"

"Trust me," Isabelle said, placing a hand on his chest, just over his unbeating heart. "I feel better already."

Clary lay awake in bed, staring up at a single patch of moonlight as it made its way across the ceiling. Her nerves were still too jangled from the events of the day for her to sleep, and it didn't help that Simon hadn't come back before dinner—or after it. Eventually she'd voiced her concern to Luke, who'd thrown on a coat and headed over to the Lightwoods'. He'd returned looking amused. "Simon's fine, Clary," he said. "Go to bed." And then he'd left again, with Amatis, off to another one of their interminable meetings at the Accords Hall. She wondered if anyone had cleaned up the Inquisitor's blood yet.

With nothing else to do, she'd gone to bed, but sleep had remained stubbornly out of reach. Clary kept seeing Valentine in her head, reaching into the Inquisitor and ripping his heart out. The way he had turned to her and said, *You'd keep your mouth shut. For your brother's sake, if not your own.* Above all, the secrets she had learned from Ithuriel lay like a weight on her chest. Under all these anxieties was the fear, constant as a heartbeat, that her mother would die. Where was Magnus?

There was a rustling sound by the curtains, and a sudden wash of moonlight poured into the room. Clary sat bolt upright, scrabbling for the seraph blade she kept on her bedside table.

"It's all right." A hand came down on hers—a slender, scarred, familiar hand. "It's me."

Clary drew her breath in sharply, and he took his hand back. "Jace," she said. "What are you doing here? What's wrong?"

For a moment he didn't answer, and she twisted to look at him, pulling the bedclothes up around her. She felt herself flush, acutely conscious of the fact that she was wearing only pajama bottoms and a flimsy camisole—and then she saw his expression, and her embarrassment faded.

"Jace?" she whispered. He was standing by the head of her bed, still wearing his white mourning clothes, and there was nothing light or sarcastic or distant in the way he was looking down at her. He was very pale, and his eyes looked haunted and nearly black with strain. "Are you all right?"

"I don't know," he said in the dazed manner of someone just waking up from a dream. "I wasn't going to come here. I've been wandering around all night—I couldn't sleep—and I kept finding myself walking here. To you."

She sat up straighter, letting the bedclothes fall down around her hips. "Why can't you sleep? Did something happen?" she asked, and immediately felt stupid. What *hadn't* happened?

Jace, however, barely seemed to hear the question. "I had to see you," he said, mostly to himself. "I know I shouldn't. But I *had* to."

"Well, sit down, then," she said, pulling her legs back to make a space for him to sit at the edge of the bed. "Because you're freaking me out. Are you sure nothing's happened?"

"I didn't say nothing happened." He sat down on the bed, facing her. He was close enough that she could have just leaned forward and kissed him—

Her chest tightened. "Is there bad news? Is everything—is everyone—"

"It's not bad," said Jace, "and it's not news. It's the opposite of news. It's something I've always known, and you—you probably know it too. God knows I haven't hid it all that well." His eyes searched her face, slowly, as if he meant to memorize it. "What happened," he said, and hesitated—"is that I realized something."

"Jace," she whispered suddenly, and for no reason she could identify, she was frightened of what he was about to say. "Jace, you don't have to—"

"I was trying to go . . . somewhere," Jace said. "But I kept getting pulled back here. I couldn't stop walking, couldn't stop thinking. About the first time I ever saw you, and how after that I couldn't forget you. I wanted to, but I couldn't stop myself. I forced Hodge to let me be the one who came to find you and bring you back to the Institute. And even back then, in that stupid coffee shop, when I saw you sitting on that couch with Simon, even *then* that felt wrong to me—*I* should have been the one sitting with you. The one who made you laugh like that. I couldn't get rid of that feeling. That it should have been me. And the more I knew you, the more I felt it—it had never been like that for me before. I'd always wanted a girl and then gotten to know her and not wanted her anymore, but with you the feeling just got stronger and stronger until that night when you showed up at Renwick's and I *knew*.

"And then to find out that the reason I felt like that—like you were some part of me I'd lost and never even knew I was missing until I saw you again—that the reason was that you were *my sister*, it felt like some sort of cosmic joke. Like God was spitting on me. I don't even know for what—for thinking that I could actually get to *have* you, that I would deserve something like that, to be that happy. I couldn't imagine what it was I'd done that I was being punished for—"

"If you're being punished," Clary said, "then so am I. Because all those things you felt, I felt them too, but we can't—we *have* to stop feeling this way, because it's our only chance."

Jace's hands were tight at his sides. "Our only chance for what?"

"To be together at all. Because otherwise we can't ever be around each other, not even just in the same room, and I can't stand that. I'd rather have you in my life even as a brother than not at all—"

"And I'm supposed to sit by while you date boys, fall in love with someone else, get married . . . ?" His voice tightened. "And meanwhile, I'll die a little bit more every day, watching."

"No. You won't care by then," she said, wondering even as she said it if she could stand the idea of a Jace who didn't care. She hadn't thought as far ahead as he had, and when she tried to imagine watching him fall in love with someone else, marry someone else, she couldn't even picture it, couldn't picture anything but an empty black tunnel that stretched out ahead of her, forever. "Please. If we don't say anything—if we just pretend—"

"There is no pretending," Jace said with absolute clarity. "I love you, and I will love you until I die, and if there's a life after that, I'll love you then."

She caught her breath. He had said it—the words there was no going back from. She struggled for a reply, but none came.

"And I know you think I just want to be with you to—to show myself what a monster I am," he said. "And maybe I am a monster. I don't know the answer to that. But what I do know is that even if there's demon blood inside me, there is human blood inside me as well. And I couldn't love you like I do if I wasn't at least a little bit human. Because demons *want*. But they don't love. And I—"

He stood up then, with a sort of violent suddenness, and crossed the room to the window. He looked lost, as lost as he had in the Great Hall standing over Max's body.

"Jace?" Clary said, alarmed, and when he didn't answer, she scrambled to her feet and went to him, laying her hand on his arm. He continued staring out the window; their reflections in the glass were nearly transparent—ghostly outlines of a tall boy and a smaller girl, her hand clamped anxiously on his sleeve. "What's wrong?"

"I shouldn't have told you like that," he said, not looking at her. "I'm sorry. That was probably a lot to take in. You looked so . . . shocked." The tension underlying his voice was a live wire.

"I was," she said. "I've spent the past few days wondering if you hated me. And then I saw you tonight and I was pretty sure you did."

"Hated you?" he echoed, looking bewildered. He reached out then and touched her face, lightly, just the tips of his fingers against her skin. "I told you I couldn't sleep. Tomorrow by midnight we'll be either at war or under Valentine's rule. This could be the last night of our lives, certainly the last even barely ordinary one. The last night we go to sleep and get up just as we always have. And all I could think of was that I wanted to spend it with you."

Her heart skipped a beat. "Jace—"

"I don't mean it like that," he said. "I won't touch you, not if you don't want me to. I know it's wrong—God, it's all kinds of wrong—but I just want to lie down with you and wake up with you, just once, just once ever in my life." There was desperation in his voice. "It's just this one night. In the grand scheme of things, how much can one night matter?"

Because think how we'll feel in the morning. Think how much worse it will be pretending that we don't mean anything to each other in front of everyone else after we've spent the night together, even if all we do is sleep. It's like having just a little bit of a drug—it only makes you want more.

But that was why he had told her what he had, she realized.

Because it wasn't true, not for him; there was nothing that could make it worse, just as there was nothing that could make it better. What he felt was as final as a life sentence, and could she really say it was so different for her? And even if she hoped it might be, even if she hoped she might someday be persuaded by time or reason or gradual attrition not to feel this way anymore, it didn't matter. There was nothing she had ever wanted in her life more than she wanted this night with Jace.

"Close the curtains, then, before you come to bed," she said. "I can't sleep with this much light in the room."

The look that washed over his face was pure incredulity. He really hadn't expected her to say yes, Clary realized in surprise, and a moment later he had caught her and hugged her to him, his face buried in her still-messy-from-sleep hair. "Clary . . ."

"Come to bed," she said softly. "It's late." She drew away from him and returned to the bed, crawling up onto it and drawing the covers up to her waist. Somehow, looking at him like this, she could almost imagine that things were different, that it was many years from now and they'd been together so long that they'd done this a hundred times, that every night belonged to them, and not just this one. She propped her chin on her hands and watched him as he reached to jerk the curtains shut and then unzipped his white jacket and hung it over the back of a chair. He was wearing a pale gray T-shirt underneath, and the Marks that twined his bare arms shone darkly as he unbuckled his weapons belt and laid it on the floor. He unlaced his boots and stepped out of them as he came toward the bed, and he stretched out very carefully beside Clary. Lying on his back, he turned his head to look at her. A very little light filtered into the room past the edge of the curtains, just enough for her to see the outline of his face and the bright gleam of his eyes.

"Good night, Clary," he said.

His hands lay flat on either side of him, his arms at his sides. He seemed barely to be breathing; she wasn't sure she was breathing herself. She slid her own hand across the bedsheet, just far enough that their fingers touched—so lightly that she would probably hardly have been aware of it had she been touching anyone but Jace; as it was, the nerve endings in her fingertips prickled softly, as if she were holding them over a low flame. She felt him tense beside her and then relax. He had shut his eyes, and his lashes cast fine shadows against the curve of his cheekbones. His mouth curled into a smile as if he sensed her watching him, and she wondered how he would look in the morning, with his hair messed and sleep circles under his eyes. Despite everything, the thought gave her a jolt of happiness.

She laced her fingers through his. "Good night," she whispered. With their hands clasped like children in a fairy tale, she fell asleep beside him in the dark.

15

Things Fall Apart

Luke had spent most of the night watching the moon's progress across the translucent roof of the Hall of Accords like a silver coin rolling across the clear surface of a glass table. When the moon was close to full, as it was right now, he felt a corresponding sharpening in his vision and sense of smell, even when he was in human form. Now, for instance, he could smell the sweat of doubt in the room, and the underlying sharp tang of fear. He could sense the restless worry of his pack of wolves out in Brocelind Forest as they paced the darkness beneath the trees and waited for news from him.

"Lucian." Amatis's voice in his ear was low but piercing. *"Lucian!"*

Snapped out of his reverie, Luke fought to focus his

exhausted eyes on the scene in front of him. It was a ragged little group, those who had agreed to at least listen to his plan. Fewer than he had hoped for. Many he knew from his old life in Idris—the Penhallows, the Lightwoods, the Ravenscars—and just as many he had just met, like the Monteverdes, who ran the Lisbon Institute and spoke in a mixture of Portuguese and English, or Nasreen Chaudhury, the stern-featured head of the Mumbai Institute. Her dark green sari was patterned in elaborate runes of such a bright silver that Luke instinctively flinched when she passed too close.

"Really, Lucian," said Maryse Lightwood. Her small white face was pinched by exhaustion and grief. Luke hadn't really expected either her or her husband to come, but they had agreed almost as soon as he'd mentioned it to them. He supposed he ought to be grateful they were here at all, even if grief did tend to make Maryse more sharp-tempered than usual. "You're the one who wanted us all here; the least you can do is pay attention."

"He *has* been." Amatis sat with her legs drawn under her like a young girl, but her expression was firm. "It's not Lucian's fault that we've been going around in circles for the past hour."

"And we'll keep going around and around until we figure out a solution," said Patrick Penhallow, an edge to his voice.

"With all due respect, Patrick," said Nasreen, in her clipped accent, "there may be no *solution* to this problem. The best we can hope for is a plan."

"A plan that doesn't involve either mass slavery or—," began Jia, Patrick's wife, and then she broke off, biting her lip. She was a pretty, slender woman who looked very like her daughter, Aline. Luke remembered when Patrick had run off to the Beijing Institute and married her. It had been something of a scandal, as he'd been supposed to marry a girl his parents had already picked out for him in Idris. But Patrick never had liked to do what he was told, a quality for which Luke was now grateful.

"Or allying ourselves with Downworlders?" said Luke. "I'm afraid there's no way around that."

"That's not the problem, and you know it," said Maryse. "It's the whole business about seats on the Council. The Clave will never agree to it. You know that. *Four* whole seats—"

"Not four," Luke said. "One each for the Fair Folk, the Moon's Children, and the children of Lilith."

"The warlocks, the fey, and the lycanthropes," said soft-voiced Senhor Monteverde, his eyebrows arched. "And what of the vampires?"

"They haven't promised me anything," Luke admitted. "And I haven't promised them anything either. They may not be eager to join the Council; they're none too fond of my kind, and none too fond of meetings and rules. But the door is open to them should they change their minds."

"Malachi and his lot will never agree to it, and we may not have enough Council votes without them," muttered Patrick. "Besides, without the vampires, what chance do we have?"

"A very good one," snapped Amatis, who seemed to believe in Luke's plan even more than he did. "There are many Downworlders who *will* fight with us, and they are powerful indeed. The warlocks alone—"

With a shake of her head Senhora Monteverde turned to her husband. "This plan is mad. It will never work. Downworlders cannot be trusted."

"It worked during the Uprising," said Luke.

The Portuguese woman's lips curled back. "Only because Valentine was fighting with fools for an army," she said. "Not demons. And how are we to know his old Circle members will not go back to him the moment he calls them to his side?"

"Be careful what you say, Senhora," rumbled Robert Lightwood. It was the first time he had spoken in more than an hour; he'd spent most of the evening motionless, immobilized by sorrow. There were lines in his face Luke could have sworn hadn't been there three days ago. His torment was plain in his taut shoulders and clenched fists; Luke could hardly blame him. He had never much liked Robert, but there was something about the sight of such a big man made helpless by grief that was painful to witness. "If you think I would join with Valentine after Max's death—he had my boy *murdered*—"

"Robert," Maryse murmured. She put her hand on his arm.

"If we do not join with him," said Senhor Monteverde, "*all* our children may die."

"If you think that, then why are you here?" Amatis rose to her feet. "I thought we had agreed—"

So did I. Luke's head ached. It was always like this with them, he thought, two steps forward and a step back. They were as bad as warring Downworlders themselves, if only they could see it. Maybe they'd all be better off if they solved their problems with combat, the way the pack did—

A flash of movement at the doors of the Hall caught his eye. It was momentary, and if it had not been so close to the full moon, he might not have seen it, or recognized the figure who passed quickly before the doors. He wondered for a moment if he was imagining things. Sometimes, when he was very tired, he thought he saw Jocelyn—in the flicker of a shadow, in the play of light on a wall.

But this wasn't Jocelyn. Luke rose to his feet. "I'm taking five minutes for some air. I'll be back." He felt them watching him as he made his way to the front doors—all of them, even Amatis. Senhor Monteverde whispered something to his wife in Portuguese; Luke caught "*lobo*," the word for "wolf," in the stream of words. *They probably think I'm going outside to run in circles and bark at the moon.*

The air outside was fresh and cold, the sky a slate-steel gray. Dawn reddened the sky in the east and gave a pale pink cast to the white marble steps leading down from the Hall doors. Jace was waiting for him, halfway down the stairs. The white mourning clothes he wore hit Luke like a slap in the face, a reminder of all the death they'd just endured here, and were about to endure again.

Luke paused several steps above Jace. "What are you doing here, Jonathan?"

Jace said nothing, and Luke mentally cursed his forgetfulness—Jace didn't like being called Jonathan and usually responded to the name with a sharp objection. This time, though, he didn't seem to care. The face he raised to Luke was as grimly set as the faces of any of the adults in the Hall. Though Jace was still a year away from being an adult under Clave law, he'd already seen worse things in his short life than most adults could even imagine.

"Were you looking for your parents?"

"You mean the Lightwoods?" Jace shook his head. "No. I don't want to talk to them. I was looking for you."

"Is it about Clary?" Luke descended several steps until he stood just above Jace. "Is she all right?"

"She's fine." The mention of Clary seemed to make Jace tense all over, which in turn sparked Luke's nerves—but Jace would never say Clary was all right if she weren't.

"Then what is it?"

Jace looked past him, toward the doors of the Hall. "How is it going in there? Any progress?"

"Not really," Luke admitted. "As much as they don't want to surrender to Valentine, they like the idea of Downworlders on the Council even less. And without the promise of seats on the Council, my people won't fight."

Jace's eyes sparked. "The Clave is going to *hate* that idea."

"They don't have to love it. They only have to like it better than they like the idea of suicide."

"They'll stall," Jace advised him. "I'd give them a deadline if I were you. The Clave works better with deadlines."

Luke couldn't help but smile. "All the Downworlders I can summon will be approaching the North Gate at twilight. If the Clave agrees to fight with them by then, they'll enter the city. If not, they'll turn around. I couldn't leave it any later than that—it barely gives us enough time to get to Brocelind by midnight as it is."

Jace whistled. "That's theatrical. Hoping the sight of all those Downworlders will inspire the Clave, or scare them?"

"Probably a little of both. Many of the Clave members are associated with Institutes, like you; they're a lot more used to the sight of Downworlders. It's the native Idrisians I'm worried about. The sight of Downworlders at their gates might send them into a panic. On the other hand, it can't hurt for them to be reminded how vulnerable they are."

As if on cue, Jace's gaze flicked up to the ruins of the Gard, a black scar on the hillside over the city. "I'm not sure anyone needs more reminders of that." He glanced back at Luke, his clear eyes very serious. "I want to tell you something, and I want it to be in confidence."

Luke couldn't hide his surprise. "Why tell me? Why not the Lightwoods?"

"Because you're the one who's in charge here, really. You know that."

Luke hesitated. Something about Jace's white and tired face drew sympathy out of his own exhaustion—sympathy and a desire to show this boy, who had been so betrayed and badly used by the adults in his life, that not all adults were like that, that there were some he could rely on. "All right."

"And," Jace said, "because I trust you to know how to explain it to Clary."

"Explain *what* to Clary?"

"Why I had to do it." Jace's eyes were wide in the light of the rising sun; it made him look years younger. "I'm going after Sebastian, Luke. I know how to find him, and I'm going to follow him until he leads me to Valentine."

Luke let his breath out in surprise. "You *know how to find him*? I thought there was nothing left to track him with."

"I found something," said Jace. "A thread soaked in his blood. It's not much, but it's enough. I tried it, and it worked."

"You can't go haring off after Valentine on your own, Jace. I won't let you."

"You can't stop me. Not really. Unless you want to fight me right here on these steps. You won't win, either. You know that as well as I do." There was a strange note in Jace's voice, a mixture of certainty and self-hatred.

"Look, however determined you may be to play the solitary hero—"

"I am not a hero," Jace said. His voice was clear and toneless, as if he were stating the simplest of facts.

"Think of what this will do to the Lightwoods, even if nothing happens to you. Think of Clary—"

"You think I *haven't* thought of Clary? You think I haven't thought of my family? Why do you think I'm doing this?"

"Do you think I don't remember what it's like to be seventeen?" Luke answered. "To think you have the power to save the world—and not just the power but the responsibility—"

"Look at me," said Jace. "Look at me and tell me I'm an ordinary seventeen-year-old."

Luke sighed. "There's nothing ordinary about you."

"Now tell me it's impossible. Tell me what I'm suggesting can't be done." When Luke said nothing, Jace went on, "Look, your plan is fine, as far as that goes. Bring in Downworlders, fight Valentine all the way to the gates of Alicante. It's better than just lying down and letting him walk over you. But he'll expect it. You won't be catching him by surprise. I—I could catch him by surprise. He may not know Sebastian's being followed. It's a chance at least, and we have to take whatever chances we can get."

"That may be true," said Luke. "But this is too much to expect of any one person. Even you."

"But don't you see—it can only *be* me," Jace said, desperation creeping into his voice. "Even if Valentine senses I'm following him, he might let me get close enough—"

"Close enough to do what?"

"To kill him," said Jace. "What else?"

Luke looked at the boy standing below him on the stairs. He wished in some way he could reach through and see Jocelyn in her son, the way he saw her in Clary, but Jace was only, and always, himself—contained, alone, and separate. "You could do that?" Luke said. "You could kill your own father?"

"Yes," Jace said, his voice as distant as an echo. "Now is this where you tell me I can't kill him because he is, after all, my father, and patricide is an unforgivable crime?"

"No. This is where I tell you that you have to be sure you're capable of it," said Luke, and realized, to his own surprise, that some part of him had already accepted that Jace was going to do exactly what he said he was going to do, and that he would let him. "You can't do all this, cut your ties here and hunt Valentine down on your own, just to fail at the final hurdle."

"Oh," said Jace, "I'm capable of it." He looked away from Luke, down the steps toward the square that until yesterday morning had been full of bodies. "My father made me what I am. And I hate him for it. I can kill him. He made sure of that."

Luke shook his head. "Whatever your upbringing, Jace, you've fought it. He didn't corrupt you—"

"No," Jace said. "He didn't have to." He glanced up at the sky, striped with blue and gray; birds had begun their morning songs in the trees lining the square. "I'd better go."

"Is there something you wanted me to tell the Lightwoods?"

"No. No, don't tell them anything. They'll just blame you if they find out you knew what I was going to do and you let me go. I left notes," he added. "They'll figure it out."

"Then why—"

"Did I tell you all this? Because I want you to know. I want you to keep it in mind while you make your battle plans. That I'm out there, looking for Valentine. If I find him, I'll send you a message." He smiled fleetingly. "Think of me as your backup plan."

Luke reached out and clasped the boy's hand. "If your father weren't who he is," he said, "he'd be proud of you."

Jace looked surprised for a moment, and then just as quickly he flushed and drew his hand back. "If you knew—," he began, and bit his lip. "Never mind. Good luck to you, Lucian Graymark. *Ave atque vale.*"

"Let us hope there will be no real farewell," Luke said. The sun was rising fast now, and as Jace lifted his head, frowning at the sudden intensification of the light, there was something in his face that struck Luke—something in that mixture of vulnerability and stubborn pride. "You remind me of someone," he said without thinking. "Someone I knew years ago."

"I know," Jace said with a bitter twist to his mouth. "I remind you of Valentine."

"No," said Luke, in a wondering voice; but as Jace turned away, the resemblance faded, banishing the ghosts of memory. "No—I wasn't thinking of Valentine at all."

The moment Clary awoke, she knew Jace was gone, even before she opened her eyes. Her hand, still outstretched across the bed, was empty; no fingers returned the pressure of her own. She sat up slowly, her chest tight.

He must have drawn the curtains back before he left, because the windows were open and bright bars of sunlight striped the bed. Clary wondered why the light hadn't woken her. From the position of the sun, it had to be afternoon. Her head felt heavy and thick, her eyes bleary. Maybe it was just that she hadn't had nightmares last night, for the first time in so long, and her body was catching up on sleep.

It was only when she stood up that she noticed the folded piece of paper on the nightstand. She picked it up with a smile hovering around her lips—so Jace had left a note—and when something heavy slid from beneath the paper and rattled to the floor at her feet, she was so surprised that she jumped back, thinking it was alive.

It lay at her feet, a coil of bright metal. She knew what it was before she bent and picked it up. The chain and silver ring that Jace had worn around his neck. The family ring. She had rarely seen him without it. A sudden sensation of dread washed over her.

She opened the note and scanned the first lines: *Despite everything, I can't bear the thought of this ring being lost forever, any more than I can bear the thought of leaving you forever. And though I have no choice about the one, at least I can choose about the other.*

The rest of the letter seemed to wash together into a meaningless blur of letters; she had to read it over and over to make any sense of it. When she did finally understand, she stood staring down, watching the paper flutter as her hand shook. She understood now why Jace had told her everything he had, and why he had said one night didn't matter. You could say anything you wanted to someone you thought you were never going to see again.

She had no recollection, later, of having decided what to do next, or of having hunted for something to wear, but somehow she was hurrying down the stairs, dressed in Shadowhunter gear, the letter in one hand and the chain with the ring clasped hastily around her throat.

The living room was empty, the fire in the grate burned down to gray ash, but noise and light emanated from the kitchen: a chatter of voices, and the smell of something cooking. *Pancakes?* Clary thought in surprise. She wouldn't have thought Amatis knew how to make them.

And she was right. Stepping into the kitchen, Clary felt her eyes widen—Isabelle, her glossy dark hair swept up in a knot at the back of her neck, stood at the stove, an apron around her waist and a metal spoon in her hand. Simon was sitting on the table behind her, his feet up on a chair, and Amatis, far from telling him to get off the furniture, was leaning against the counter, looking highly entertained.

Isabelle waved her spoon at Clary. "Good morning," she said. "Would you like breakfast? Although, I guess it's more like lunchtime."

Speechless, Clary looked at Amatis, who shrugged. "They just showed up and wanted to make breakfast," she said, "and I have to admit, I'm not that good a cook."

Clary thought of Isabelle's awful soup back at the Institute and suppressed a shudder. "Where's Luke?"

"In Brocelind, with his pack," said Amatis. "Is everything all right, Clary? You look a little . . ."

"Wild-eyed," Simon finished for her. "*Is* everything all right?"

For a moment Clary couldn't think of a reply. *They just showed up*, Amatis had said. Which meant Simon had spent the *entire* night at Isabelle's. She stared at him. He didn't *look* any different.

"I'm fine," she said. Now was hardly the time to be worrying about Simon's love life. "I need to talk to Isabelle."

"So talk," Isabelle said, poking at a misshapen object in the bottom of the frying pan that was, Clary feared, a pancake. "I'm listening."

"*Alone,*" said Clary.

Isabelle frowned. "Can't it wait? I'm almost done—"

"No," Clary said, and there was something in her tone that made Simon, at least, sit up straight. "It can't."

Simon slid off the table. "Fine. We'll give you two some privacy," he said. He turned to Amatis. "Maybe you could show me those baby pictures of Luke you were talking about."

Amatis shot a worried glance at Clary but followed Simon out of the room. "I suppose I could. . . ."

Isabelle shook her head as the door closed behind them. Something glinted at the back of her neck: a bright, delicately thin knife was thrust through the coil of her hair, holding it in place. Despite the tableau of domesticity, she was still a Shadowhunter. "Look," she said. "If this is about Simon—"

"It's not about Simon. It's about Jace." She thrust the note at Isabelle. "Read this."

With a sigh Isabelle turned off the stove, took the note, and sat down to read it. Clary took an apple out of the basket on the table and sat down as Isabelle, across from her at the table, scanned the note silently. Clary picked at the apple peel in silence—she couldn't imagine actually eating the apple, or, in fact, eating anything at all, ever again.

Isabelle looked up from the note, her eyebrows arched. "This seems kind of—personal. Are you sure I should be reading it?"

Probably not. Clary could barely even remember the words in the letter now; in any other situation, she would never have showed it to Isabelle, but her panic about Jace overrode every other concern. "Just read to the end."

Isabelle turned back to the note. When she was done, she set the paper down on the table. "I thought he might do something like this."

"You see what I mean," Clary said, her words stumbling over themselves, "but he can't have left that long ago, or gotten that far. We have to go after him and—" She broke off, her brain finally processing what Isabelle had said and catching up with her mouth. "What do you mean, you thought he might do something like this?"

"Just what I said." Isabelle pushed a dangling lock of hair behind her ears. "Ever since Sebastian disappeared, everyone's been talking about how to find him. I tore his room at the Penhallows' apart looking for anything we could use to track him—but there was nothing. I might have known that if Jace found anything that would allow him to track Sebastian, he'd be off like a shot." She bit her lip. "I just would have hoped that he'd have brought Alec with him. Alec won't be happy."

"So you think Alec will want to go after him, then?" Clary asked, with renewed hope.

"Clary." Isabelle sounded faintly exasperated. "*How* are we supposed to go after him? How are we supposed to have the slightest idea where he's gone?"

"There must be some way—"

"We can try to track him. Jace is smart, though. He'll have figured out some way to block the tracking."

A cold anger stirred in Clary's chest. "Do you even *want* to find him? Do you even care that he's gone off on what's practically a suicide mission? He can't face down Valentine all by himself."

"Probably not," said Isabelle. "But I trust that Jace has his reasons for—"

"For what? For wanting to die?"

"Clary." Isabelle's eyes blazed up with a sudden light of anger. "Do you think the rest of us are *safe*? We're all waiting to die or be enslaved. Can you really see Jace doing that, just sitting around waiting for something awful to happen? Can you really see—"

"All I see is that Jace is your brother just like Max was," said Clary, "and you cared what happened to *him*."

She regretted it the moment she said it; Isabelle's face went white, as if Clary's words had bleached the color out of the other girl's skin. "Max," Isabelle said with a tightly controlled fury, "was a *little boy*, not a fighter—he was *nine years old*. Jace is a Shadowhunter, a warrior. If we fight Valentine, do you think Alec won't be in the battle? Do you think we're not all of us, at all times, prepared to die if we have to, if the cause is great enough? Valentine is Jace's father; Jace probably has the best chance of all of us of getting close to him to do what he has to do—"

"Valentine will kill Jace if he has to," Clary said. "He won't spare him."

"I know."

"But all that matters is if he goes out in glory? Won't you even miss him?"

"I will miss him *every day*," Isabelle said, "for the rest of my life, which, let's face it, if Jace fails, will probably be about a week long." She shook her head. "You don't get it, Clary. You don't understand what it's like to live always at war, to grow up with battle and sacrifice. I guess it's not your fault. It's just how you were brought up—"

Clary held her hands up. "I *do* get it. I know you don't like me, Isabelle. Because I'm a mundane to you."

"You think *that's* why—" Isabelle broke off, her eyes bright; not just with anger, Clary saw with surprise, but with tears. "God, you don't understand *anything*, do you? You've known Jace what, a month? I've known him for seven years. And all the time I've known him, I've never seen him fall in love, never seen him even *like* anyone. He'd hook up with girls, sure. Girls always fell in love with him, but he never *cared.* I think that's why Alec thought—" Isabelle stopped for a moment, holding herself very still. *She's trying not to cry*, Clary thought in wonder—Isabelle, who seemed like she *never* cried. "It always worried me, and my mom, too—I mean, what kind of teenage boy never even gets a crush on anyone? It was like he was always half-awake where other people were concerned. I thought maybe what had happened with his father had done some sort of permanent damage to him, like maybe he never really could love anyone. If I'd only known what had *really* happened with his father—but then I probably would have thought the same thing, wouldn't I? I mean, who *wouldn't* have been damaged by that?

"And then we met you, and it was like he woke up. You couldn't see it, because you'd never known him any different. But I saw it. Hodge saw it. Alec saw it—why do you think he hated you so much? It was like that from the second we met you. You thought it was amazing that you could see us, and it was, but what was amazing to me was that Jace *could see you, too.* He kept talking about you all the way back to the Institute; he made Hodge send him out to get you; and once he brought you back, he didn't want you to leave again. Wherever you were in the room, he watched you. . . . He was even jealous of Simon. I'm not sure he realized it himself, but he was. I could tell. Jealous of a mundane. And then after what happened to Simon at the party, he was willing to go with you to the Dumort, to break Clave Law, just to save a mundane he didn't even like. He did it for you. Because if anything had happened to Simon, *you* would have been hurt. You were the first person outside our family whose happiness I'd ever seen him take into consideration. Because he *loved* you."

Clary made a noise in the back of her throat. "But that was before—"

"Before he found out you were his sister. I know. And I don't blame you for *that*. You couldn't have known. And I guess you couldn't have helped that you just went right on ahead and dated Simon afterward like you didn't even care. I thought once Jace knew you were his sister, he'd give up and get over it, but he didn't, and he couldn't. I don't know what Valentine did to him when he was a child. I don't know if that's why he is the way he is, or if it's just the way he's made, but he won't get over you, Clary. He can't. I started to hate seeing you. I hated for *Jace* to see you. It's like an injury you get from demon poison—you have to leave it alone and let it heal. Every time you rip the bandages off, you just open the wound up again. Every time he sees you, it's like tearing off the bandages."

"I know," Clary whispered. "How do you think it is for me?"

"I don't know. I can't tell what you're feeling. You're not *my* sister. I don't hate you, Clary. I even like you. If it were possible, there isn't anyone I'd rather Jace be with. But I hope you can understand when I say that if by some miracle we all get through this, I hope my family moves itself somewhere so far away that we never see you again."

Tears stung the backs of Clary's eyes. It was strange, she and Isabelle sitting here at this table, crying over Jace for reasons that were both very different and strangely the same. "Why are you telling me all this now?"

"Because you're accusing me of not wanting to protect Jace. But I do want to protect him. Why do you think I was so upset when you suddenly showed up at the Penhallows'? You act as if you're not a part of all this, of our world; you stand on the sidelines, but you *are* a part of it. You're central to it. You can't just pretend to be a bit player forever, Clary, not when you're Valentine's daughter. Not when Jace is doing what he's doing partly because of you."

"Because of *me*?"

"Why do you think he's so willing to risk himself? Why do you think he doesn't care if he dies?" Isabelle's words drove into Clary's ears like sharp needles. *I know why*, she thought. *It's because he thinks he's a demon, thinks he isn't really human, that's why—but I can't tell you that, can't tell you the one thing that would make you understand.* "He's always thought there was something wrong with him, and now, because of you, he thinks he's cursed forever. I heard him say so to Alec. Why *not* risk your life, if you don't want to live anyway? Why *not* risk your life if you'll never be happy no matter what you do?"

"Isabelle, that's enough." The door opened, almost silently, and Simon stood in the doorway. Clary had nearly forgotten how much better his hearing was now. "It's not Clary's fault."

Color rose in Isabelle's face. "Stay out of this, Simon. You don't know what's going on."

Simon stepped into the kitchen, shutting the door behind him. "I heard most of what you've been saying," he told them matter-of-factly. "Even through the wall. You said you don't know what Clary's feeling because you haven't known her long enough. Well, I have. If you think Jace is the only one who's suffered, you're wrong there."

There was a silence; the fierceness in Isabelle's expression was fading slightly. In the distance, Clary thought she heard the sound of someone knocking on the front door: Luke, probably, or Maia bringing more blood for Simon.

"It's not because of me that he left," Clary said, and her heart began to pound. *Can I tell them Jace's secret, now that he's gone? Can I tell them the real reason he left, the real reason he doesn't care if he dies?* Words started to pour out of her, almost against her will. "When Jace and I went to the Wayland manor—when we went to find the Book of the White—"

She broke off as the kitchen door swung open. Amatis stood there, the strangest expression on her face. For a moment Clary thought she was frightened, and her heart skipped a beat. But it wasn't fright on Amatis's face, not really. She looked as she had when Clary and Luke had suddenly showed up at her front door. She looked as if she'd seen a ghost. "Clary," she said slowly. "There's someone here to see you—"

Before she could finish, that someone pushed past her into the kitchen. Amatis stood back, and Clary got her first good look at the intruder—a slender woman, dressed in black. At first all Clary saw was the Shadowhunter gear and she almost didn't recognize her, not until her eyes reached the woman's face and she felt her stomach drop out of her body the way it had when Jace had driven their motorcycle off the edge of the Dumort roof, a ten-story fall.

It was her mother.

Part Three

The Way to Heaven

Oh yes, I know the way to heaven was easy.
—Siegfried Sassoon, "The Imperfect Lover"

16

Articles of Faith

Since the night she'd come home to find her mother gone, Clary had imagined seeing her again, well and healthy, so often that her imaginings had taken on the quality of a photograph that had become faded from being taken out and looked at too many times. Those images rose up before her now, even as she stared in disbelief—images in which her mother, looking healthy and happy, hugged Clary and told her how much she'd missed her but that everything was going to be all right now.

The mother in her imaginings bore very little resemblance to the woman who stood in front of her now. She'd remembered Jocelyn as gentle and artistic, a little bohemian with her paint-splattered overalls, her red hair in pigtails or fastened up with a pencil into a messy bun. This Jocelyn was as bright and sharp as a knife, her hair drawn back sternly, not a wisp out of place; the harsh black of her gear made her face look pale and hard. Nor was her expression the one Clary had imagined: Instead of delight, there was something very like horror in the way she looked at Clary, her green eyes wide. "Clary," she breathed. "Your *clothes*."

Clary looked down at herself. She had on Amatis's black Shadowhunter gear, exactly what her mother had spent her whole life making sure her daughter would never have to wear. Clary swallowed hard and stood up, clutching the edge of the table with her hands. She could see how white her knuckles were, but her hands felt disconnected from her body somehow, as if they belonged to someone else.

Jocelyn stepped toward her, reaching her arms out. "Clary—"

And Clary found herself backing up, so hastily that she hit the counter with the small of her back. Pain flared through her, but she hardly noticed; she was staring at her mother. So was Simon, his mouth slightly open; Amatis, too, looked stricken.

Isabelle stood up, putting herself between Clary and her mother. Her hand slid beneath her apron, and Clary had a feeling that when she drew it out, she'd be holding her slender electrum whip. "What's going on here?" Isabelle demanded. "Who are you?"

Her strong voice wavered slightly as she seemed to catch the expression on Jocelyn's face; Jocelyn was staring at her, her hand over her heart.

"*Maryse.*" Jocelyn's voice was barely a whisper.

Isabelle looked startled. "How do you know my mother's name?"

Color came into Jocelyn's face in a rush. "Of course. You're

Maryse's daughter. It's just—you look so much like her." She lowered her hand slowly. "I'm Jocelyn Fr—Fairchild. I'm Clary's mother."

Isabelle took her hand out from under the apron and glanced at Clary, her eyes full of confusion. "But you were in the hospital . . . in New York . . ."

"I was," Jocelyn said in a firmer voice. "But thanks to my daughter, I'm fine now. And I'd like a moment with her."

"I'm not sure," said Amatis, "that she wants a moment with you." She reached out to put her hand on Jocelyn's shoulder. "This must be a shock for her—"

Jocelyn shook off Amatis and moved toward Clary, reaching her hands out. "Clary—"

At last Clary found her voice. It was a cold, icy voice, so angry it surprised her. "How did you get here, Jocelyn?"

Her mother stopped dead, a look of uncertainty passing over her face. "I Portaled to just outside the city with Magnus Bane. Yesterday he came to me in the hospital—he brought the antidote. He told me everything you did for me. All I've wanted since I woke up was to see you. . . ." Her voice trailed off. "Clary, is something wrong?"

"Why didn't you ever tell me I had a brother?" Clary said. It wasn't what she'd expected to say, wasn't even what she'd planned to have come out of her mouth. But there it was.

Jocelyn dropped her hands. "I thought he was dead. I thought it would only hurt you to know."

"Let me tell you something, Mom," Clary said. "Knowing is better than not knowing. Every time."

"I'm sorry—," Jocelyn began.

"*Sorry?*" It was as if something inside Clary had torn open, and everything was pouring out, all her bitterness, all her pent-up rage. "Do you want to explain why you never told me I was a Shadowhunter? Or that my father was still alive? Oh, and how about that bit where you paid Magnus to steal my memories?"

"I was trying to protect you—"

"Well, you did a *terrible* job!" Clary's voice rose. "What did you expect to happen to me after you disappeared? If it hadn't been for Jace and the others, I'd be dead. You never showed me how to protect myself. You never told me how dangerous things really were. What did you think? That if I couldn't see the bad things, that meant they couldn't see me?" Her eyes burned. "You knew Valentine wasn't dead. You told Luke you thought he was still alive."

"That's why I had to hide you," Jocelyn said. "I couldn't risk letting Valentine know where you were. I couldn't let him touch you—"

"Because he turned your first child into a monster," said Clary, "and you didn't want him to do the same to me."

Shocked speechless, Jocelyn could only stare at her. "Yes," she said finally. "Yes, but that's not all it was, Clary—"

"You stole my memories," Clary said. "You took them away from me. You took away who I was."

"That's not who you are!" Jocelyn cried. "I never wanted it to be who you were—"

"It doesn't matter what you wanted!" Clary shouted. "It is who I am! You took all that away from me and *it didn't belong to you!*"

Jocelyn was ashen. Tears rose up in Clary's eyes—she couldn't bear seeing her mother like this, seeing her so hurt, and yet she was the one doing the hurting—and she knew that if she opened her mouth again, more terrible words would come out, more hateful, angry things. She clapped her hand over her mouth and darted for the hallway, pushing past her mother, past Simon's outstretched hand. All she wanted was to get away. Blindly pushing at the front door, she half-fell out into the street. Behind her, someone called her name, but she didn't turn around. She was already running.

Jace was somewhat surprised to discover that Sebastian had left the Verlac horse in the stables rather than galloping away on it the night he fled. Perhaps he had been afraid that Wayfarer might in some manner be tracked.

It gave Jace a certain satisfaction to saddle the stallion up and ride him out of the city. True, if Sebastian had really wanted Wayfarer, he wouldn't have left him behind—and besides, the horse hadn't really been Sebastian's to begin with. But the fact was, Jace liked horses. He'd been ten the last time he'd ridden one, but the memories, he was pleased to note, came back fast.

It had taken him and Clary six hours to walk from the Wayland manor to Alicante. It took about two hours to get back, riding at a near gallop. By the time they drew up on the ridge overlooking the house and gardens, both he and the horse were covered in a light sheen of sweat.

The misdirection wards that had hidden the manor had been destroyed along with the manor's foundation. What was left of the once elegant building was a heap of smoldering stone. The gardens, singed at the edges now, still brought back memories of the time he'd lived there as a child. There were the rosebushes, denuded of their blossoms now and threaded with green weeds; the stone benches that sat by empty pools; and the hollow in the ground where he'd lain with Clary the night the manor collapsed. He could see the blue glint of the nearby lake through the trees.

A surge of bitterness caught him. He jammed his hand into his pocket and drew out first a stele—he'd "borrowed" it from Alec's room before he'd left, as a replacement for the one Clary had lost, since Alec could always get another—and then the thread he'd taken from the sleeve of Clary's coat. It lay in his palm, stained red-brown at one end. He closed his fist around it, tightly enough to make the bones jut out under his skin, and with his stele retraced the rune on the back of his hand. The faint sting was more familiar than painful. He watched the rune sink into his skin like a stone sinking through water, and closed his eyes.

Instead of the backs of his eyelids he saw a valley. He was standing on a ridge looking down over it, and as if he were gazing at a map that pinpointed his location, he knew exactly where he was. He remembered how the Inquisitor had known exactly where Valentine's boat was in the middle of the East River and realized, *This is how she did it*. Every detail was clear—every blade of grass, the scatter of browning leaves at his feet—but there was no sound. The scene was eerily silent.

The valley was a horseshoe with one end narrower than the other. A bright silver rill of water—a creek or stream—ran through the center of it and disappeared among rocks at the narrow end. Beside the stream sat a gray stone house, white smoke puffing from the square chimney. It was an oddly pastoral scene, tranquil under the blue gaze of the sky. As he watched, a slender figure swung into view. Sebastian. Now that he was no longer bothering to pretend, his arrogance was plain in the way he walked, in the jut of his shoulders, the faint smirk on his face. Sebastian knelt down by the side of the stream and plunged his hands in, splashing water up over his face and hair.

Jace opened his eyes. Beneath him Wayfarer was contentedly cropping grass. Jace shoved the stele and thread back into his pocket, and with a single last glance at the ruins of the house he'd grown up in, he gathered up the reins and dug his heels into the horse's sides.

Clary lay in the grass near the edge of Gard Hill and stared morosely down at Alicante. The view from here was pretty spectacular, she had to admit. She could look out over the rooftops of the city, with their elegant carvings and rune-Marked weather vanes, past the spires of the Hall of Accords, out toward something that gleamed in the far distance like the edge of a silver coin—Lake Lyn? The black ruins of the Gard hulked behind her, and the demon towers shone like crystal. Clary almost thought she could see the wards, shimmering like an invisible net woven around the borders of the city.

She looked down at her hands. She had torn up several fistfuls of grass in the last spasms of her anger, and her fingers were sticky with dirt and blood where she'd ripped a nail half off. Once the fury had passed, a feeling of utter emptiness had replaced it. She hadn't realized how angry she'd been with her mother, not until she'd stepped through the door and Clary had set her panic about Jocelyn's life aside and realized what lay under it. Now that she was calmer, she wondered if a part of her had wanted to punish her mother for what had happened to

Jace. If he hadn't been lied to—if they *both* hadn't been—then perhaps the shock of finding out what Valentine had done to him when he was only a baby wouldn't have driven him to a gesture Clary couldn't help feeling was close to suicide.

"Mind if I join you?"

She jumped in surprise and rolled onto her side to look up. Simon stood over her, his hands in his pockets. Someone—Isabelle, probably—had given him a dark jacket of the tough black stuff Shadowhunters used for their gear. A vampire in gear, Clary thought, wondering if it was a first. "You snuck up on me," she said. "I guess I'm not much of a Shadowhunter, huh."

Simon shrugged. "Well, in your defense, I do move with a silent, pantherlike grace."

Despite herself, Clary smiled. She sat up, brushing dirt off her hands. "Go ahead and join me. This mope-fest is open to all."

Sitting beside her, Simon looked out over the city and whistled. "Nice view."

"It is." Clary looked at him sidelong. "How did you find me?"

"Well, it took me a few hours." He smiled, a little crookedly. "Then I remembered how when we used to fight, back in first grade, you'd go and sulk on my roof and my mom would have to get you down?"

"So?"

"I know you," he said. "When you get upset, you head for high ground."

He held something out to her—her green coat, neatly folded. She took it and shrugged it on—the poor thing was already showing distinct signs of wear. There was even a small hole in the elbow big enough to wiggle a finger through.

"Thanks, Simon." She laced her hands around her knees and stared out at the city. The sun was low in the sky, and the towers had begun to glow a faint reddish pink. "Did my mom send you up here to get me?"

Simon shook his head. "Luke, actually. And he just asked me to tell you that you might want to head back before sunset. Some pretty important stuff is happening."

"What kind of stuff?"

"Luke gave the Clave until sunset to decide whether they'd agree to give the Downworlders seats on the Council. The Downworlders are all coming to the North Gate at twilight. If the Clave agrees, they can come into Alicante. If not . . ."

"They get sent away," Clary finished. "And the Clave gives itself up to Valentine."

"Yeah."

"They'll agree," said Clary. "They *have* to." She hugged her knees. "They'd never pick Valentine. No one would."

"Glad to see your idealism hasn't been damaged," said Simon, and though his voice was light, Clary heard another voice through it. Jace's, saying he wasn't an idealist, and she shivered, despite the coat she was wearing.

"Simon?" she said. "I have a stupid question."

"What is it?"

"Did you sleep with Isabelle?"

Simon made a choking sound. Clary swiveled slowly around to look at him.

"Are you okay?" she asked.

"I think so," he said, recovering his poise with apparent effort. "Are you serious?"

"Well, you *were* gone all night."

Simon was silent for a long moment. Finally he said, "I'm not sure it's your business, but no."

"Well," said Clary, after a judicious pause, "I guess you wouldn't have taken advantage of her when she's so grief-stricken and all."

Simon snorted. "If you ever meet the man who could take advantage of Isabelle, you'll have to let me know. I'd like to shake his hand. Or run away from him very fast, I'm not sure which."

"So you're not dating Isabelle."

"Clary," Simon said, "why are you asking me about Isabelle? Don't you want to talk about your mom? Or about Jace? Izzy told me that he left. I know how you must be feeling."

"No," Clary said. "No, I don't think you do."

"You're not the only person who's ever felt abandoned." There was an edge of impatience to Simon's voice. "I guess I just thought—I mean, I've never seen you so angry. And at your mom. I thought you missed her."

"Of course I missed her!" Clary said, realizing even as she said it how the scene in the kitchen must have looked. Especially to her mother. She pushed the thought away. "It's just that I've been so focused on rescuing her—saving her from Valentine, then figuring out a way to cure her—that I never even stopped to think about how angry I was that she lied to me all these years. That she kept all of this from me, kept the truth from me. Never let me know who I really was."

"But that's not what you said when she walked into the room," said Simon quietly. "You said, 'Why didn't you ever tell me I had a brother?'"

"I know." Clary yanked a blade of grass out of the dirt,

worrying it between her fingers. "I guess I can't help thinking that if I'd known the truth, I wouldn't have met Jace the way I did. I wouldn't have fallen in love with him."

Simon was silent for a moment. "I don't think I've ever heard you say that before."

"That I love him?" She laughed, but it sounded dreary even to her ears. "Seems useless to pretend like I don't, at this point. Maybe it doesn't matter. I probably won't ever see him again, anyway."

"He'll come back."

"Maybe."

"He'll come back," Simon said again. "For you."

"I don't know." Clary shook her head. It was getting colder as the sun dipped to touch the edge of the horizon. She narrowed her eyes, leaning forward, staring. "Simon. Look."

He followed her gaze. Beyond the wards, at the North Gate of the city, hundreds of dark figures were gathering, some huddled together, some standing apart: the Downworlders Luke had called to the city's aid, waiting patiently for word from the Clave to let them in. A shiver sizzled down Clary's spine. She was poised not just on the crest of this hill, looking down over a steep drop to the city below, but at the edge of a crisis, an event that would change the workings of the whole Shadowhunting world.

"They're here," Simon said, half to himself. "I wonder if that means the Clave's decided?"

"I hope so." The grass blade Clary had been worrying at was a mangled green mess; she tossed it aside and yanked up another one. "I don't know what I'll do if they decide to give in to Valentine. Maybe I can create a Portal that'll take us all away to somewhere Valentine will never find us. A deserted island, or something."

"Okay, I have a stupid question myself," Simon said. "You can create new runes, right? Why can't you just create one to destroy every demon in the world? Or kill Valentine?"

"It doesn't work like that," Clary said. "I can only create runes I can visualize. The whole image has to come into my head, like a picture. When I try to visualize 'kill Valentine' or 'rule the world' or something, I don't get any images. Just white noise."

"But where do the images of the runes come from, do you think?"

"I don't know," Clary said. "All the runes the Shadowhunters know come from the Gray Book. That's why they can only be put on Nephilim; that's what they're for. But there are other, older runes. Magnus told me that. Like the Mark of Cain. It was a protection Mark, but not one from the Gray Book. So when I think of these runes, like the Fearless rune, I don't know if it's something I'm inventing, or something I'm *remembering*—runes older than Shadowhunters. Runes as old as angels themselves." She thought of the rune Ithuriel had showed her, the one as simple as a knot. Had it come from her own mind, or the angel's? Or was it just something that had always existed, like the sea or the sky? The thought made her shiver.

"Are you cold?" Simon asked.

"Yes—aren't you?"

"I don't get cold anymore." He put an arm around her, his hand rubbing her back in slow circles. He chuckled ruefully. "I guess this probably doesn't help much, what with me having no body heat and all."

"No," Clary said. "I mean—yes, it does help. Stay like that." She glanced up at him. He was staring down at the North Gate, around which the dark figures of Downworlders still crowded, almost motionless. The red light of the demon towers reflected in his eyes; he looked like someone in a photograph taken with a flash. She could see faint blue veins spidering just under the surface of his skin where it was thinnest: at his temples, at the base of his collarbone. She knew enough about vampires to know that this meant it had been a while since he'd fed. "Are you hungry?"

Now he did glance down at her. "Afraid I'm going to bite you?"

"You know you're welcome to my blood whenever you want it."

A shiver, not from cold, passed over him, and he pulled her more tightly against his side. "I'd never do that," he said. And then, more lightly, "Besides, I've already drunk Jace's blood—I've had enough of feeding off my friends."

Clary thought of the silver scar on the side of Jace's throat. Slowly, her mind still full of the image of Jace, she said, "Do you think that's why . . . ?"

"Why what?"

"Why sunlight doesn't hurt you. I mean, it did hurt you before that, didn't it? Before that night on the boat?"

He nodded reluctantly.

"So what else changed? Or is it just that you drank his blood?"

"You mean because he's Nephilim? Yes, but not just because of that. You and Jace—you're not quite normal, are you? I mean, not normal Shadowhunters. Whatever makes you different, it's what makes me different as well. There's something special about you both. Like the Seelie Queen said. You were experiments." He smiled at her startled look. "I'm not stupid. I can put these things together. You with your rune powers, and Jace, well . . . no one could be that annoying without some kind of supernatural assistance."

"Do you really dislike him that much?"

"I don't dislike Jace," Simon protested. "I mean, I hated him at first, sure. He seemed so arrogant and sure of himself, and you acted like he hung the moon—"

"I did not."

"Let me finish, Clary." There was a breathless undercurrent in Simon's voice, if someone who never breathed could be said to be breathless. He sounded as if he were racing toward something. "I could tell how much you liked him, and I thought he was using you, that you were just some stupid mundane girl he could impress with his Shadowhunter tricks. First I told myself that you'd never fall for it, and then that even if you did, he'd get tired of you eventually and you'd come back to me. I'm not proud of that, but when you're desperate, you'll believe anything, I guess. And then when he turned out to be your brother, it seemed like a last-minute reprieve—and I was glad. I was even glad to see how much he seemed to be suffering, until that night in the Seelie Court when you kissed him. I could see . . ."

"See what?" Clary said, unable to bear the pause.

"The way he looked at you. I got it then. He was never using you. He loved you, and it was killing him."

"Is that why you went to the Dumort?" Clary whispered. It was something she'd always wanted to know but had never been able to bring herself to ask.

"Because of you and Jace? Not in any real way, no. Ever since that night in the hotel, I'd been wanting to go back. I dreamed about it. And I'd wake up out of bed, getting dressed, or already on the street, and I knew I wanted to go back to the hotel. It was always worse at night, and worse the closer I got to the hotel. It didn't even occur to me that it was something supernatural—I thought it was posttraumatic stress or something. That night, I was so exhausted and angry, and we were so close to the hotel, and it was night—I barely even remember what happened. I just remember walking away from the park, and then—nothing."

"But if you hadn't been angry at me—if we hadn't upset you—"

"It's not like you had a choice," Simon said. "And it's not like I didn't know. You can only push the truth down for so long, and then it bubbles back up. The mistake I made was not telling you what was going on with me, not telling you about the dreams. But I don't regret dating you. I'm glad we tried. And I love you for trying, even if it was never going to work."

"I wanted it to work so much," Clary said softly. "I never wanted to hurt you."

"I wouldn't change it," Simon said. "I wouldn't give up loving you. Not for anything. You know what Raphael told me? That I didn't know how to be a good vampire, that vampires accept that they're dead. But as long as I remember what it was like to love you, I'll always feel like I'm alive."

"Simon—"

"Look." He cut her off with a gesture, his dark eyes widening. "Down there."

The sun was a red sliver on the horizon; as she looked, it flickered and vanished, disappearing past the dark rim of the world. The demon towers of Alicante blazed into sudden incandescent life. In their light Clary could see the dark crowd swarming restlessly around the North Gate. "What's going on?" she whispered. "The sun's set; why aren't the gates opening?"

Simon was motionless. "The Clave," he said. "They must have said no to Luke."

"But they can't have!" Clary's voice rose sharply. "That would mean—"

"They're going to give themselves up to Valentine."

"They *can't*!" Clary cried again, but even as she stared, she saw the groups of dark figures surrounding the wards turn and move away from the city, streaming like ants out of a destroyed anthill.

Simon's face was waxy in the fading light. "I guess," he said, "they really hate us that much. They'd really rather choose Valentine."

"It's not hate," Clary said. "It's that they're afraid. Even Valentine was afraid." She said it without thinking, and realized as she said it that it was true. "Afraid and jealous."

Simon flicked a glance toward her in surprise. "Jealous?"

But Clary was back in the dream Ithuriel had showed her, Valentine's voice echoing in her ears. *I dreamed that you would tell me* why. *Why Raziel created us, his race of Shadowhunters, yet did not give us the powers Downworlders have—the speed of the wolves, the immortality of the Fair Folk, the magic of warlocks, even the endurance of vampires. He left us naked before the hosts of hell but for these painted lines on our skin. Why should their powers be greater than ours? Why can't we share in what they have?*

Her lips parted and she stared unseeing down at the city below. She was vaguely aware that Simon was saying her name, but her mind was racing. The angel could have showed her anything, she thought, but he'd chosen to show her these scenes, these memories, for a reason. She thought of Valentine crying, *That we should be* bound *to Downworlders, tied to those creatures!*

And the rune. The one she had dreamed of. The rune as simple as a knot.

Why can't we share in what they have?

"Binding," she said out loud. "It's a binding rune. It joins like and unlike."

"What?" Simon stared up at her in confusion.

She scrambled to her feet, brushing off the dirt. "I have to get down there. Where are they?"

"Where are who? Clary—"

"The *Clave*. Where are they meeting? Where's Luke?"

Simon rose to his feet. "The Accords Hall. Clary—"

But she was already racing toward the winding path that led to the city. Swearing under his breath, Simon followed.

They say all roads lead to the Hall. Sebastian's words pounded over and over in Clary's head and she sprinted down the narrow streets of Alicante. She hoped it was true, because otherwise she was definitely going to get lost. The streets twisted at odd angles, not like the lovely, straight, gridded streets of Manhattan. In Manhattan you always knew where you were. Everything was clearly numbered and laid out. This was a labyrinth.

She darted through a tiny courtyard and down one of the narrow canal paths, knowing that if she followed the water, she'd eventually come out in Angel Square. Somewhat to her surprise, the path took her by Amatis's house, and then she was racing, panting, down a wider, curving, familiar street. It opened out onto the square, the Accords Hall rising up wide and white before her, the angel statue shining at the square's center. Standing beside the statue was Simon, his arms crossed, regarding her darkly.

"You could have waited," he said.

She leaned forward, her hands on her knees, catching her breath. "You . . . can't really say that . . . since you got here before me anyway."

"Vampire speed," Simon said with some satisfaction. "When we get home, I ought to go out for track."

"That would be . . . cheating." With a last deep breath Clary straightened up and pushed her sweaty hair out of her eyes. "Come on. We're going in."

The Hall was full of Shadowhunters, more Shadowhunters than Clary had ever seen in one place before, even on the night of Valentine's attack. Their voices rose in a roar like a crashing avalanche; most of them had gathered into contentious, shouting groups—the dais was deserted, the map of Idris hanging forlornly behind it.

She looked around for Luke. It took her a moment to find him, leaning against a pillar with his eyes half-closed. He looked awful—half-dead, his shoulders slumped. Amatis stood behind him, patting his shoulder worriedly. Clary looked around, but Jocelyn was nowhere to be seen in the crowd.

For just a moment she hesitated. Then she thought of Jace, going after Valentine, doing it alone, knowing that he might well get himself killed. He knew he was a part of this, a part of all of it, and she was too—she always had been, even when she hadn't known it. Adrenaline was still coursing through her in spikes, sharpening her perception, making everything seem clear. Almost too clear. She squeezed Simon's hand. "Wish me luck," she said, and then her feet were carrying her toward the dais steps, almost without her volition, and then she was standing on the dais and turning to face the crowd.

She wasn't sure what she'd expected. Gasps of surprise? A sea of hushed, expectant faces? They barely noticed her—only Luke looked up, as if he sensed her there, and froze with a look of astonishment on his face. And there was someone coming toward her through the crowd—a tall man with bones as prominent as the prow of a sailing ship. Consul Malachi. He was gesturing at her to get down from the dais, shaking his head and shouting something she couldn't hear. More Shadowhunters were turning toward her now as he made his way through the throng.

Clary had what she wanted now, all eyes riveted on her. She heard the whispers running through the crowd: *That's her. Valentine's daughter.*

"You're right," she said, casting her voice as far and as loudly as she could, "I *am* Valentine's daughter. I never even knew he was my father until a few weeks ago. I never even knew he *existed* until a few weeks ago. I know a lot of you are going to believe that's not true, and that's fine. Believe what you want. Just as long as you also believe I know things about Valentine you don't know, things that could help you win this battle against him—*if only you let me tell you what they are.*"

"Ridiculous." Malachi stood at the foot of the dais steps. "This is ridiculous. You're just a little girl—"

"She's Jocelyn Fairchild's daughter." It was Patrick Penhallow. Having pushed his way to the front of the crowd, he held up a hand. "Let the girl say her piece, Malachi."

The crowd was buzzing. "You," Clary said to the Consul. "You and the Inquisitor threw my friend Simon into prison—"

Malachi sneered. "Your friend the vampire?"

"He told me you asked him what happened to Valentine's ship that night on the East River. You thought Valentine must have done something, some kind of black magic. Well, he didn't. If you want to know what destroyed that ship, the answer is me. I did it."

Malachi's disbelieving laugh was echoed by several others in the crowd. Luke was looking at her, shaking his head, but Clary plowed on.

"I did it with a rune," she said. "It was a rune so strong it made the ship come apart in pieces. I can create new runes. Not just the ones in the Gray Book. Runes no one's ever seen before—powerful ones—"

"That's enough," Malachi roared. "This is ridiculous. No one can create new runes. It's a complete impossibility." He turned to the crowd. "Like her father, this girl is nothing but a liar."

"She's not lying." The voice came from the back of the crowd. It was clear, strong, and purposeful. The crowd turned, and Clary saw who had spoken: It was Alec. He stood with Isabelle on one side of him and Magnus on the other. Simon was with them, and so was Maryse Lightwood. They formed a small, determined-looking knot by the front doors. "I've seen her create a rune. She even used it on me. It worked."

"You're lying," the Consul said, but doubt had crept into his eyes. "To protect your friend—"

"Really, Malachi," Maryse said crisply. "Why would my son

lie about something like this, when the truth can so easily be discovered? Give the girl a stele and let her create a rune."

A murmur of assent ran around the Hall. Patrick Penhallow stepped forward and held a stele up to Clary. She took it gratefully and turned back to the crowd.

Her mouth went dry. Her adrenaline was still up, but it wasn't enough to completely drown her stage fright. What was she supposed to do? What kind of rune could she create that would convince this crowd she was telling the truth? What would *show* them the truth?

She looked out then, through the crowd, and saw Simon with the Lightwoods, looking at her across the empty space that separated them. It was the same way that Jace had looked at her at the manor. It was the one thread that bound these two boys that she loved so much, she thought, their one commonality: They both believed in her even when she didn't believe in herself.

Looking at Simon, and thinking of Jace, she brought the stele down and drew its stinging point against the inside of her wrist, where her pulse beat. She didn't look down as she was doing it but drew blindly, trusting herself and the stele to create the rune she needed. She drew it faintly, lightly—she would need it only for a moment—but without a second's hesitation.

The first thing she saw when she'd finished was Malachi. His face had gone white, and he was backing away from her with a look of horror. He said something—a word in a language she didn't recognize—and then behind him she saw Luke, staring at her, his mouth slightly open. "Jocelyn?" Luke said.

She shook her head at him, just slightly, and looked out at

the crowd. It was a blur of faces, fading in and out as she stared. Some were smiling, some glancing around the crowd in surprise, some turning to the person who stood next to them. A few wore expressions of horror or amazement, hands clamped over their mouths. She saw Alec glance quickly at Magnus, and then at her, in disbelief, and Simon looking on in puzzlement, and then Amatis came forward, shoving her way past Patrick Penhallow's bulk, and ran up to the edge of the dais. "Stephen!" she said, looking up at Clary with a sort of dazzled amazement. *"Stephen!"*

"Oh," Clary said. "Oh, Amatis, no," and then she felt the rune magic slip from her, as if she'd shed a thin, invisible garment. Amatis's eager face dropped, and she backed away from the dais, her expression half-crestfallen and half-amazed.

Clary looked out across the crowd. They were utterly silent, every face turned to her. "I know what you all just saw," she said. "And I know that you know that that kind of magic is beyond any glamour or illusion. And I did that with one rune, a single rune, a rune *that I created*. There are reasons why I have this ability, and I know you might not like them or even believe them, but it doesn't matter. What matters is that I can help you win this battle against Valentine, if you'll let me."

"There will be no battle against Valentine," Malachi said. He didn't meet her eyes as he spoke. "The Clave has decided. We will agree to Valentine's terms and lay down our arms tomorrow morning."

"You can't do that," she said, a tinge of desperation entering her voice. "You think everything will be all right if you just give up? You think Valentine will let you keep on living like you have already? You think he'll confine his killing to demons and

Downworlders?" She swept her gaze across the room. "Most of you haven't seen Valentine in fifteen years. Maybe you've forgotten what he's really like. But I know. I've heard him talk about his plans. You think you can still live your lives under Valentine's rule, but you won't be able to. He'll control you completely, because he'll always be able to threaten to destroy you with the Mortal Instruments. He'll start with Downworlders, of course. But then he'll go to the Clave. He'll kill them first because he thinks they're weak and corrupt. Then he'll start in on anyone who has a Downworlder anywhere in their family. Maybe a werewolf brother"—her eyes swept over Amatis—"or a rebellious teenage daughter who dates the occasional faerie knight"—her eyes went to the Lightwoods—"or anyone who's ever so much as befriended a Downworlder. And then he'll go after anyone who's ever employed the services of a warlock. How many of you would that be?"

"This is nonsense," Malachi said crisply. "Valentine is not interested in destroying Nephilim."

"But he doesn't think anyone who associates with Downworlders is worthy of being called Nephilim," Clary insisted. "Look, your war isn't against Valentine. It's against demons. Keeping demons from this world is your mandate, a mandate from heaven. And a mandate from heaven isn't something you can just *ignore*. Downworlders hate demons too. They destroy them too. If Valentine has his way, he'll spend so much of his time trying to murder every Downworlder, and every Shadowhunter who's ever associated with them, that he'll forget all about the demons, and so will you, because you'll be so busy being afraid of Valentine. And they'll overrun the world, and that will be that."

"I see where this is going," Malachi said through gritted

teeth. "We will not fight beside Downworlders in the service of a battle we can't possibly win—"

"But you can win it," Clary said. "You can." Her throat was dry, her head aching, and the faces in the crowd before her seemed to meld into a featureless blur, punctuated here and there by soft white explosions of light. *But you can't stop now. You have to keep going. You have to try.* "My father hates Downworlders because he's jealous of them," she went on, her words tripping over one another. "Jealous and afraid of all the things they can do that he can't. He hates that in some ways they're more powerful than Nephilim, and I'd bet he's not alone in that. It's easy to be afraid of what you don't share." She took a breath. "But what if you *could* share it? What if I could make a rune that could bind each of you, each Shadowhunter, to a Downworlder who was fighting by your side, and you could *share your powers*—you could be as fast-healing as a vampire, as tough as a werewolf, or as swift as a faerie knight. And they, in turn, could share your training, your fighting skills. You could be an unbeatable force—if you'll let me Mark you, and if you'll fight with the Downworlders. Because if you don't fight beside them, the runes won't work." She paused. "Please," she said, but the word came almost inaudibly out of her dry throat. "Please let me Mark you."

Her words fell into a ringing silence. The world moved in a shifting blur, and she realized that she'd delivered the last half of her speech staring up at the ceiling of the Hall and that the soft white explosions she'd seen had been the stars coming out in the night sky, one by one. The silence went on and on as her hands, at her sides, curled themselves slowly into fists. And then slowly, very slowly, she lowered her gaze and met the eyes of the crowd staring back at her.

17

The Shadowhunter's Tale

Clary sat on the top step of the Accords Hall, looking out over Angel Square. The moon had come up earlier and was just visible over the roofs of the houses. The demon towers reflected back its light, silver-white. The darkness hid the scars and bruises of the city well; it looked peaceful under the night sky—if one didn't look up at Gard Hill and the ruined outline of the citadel. Guards patrolled the square below, appearing and disappearing as they moved in and out of the illumination of the witchlight lamps. They studiously ignored Clary's presence.

A few steps below her Simon was pacing back and forth, his footsteps utterly soundless. He had his hands in his pockets, and when he turned at the end of the stairs to walk back toward her, the moonlight glossed off his pale skin as if it were a reflective surface.

"Quit pacing," she told him. "You're just making me more nervous."

"Sorry."

"I feel like we've been out here forever." Clary strained her ears, but she couldn't hear more than the dull murmur of many voices coming through the closed double doors of the Hall. "Can you hear what they're saying inside?"

Simon half-closed his eyes; he appeared to be concentrating hard. "A little," he said after a pause.

"I wish I were in there," Clary said, kicking her heels irritably against the steps. Luke had asked her to wait outside the doors while the Clave deliberated; he'd wanted to send Amatis out with her, but Simon had insisted on coming instead, saying it would be better to have Amatis inside, supporting Clary. "I wish I were part of the meeting."

"No," Simon said. "You don't."

She knew why Luke had asked her to wait outside. She could imagine what they were saying about her in there. *Liar. Freak. Fool. Crazy. Stupid. Monster. Valentine's daughter.* Perhaps she was better off outside the Hall, but the tension of anticipating the Clave's decision was almost painful.

"Maybe I can climb one of those," Simon said, eyeing the fat white pillars that held up the slanted roof of the Hall. Runes were carved on them in overlapping patterns, but otherwise there were no visible handholds. "Work off steam that way."

"Oh, come on," Clary said. "You're a vampire, not Spider-Man."

Simon's only response was to jog lightly up the steps to the base of a pillar. He eyed it thoughtfully for a moment before putting his hands to it and starting to climb. Clary watched him, openmouthed, as his fingertips and feet found impossible holds on the ridged stone. "You *are* Spider-Man!" she exclaimed.

Simon glanced down from his perch halfway up the pillar. "That makes you Mary Jane. She has red hair," he said. He glanced out across the city, frowning. "I was hoping I could see the North Gate from here, but I'm not high enough."

Clary knew why he wanted to see the gate. Messengers had been dispatched there to ask the Downworlders to wait while the Clave deliberated, and Clary could only hope they were willing to do it. And if they were, what was it like out there? Clary pictured the crowd waiting, milling, wondering. . . .

The double doors of the Hall cracked open. A slim figure slipped through the gap, closed the door, and turned to face Clary. She was in shadow, and it was only when she moved forward, closer to the witchlight that illuminated the steps, that Clary saw the bright blaze of her red hair and recognized her mother.

Jocelyn looked up, her expression bemused. "Well, hello, Simon. Glad to see you're . . . adjusting."

Simon let go of the pillar and dropped, landing lightly at its base. He looked mildly abashed. "Hey, Mrs. Fray."

"I don't know if there's any point in calling me that now," said Clary's mother. "Maybe you should just call me Jocelyn." She hesitated. "You know, strange as this—situation—is, it's good to see you here with Clary. I can't remember the last time you two were apart."

Simon looked acutely embarrassed. "It's good to see you, too."

"Thank you, Simon." Jocelyn glanced at her daughter. "Now, Clary, would it be all right for us to talk for a moment? Alone?"

Clary sat motionless for a long moment, staring at her mother. It was hard not to feel like she was staring at a stranger. Her throat felt tight, almost too tight to speak. She glanced toward Simon, who was clearly waiting for a signal from her to tell him whether to stay or go. She sighed. "Okay."

Simon gave Clary an encouraging thumbs-up before vanishing back into the Hall. Clary turned away and stared fixedly down into the square, watching the guards do their rounds, as Jocelyn came and sat down next to her. Part of Clary wanted to lean sideways and put her head on her mother's shoulder. She could even close her eyes, pretend everything was all right. The other part of her knew that it wouldn't make a difference; she couldn't keep her eyes closed forever.

"Clary," Jocelyn said at last, very softly. "I am so sorry."

Clary stared down at her hands. She was, she realized, still holding Patrick Penhallow's stele. She hoped he didn't think she'd meant to steal it.

"I never thought I'd see this place again," Jocelyn went on. Clary stole a sideways glance at her mother and saw that she was looking out over the city, at the demon towers casting their pale whitish light over the skyline. "I dreamed about it sometimes. I even wanted to paint it, to paint my memories of it, but I couldn't do that. I thought if you ever saw the paintings, you might ask questions, might wonder how those images had ever come into my head. I was so frightened you'd find out where I was really from. Who I really was."

"And now I have."

"And now you have." Jocelyn sounded wistful. "And you have every reason to hate me."

"I don't hate you, Mom," Clary said. "I just . . ."

"Don't trust me," said Jocelyn. "I can't blame you. I should have told you the truth." She touched Clary's shoulder lightly and seemed encouraged when Clary didn't move away. "I can tell you I did it to protect you, but I know how that must sound. I was there, just now, in the Hall, watching you—"

"You were there?" Clary was startled. "I didn't see you."

"I was in the very back of the Hall. Luke had told me not to come to the meeting, that my presence would just upset everyone and throw everything off, and he was probably right, but I so badly wanted to be there. I slipped in after the meeting started and hid in the shadows. But I was there. And I just wanted to tell you—"

"That I made a fool out of myself?" Clary said bitterly. "I already know that."

"No. I wanted to tell you that I was proud of you."

Clary slewed around to look at her mother. "You were?"

Jocelyn nodded. "Of course I was. The way you stood up in front of the Clave like that. The way you showed them what you could do. You made them look at you and see the person they loved most in the world, didn't you?"

"Yeah," Clary said. "How did you know?"

"Because I heard them all calling out different names," Jocelyn said softly. "But I still saw you."

"Oh." Clary looked down at her feet. "Well, I'm still not sure they believe me about the runes. I mean, I hope so, but—"

"Can I see it?" Jocelyn asked.

"See what?"

"The rune. The one that you created to bind Shadowhunters and Downworlders." She hesitated. "If you can't show me . . ."

"No, it's all right." With the stele Clary traced the lines of the rune the angel had showed her across the marble of the Accords Hall step, and they blazed up in hot gold lines as she drew. It was a strong rune, a map of curving lines overlapping a matrix of straight ones. Simple and complex at the same time. Clary knew now why it had seemed somehow unfinished to her when she had visualized it before: It needed a matching rune to make it work. A twin. A partner. "Alliance," she said, drawing the stele back. "That's what I'm calling it."

Jocelyn watched silently as the rune flared and faded, leaving faint black lines on the stone. "When I was a young woman," she said finally, "I fought so hard to bind Downworlders and Shadowhunters together, to protect the Accords. I thought I was chasing a sort of dream—something most Shadowhunters could hardly imagine. And now you've made it concrete and literal and *real*." She blinked hard. "I realized something, watching you there in the Hall. You know, all these years I've tried to protect you by hiding you away. It's why I hated you going to Pandemonium. I knew it was a place where Downworlders and mundanes mingled—and that that meant there would be Shadowhunters there. I imagined it was something in your blood that drew you to the place, something that recognized the shadow world even without your Sight. I thought you would be safe if only I could keep that world hidden from you. I never thought about trying to protect you by helping you to be strong and to fight." She sounded sad. "But somehow you got to be strong anyway. Strong enough for me to tell you the truth, if you still want to hear it."

"I don't know." Clary thought of the images the angel had showed her, how terrible they had been. "I know I was angry with you for lying. But I'm not sure I want to find out any more horrible things."

"I talked to Luke. He thought you should know what I have to tell you. The whole story. All of it. Things I've never told anyone, never told him, even. I can't promise you that the whole truth is pleasant. But it is the truth."

The Law is hard, but it is the Law. She owed it to Jace to find out the truth as much as she owed it to herself. Clary tightened her grip on the stele in her hand, her knuckles whitening. "I want to know everything."

"Everything . . ." Jocelyn took a deep breath. "I don't even know where to start."

"How about starting with how you could marry Valentine? How you could have married a man like that, made him my father—he's a *monster*."

"No. He's a man. He's not a good man. But if you want to know why I married him, it was because I loved him."

"You can't have," Clary said. "Nobody could."

"I was your age when I fell in love with him," Jocelyn said. "I thought he was perfect—brilliant, clever, wonderful, funny, charming. I know, you're looking at me as if I've lost my mind. You only know Valentine the way he is now. You can't imagine what he was like then. When we were at school together, *everyone* loved him. He seemed to give off light, in a way, like there was some special and brilliantly illuminated part of the universe that only he had access to, and if we were lucky, he might share it with us, even just a little. Every girl loved him, and I thought I didn't have a chance. There was nothing special about me. I wasn't even that popular; Luke was one of my closest friends, and I spent most of my time with him. But still, somehow, Valentine chose me."

Gross, Clary wanted to say. But she held back. Maybe it was the wistfulness in her mother's voice, mixed with regret. Maybe it was what she had said about Valentine giving off light. Clary had thought the same thing about Jace before, and then felt stupid for thinking it. But maybe everyone in love felt that way.

"Okay," she said, "I get it. But you were sixteen then. That doesn't mean you had to marry him later."

"I was eighteen when we got married. He was nineteen," Jocelyn said in a matter-of-fact tone.

"Oh my God," Clary said in horror. "You'd *kill* me if I wanted to get married when I was eighteen."

"I would," Jocelyn agreed. "But Shadowhunters tend to get married earlier than mundanes. Their—*our*—life spans are shorter; a lot of us die violent deaths. We tend to do everything earlier because of it. Even so, I was young to get married. Still, my family was happy for me—even Luke was happy for me. Everyone thought Valentine was a wonderful boy. And he was, you know, just a boy then. The only person who ever told me I shouldn't marry him was Madeleine. We'd been friends in school, but when I told her I was engaged, she said that Valentine was selfish and hateful, that his charm masked a terrible amorality. I told myself she was jealous."

"Was she?"

"No," said Jocelyn, "she was telling the truth. I just didn't want to hear it." She glanced down at her hands.

"But you were sorry," Clary said. "After you married him, you were sorry you did it, right?"

"Clary," Jocelyn said. She sounded tired. "We were *happy*. At least for the first few years. We went to live in my parents' manor house, where I grew up; Valentine didn't want to be in the city, and he wanted the rest of the Circle to avoid Alicante and the prying eyes of the Clave as well. The Waylands lived in the manor just a mile or two from ours, and there were others close by—the Lightwoods, the Penhallows. It was like being at the center of the world, with all this activity swirling around us, all this passion, and through it all I was by Valentine's side. He never made me feel dismissed or inconsequential. No, I was a key part of the Circle. I was one of the few whose opinions he trusted. He told me over and over that without me, he couldn't do any of it. Without me, he'd be nothing."

"He *did*?" Clary couldn't imagine Valentine saying anything like that, anything that made him sound . . . vulnerable.

"He did, but it wasn't true. Valentine could never have been nothing. He was born to be a leader, to be the center of a revolution. More and more converts came to him. They were drawn by his passion and the brilliance of his ideas. He rarely even spoke of Downworlders in those early days. It was all about reforming the Clave, changing laws that were ancient and rigid and wrong. Valentine said there should be more Shadowhunters, more to fight the demons, more Institutes, that we should worry less about hiding and more about protecting the world from demonkind. That we should walk tall and proud in the world. It was seductive, his vision: a world full of Shadowhunters, where demons ran scared and mundanes, instead of believing we didn't exist, thanked us for what we did for them. We were young; we thought *thanks* were important. We didn't know." Jocelyn took a deep breath, as if she were about to dive underwater. "Then I got pregnant."

Clary felt a cold prickle at the back of her neck and suddenly—she couldn't have said why—she was no longer sure she wanted the truth from her mother, no longer sure she wanted to hear, again, how Valentine had made Jace into a monster. "Mom . . ."

Jocelyn shook her head blindly. "You asked me why I never told you that you had a brother. *This* is why." She took a ragged breath. "I was so happy when I found out. And Valentine—he'd always wanted to be a father, he said. To train his son to be a warrior the way his father had trained him. 'Or your daughter,' I'd say, and he'd smile and say a daughter could be a warrior just as well as a boy, and he would be happy with either. I thought everything was perfect.

"And then Luke was bitten by a werewolf. They'll tell you there's a one in two chance that a bite will pass on lycanthropy. I think it's more like three in four. I've rarely seen anyone escape the disease, and Luke was no exception. At the next full moon he Changed. He was there on our doorstep in the morning, covered in blood, his clothes torn to rags. I wanted to comfort him, but Valentine shoved me aside. 'Jocelyn,' he said, 'the baby. ' As if Luke were about to run at me and tear the baby out of my stomach. It was *Luke*, but Valentine pushed me away and dragged Luke down the steps and into the woods. When he came back much later, he was alone. I ran to him, but he told me that Luke had killed himself in despair over his lycanthropy. That he was . . . dead."

The grief in Jocelyn's voice was raw and ragged, Clary thought, even now, when she knew Luke hadn't died. But Clary remembered her own despair when she'd held Simon as he'd died on the steps of the Institute. There were some feelings you never forgot.

"But he gave Luke a knife," Clary said in a small voice. "He told him to kill himself. He made Amatis's husband divorce her, just because her brother had become a werewolf."

"I didn't know," Jocelyn said. "After Luke died, it was like I fell into a black pit. I spent months in my bedroom, sleeping all the time, eating only because of the baby. Mundanes would call what I had depression, but Shadowhunters don't have those kinds of terms. Valentine believed I was having a difficult pregnancy. He told everyone I was ill. I *was* ill—I couldn't sleep. I kept thinking I heard strange noises, cries in the night. Valentine gave me sleeping drafts, but those just gave me nightmares. Terrible dreams that Valentine was holding me down, was forcing a knife into me, or that I was choking on poison. In the morning I'd be exhausted, and I'd sleep all day. I had no idea what was going on outside, no idea that he'd forced Stephen to divorce Amatis and marry Céline. I was in a daze. And then . . ." Jocelyn knotted her hands together in her lap. They were shaking. "And then I had the baby."

She fell silent, for so long that Clary wondered if she was going to speak again. Jocelyn was staring sightlessly toward the demon towers, her fingers beating a nervous tattoo against her knees. At last she said, "My mother was with me when the baby was born. You never knew her. Your grandmother. She was such a kind woman. You would have liked her, I think. She handed me my son, and at first I knew only that he fit perfectly into my arms, that the blanket wrapping him was soft, and that he was so small and delicate, with just a wisp of fair hair on the top of his head. And then he opened his eyes."

Jocelyn's voice was flat, almost toneless, yet Clary found herself shivering, dreading what her mother might say next. *Don't*, she wanted to say. *Don't tell me.* But Jocelyn went on, the words pouring out of her like cold poison.

"Horror washed over me. It was like being bathed in

acid—my skin seemed to burn off my bones, and it was all I could do not to drop the baby and begin screaming. They say every mother knows her own child instinctively. I suppose the opposite is true as well. Every nerve in my body was crying out that this was not my baby, that it was something horrible and unnatural, as inhuman as a parasite. How could my mother not see it? But she was smiling at me as if nothing were wrong.

"'His name is Jonathan,' said a voice from the doorway. I looked up and saw Valentine regarding the scene before him with a look of pleasure. The baby opened his eyes again, as if recognizing the sound of his name. His eyes were black, black as night, fathomless as tunnels dug into his skull. There was nothing human in them at all."

There was a long silence. Clary sat frozen, staring at her mother in openmouthed horror. *That's Jace she's talking about*, she thought. *Jace when he was a baby. How could you feel like that about a* baby?

"Mom," she whispered. "Maybe—maybe you were in shock or something. Or maybe you were sick—"

"That's what Valentine told me," Jocelyn said emotionlessly. "That I was sick. Valentine adored Jonathan. He couldn't understand what was wrong with me. And I knew he was right. I was a monster, a mother who couldn't stand her own child. I thought about killing myself. I might have done it too—and then I got a message, delivered by fire-letter, from Ragnor Fell. He was a warlock who had always been close to my family; he was the one we called on when we needed a healing spell, that sort of thing. He'd found out that Luke had become the leader of a pack of werewolves in the Brocelind Forest, by the eastern border. I burned the note once I got it. I knew Valentine could never know. But it wasn't until I went to the werewolf encampment and *saw* Luke that I knew for certain that Valentine had lied to me, lied to me about Luke's suicide. It was then that I started to truly hate him."

"But Luke said you knew there was something wrong with Valentine—that you knew he was doing something terrible. He said you knew it even before he was Changed."

For a moment Jocelyn didn't reply. "You know, Luke should never have been bitten. It shouldn't have happened. It was a routine patrol of the woods, he was out with Valentine—it shouldn't have happened."

"Mom . . ."

"Luke says I told him I was afraid of Valentine even before he was Changed. He says I told him I could hear screams through the walls of the manor, that I suspected something, dreaded something. And Luke—trusting Luke—asked Valentine about it the very next day. That night Valentine took Luke hunting, and he was bitten. I think—I think Valentine made me forget what I'd seen, whatever had made me afraid. He made me believe it was all bad dreams. And I think he made sure Luke got bitten that night. I think he wanted Luke out of the way so no one could remind me that I was afraid of my husband. But I didn't realize that, not right away. Luke and I saw each other so briefly that first day, and I wanted so badly to tell him about Jonathan, but I couldn't, I couldn't. Jonathan was my son. Still, seeing Luke, even just seeing him, made me stronger. I went home telling myself that I would make a new effort with Jonathan, would learn to love him. Would make myself love him.

"That night I was woken by the sound of a baby crying. I sat bolt upright, alone in the bedroom. Valentine was out at a

Circle meeting, so I had no one to share my amazement with. Jonathan, you see, never cried—never made a noise. His silence was one of the things that most upset me about him. I dashed down the hall to his room, but he was sleeping silently. Still, I could *hear* a baby crying, I was sure of it. I raced down the stairs, following the sound of the crying. It seemed to be coming from inside the empty wine cellar, but the door was locked, the cellar never used. But I had grown up in the manor. I knew where my father hid the key. . . ."

Jocelyn didn't look at Clary as she spoke; she seemed lost in the story, in her memories.

"I never told you the story of Bluebeard's wife, did I, when you were a little girl? The husband told his wife never to look in the locked room, and she looked, and found the remains of all the wives he had murdered before her, displayed like butterflies in a glass case. I had no idea when I unlocked that door what I would find inside. If I had to do it again, would I be able to bring myself to open the door, to use my witchlight to guide me down into the darkness? I don't know, Clary. I just don't know.

"The smell—oh, the smell down there, like blood and death and rot. Valentine had hollowed out a place under the ground, in what had once been the wine cellar. It wasn't a child I had heard crying, after all. There were cells down there now, with things imprisoned in them. Demon-creatures, bound with electrum chains, writhed and flopped and gurgled in their cells, but there was more, much more—the bodies of Downworlders, in different stages of death and dying. There were werewolves, their bodies half-dissolved by silver powder. Vampires held head-down in holy water until their skin peeled off the bones. Faeries whose skin had been pierced with cold iron.

"Even now I don't think of him as a torturer. Not really. He seemed to be pursuing an almost scientific end. There were ledgers of notes by each cell door, meticulous recordings of his experiments, how long it had taken each creature to die. There was one vampire whose skin he had burned off over and over again to see if there was a point beyond which the poor creature could no longer regenerate. It was hard to read what he had written without wanting to faint, or throw up. Somehow I did neither.

"There was one page devoted to experiments he had done on himself. He had read somewhere that the blood of demons might act as an amplifier of the powers Shadowhunters are naturally born with. He had tried injecting himself with the blood, to no end. Nothing had happened except that he had made himself sick. Eventually he came to the conclusion that he was too old for the blood to affect him, that it must be given to a child to take full effect—preferably one as yet unborn.

"Across from the page recording those particular conclusions he had written a series of notes with a heading I recognized. My name. *Jocelyn Morgenstern.*

"I remember the way my fingers shook while I turned the pages, the words burning themselves into my brain. 'Jocelyn drank the mixture again tonight. No visible changes in her, but again it is the child that concerns me. . . . With regular infusions of demonic ichor such as I have been giving her, the child may be capable of any feats. . . . Last night I heard the child's heart beat, more strongly than any human heart, the sound like a mighty bell, tolling the beginning of a new generation of Shadowhunters, the blood of angels and demons mixed to produce powers beyond any previously imagined possible. . . . No longer will the power of Downworlders be the greatest on this earth. . . .'

"There was more, much more. I clawed at the pages, my fingers trembling, my mind racing back, seeing the mixtures Valentine had given me to drink each night, the nightmares about being stabbed, choked, poisoned. But I wasn't the one he'd been poisoning. It was Jonathan. Jonathan, whom he'd turned into some kind of half-demon *thing*. And that, Clary—*that* was when I realized what Valentine really was."

Clary let out the breath she hadn't realized she'd been holding. It was horrible—so horrible—and yet it all matched up with the vision Ithuriel had showed her. She wasn't sure whom she felt more pity for, her mother or Jonathan. Jonathan—she couldn't think of him as Jace, not with her mother there, not with the story so fresh in her mind—doomed to be not quite human by a father who'd cared more about murdering Downworlders than he had about his own family.

"But—you didn't leave then, did you?" Clary asked, her voice sounding small to her ears. "You stayed. . . ."

"For two reasons," Jocelyn said. "One was the Uprising. What I found in the cellar that night was like a slap in the face. It woke me up out of my misery and made me see what was going on around me. Once I realized what Valentine was planning—the wholesale slaughter of Downworlders—I knew I couldn't let it happen. I began meeting in secret with Luke. I couldn't tell him what Valentine had done to me and to our child. I knew it would just drive him mad, that he'd be unable to stop himself from trying to hunt down Valentine and kill him, and he'd only get himself killed in the process. And I couldn't let anyone else know what had been done to Jonathan either. Despite everything, he was still my child. But I did tell Luke about the horrors in the cellar, of my conviction that Valentine was losing his mind, becoming progressively more insane. Together, we planned to thwart the Uprising. I felt driven to do it, Clary. It was a sort of expiation, the only way I could make myself feel like I had paid for the sin of ever having joined the Circle, of having trusted Valentine. Of having loved him."

"And he didn't know? Valentine, I mean. He didn't figure out what you were doing?"

Jocelyn shook her head. "When people love you, they trust you. Besides, at home I tried to pretend everything was normal. I behaved as though my initial revulsion at the sight of Jonathan was gone. I would bring him over to Maryse Lightwood's house, let him play with her baby son, Alec. Sometimes Céline Herondale would join us—she was pregnant by that time. 'Your husband is so kind,' she would tell me. 'He is so concerned about Stephen and me. He gives me potions and mixtures for the health of the baby; they are wonderful.'"

"Oh," said Clary. "Oh my God."

"That's what I thought," said Jocelyn grimly. "I wanted to tell her not to trust Valentine or to accept anything he gave her, but I couldn't. Her husband was Valentine's closest friend, and she would have betrayed me to him immediately. I kept my mouth shut. And then—"

"She killed herself," said Clary, remembering the story. "But—was it because of what Valentine did to her?"

Jocelyn shook her head. "I honestly don't think so. Stephen was killed in a raid, and she slit her wrists when she found out the news. She was eight months pregnant. She bled to death. . . ." She paused. "Hodge was the one who found her body. And Valentine actually did seem distraught over their deaths. He vanished for almost an entire day afterward, and came home bleary-eyed and staggering. And yet in a way, I was almost grateful for his distraction. At least it meant he wasn't paying attention to what *I* was doing. Every day I became more and more frightened that Valentine would discover the conspiracy and try to torture the truth out of me: Who was in our secret alliance? How much had I betrayed of his plans? I wondered how I would withstand torture, whether I could hold up against it. I was terribly afraid that I couldn't. I resolved finally to take steps to make sure that this never happened. I went to Fell with my fears and he created a potion for me—"

"The potion from the Book of the White," Clary said, realizing. "That's why you wanted it. And the antidote—how did it wind up in the Waylands' library?"

"I hid it there one night during a party," said Jocelyn with the trace of a smile. "I didn't want to tell Luke—I knew he'd hate the whole idea of the potion, but everyone else I knew was in the Circle. I sent a message to Ragnor, but he was leaving Idris and wouldn't say when he'd be back. He said he could always be reached with a message—but who would send it? Eventually I realized there was one person I could tell, one person who hated Valentine enough that she'd never betray me to him. I sent a letter to Madeleine explaining what I planned to do and that the only way to revive me was to find Ragnor Fell. I never heard a word back from her, but I had to believe she had read it and understood. It was all I had to hold on to."

"Two reasons," Clary said. "You said there were two reasons that you stayed. One was the Uprising. What was the other?"

Jocelyn's green eyes were tired, but luminous and wide. "Clary," she said, "can't you guess? The second reason is that I was pregnant again. Pregnant with you."

"Oh," Clary said in a small voice. She remembered Luke saying, *She was carrying another child and had known it for weeks.* "But didn't that make you want to run away even more?"

"Yes," Jocelyn said. "But I knew I couldn't. If I'd run away from Valentine, he would have moved heaven and hell to get me back. He would have followed me to the ends of the earth, because I belonged to him and he would never have let me go. And maybe I would have let him come after me, and taken my chances, but I would never have let him come after you." She pushed her hair back from her tired-looking face. "There was only one way I could make sure he never did. And that was for him to die."

Clary looked at her mother in surprise. Jocelyn still looked tired, but her face was shining with a fierce light.

"I thought he'd be killed during the Uprising," she said. "I couldn't have killed him myself. I couldn't have brought myself to, somehow. But I never thought he'd survive the battle. And later, when the house burned, I wanted to believe he was dead. I told myself over and over that he and Jonathan had burned to death in the fire. But I knew . . ." Her voice trailed off. "It was why I did what I did. I thought it was the only way to protect you—taking your memories, making you into as much of a mundane as I could. Hiding you in the mundane world. It was stupid, I realize that now, stupid and wrong. And I'm sorry, Clary. I just hope you can forgive me—if not now, then in the future."

"Mom." Clary cleared her throat. She'd felt like she was about to cry for pretty much the last ten minutes. "It's okay. It's just—there's one thing I don't get." She knotted her fingers into the material of her coat. "I mean, I knew already a little of what Valentine did to Jace—I mean, to Jonathan. But the way you describe Jonathan, it's like he was a monster. And, Mom, Jace isn't like that. He's nothing like that. If you knew him—if you could just meet him—"

"Clary." Jocelyn reached out and took Clary's hand in hers. "There's more that I have to tell you. There's nothing more that I hid from you, or lied about. But there are things I never knew, things I only just discovered. And they may be very hard to hear."

Worse than what you've already told me? Clary thought. She bit her lip and nodded. "Go ahead and tell me. I'd rather know."

"When Dorothea told me that Valentine had been sighted in the city, I knew he was there for me—for the Cup. I wanted to flee, but I couldn't bring myself to tell you why. I don't blame you at all for running from me that awful night, Clary. I was just glad you weren't there when your father—when Valentine and his demons broke into our apartment. I just had time to swallow the potion—I could hear them breaking the door down . . ." She trailed off, her voice tight. "I hoped Valentine would leave me for dead, but he didn't. He brought me to Renwick's with him. He tried various methods to wake me up, but nothing worked. I was in a sort of dream state; I was half-conscious that he was there, but I couldn't move or respond to him. I doubt he thought I could hear or understand him. And yet he would sit by the bed while I slept and talk to me."

"Talk to you? About what?"

"About our past. Our marriage. How he had loved me and I had betrayed him. How he hadn't loved anyone since. I think he meant it too, as much as he could mean these things. I had always been the one he'd talked to about the doubts he had, the guilt he felt, and in the years since I'd left him I don't think there'd ever been anyone else. I think he couldn't stop himself from talking to me, even though he knew he shouldn't. I think he just wanted to talk to someone. You'd have thought that what was on his mind would be what he'd done to those poor people, making them Forsaken, and what he was planning to do to the Clave. But it wasn't. What he wanted to talk about was Jonathan."

"What about him?"

Jocelyn's mouth tightened. "He wanted to tell me he was sorry for what he'd done to Jonathan before he'd been born, because he knew it had nearly destroyed me. He'd known I was close to suicide over Jonathan—though he didn't know I was also despairing over what I'd discovered about *him.* He'd somehow gotten hold of angel blood. It's an almost legendary substance for Shadowhunters. Drinking it is supposed to give you incredible strength. Valentine had tried it on himself and discovered that it gave him not just increased strength but a feeling of euphoria and happiness every time he injected it into his blood. So he took some, dried it to powder, and mixed it into my food, hoping it would help my despair."

I know where he got hold of angel blood, Clary thought, thinking of Ithuriel with a sharp sadness. "Do you think it worked at all?"

"I do wonder now if that was why I suddenly found the focus and the ability to go on, and to help Luke thwart the Uprising. It would be ironic if that was the case, considering why Valentine did it in the first place. But what he didn't know was that while he was doing this, I was pregnant with you. So while it may have affected me slightly, it affected you much more. I believe that's why you can do what you can with runes."

"And maybe," Clary said, "why you can do things like trap the image of the Mortal Cup in a tarot card. And why Valentine can do things like take the curse off Hodge—"

"Valentine has had years of experimenting on himself in a myriad of ways," said Jocelyn. "He's as close now as a human being, a Shadowhunter, can get to a warlock. But nothing he can do to himself would have the kind of profound effect on him it would have on you or Jonathan, because you were so young. I'm not sure anyone's ever before done what Valentine did, not to a baby before it was born."

"So Jace—Jonathan—and I really were both experiments."

"You were an unintentional one. With Jonathan, Valentine wanted to create some kind of superwarrior, stronger and faster and better than other Shadowhunters. At Renwick's, Valentine told me that Jonathan really was all those things. But that he was also cruel and amoral and strangely empty. Jonathan was loyal enough to Valentine, but I suppose Valentine realized that somewhere along the way, in trying to create a child who was superior to others, he'd created a son who could never really love him."

Clary thought of Jace, of the way he'd looked at Renwick's, the way he'd clutched that piece of the broken Portal so hard that blood had run down his fingers. "No," she said. "No and no. Jace is not like that. He does love Valentine. He shouldn't, but he does. And he isn't empty. He's the opposite of everything you're saying."

Jocelyn's hands twisted in her lap. They were laced all over with fine white scars—the fine white scars all Shadowhunters bore, the memory of vanished Marks. But Clary had never really seen her mother's scars before. Magnus's magic had always made her forget them. There was one, on the inside of her mother's wrist, that was very like the shape of a star. . . .

Her mother spoke then, and all thoughts of anything else fled from Clary's mind.

"I am not," Jocelyn said, "talking about Jace."

"But . . . ," Clary said. Everything seemed to be happening very slowly, as if she were dreaming. *Maybe I am dreaming*, she thought. *Maybe my mother never woke up at all, and all of this is a dream.* "Jace is Valentine's son. I mean, who else could he be?"

Jocelyn looked straight into her daughter's eyes. "The night Céline Herondale died, she was eight months pregnant. Valentine had been giving her potions, powders—he was trying on her what he'd tried on himself, with angel blood, hoping that Stephen's child would be as strong and powerful as he suspected Jonathan would be, but without Jonathan's worse qualities. He couldn't bear that his experiment would go to waste, so with Hodge's help he cut the baby out of Céline's stomach. She'd only been dead a short time—"

Clary made a gagging noise. "That isn't possible."

Jocelyn went on as if Clary hadn't spoken. "Valentine took that baby and had Hodge bring it to his own childhood home, in a valley not far from Lake Lyn. It was why he was gone all that night. Hodge took care of the baby until the Uprising. After that, because Valentine was pretending to be Michael Wayland, he moved the child to the Wayland manor and raised him as Michael Wayland's son."

"So Jace," Clary whispered. "Jace is *not* my brother?"

She felt her mother squeeze her hand—a sympathetic squeeze. "No, Clary. He's not."

Clary's vision darkened. She could feel her heart pounding in separate, distinct beats. *My mom feels sorry for me*, she thought distantly. *She thinks this is* bad *news*. Her hands were shaking. "Then whose bones were those in the fire? Luke said there were a child's bones—"

Jocelyn shook her head. "Those were Michael Wayland's bones, and his son's bones. Valentine killed them both and burned their bodies. He wanted the Clave to believe that both he and his son were dead."

"Then Jonathan—"

"Is alive," said Jocelyn, pain flashing across her face. "Valentine told me as much at Renwick's. Valentine brought Jace up in the Wayland manor, and Jonathan in the house near the lake. He managed to divide his time between the two of them, traveling from one house to the other, sometimes leaving one or both alone for long periods of time. It seems that Jace never knew about Jonathan, though Jonathan may have known about Jace. They never met, though they probably lived only miles from each other."

"And Jace doesn't have demon blood in him? He's not—cursed?"

"Cursed?" Jocelyn looked surprised. "No, he doesn't have demon blood. Clary, Valentine experimented on Jace when he was a baby with the same blood he used on me, on you. *Angel* blood. Jace isn't cursed. The opposite, if anything. All Shadowhunters have some of the Angel's blood in them—you two just have a bit more."

Clary's mind whirled. She tried to imagine Valentine raising two children at the same time, one part demon, one part angel. One shadow boy, and one light. Loving them both, perhaps, as much as Valentine could love anything. Jace had never known about Jonathan, but what had the other boy known about him? His complementary part, his opposite? Had he hated the thought of him? Yearned to meet him? Been indifferent? They had both been so alone. And one of them was her brother—her real, full-blooded brother. "Do you think he's still the same? Jonathan, I mean? Do you think he could have gotten . . . better?"

"I don't think so," Jocelyn said gently.

"But what makes you so sure?" Clary spun to look at her mother, suddenly eager. "I mean, maybe he's changed. It's been years. Maybe—"

"Valentine told me he had spent years teaching Jonathan how to appear pleasant, even charming. He wanted him to be a spy, and you can't be a spy if you terrify everyone you meet. Jonathan even learned a certain ability to cast slight glamours, to convince people he was likable and trustworthy." Jocelyn sighed. "I'm telling you this so you won't feel bad that you were taken in. Clary, you've met Jonathan. He just never told you his real name, because he was posing as someone else. Sebastian Verlac."

Clary stared at her mother. *But he's the Penhallows' cousin*, part of her mind insisted, but of course Sebastian had never been who he'd claimed he was; everything he'd said had been a lie. She thought of the way she'd felt the first time she'd seen him, as if she were recognizing someone she'd known all her life, someone as intimately familiar to her as her own self. She had never felt that way about Jace. "Sebastian's my brother?"

Jocelyn's fine-boned face was drawn, her hands laced together. Her fingertips were white, as if she were pressing them too hard against one another. "I spoke to Luke for a long time today about everything that's happened in Alicante since you arrived. He told me about the demon towers, and his suspicion that Sebastian had destroyed the wards, though he had no idea how. I realized then who Sebastian really was."

"You mean because he lied about being Sebastian Verlac? And because he's a spy for Valentine?"

"Those two things, yes," said Jocelyn, "but it actually wasn't until Luke said that you'd told him Sebastian dyed his hair that I guessed. And I could be wrong, but a boy just a little older than you, fair-haired and dark-eyed, with no apparent parents, utterly loyal to Valentine—I couldn't help but think he must be Jonathan. And there's more than that. Valentine was always trying to find a way to bring the wards down, always determined that there was a way to do it. Experimenting on Jonathan with demon blood—he said it was to make him stronger, a better fighter, but there was more to it than that—"

Clary stared. "What do you mean, more to it?"

"It was his way of bringing down the wards," Jocelyn said. "You can't bring a demon into Alicante, but you need demons' blood to take down the wards. Jonathan has demon blood; it's in his veins. And his being a Shadowhunter means he's granted automatic entrance to the city whenever he wants to get in, no matter what. He used his own blood to take the wards down, I'm sure of it."

Clary thought of Sebastian standing across from her in the grass near the ruins of Fairchild manor. The way his dark hair had blown across his face. The way he'd held her wrists, his nails digging into her skin. The way he'd said it was impossible that Valentine had ever loved Jace. She'd thought it was because he hated Valentine. But it wasn't, she realized. He'd been . . . jealous.

She thought of the dark prince of her drawings, the one who had looked so much like Sebastian. She had dismissed the resemblance as coincidence, a trick of imagination, but now she wondered if it was the tie of their shared blood that had driven her to give the unhappy hero of her story her brother's face. She tried to visualize the prince again, but the image seemed to shatter and dissolve before her eyes, like ash blown away on the wind. She could only see Sebastian now, the red light of the burning city reflected in his eyes.

"Jace," she said. "Someone has to tell him. Has to tell him the truth." Her thoughts tumbled over themselves, helter-skelter; if Jace had known, known he didn't have demon blood, maybe he wouldn't have gone after Valentine. If he'd known he wasn't Clary's brother after all . . .

"But I thought," said Jocelyn, with a mixture of sympathy and puzzlement, "that nobody knew where he was . . . ?"

Before Clary could answer, the double doors of the Hall swung open, spilling light out over the pillared arcade and the steps below it. The dull roar of voices, no longer muffled, rose as Luke came through the doors. He looked exhausted, but there was a lightness about him that hadn't been there before. He seemed almost relieved.

Jocelyn rose to her feet. "Luke. What is it?"

He took a few steps toward them, then paused between the doorway and the stairs. "Jocelyn," he said, "I'm sorry to interrupt you."

"That's all right, Luke." Even through her daze Clary thought, *Why do they keep saying each other's* names *like that?* There was a sort of awkwardness between them now, an awkwardness that hadn't been there before. "Is something wrong?"

He shook his head. "No. For a change, something's right." He smiled at Clary, and there was nothing awkward about it: He looked pleased with her, and even proud. "You did it, Clary," he said. "The Clave's agreed to let you Mark them. There will be no surrender after all."

18

Hail and Farewell

The valley was more beautiful in reality than it had been in Jace's vision. Maybe it was the bright moonlight silvering the river that cut across the green valley floor. White birch and aspen dotted the valley's sides, shivering their leaves in the cool breeze—it was chilly up on the ridge, with no protection from the wind.

This was without a doubt the valley where he'd last seen Sebastian. Finally he was catching up. After securing Wayfarer to a tree, Jace took the bloody thread from his pocket and repeated the tracking ritual, just to be sure.

He closed his eyes, expecting to see Sebastian, hopefully somewhere very close by—maybe even still in the valley—

Instead he saw only darkness.

His heart began to pound.

He tried again, moving the thread to his left fist and awkwardly carving the tracking rune onto the back of it with his right, less agile, hand. He took a deep breath before closing his eyes this time.

Nothing, again. Just a wavering, shadowy blackness. He stood there for a full minute, his teeth gritted, the wind slicing through his jacket, making goose bumps rise on his skin. Eventually, cursing, he opened his eyes—and then, in a fit of desperate anger, his fist; the wind picked up the thread and carried it away, so fast that even if he'd regretted it immediately he couldn't have caught it back.

His mind raced. Clearly the tracking rune was no longer working. Perhaps Sebastian had realized he was being followed and done something to break the charm—but what *could* you do to stop a tracking? Maybe he'd found a large body of water. Water disrupted magic.

Not that that helped Jace much. It wasn't as if he could go to every lake in the country and see if Sebastian was floating around in the middle of it. He'd been so close, too—so close. He'd *seen* this valley, seen Sebastian in it. And there the house was, just barely visible, nestled against a copse of trees on the valley floor. At least it would be worth going down to look around the house to see if there was anything that might point toward Sebastian's, or Valentine's, location.

With a feeling of resignation, Jace used the stele to Mark himself with a number of fast-acting, fast-disappearing battle Marks: one to give him silence, and one swiftness, and another for sure-footed walking. When he was done—and feeling the familiar, stinging pain hot against his skin—he slid the stele into his pocket, gave Wayfarer a brisk pat on the neck, and headed down into the valley.

The sides of the valley were deceptively steep, and treacherous with loose scree. Jace alternated picking his way down it carefully and sliding on the scree, which was fast but dangerous. By the time he reached the valley floor, his hands were bloody where he'd fallen onto the loose gravel more than once. He washed them in the clear, fast-flowing stream; its water was numbingly cold.

When he straightened up and looked around, he realized he was now regarding the valley from a different angle than he'd had in the tracking vision. There was the gnarled copse of trees, their branches intertwining, the valley walls rising all around, and there was the small house. Its windows were dark now, and no smoke rose out of the chimney. Jace felt a mingled stab of relief and disappointment. It would be easier to search the house if no one was in it. On the other hand, no one was in it.

As he approached, he wondered what about the house in the vision had seemed eerie. Up close, it was just an ordinary Idris farmhouse, made of squares of white and gray stone. The shutters had once been painted a bright blue, but it looked as if it had been years since anyone had repainted them. They were pale and peeling with age.

Reaching one of the windows, Jace hoisted himself onto the sill and peered through the cloudy pane. He saw a big, slightly dusty room with a workbench of sorts running along one wall. The tools on it weren't anything you'd do handiwork with—they were a warlock's tools: stacks of smeared parchment; black, waxy candles; fat copper bowls with dried dark liquid stuck to the rims; an assortment of knives, some as thin as awls, some with wide square blades. A pentagram was chalked on the floor, its outlines blurred, each of its five points decorated with a different rune. Jace's stomach tightened—the runes looked like the ones that had been carved around Ithuriel's feet. Could Valentine have done this—could these be *his* things? Was this his hideaway—a hideaway Jace had never visited or known about?

Jace slid off the sill, landing in a dry patch of grass—just as a shadow passed across the face of the moon. But there were no birds here, he thought, and glanced up just in time to see a raven wheeling overhead. He froze, then stepped hastily into the shadow of a tree and peered up through its branches. As the raven dipped closer to the ground, Jace knew his first instinct had been right. This wasn't just any raven—this was Hugo, the raven that had once been Hodge's; Hodge had used him on occasion to carry messages outside the Institute. Since then Jace had learned that Hugo had originally been his father's.

Jace pressed himself closer to the tree trunk. His heart was pounding again, this time with excitement. If Hugo was here, it could only mean that he was carrying a message, and this time the message wouldn't be for Hodge. It would be for Valentine. It *had* to be. If Jace could only manage to follow him—

Perching on a sill, Hugo peered through one of the house's windows. Apparently realizing that the house was empty, the bird rose into the air with an irritable caw and flapped off in the direction of the stream.

Jace stepped out from the shadows and set out in pursuit of the raven.

"So, technically," Simon said, "even though Jace isn't actually related to you, you *have* kissed your brother."

"Simon!" Clary was appalled. "Shut UP." She spun in her

seat to see if anyone was listening, but, fortunately, nobody seemed to be. She was sitting in a high seat on the dais in the Accords Hall, Simon by her side. Her mother stood at the edge of the dais, leaning down to speak to Amatis.

All around them the Hall was chaos as the Downworlders who had come from the North Gate poured in, spilling in through the doors, crowding against the walls. Clary recognized various members of Luke's pack, including Maia, who grinned across the room at her. There were faeries, pale and cold and lovely as icicles and warlocks with bat wings and goat feet and even one with antlers, blue fire sparking from their fingertips as they moved through the room. The Shadowhunters milled among them, looking nervous.

Clutching her stele in both hands, Clary looked around anxiously. Where was Luke? He'd vanished into the crowd. She picked him out after a moment, talking with Malachi, who was shaking his head violently. Amatis stood nearby, shooting the Consul dagger glances.

"Don't make me sorry I ever told you any of this, Simon," Clary said, glaring at him. She'd done her best to give him a pared-down version of Jocelyn's tale, mostly hissed under her breath as he'd helped her plow through the crowds to the dais and take her seat there. It was weird being up here, looking down on the room as if she were the queen of all she surveyed. But a queen wouldn't be nearly so panicked. "Besides. He was a horrible kisser."

"Or maybe it was just gross, because he was, you know, *your brother*." Simon seemed more amused by the whole business than Clary thought he had any right to be.

"Do *not* say that where my mother can hear you, or I'll kill you," she said with a second glare. "I already feel like I'm going to throw up or pass out. Don't make it worse."

Jocelyn, returning from the edge of the dais in time to hear Clary's last words—though, fortunately, not what she and Simon had been discussing—dropped a reassuring pat onto Clary's shoulder. "Don't be nervous, baby. You were so great before. Is there anything you need? A blanket, some hot water . . ."

"I'm not cold," Clary said patiently, "and I don't need a bath, either. I'm fine. I just want Luke to come up here and tell me what's going on."

Jocelyn waved toward Luke to get his attention, silently mouthing something Clary couldn't quite decipher. "Mom," she spat, "*don't*," but it was already too late. Luke glanced up—and so did quite a few of the other Shadowhunters. Most of them looked away just as quickly, but Clary sensed the fascination in their stares. It was weird thinking that her mother was something of a legendary figure here. Just about everyone in the room had heard her name and had some kind of opinion about her, good or bad. Clary wondered how her mother kept it from bothering her. She didn't *look* bothered—she looked cool and collected and dangerous.

A moment later Luke had joined them on the dais, Amatis at his side. He still looked tired, but also alert and even a little excited. He said, "Just hang on a second. Everyone's coming."

"Malachi," said Jocelyn, not quite looking directly at Luke while she spoke, "was he giving you trouble?"

Luke made a dismissive gesture. "He thinks we should send a message to Valentine, refusing his terms. I say we shouldn't tip our hand. Let Valentine show up with his army on

Brocelind Plain expecting a surrender. Malachi seemed to think that wouldn't be sporting, and when I told him war wasn't an English schoolboy cricket game, he said that if any of the Downworlders here got out of hand, he'd step in and end the whole business. I don't know what he thinks is going to happen—as if Downworlders can't stop fighting even for five minutes."

"That's exactly what he thinks," said Amatis. "It's Malachi. He's probably worried you'll start eating each other."

"Amatis," Luke said. "Someone might hear you." He turned, then, as two men mounted the steps behind him: one was a tall, slender faerie knight with long dark hair that fell in sheets on either side of his narrow face. He wore a tunic of white armor: pale, hard metal made of tiny overlapping circles, like the scales of a fish. His eyes were leaf green.

The other man was Magnus Bane. He didn't smile at Clary as he came to stand beside Luke. He wore a long, dark coat buttoned up to the throat, and his black hair was pulled back from his face.

"You look so *plain*," Clary said, staring.

Magnus smiled faintly. "I heard you had a rune to show us," was all he said.

Clary looked at Luke, who nodded. "Oh, yes," she said. "I just need something to write on—some paper."

"I *asked* you if you needed anything," Jocelyn said under her breath, sounding very much like the mother Clary remembered.

"I've got paper," said Simon, fishing something out of his jeans pocket. He handed it to her. It was a crumpled flyer for his band's performance at the Knitting Factory in July. She shrugged and flipped it over, raising her borrowed stele. It sparked slightly when she touched the tip to the paper, and she worried for a moment that the flyer might burn, but the tiny flame subsided. She set to drawing, doing her best to shut everything else out: the noise of the crowd, the feeling that everyone was staring at her.

The rune came out as it had before—a pattern of lines that curved strongly into one another, then stretched across the page as if expecting a completion that wasn't there. She brushed dust from the page and held it up, feeling absurdly as if she were in school and showing off some sort of presentation to her class. "This is the rune," she said. "It requires a second rune to complete it, to work properly. A—partner rune."

"One Downworlder, one Shadowhunter. Each half of the partnership has to be Marked," Luke said. He scribbled a copy of the rune on the bottom of the page, tore the paper in half, and handed one illustration to Amatis. "Start circulating the rune," he said. "Show the Nephilim how it works."

With a nod Amatis vanished down the steps and into the crowd. The faerie knight, glancing after her, shook his head. "I have always been told that only the Nephilim can bear the Angel's Marks," he said, with a measure of distrust. "That others of us will run mad, or die, should we wear them."

"This isn't one of the Angel's Marks," said Clary. "It's not from the Gray Book. It's safe, I promise."

The faerie knight looked unimpressed.

With a sigh Magnus flipped his sleeve back and reached a hand out to Clary. "Go ahead."

"I can't," she said. "The Shadowhunter who Marks you will be your partner, and I'm not fighting in the battle."

"I should hope not," said Magnus. He glanced over at Luke and Jocelyn, who were standing close together. "You two," he said. "Go on, then. Show the faerie how it works."

Jocelyn blinked in surprise. "What?"

"I assumed," Magnus said, "that you two would be partners, since you're practically married anyway."

Color flooded up into Jocelyn's face, and she carefully avoided looking at Luke. "I don't have a stele—"

"Take mine." Clary handed it over. "Go ahead, show them."

Jocelyn turned to Luke, who seemed entirely taken aback. He thrust out his hand before she could ask for it, and she Marked his palm with a hasty precision. His hand shook as she drew, and she took his wrist to steady it; Luke looked down at her as she worked, and Clary thought of their conversation about her mother and what he had told her about his feelings for Jocelyn, and she felt a pang of sadness. She wondered if her mother even knew that Luke loved her, and if she knew, what she would say.

"There." Jocelyn drew the stele back. "Done."

Luke raised his hand, palm out, and showed the swirling black mark in its center to the faerie knight. "Is that satisfactory, Meliorn?"

"*Meliorn?*" said Clary. "I've *met* you, haven't I? You used to go out with Isabelle Lightwood."

Meliorn was almost expressionless, but Clary could have sworn he looked ever so slightly uncomfortable. Luke shook his head. "Clary, Meliorn is a knight of the Seelie Court. It's very unlikely that he—"

"He was *totally* dating Isabelle," Simon said, "and she dumped him too. At least she said she was going to. Tough break, man."

Meliorn blinked at him. "You," he said with distaste, "*you* are the chosen representative of the Night Children?"

Simon shook his head. "No. I'm just here for her." He pointed at Clary.

"The Night Children," said Luke, after a brief hesitation, "aren't participating, Meliorn. I did convey that information to your Lady. They've chosen to—to go their own way."

Meliorn's delicate features drew down into a scowl. "Would that I had known that," he said. "The Night Children are a wise and careful people. Any scheme that draws their ire draws *my* suspicions."

"I didn't say anything about ire," Luke began, with a mixture of deliberate calm and faint exasperation—Clary doubted that anyone who didn't know him well would know he was irritated at all. She could sense the shift in his attention: He was looking down toward the crowd. Following his gaze, Clary saw a familiar figure cut a path across the room—Isabelle, her black hair swinging, her whip wrapped around her wrist like a series of golden bracelets.

Clary caught Simon's wrist. "The *Lightwoods*. I just saw Isabelle."

He glanced toward the crowd, frowning. "I didn't realize you were looking for them."

"Please go talk to her for me," she whispered, glancing over to see if anyone was paying attention to them; nobody was. Luke was gesturing toward someone in the crowd; meanwhile, Jocelyn was saying something to Meliorn, who was looking at her with something approaching alarm. "I have to stay here, but—please, I need you to tell her and Alec what my mother told me. About Jace and who he really is, and Sebastian. They have to know. Tell them to come and talk to me as soon as they can. Please, Simon."

"All right." Clearly worried by the intensity of her tone,

Simon freed his wrist from her grasp and touched her reassuringly on the cheek. "I'll be back."

He went down the steps and vanished into the throng; when she turned back, she saw that Magnus was looking at her, his mouth set in a crooked line. "It's fine," he said, obviously answering whatever question Luke had just asked him. "I'm familiar with Brocelind Plain. I'll set the Portal up in the square. I can't promise how long it will last, so you'd better get everyone through it pretty quickly once they're Marked."

As Luke nodded and turned to say something to Jocelyn, Clary leaned forward and said quietly, "Thanks, by the way. For everything you did for my mom."

Magnus's uneven smile broadened. "You didn't think I was going to do it, did you?"

"I wondered," Clary admitted. "Especially considering that when I saw you at the cottage, you didn't even see fit to tell me that Jace brought Simon through the Portal with him when he came to Alicante. I didn't have a chance to yell at you about that before, but *what* were you thinking? That I wouldn't be interested?"

"That you'd be too interested," said Magnus. "That you'd drop everything and go rushing off to the Gard. And I needed you to look for the Book of the White."

"That's ruthless," Clary said angrily. "And you're wrong. I would have—"

"Done what anyone would have done. What I would have done if it were someone *I* cared about. I don't blame you, Clary, and I didn't do it because I thought you were weak. I did it because you're human, and I know humanity's ways. I've been alive a long time."

"Like you never do anything stupid because you have feelings," Clary said. "Where's Alec, anyway? Why aren't you off choosing him as your partner right now?"

Magnus seemed to wince. "I wouldn't approach him with his parents there. You know that."

Clary propped her chin on her hand. "Doing the right thing because you love someone sucks sometimes."

"It does," Magnus said, "at that."

The raven flew in slow, lazy circles, making its way over the treetops toward the western wall of the valley. The moon was high, eliminating the need for witchlight as Jace followed, keeping to the edges of the trees.

The valley wall rose above, a sheer wall of gray rock. The raven's path seemed to be following the curve of the stream as it wended its way west, disappearing finally into a narrow fissure in the wall. Jace nearly twisted his ankle several times on wet rock and wished he could swear out loud, but Hugo would be sure to hear him. Bent into an uncomfortable half crouch, he concentrated on not breaking a leg instead.

His shirt was soaked with sweat by the time he reached the edge of the valley. For a moment he thought he'd lost sight of Hugo, and his heart fell—then he saw the black sinking shape as the raven swooped low and disappeared into the dark, fissured hole in the valley's rock wall. Jace ran forward—it was such a relief to run instead of crawl. As he neared the fissure, he could see a much larger, darker gap beyond it—a cove. Fumbling his witchlight stone out of his pocket, Jace dived in after the raven.

Only a little light seeped in through the cave's mouth, and after a few steps even that was swallowed up by the oppressive darkness. Jace raised his witchlight and let the illumination bleed out between his fingers.

At first he thought he'd somehow found his way outside again, and that the stars were visible overhead in all their glittering glory. The stars never shone anywhere else the way they shone in Idris—and they weren't shining now. The witchlight had picked out dozens of sparkling deposits of mica in the rock around him, and the walls had come alive with brilliant points of light.

They showed him that he was standing in a narrow space carved out of sheer rock, the cave entrance behind him, two branching dark tunnels ahead. Jace thought of the stories his father had told him about heroes lost in mazes who used rope or twine to find their way back. He didn't have either of those on him, though. He moved closer to the tunnels and stood silent for a long moment, listening. He heard the drip of water, faintly, from somewhere far away; the rush of the stream, a rustling like wings, and—voices.

He jerked back. The voices were coming from the left-hand tunnel, he was sure of it. He ran his thumb over the witchlight to dim it, until it was giving off a faint glow that was just enough to light his way. Then he plunged forward into the darkness.

"Are you serious, Simon? It's really true? That's fantastic! It's wonderful!" Isabelle reached out for her brother's hand. "Alec, did you hear what Simon said? Jace *isn't* Valentine's son. He never was."

"So whose son *is* he?" Alec replied, though Simon had the feeling that he was only partly paying attention. He seemed to be casting around the room for something. His parents stood a little distance away, frowning in their direction; Simon had been worried he'd have to explain the whole business to them, too, but they'd nicely allowed him a few minutes with Isabelle and Alec alone.

"Who cares!" Isabelle threw her hands up in delight, then frowned. "Actually, that's a good point. Who *was* his father? Michael Wayland after all?"

Simon shook his head. "Stephen Herondale."

"So he was the Inquisitor's grandson," Alec said. "*That* must be why she—" He broke off, staring into the distance.

"Why she *what*?" Isabelle demanded. "Alec, pay attention. Or at least tell us what you're looking for."

"Not what," said Alec. "Who. Magnus. I wanted to ask him if he'd be my partner in the battle. But I've no idea where he is. Have *you* seen him?" he asked, directing his question at Simon.

Simon shook his head. "He was up on the dais with Clary, but"—he craned his neck to look—"he's not now. He's probably in the crowd somewhere."

"Really? Are you going to ask him to be your partner?" Isabelle asked. "It's like a cotillion, this partners business, except with killing."

"So, exactly like a cotillion," said Simon.

"Maybe I'll ask you to be my partner, Simon," Isabelle said, raising an eyebrow delicately.

Alec frowned. He was, like the rest of the Shadowhunters in the room, entirely geared up—all in black, with a belt from which dangled multiple weapons. A bow was strapped across his back; Simon was happy to see he'd found a replacement for the one Sebastian had smashed. "Isabelle, you don't need a partner, because you're not fighting. You're too young. And if you even think about it, I'll kill you." His head jerked up. "Wait—is *that* Magnus?"

Isabelle, following his gaze, snorted. "Alec, that's a werewolf. A *girl* werewolf. In fact, it's what's-her-name. May."

"Maia," Simon corrected. She was standing a little ways away, wearing brown leather pants and a tight black T-shirt that said WHATEVER DOESN'T KILL ME . . . HAD BETTER START RUNNING. A cord held back her braided hair. She turned, as if sensing their eyes on her, and smiled. Simon smiled back. Isabelle glowered. Simon stopped smiling hastily—when exactly had his life gotten so complicated?

Alec's face lit up. "There's Magnus," he said, and took off without a backward glance, shearing a path through the crowd to the space where the tall warlock stood. Magnus's surprise as Alec approached him was visible, even from this distance.

"It's sort of sweet," said Isabelle, looking at them, "you know, in kind of a lame way."

"Why lame?"

"Because," Isabelle explained, "Alec's trying to get Magnus to take him seriously, but he's never told our parents about Magnus, or even that he likes, you know—"

"Warlocks?" Simon said.

"Very funny." Isabelle glared at him. "You know what I mean. What's going on here is—"

"What is going on, exactly?" asked Maia, striding into earshot. "I mean, I don't quite get this partners thing. How is it supposed to work?"

"Like that." Simon pointed toward Alec and Magnus, who stood a bit apart from the crowd, in their own small space. Alec was drawing on Magnus's hand, his face intent, his dark hair falling forward to hide his eyes.

"So we all have to do that?" Maia said. "Get drawn on, I mean."

"Only if you're going to fight," Isabelle said, looking at the other girl coldly. "You don't look eighteen yet."

Maia smiled tightly. "I'm not a Shadowhunter. Lycanthropes are considered adults at sixteen."

"Well, you have to get drawn on, then," said Isabelle. "By a Shadowhunter. So you'd better look for one."

"But—" Maia, still looking over at Alec and Magnus, broke off and raised her eyebrows. Simon turned to see what she was looking at—and stared.

Alec had his arms around Magnus and was kissing him, full on the mouth. Magnus, who appeared to be in a state of shock, stood frozen. Several groups of people—Shadowhunters and Downworlders alike—were staring and whispering. Glancing to the side, Simon saw the Lightwoods, their eyes wide, gaping at the display. Maryse had her hand over her mouth.

Maia looked perplexed. "Wait a second," she said. "Do we all have to do that, too?"

For the sixth time Clary scanned the crowd, looking for Simon. She couldn't find him. The room was a roiling mass of Shadowhunters and Downworlders, the crowd spilling through the open doors and onto the steps outside. Everywhere was the flash of steles as Downworlders and Shadowhunters came together in pairs and Marked each other. Clary saw Maryse Lightwood holding out her hand to a tall green-skinned faerie woman who was just as pale and regal as she was. Patrick Penhallow was solemnly exchanging Marks with a warlock whose hair shone with blue sparks. Through the Hall doors Clary could see the bright glimmer of the Portal in the square. The starlight shining down through the glass skylight lent a surreal air to all of it.

"Amazing, isn't it?" Luke said. He stood at the edge of the dais, looking down over the room. "Shadowhunters and Downworlders, mingling together in the same room. Working together." He sounded awed. All Clary could think was that she wished Jace were here to see what was happening. She couldn't put aside her fear for him, no matter how hard she tried. The idea that he might face down Valentine, might risk his life because he thought he was cursed—that he might die without ever knowing it wasn't true—

"Clary," Jocelyn said, with a trace of amusement, "did you hear what I said?"

"I did," said Clary, "and it *is* amazing, I know."

Jocelyn put her hand on top of Clary's. "That's not what I was saying. Luke and I will both be fighting. I know you know that. You'll be staying here with Isabelle and the other children."

"I'm not a child."

"I know you're not, but you're too young to fight. And even if you weren't, you've never been trained."

"I don't want to just sit here and do nothing."

"Nothing?" Jocelyn said in amazement. "Clary, none of this would be happening if it wasn't for you. We wouldn't even have a chance to fight if it wasn't for you. I'm so proud of you. I just wanted to tell you that even though Luke and I will be gone, we'll be coming back. Everything's going to be fine."

Clary looked up at her mother, into the green eyes so like her own. "Mom," she said. "Don't lie."

Jocelyn took a sharp breath and stood up, drawing her hand back. Before she could say anything, something caught Clary's eye—a familiar face in the crowd. A slim, dark figure, moving purposely toward them, slipping through the thronged Hall with deliberate and surprising ease—as if he could drift *through* the crowd, like smoke through the gaps in a fence.

And he *was*, Clary realized, as he neared the dais. It was Raphael, dressed in the same white shirt and black pants she'd first seen him in. She had forgotten how slight he was. He looked barely fourteen as he climbed the stairs, his thin face calm and angelic, like a choirboy mounting the steps to the chancel.

"Raphael." Luke's voice held amazement, mixed with relief. "I didn't think you were coming. Have the Night Children reconsidered joining us in fighting Valentine? There's still a Council seat open for you, if you'd like to take it." He held a hand out to Raphael.

Raphael's clear and lovely eyes regarded him expressionlessly. "I cannot shake hands with you, werewolf." When Luke looked offended, he smiled, just enough to show the white tips of his fang teeth. "I am a Projection," he said, raising his hand so that they could all see how the light shone through it. "I can touch nothing."

"But—" Luke glanced up at the moonlight pouring through the roof. "Why—" He lowered his hand. "Well, I'm glad you're here. However you choose to appear."

Raphael shook his head. For a moment his eyes lingered on Clary—a look she really didn't like—and then he turned his gaze to Jocelyn, and his smile widened. "You," he said, "Valentine's wife. Others of my kind, who fought with you at the Uprising, told me of you. I admit I never thought I would see you myself."

Jocelyn inclined her head. "Many of the Night Children fought very bravely then. Does your presence here indicate that we might fight alongside each other once again?"

It was odd, Clary thought, to hear her mother speak in that cool and formal way, and yet it seemed natural to Jocelyn. As natural in its way as sitting on the ground in ancient overalls, holding a paint-splattered brush.

"I hope so," Raphael said, and his gaze brushed Clary again, like the touch of a cold hand. "We have only one requirement, one simple—and small—request. If that is honored, the Night Children of many lands will happily go to battle at your side."

"The Council seat," said Luke. "Of course—it can be formalized, the documents drawn up within the hour—"

"Not," said Raphael, "the Council seat. Something else."

"Something—else?" Luke echoed blankly. "What is it? I assure you, if it's in our power—"

"Oh, it is." Raphael's smile was blinding. "In fact, it is something that is within the walls of this Hall as we speak." He turned and gestured gracefully toward the crowd. "It is the boy Simon that we want," he said. "It is the Daylighter."

The tunnel was long and twisting, switchbacking on itself over and over as if Jace were crawling through the entrails of an enormous monster. It smelled like wet rock and ashes and something else, something dank and odd that reminded Jace ever so slightly of the smell of the Bone City.

At last the tunnel opened out into a circular chamber. Huge stalactites, their surfaces as burnished as gems, hung down from a ridged, stony ceiling high above. The floor was as smooth as if it had been polished, alternating here and there with arcane patterns of gleaming inlaid stone. A series of rough stalagmites circled the chamber. In the very center of the room stood a single massive quartz stalagmite, rearing up from the floor like a gigantic fang, patterned here and there with a reddish design. Peering closer, Jace saw that the sides of the stalagmite were transparent, the reddish pattern the result of something swirling and moving *inside* it, like a glass test tube full of colored smoke.

High above, light filtered down from a circular hole in the stone, a natural skylight. The chamber had certainly been a product of design rather than accident—the intricate patterns tracing the floor made that much obvious—but who would have hollowed out such an enormous underground chamber, and why?

A sharp caw echoed through the room, sending a shock through Jace's nerves. He ducked behind a bulky stalagmite, dousing his witchlight, just as two figures emerged from the shadows at the far end of the room and moved toward him, their heads bent together in conversation. It was only when they reached the center of the room and the light struck them that he recognized them.

Sebastian.

And Valentine.

Hoping to avoid the crowd, Simon took the long way back toward the dais, ducking behind the rows of pillars that lined the sides of the Hall. He kept his head down as he went, lost in thought. It seemed strange that Alec, only a year or two older than Isabelle, was heading off to fight in a war, and the rest of them were going to stay behind. And Isabelle seemed calm about it. No crying, no hysterics. It was as if she'd expected it. Maybe she had. Maybe they all had.

He was close to the dais steps when he glanced up and saw, to his surprise, Raphael standing across from Luke, looking his usual near-expressionless self. Luke, on the other hand, looked agitated—he was shaking his head, his hands up in protest, and Jocelyn, beside him, looked outraged. Simon couldn't see Clary's face—her back was to him—but he knew her well enough to recognize her tension just from the set of her shoulders.

Not wanting Raphael to see him, Simon ducked behind a pillar, listening. Even over the babble of the crowd, he was able to hear Luke's rising voice.

"It's out of the question," Luke was saying. "I can't believe you'd even ask."

"And I can't believe you would refuse." Raphael's voice was cool and clear, the sharp, still-high voice of a young boy. "It is such a small thing."

"It's not a *thing*." Clary sounded angry. "It's Simon. He's a *person*."

"He's a vampire," said Raphael. "Which you seem to keep forgetting."

"Aren't you a vampire as well?" asked Jocelyn, her tone as freezing as it had been every time Clary and Simon had ever gotten in trouble for doing something stupid. "Are you saying *your* life has no worth?"

Simon pressed himself back against the pillar. What was going on?

"My life has great worth," said Raphael, "being, unlike yours, eternal. There is no end to what I might accomplish, while there is a clear end where you are concerned. But that is not the issue. He is a vampire, one of my own, and I am asking for him back."

"You can't have him *back*," Clary snapped. "You never had him in the first place. You were never even interested in him either, till you found out he could walk around in daylight—"

"Possibly," said Raphael, "but not for the reason you think." He cocked his head, his bright, soft eyes dark and darting as a bird's. "No vampire should have the power he has," he said, "just as no Shadowhunter should have the power that you and your brother do. For years we have been told that we are wrong and unnatural. But this—*this* is unnatural."

"Raphael." Luke's tone was warning. "I don't know what you were hoping for. But there's no chance we'll let you hurt Simon."

"But you will let Valentine and his army of demons hurt all these people, your allies." Raphael made a sweeping gesture that encompassed the room. "You will let them risk their lives at their own discretion but won't give Simon the same choice? Perhaps he would make a different one than you will." He lowered his arm. "You know we will not fight with you otherwise. The Night Children will have no part in this day."

"Then have no part in it," said Luke. "I won't buy your cooperation with an innocent life. I'm not Valentine."

Raphael turned to Jocelyn. "What about you, Shadowhunter? Are you going to let this werewolf decide what's best for your people?"

Jocelyn was looking at Raphael as if he were a roach she'd found crawling across her clean kitchen floor. Very slowly she said, "If you lay one hand on Simon, vampire, I'll have you chopped up into tiny pieces and fed to my cat. Understand?"

Raphael's mouth tightened. "Very well," he said. "When you lie dying on Brocelind Plain, you may ask yourself whether one life was truly worth so many."

He vanished. Luke turned quickly to Clary, but Simon was no longer watching them: He was looking down at his hands. He had thought they would be shaking, but they were as motionless as a corpse's. Very slowly, he closed them into fists.

Valentine looked as he always had, a big man in modified Shadowhunter gear, his broad, thick shoulders at odds with his sharply planed, fine-featured face. He had the Mortal Sword strapped across his back along with a bulky satchel. He wore a wide belt with numerous weapons thrust through it: thick hunting daggers, narrow dirks, and skinning knives. Staring at Valentine from behind the rock, Jace felt as he always did now when he thought of his father—a persistent familial affection corroded through with bleakness, disappointment, and mistrust.

It was strange seeing his father with Sebastian, who looked—different. He wore gear as well, and a long silver-hilted sword strapped at his waist, but it wasn't what he was wearing that struck Jace as odd. It was his hair, no longer a cap of dark curls but fair, shining-fair, a sort of white gold. It suited him, actually, better than the dark hair had; his skin no longer looked so startlingly pale. He must have dyed his hair to resemble the real Sebastian Verlac, and this was what he really looked like. A sour, roiling wave of hatred coursed through Jace, and it was all he could do to stay hidden behind the rock and not lunge forward to wrap his hands around Sebastian's throat.

Hugo cawed again and swooped down to land on Valentine's shoulder. An odd pang went through Jace, seeing the raven in the posture that had become so familiar to him over the years he'd known Hodge. Hugo had practically lived on the tutor's shoulder, and seeing him on Valentine's felt oddly foreign, even wrong, despite everything Hodge had done.

Valentine reached up and stroked the bird's glossy feathers, nodding as if the two of them were deep in conversation. Sebastian watched, his pale eyebrows arched. "Any word from Alicante?" he said as Hugo lifted himself from Valentine's shoulder and soared into the air again, his wings brushing the gemlike tips of the stalactites.

"Nothing as comprehensible as I would like," Valentine said. The sound of his father's voice, cool and unruffled as ever, went through Jace like an arrow. His hands twitched involuntarily and he pressed them hard against his sides, grateful for the bulk of the rock hiding him from view. "One thing is certain. The Clave is allying itself with Lucian's force of Downworlders."

Sebastian frowned. "But Malachi said—"

"Malachi has failed." Valentine's jaw was set.

To Jace's surprise Sebastian moved forward and put a hand on Valentine's arm. There was something about that touch—something intimate and confident—that made Jace's stomach feel as if it had been invaded by a nest of worms. No one touched Valentine like that. Even he would not have touched his father like that. "Are you upset?" Sebastian asked, and the same tone was in his voice, the same grotesque and peculiar assumption of closeness.

"The Clave is further gone than I had thought. I knew the Lightwoods were corrupted beyond hope, and that sort of corruption is contagious. It's why I tried to keep them from entering Idris. But for the rest to have so easily had their minds filled with Lucian's poison, when he is not even Nephilim . . ." Valentine's disgust was plain, but he didn't move away from Sebastian, Jace saw with growing disbelief, didn't move to brush the boy's hand from his shoulder. "I am disappointed. I thought they would see reason. I would have preferred not to end things this way."

Sebastian looked amused. "*I* don't agree," he said. "Think of them, ready to do battle, riding out to glory, only to find that none of it matters. That their gesture is futile. Think of the looks on their faces." His mouth stretched into a grin.

"Jonathan." Valentine sighed. "This is ugly necessity, nothing to take delight in."

Jonathan? Jace clutched at the rock, his hands suddenly slippery. Why would Valentine call Sebastian by *his* name? Was it a mistake? But Sebastian didn't look surprised.

"Isn't it better if I enjoy what I'm doing?" Sebastian said. "I certainly enjoyed myself in Alicante. The Lightwoods were better company than you led me to believe, especially that Isabelle. We certainly parted on a high note. And as for Clary—"

Just hearing Sebastian say Clary's name made Jace's heart skip a sudden, painful beat.

"She wasn't at all like I thought she'd be," Sebastian went on petulantly. "She wasn't anything like me."

"There is no one else in the world like you, Jonathan. And as for Clary, she has always been exactly like her mother."

"She won't admit what she really wants," Sebastian said. "Not yet. But she'll come around."

Valentine raised an eyebrow. "What do you mean, come around?"

Sebastian grinned, a grin that filled Jace with an almost uncontrollable rage. He bit down hard on his lip, tasting blood. "Oh, you know," Sebastian said. "To our side. I can't wait. Tricking her was the most fun I've had in ages."

"You weren't supposed to be having fun. You were supposed to be finding out what it was she was looking for. And when she did find it—without you, I might add—you let her give it to a warlock. And then you failed to bring her with you when you left, despite the threat she poses to us. Not exactly a glorious success, Jonathan."

"I *tried* to bring her. They wouldn't let her out of their sight, and I couldn't exactly kidnap her in the middle of the Accords Hall." Sebastian sounded sulky. "Besides, I told you, she doesn't have any idea how to use that rune power of hers. She's too naive to pose any danger—"

"Whatever the Clave is planning now, she's at the center of it," Valentine said. "Hugin says as much. He saw her there on the dais in the Accords Hall. If she can show the Clave her power . . ."

Jace felt a flash of fear for Clary, mixed with an odd sort of pride—of course she was at the center of things. That was his Clary.

"Then they'll fight," said Sebastian. "Which is what we want, isn't it? Clary doesn't matter. It's the battle that matters."

"You underestimate her, I think," Valentine said quietly.

"I was watching her," said Sebastian. "If her power was as unlimited as you seem to think, she could have used it to get her little vampire friend out of his prison—or save that fool Hodge when he was dying—"

"Power doesn't have to be unlimited to be deadly," Valentine said. "And as for Hodge, perhaps you might show a bit more reserve regarding his death, since you're the one who killed him."

"He was about to tell them about the Angel. I *had* to."

"You *wanted* to. You always do." Valentine took a pair of heavy leather gloves from his pocket and drew them on slowly. "Perhaps he would have told them. Perhaps not. All those years he looked after Jace in the Institute and must have wondered what it was he was raising. Hodge was one of the few who knew there was more than one boy. I knew he wouldn't betray me—he was too much of a coward for that." He flexed his fingers inside the gloves, frowning.

More than one boy? What was Valentine talking about?

Sebastian dismissed Hodge with a wave of his hand. "Who cares what he thought? He's dead, and good riddance." His eyes gleamed blackly. "Are you going to the lake now?"

"Yes. You're clear on what must be done?" Valentine jerked his chin toward the sword at Sebastian's waist. "Use that. It's not the Mortal Sword, but its alliance is sufficiently demonic for this purpose."

"I can't go to the lake with you?" Sebastian's voice had taken on a distinct whining tone. "Can't we just release the army now?"

"It's not midnight yet. I said I would give them until midnight. They may yet change their minds."

"They're not going to—"

"I gave my word. I'll stand by it." Valentine's tone was final. "If you hear nothing from Malachi by midnight, open the gate." Seeing Sebastian's hesitation, Valentine looked impatient. "I need you to do this, Jonathan. I can't wait here for midnight; it'll take me nearly an hour to get to the lake through the tunnels, and I have no intention of letting the battle drag on very long. Future generations must know how quickly the Clave lost, and how decisive our victory was."

"It's just that I'll be sorry to miss the summoning. I'd like to be there when you do it." Sebastian's look was wistful, but there was something calculated beneath it, something sneering and grasping and planning and strangely, deliberately . . . *cold*. Not that Valentine seemed bothered.

To Jace's bafflement, Valentine touched the side of Sebastian's face, a quick, undisguisedly affectionate gesture, before turning away and moving toward the far end of the cavern, where thick clots of shadows gathered. He paused there, a pale figure against the darkness. "Jonathan," he called back, and Jace glanced up, unable to help himself. "You will look upon the Angel's face someday. After all, you will inherit the Mortal Instruments once I am gone. Perhaps one day you, too, will summon Raziel."

"I'd like that," Sebastian said, and stood very still as Valentine, with a final nod, disappeared into the darkness. Sebastian's voice dropped to a half whisper. "I'd like it very much," he snarled. "I'd like to spit in his bastard face." He whirled, his face a white mask in the dim light. "You might as well come out, Jace," he said. "I know you're here."

Jace froze—but only for a second. His body moved before his mind had time to catch up, catapulting him to his feet. He ran for the tunnel entrance, thinking only of making it outside, of getting a message, somehow, to Luke.

But the entrance was blocked. Sebastian stood there, his expression cool and gloating, his arms outstretched, his fingers almost touching the tunnel walls. "Really," he said, "you didn't actually think you were faster than me, did you?"

Jace skidded to a halt. His heart beat unevenly in his chest, like a broken metronome, but his voice was steady. "Since I'm better than you in every other conceivable way, it did stand to reason."

Sebastian just smiled. "I could hear your heart beating," he said softly. "When you were watching me with Valentine. Did it bother you?"

"That you seem to be dating my dad?" Jace shrugged. "You're a little young for him, to be honest."

"*What?*" For the first time since Jace had met him, Sebastian seemed flabbergasted. Jace was able to enjoy it for only a moment, though, before Sebastian's composure returned. But there was a dark glint in his eye that indicated he hadn't forgiven Jace for making him lose his calm. "I wondered about you sometimes," Sebastian went on, in the same soft voice. "There seemed to be something to you, on occasion, something behind those yellow eyes of yours. A flash of intelligence, unlike the rest of your mud-stupid adoptive family. But I suppose it was only a pose, an attitude. You're as foolish as the rest, despite your decade of good upbringing."

"What do you know about my upbringing?"

"More than you might think." Sebastian lowered his hands. "The same man who brought you up, brought me up. Only he didn't tire of me after the first ten years."

"What do you mean?" Jace's voice came out in a whisper, and then, as he stared at Sebastian's unmoving, unsmiling face, he seemed to see the other boy as if for the first time—the white hair, the black anthracite eyes, the hard lines of his face, like something chiseled out of stone—and he saw in his mind the face of his father as the angel had showed it to him, young and sharp and alert and hungry, and he *knew*. "You," he said. "Valentine's your father. You're my *brother*."

But Sebastian was no longer standing in front of him; he was suddenly behind him, and his arms were around Jace's shoulders as if he meant to embrace him, but his hands were clenched into fists. "Hail and farewell, my brother," he spat, and then his arms jerked up and tightened, cutting off Jace's breath.

Clary was exhausted. A dull, pounding headache, the aftereffect of drawing the Alliance rune, had taken up residence in her frontal lobe. It felt like someone trying to kick a door down from the wrong side.

"Are you all right?" Jocelyn put her hand on Clary's shoulder. "You look like you aren't feeling well."

Clary glanced down—and saw the spidering black rune that crossed the back of her mother's hand, the twin of the one on Luke's palm. Her stomach tightened. She was managing to deal with the fact that within a few hours her mother might actually be *fighting an army of demons*—but only by willfully pushing down the thought every time it surfaced.

"I'm just wondering where Simon is." Clary rose to her feet. "I'm going to go get him."

"Down there?" Jocelyn gazed worriedly down at the crowd. It was thinning out now, Clary noted, as those who had been Marked flooded out the front doors into the square outside. Malachi stood by the doors, his bronze face impassive as he directed Downworlders and Shadowhunters where to go.

"I'll be fine." Clary edged past her mother and Luke toward the dais steps. "I'll be right back."

People turned to stare as she descended the steps and slipped into the crowd. She could feel the eyes on her, the *weight* of the staring. She scanned the crowd, looking for the

Lightwoods or Simon, but saw nobody she knew—and it was hard enough seeing anything over the throng, considering how short she was. With a sigh Clary slipped away toward the west side of the Hall, where the crowd was thinner.

The moment she neared the tall line of marble pillars, a hand shot out from between two of them and pulled her sideways. Clary had time to gasp in surprise, and then she was standing in the darkness behind the largest of the pillars, her back against the cold marble wall, Simon's hands gripping her arms. "*Don't* scream, okay? It's just me," he said.

"Of course I'm not going to scream. Don't be ridiculous." Clary glanced from side to side, wondering what was going on—she could see only bits and pieces of the larger Hall, in between the pillars. "But what's with the James Bond spy stuff? I was coming to find you anyway."

"I know. I've been waiting for you to come down off the dais. I wanted to talk to you where no one else could hear us." He licked his lips nervously. "I heard what Raphael said. What he wanted."

"Oh, Simon." Clary's shoulders sagged. "Look, nothing happened. Luke sent him away—"

"Maybe he shouldn't have," Simon said. "Maybe he should have given Raphael what he wanted."

She blinked at him. "You mean *you*? Don't be stupid. There's no way—"

"There is a way." His grip on her arms tightened. "I want to do this. I want Luke to tell Raphael that the deal is on. Or I'll tell him myself."

"I know what you're doing," Clary protested. "And I respect it and I admire you for it, but you don't have to do it, Simon, you don't have to. What Raphael's asking for is wrong, and nobody will judge you for not sacrificing yourself for a war that isn't yours to fight—"

"But that's just it," Simon said. "What Raphael said was right. I *am* a vampire, and you keep forgetting it. Or maybe you just want to forget. But I'm a Downworlder and you're a Shadowhunter, and this fight is both of ours."

"But you're not like them—"

"I am one of them." He spoke slowly, deliberately, as if to make absolutely sure that she understood every word he was saying. "And I always will be. If the Downworlders fight this war with the Shadowhunters, without the participation of Raphael's people, then there will be no Council seat for the Night Children. They won't be a part of the world Luke's trying to create, a world where Shadowhunters and Downworlders work together. Are together. The vampires will be shut out of that. They'll be the enemies of the Shadowhunters. I'll be *your* enemy."

"I could never be your enemy."

"It would kill me," Simon said simply. "But I can't help anything by standing back and pretending I'm not part of this. And I'm not asking your permission. I would like your help. But if you won't give it to me, I'll get Maia to take me to the vampire camp anyway, and I'll give myself up to Raphael. Do you understand?"

She stared at him. He was holding her arms so tightly she could feel the blood beating in the skin under his hands. She ran her tongue over her dry lips; her mouth tasted bitter. "What can I do," she whispered, "to help you?"

She looked up at him incredulously as he told her. She was already shaking her head before he finished, her hair whipping back and forth, nearly covering her eyes. "No," she said, "that's a crazy idea, Simon. It's not a gift; it's a *punishment*—"

"Maybe not for me," Simon said. He glanced toward the crowd, and Clary saw Maia standing there, watching them, her expression openly curious. She was clearly waiting for Simon. *Too fast*, Clary thought. *This is all happening much too fast.*

"It's better than the alternative, Clary."

"No . . ."

"It might not hurt me at all. I mean, I've *already* been punished, right? I already can't go into a church, a synagogue, I can't say—I can't say holy names, I can't get older, I'm already shut out from normal life. Maybe this won't change anything."

"But maybe it will."

He let go of her arms, slid his hand around her side, and drew Patrick's stele from her belt. He held it out to her. "Clary," he said. "Do this for me. Please."

She took the stele with numb fingers and raised it, touching the end of it to Simon's skin, just above his eyes. *The first Mark*, Magnus had said. The very first. She thought of it, and her stele began to move the way a dancer begins to move when the music starts. Black lines traced themselves across his forehead like a flower unfolding on a speeded-up roll of film. When she was done, her right hand ached and stung, but as she drew back and stared, she knew she had drawn something perfect and strange and ancient, something from the very beginning of history. It blazed like a star above Simon's eyes as he brushed his fingers across his forehead, his expression dazzled and confused.

"I can feel it," he said. "Like a burn."

"I don't know what'll happen," she whispered. "I don't know what long-term side effects it'll have."

With a twisted half smile, he raised his hand to touch her cheek. "Let's hope we get the chance to find out."

19

Peniel

Maia was silent most of the way to the forest, keeping her head down and glancing from side to side only occasionally, her nose wrinkled in concentration. Simon wondered if she was *smelling* their way, and he decided that although that might be a little weird, it certainly counted as a useful talent. He also found that he didn't have to hurry to keep up with her, no matter how fast she moved. Even when they reached the beaten-down path that led into the forest and Maia started to run—swiftly, quietly, and staying low to the ground—he had no trouble matching her pace. It was one thing about being a vampire that he could honestly say he enjoyed.

It was over too soon; the woods thickened and they were running among the trees, over scuffed, thick-rooted ground dense with fallen leaves. The branches overhead made lace-like patterns against the starlit sky. They emerged from the trees in a clearing strewn with large boulders that gleamed like square white teeth. There were heaped piles of leaves here and there, as if someone had been over the place with a gigantic rake.

"Raphael!" Maia had cupped her hands around her mouth and was calling out in a voice loud enough to startle the birds out of the treetops high overhead. "Raphael, show yourself!"

Silence. Then the shadows rustled; there was a soft pattering sound, like rain hitting a tin roof. The piled leaves on the ground blew up into the air in tiny cyclones. Simon heard Maia cough; she had her hands up, as if to brush the leaves away from her face, her eyes.

As suddenly as the wind had come up, it settled. Raphael stood there, only a few feet from Simon. Surrounding him was a group of vampires, pale and still as trees in the moonlight. Their expressions were cold, stripped down to a bare hostility. He recognized some of them from the Hotel Dumort: the petite Lily and the blond Jacob, his eyes as narrow as knives. But just as many of them he had never seen before.

Raphael stepped forward. His skin was sallow, his eyes ringed with black shadow, but he smiled when he saw Simon.

"Daylighter," he breathed. "You came."

"I came," Simon said. "I'm here, so—it's done."

"It's far from done, Daylighter." Raphael looked toward Maia. "Lycanthrope," he said. "Return to your pack leader and thank him for changing his mind. Tell him that the Night Children will fight beside his people on Brocelind Plain."

Maia's face was tight. "Luke didn't change—"

Simon interrupted her hastily. "It's fine, Maia. Go."

Her eyes were luminous and sad. "Simon, think," she said. "You don't have to do this."

"Yes, I do." His tone was firm. "Maia, thank you so much for bringing me here. Now go."

"Simon—"

He dropped his voice. "If you *don't* go, they'll kill us both, and all this will have been for nothing. Go. Please."

She nodded and turned away, Changing as she turned, so that one moment she was a human girl, her bead-tied braids bouncing on her shoulders, and the next she had hit the ground running on all fours, a swift and silent wolf. She darted from the clearing and vanished into the shadows.

Simon turned back to the vampires—and almost shouted out loud; Raphael was standing directly in front of him, inches away. Up close his skin bore the telltale dark traceries of hunger. Simon thought of that night in the Hotel Dumort—faces appearing out of shadow, fleeting laughter, the smell of blood—and shivered.

Raphael reached out to Simon and took hold of his shoulders, the grip of his deceptively slight hands like iron. "Turn your head," he said, "and look at the stars; it will be easier that way."

"So you *are* going to kill me," Simon said. To his surprise he didn't feel afraid, or even particularly agitated; everything seemed to have slowed down to a perfect clarity. He was simultaneously aware of every leaf on the branches above him, every tiny pebble on the ground, every pair of eyes that rested on him.

"What did you think?" Raphael said—a little sadly, Simon

thought. "It's not personal, I assure you. It's as I said before—you are too dangerous to be allowed to continue as you are. If I had known what you'd become—"

"You'd never have let me crawl out of that grave. I know," said Simon.

Raphael met his eyes. "Everyone does what they must to survive. In that way even we are just like humans." His needle teeth slid from their sheaths like delicate razors. "Hold still," he said. "This will be quick." He leaned forward.

"Wait," Simon said, and when Raphael drew back with a scowl, he said it again, with more force: "Wait. There's something I have to show you."

Raphael made a low hissing sound. "You had better be doing more than trying to delay me, Daylighter."

"I am. There's something I thought you should see." Simon reached up and brushed the hair back from his forehead. It felt like a foolish, even theatrical, gesture, but as he did it, he saw Clary's desperate white face as she stared up at him, the stele in her hand, and thought, *Well, for her sake, at least I've* tried.

The effect on Raphael was both startling and instantaneous. He jerked back as if Simon had brandished a crucifix at him, his eyes widening. "Daylighter," he spat, "who did this to you?"

Simon only stared. He wasn't sure what reaction he'd expected, but it hadn't been this one.

"Clary," Raphael said, answering his own inquiry, "of course. Only a power like hers would allow this—a vampire, Marked, and with a Mark like that one—"

"A Mark like *what?*" said Jacob, the slender blond boy standing just behind Raphael. The rest of the vampires were staring as well, with expressions that mingled confusion and a growing fear. Anything that frightened Raphael, Simon thought, was sure to frighten them, too.

"This Mark," Raphael said, still looking only at Simon, "is not one of those from the Gray Book. It is an even older Mark than that. One of the ancients, drawn by the Maker's own hand." He made as if to touch Simon's forehead but didn't seem quite able to bring himself to do it; his hand hovered for a moment, then fell to his side. "Such Marks are mentioned, but I have never seen one. And this one . . ."

Simon said, "'Therefore whosoever slayeth Cain, vengeance shall be taken on him sevenfold. And the Lord set a Mark upon Cain, lest any finding him should kill him.' You can *try* to kill me, Raphael. But I wouldn't advise it."

"The Mark of Cain?" Jacob said in disbelief. "This Mark on you is the Mark of *Cain*?"

"Kill him," said a redheaded female vampire who stood close to Jacob. She spoke with a heavy accent—Russian, Simon thought, though he wasn't sure. "Kill him anyway."

Raphael's expression was a mix of fury and disbelief. "I will not," he said. "Any harm done to him will rebound upon the doer sevenfold. That is the nature of the Mark. Of course, if any of you would like to be the one to take that risk, by all means, be my guest."

No one spoke or moved.

"I thought not," said Raphael. His eyes raked Simon. "Like the evil queen in the fairy tale, Lucian Graymark has sent me a poisoned apple. I suppose he hoped I *would* harm you, and reap the punishment that would follow."

"No," Simon said hastily. "No—Luke didn't even know

what I'd done. His gesture was made in good faith. You have to honor it."

"And so you *chose* this?" For the first time there was something other than contempt, Simon thought, in the way Raphael was looking at him. "This is no simple protection spell, Daylighter. Do you know what Cain's punishment was?" He spoke softly, as if sharing a secret with Simon. "*And now thou art cursed from the earth. A fugitive and a wanderer shalt thou be.*"

"Then," Simon said, "I'll wander, if that's what it comes to. I'll do what I have to do."

"All this," said Raphael, "all this for Nephilim."

"Not just for Nephilim," said Simon. "I'm doing this for you, too. Even if you don't want it." He raised his voice so that the silent vampires surrounding them could hear him. "You were worried that if other vampires knew what had happened to me, they'd think Shadowhunter blood could let them walk in the daylight too. But that's not why I have this power. It was something Valentine did. An experiment. He caused this, not Jace. And it isn't replicable. It won't ever happen again."

"I imagine he is telling the truth," said Jacob, to Simon's surprise. "I've certainly known one or two of the Night Children who've had a taste of Shadowhunter in the past. None of them developed a fondness for sunlight."

"It was one thing to refuse to help the Shadowhunters before," said Simon, turning back to Raphael, "but now, now that they've sent me to you—" He let the rest of the sentence hang in the air, unfinished.

"Don't try to blackmail me, Daylighter," said Raphael. "Once the Night Children have made a bargain, they honor it, no matter how badly they are dealt with." He smiled slightly, needle teeth gleaming in the dark. "There is just one thing," he said. "One last act I require from you to prove that indeed you acted here in *good faith*." The stress he put on the last two words was weighted with cold.

"What's that?" Simon asked.

"We will not be the only vampires to fight in Lucian Graymark's battle," Raphael said. "So will you."

Jace opened his eyes on a silver whirlpool. His mouth was filled with bitter liquid. He coughed, wondering for a moment if he was drowning—but if so, it was on dry land. He was sitting upright with his back against a stalagmite, and his hands were bound behind him. He coughed again and salt filled his mouth. He wasn't drowning, he realized, just choking on blood.

"Awake, little brother?" Sebastian knelt in front of him, a length of rope in his hands, his grin like an unsheathed knife. "Good. I was afraid for a moment that I'd killed you a bit too early."

Jace turned his head to the side and spat a mouthful of blood onto the ground. His head felt as if a balloon were being inflated inside it, pressing against the interior of his skull. The silvery whirling above his head slowed and stilled to the bright pattern of stars visible through the hole in the cave roof. "Waiting for a special occasion to kill me? Christmas is coming."

Sebastian gave Jace a thoughtful look. "You have a smart mouth. You didn't learn that from Valentine. What *did* you learn from him? It doesn't seem to me that he taught you much about fighting, either." He leaned closer. "You know what he gave me for my ninth birthday? A lesson. He taught me that there's a place on a man's back where, if you sink a blade in, you can pierce his heart and sever his spine, all at once. What did *you* get for your ninth birthday, little angel boy? A cookie?"

Ninth birthday? Jace swallowed hard. "So tell me, what hole was he keeping *you* in while I was growing up? Because I don't remember seeing you around the manor."

"I grew up in this valley." Sebastian jerked his chin toward the cave exit. "I don't remember seeing you around here either, come to think of it. Although I knew about you. I bet you didn't know about me."

Jace shook his head. "Valentine wasn't much given to bragging about you. I can't imagine why."

Sebastian's eyes flashed. It was easy to see, now, the resemblance to Valentine: the same unusual combination of silver-white hair and black eyes, the same fine bones that in another, less strongly molded face would have looked delicate. "I knew all about you," he said. "But you don't know anything, do you?" Sebastian got to his feet. "I wanted you alive to watch this, little brother," he said. "So watch, and watch carefully." With a movement so fast it was almost invisible, he drew the sword from its sheath at his waist. It had a silver hilt, and like the Mortal Sword it glowed with a dull dark light. A pattern of stars was etched into the surface of the black blade; it caught the true starlight as Sebastian turned the blade, and burned like fire.

Jace held his breath. He wondered if Sebastian merely meant to kill him; but no, Sebastian would have killed him already, while he was unconscious, if that were his intention. Jace watched as Sebastian moved toward the center of the chamber, the sword held lightly in his hand, though it looked to be quite heavy. His mind was whirling. How could Valentine have another son? Who was his mother? Someone else in the Circle? Was he older or younger than Jace?

Sebastian had reached the huge red-tinged stalagmite in the center of the room. It seemed to pulse as he approached, and the smoke inside it swirled faster. Sebastian half-closed his eyes and lifted the blade. He said something—a word in a harsh-sounding demon language—and brought the sword across, hard and fast, in a slicing arc.

The top of the stalagmite sheared away. Inside, it was hollow as a test tube, filled with a mass of black and red smoke, which swirled upward like gas escaping a punctured balloon. There was a roar—less a sound than a sort of explosive pressure. Jace felt his ears pop. It was suddenly hard to breathe. He wanted to claw at the neck of his shirt, but he couldn't move his hands: They were tied too tightly behind him.

Sebastian was half-hidden behind the pouring column of red and black. It was coiling, swirling upward— "Watch!" he cried, his face glowing. His eyes were alight, his white hair whipping on the rising wind, and Jace wondered if his father had looked like that when he was young: terrible and yet somehow fascinating. "Watch and behold Valentine's army!"

His voice was drowned out then by the sound. It was a sound like the tide crashing up the shore, the breaking of an enormous wave, carrying massive detritus with it, the smashed bones of whole cities, the onrush of a great and evil power. A huge column of twisting, rushing, flapping blackness poured from the smashed stalagmite, funneling up through the air, pouring toward—and through—the torn gap in the cavern roof. *Demons.* They rose shrieking, howling, and snarling, a boiling mass of claws and talons and teeth and burning eyes. Jace recalled lying on the deck of Valentine's ship as the sky and earth and sea all around turned to nightmare; this was worse. It was as if the earth had torn open and hell had poured through. The demons carried a stench like a thousand rotting corpses. Jace's hands twisted against each other, twisted until the ropes cut into his wrists and they bled. A sour taste rose in his mouth, and he choked helplessly on blood and bile as the last of the demons rose and vanished overhead, a dark flood of horror, blotting out the stars.

Jace thought he might have passed out for a minute or two. Certainly there was a period of blackness during which the shrieking and howling overhead faded and he seemed to hang in space, pinned between the earth and the sky, feeling a sense of detachment that was somehow . . . peaceful.

It was over too soon. Suddenly he was slammed back into his body, his wrists in agony, his shoulders straining backward, the stench of demon so heavy in the air that he turned his head aside and retched helplessly onto the ground. He heard a dry chuckle and looked up, swallowing hard against the acid in his throat. Sebastian knelt over him, his legs straddling Jace's, his eyes shining. "It's all right, little brother," he said. "They're gone."

Jace's eyes were streaming, his throat scraped raw. His voice came out a croak. "He said midnight. Valentine said to open the gate at midnight. It can't be midnight yet."

"I always figure it's better to ask for forgiveness than permission in these sorts of situations." Sebastian glanced up at the now empty sky. "It should take them five minutes to reach Brocelind Plain from here, quite a bit less time than it will Father to reach the lake. I want to see some Nephilim blood spilled. I want them to writhe and die on the ground. They deserve shame before they get oblivion."

"Do you really think that Nephilim have so little chance against demons? It's not as if they're unprepared—"

Sebastian dismissed him with a flick of his wrist. "I thought you were listening to us. Didn't you understand the plan? Don't you know what my father's going to do?"

Jace said nothing.

"It was good of you," said Sebastian, "to lead me to Hodge that night. If he hadn't revealed that the Mirror we sought was Lake Lyn, I'm not sure this night would have been possible. Because anyone who bears the first two Mortal Instruments and stands before the Mortal Glass can summon the Angel Raziel out of it, just as Jonathan Shadowhunter did a thousand years ago. And once you've summoned the Angel, you can demand of him one thing. One task. One . . . favor."

"A favor?" Jace felt cold all over. "And Valentine is going to demand the defeat of the Shadowhunters at Brocelind?"

Sebastian stood up. "That would be a waste," he said. "No. He's going to demand that all Shadowhunters who have not drunk from the Mortal Cup—all those who are not his followers—be stripped of their powers. They will no longer be Nephilim. And as such, bearing the Marks they do . . ." He smiled. "They will become Forsaken, easy prey for the demons, and those Downworlders who have not fled will be quickly eradicated."

Jace's ears were ringing with a harsh, tinny sound. He felt dizzy. "Even Valentine," he said, "even Valentine would never do that—"

"Please," said Sebastian. "Do you really think my father won't go through with what he's planned?"

"*Our* father," Jace said.

Sebastian glanced down at him. His hair was a white halo; he looked like the sort of bad angel who might have followed Lucifer out of heaven. "Pardon me," he said, with some amusement. "Are you *praying*?"

"No. I said *our* father. I meant Valentine. Not *your* father. Ours."

For a moment Sebastian was expressionless; then his mouth quirked up at the corner, and he grinned. "Little angel boy," he said. "You're a fool, aren't you—just like my father always said."

"Why do you keep calling me that?" Jace demanded. "Why are you blathering about angels—"

"God," said Sebastian, "you don't know *anything*, do you? Did my father ever say a word to you that wasn't a lie?"

Jace shook his head. He'd been pulling at the ropes binding his wrists, but every time he jerked at them, they seemed to get tighter. He could feel the pounding of his pulse in each of his fingers. "How do you know he wasn't lying to *you*?"

"Because I am his blood. I am just like him. When he's gone, I'll rule the Clave after him."

"I wouldn't brag about being just like him if I were you."

"There's that, too." Sebastian's voice was emotionless. "I don't pretend to be anything other than I am. I don't behave as if I'm horrified that my father does what he needs to do to save his people, even if they don't want—or, if you ask me, deserve—saving. Who would *you* rather have for a son, a boy who's proud that you're his father or one who cowers from you in shame and fear?"

"I'm not afraid of Valentine," said Jace.

"You shouldn't be," said Sebastian. "You should be afraid of me."

There was something in his voice that made Jace abandon his struggle against the bindings and look up. Sebastian was still holding his blackly gleaming sword. It was a dark, beautiful thing, Jace thought, even when Sebastian lowered the point of it so that it rested above Jace's collarbone, just nicking his Adam's apple.

Jace struggled to keep his voice steady. "So now what? You're going to kill me while I'm tied up? Does the thought of fighting me scare you that much?"

Nothing, not a flicker of emotion, passed across Sebastian's pale face. "You," he said, "are not a threat to me. You're a pest. An annoyance."

"Then why won't you untie my hands?"

Sebastian, utterly still, stared at him. He looked like a statue, Jace thought, like the statue of some long-dead prince—someone who'd died young and spoiled. And that was the difference between Sebastian and Valentine; though they shared the same cold marble looks, Sebastian had an air about him of something ruined—something eaten away from the inside. "I'm not a fool," Sebastian said, "and you can't bait me. I left you alive only long enough so that you could see the demons. When you die now, and return to your angel ancestors, you can tell them there is no place for them in this world anymore. They've failed the Clave, and the Clave no longer needs them. We have Valentine now."

"You're killing me because you want me to give a message to *God* for you?" Jace shook his head, the point of the blade scraping across his throat. "You're crazier than I thought."

Sebastian just smiled and pushed the blade in slightly deeper; when Jace swallowed, he could feel the point of it denting his windpipe. "If you have any real prayers, little brother, say them now."

"I don't have any prayers," said Jace. "I have a message, though. For our father. Will you give it to him?"

"Of course," Sebastian said smoothly, but there was something in the way he said it, a flicker of hesitation before he spoke, that confirmed what Jace was already thinking.

"You're lying," he said. "You won't give him the message, because you're not going to tell him what you've done. He never asked you to kill me, and he won't be happy when he finds out."

"Nonsense. You're nothing to him."

"You think he'll never know what happened to me if you kill me now, here. You can tell him I died in the battle, or he'll just assume that's what happened. But you're wrong if you think he won't know. Valentine always knows."

"You don't know what you're talking about," Sebastian said, but his face had tightened.

Jace kept talking, pressing home his advantage. "You can't hide what you're doing, though. There's a witness."

"A *witness?*" Sebastian looked almost surprised, which Jace counted as something of a victory. "What are you talking about?"

"The raven," Jace said. "He's been watching from the shadows. He'll tell Valentine everything."

"Hugin?" Sebastian's gaze snapped up, and though the raven was nowhere to be seen, Sebastian's face when he glanced back down at Jace was full of doubt.

"If Valentine knows you murdered me while I was tied up

and helpless, he'll be disgusted with you," Jace said, and he heard his own voice drop into his father's cadences, the way Valentine spoke when he wanted something: soft and persuasive. "He'll call you a coward. He'll never forgive you."

Sebastian said nothing. He was staring down at Jace, his lips twitching, and hatred boiled behind his eyes like poison.

"Untie me," Jace said softly. "Untie me and fight me. It's the only way."

Sebastian's lip twitched again, hard, and this time Jace thought he had gone too far. Sebastian drew the sword back and raised it, and the moonlight burst off it in a thousand silver shards, silver as the stars, silver as the color of his hair. He bared his teeth—and the sword's whistling breath cut the night air with a scream as he brought it down in a whirling arc.

Clary sat on the steps of the dais in the Hall of Accords, holding the stele in her hands. She had never felt quite so alone. The Hall was utterly, totally empty. Clary had looked everywhere for Isabelle once the fighters had all passed through the Portal, but she hadn't been able to find her. Aline had told her that Isabelle was probably back at the Penhallows' house, where Aline and a few other teenagers were meant to be looking after at least a dozen children under fighting age. She'd tried to get Clary to go there with her, but Clary had declined. If she couldn't find Isabelle, she'd rather be alone than with near strangers. Or so she'd thought. But sitting here, she found the silence and the emptiness becoming more and more oppressive. Still, she hadn't moved. She was trying as hard as she could not to think of Jace, not to think of Simon, not to think of her mother or Luke or Alec—and the only way not to think, she had found, was to remain motionless and to stare at a single square of marble on the floor instead, counting the cracks in it, over and over.

There were six. *One, two, three. Four, five, six.* She finished the count and started again, from the beginning. *One—*

The sky overhead exploded.

Or at least that was what it sounded like. Clary threw her head back and stared upward, through the clear roof of the Hall. The sky had been dark a moment ago; now it was a roiling mass of flame and blackness, shot through with an ugly orange light. *Things* moved against that light—hideous things she didn't want to see, things that made her grateful to the darkness for obscuring her view. The occasional glimpse was bad enough.

The transparent skylight overhead rippled and bent as the demon host passed, as if it were being warped by tremendous heat. At last there was a sound like a gunshot, and a huge crack appeared in the glass, spiderwebbing out into countless fissures. Clary ducked, covering her head with her hands, as glass rained down around her like tears.

They were almost to the battlefield when the sound came, ripping the night in half. One moment the woods were as silent as they were dark. The next moment the sky was lit with a hellish orange glow. Simon staggered and nearly fell; he caught at a tree trunk to steady himself and looked up, barely able to believe what he was seeing. All around him the other vampires were staring up at the sky, their white faces like night-blooming flowers, lifting to catch the moonlight as nightmare after nightmare streaked across the sky.

***

"You keep passing out on me," Sebastian said. "It's extremely tedious."

Jace opened his eyes. Pain lanced through his head. He put his hand up to touch the side of his face—and realized his hands were no longer tied behind him. A length of rope trailed from his wrist. His hand came away from his face black—blood, dark in the moonlight.

He stared around him. They were no longer in the cavern: He was lying on soft dirt and grass on the valley floor, not far from the stone house. He could hear the sound of the water in the creek, clearly close by. Knotted tree branches overhead blocked some of the moonlight, but it was still fairly bright.

"Get up," Sebastian said. "You have five seconds before I kill you where you are."

Jace stood as slowly as he thought he could get away with. He was still a little dizzy. Fighting for balance, he dug the heels of his boots into the soft dirt, trying to give himself some stability. "Why did you bring me out here?"

"Two reasons," Sebastian said. "One, I enjoyed knocking you out. Two, it would be bad for either of us to get blood on the floor of that cavern. Trust me. And I intend to spill plenty of your blood."

Jace felt at his belt, and his heart sank. Either he'd dropped most of his weapons while Sebastian was dragging him through the tunnels, or, more likely, Sebastian had thrown them away. All he had left was a dagger. It was a short blade—too short, no match for the sword.

"Not much of a weapon, that." Sebastian grinned, white in the moon-dazzled darkness.

"I can't fight with this," Jace said, trying to sound as quavering and nervous as he could.

"What a shame." Sebastian came closer to Jace, grinning. He was holding his sword loosely, theatrically unconcerned, the tips of his fingers beating a light rhythm on the hilt. If there was ever going to be an opening for him, Jace thought, this was probably it. He swung his arm back and punched Sebastian as hard as he could in the face.

Bone crunched under his knuckles. The blow sent Sebastian sprawling. He skidded backward in the dirt, the sword flying from his grip. Jace caught it up as he darted forward, and a second later was standing over Sebastian, blade in hand.

Sebastian's nose was bleeding, the blood a scarlet streak across his face. He reached up and pulled his collar aside, baring his pale throat. "So go ahead," he said. "Kill me already."

Jace hesitated. He didn't want to hesitate, but there it was: an annoying reluctance to kill anyone lying helpless on the ground in front of him. Jace remembered Valentine taunting him, back at Renwick's, daring his son to kill him, and Jace hadn't been able to do it. But Sebastian was a murderer. He'd killed Max and Hodge.

He raised the sword.

And Sebastian erupted off the ground, faster than the eye could follow. He seemed to fly into the air, performing an elegant backflip and landing gracefully on the grass barely a foot away. As he did, he kicked out, striking Jace's hand. The kick sent the sword spinning out of Jace's grasp. Sebastian caught it out of the air, laughing, and slashed out with the blade, whipping it toward Jace's heart. Jace leaped backward and the blade split the air just in front of him, slicing his shirt open down the front. There was a stinging pain and Jace felt blood welling from a shallow slice across his chest.

Sebastian chuckled, advancing toward Jace, who backed up, fumbling his insufficient dagger out of his belt as he went. He looked around, desperately hoping there was something else he could use as a weapon—a long stick, anything. There was nothing around him but the grass, the river running by, and the trees above, spreading their thick branches overhead like a green net. Suddenly he remembered the Malachi Configuration the Inquisitor had trapped him in. Sebastian wasn't the only one who could jump.

Sebastian slashed the sword toward him again, but Jace had already leaped—straight up into the air. The lowest tree branch was about twenty feet high; he caught at it, swinging himself up and over. Kneeling on the branch, he saw Sebastian, on the ground, spin around and look up. Jace flung the dagger and heard Sebastian shout. Breathless, he straightened up—

And Sebastian was suddenly on the branch beside him. His pale face was flushed angrily, his sword arm streaming blood. He had dropped the sword, evidently, in the grass, though that merely made them even, Jace thought, since his dagger was gone as well. He saw with some satisfaction that for the first time Sebastian looked *angry*—angry and surprised, as if a pet he'd thought was tame had bitten him.

"That was fun," Sebastian said. "But now it's over."

He flung himself at Jace, catching him around the waist, knocking him off the branch. They fell twenty feet through the air clutched together, tearing at each other—and hit the ground hard, hard enough that Jace saw stars behind his eyes. He grabbed for Sebastian's injured arm and dug his fingers in;

Sebastian yelled and backhanded Jace across the face. Jace's mouth filled with salty blood; he gagged on it as they rolled through the dirt together, slamming punches into each other. He felt a sudden shock of icy cold; they'd rolled down the slight incline into the river and were lying half-in, half-out of the water. Sebastian gasped, and Jace took the opportunity to grab for the other boy's throat and close his hands around it, squeezing. Sebastian choked, seizing Jace's right wrist in his hand and jerking it backward, hard enough to snap the bones. Jace heard himself scream as if from a distance, and Sebastian pressed the advantage, twisting the broken wrist mercilessly until Jace let go of him and fell back in the cold, watery mud, his arm a howl of agony.

Half-kneeling on Jace's chest, one knee digging hard into his ribs, Sebastian grinned down at him. His eyes shone out white and black from a mask of dirt and blood. Something glittered in his right hand. Jace's dagger. He must have picked it up from the ground. Its point rested directly over Jace's heart.

"And we find ourselves exactly where we were five minutes ago," Sebastian said. "You've had your chance, Wayland. Any last words?"

Jace stared up at him, his mouth streaming blood, his eyes stinging with sweat, and felt only a sense of total and empty exhaustion. Was this really how he was going to die? "Wayland?" he said. "You know that's not my name."

"You have as much of a claim to it as you have to the name of Morgenstern," said Sebastian. He bent forward, leaning his weight onto the dagger. Its tip pierced Jace's skin, sending a hot stab of pain through his body. Sebastian's face was inches away, his voice a hissing whisper. "Did you *really* think you were Valentine's son? Did you really think a whining, pathetic thing like yourself was worthy of being a Morgenstern, of being *my brother*?" He tossed his white hair back: It was lank with sweat and creek water. "You're a changeling," he said. "My father butchered a corpse to get you and make you one of his experiments. He tried to raise you as his own son, but you were too weak to be any good to him. You couldn't be a warrior. You were nothing. Useless. So he palmed you off on the Lightwoods and hoped you might be of some use to him later, as a decoy. Or as bait. *He never loved you.*"

Jace blinked his burning eyes. "Then you . . ."

"*I* am Valentine's son. Jonathan Christopher Morgenstern. You never had any right to that name. You're a ghost. A pretender." His eyes were black and glinting, like the carapaces of dead insects, and suddenly Jace heard his mother's voice, as if in a dream—but she wasn't his mother—saying *Jonathan's not a baby anymore. He isn't even human; he's a monster.*

"You're the one," Jace choked. "The one with the demon blood. Not me."

"That's right." The dagger slid another millimeter into Jace's flesh. Sebastian was still grinning, but it was a rictus grin, like a skull's. "You're the angel boy. I had to hear all about you. You with your pretty angel face and your pretty manners and your delicate, delicate feelings. You couldn't even watch a bird die without crying. No wonder Valentine was ashamed of you."

"No." Jace forgot the blood in his mouth, forgot the pain. "You're the one he's ashamed of. You think he wouldn't take you with him to the lake because he needed you to stay here and open the gate at midnight? Like he didn't know you wouldn't be able to wait. He didn't take you with him because he's ashamed to stand up in front of the Angel and show him what he's done. Show him the *thing* he made. Show him *you.*" Jace gazed up at Sebastian—he could feel a terrible, triumphant pity blazing in his own eyes. "He knows there's nothing human in you. Maybe he loves you, but he hates you too—"

"Shut up!" Sebastian pushed down on the dagger, twisting the hilt. Jace arched backward with a scream, and agony burst like lightning behind his eyes. *I'm going to die,* he thought. *I'm dying. This is it.* He wondered if his heart had already been pierced. He couldn't move, couldn't breathe. He knew now what it must be like for a butterfly pinned to a board. He tried to speak, tried to say a name, but nothing came out of his mouth but more blood.

And yet Sebastian seemed to read his eyes. "*Clary.* I'd almost forgotten. You're in love with her, aren't you? The shame of your nasty incestuous impulses must nearly have killed you. Too bad you didn't know she's not really your sister. You could have spent the rest of your life with her, if only you weren't so stupid." He bent down, pushing the knife in harder, its edge scraping bone. He spoke in Jace's ear, a voice as soft as a whisper. "She loved you, too," he said. "Keep that in mind while you die."

Darkness flooded in from the edges of Jace's vision, like dye spilling onto a photograph, blotting out the image. Suddenly there was no pain at all. He felt nothing, not even Sebastian's weight on him, as if he were floating. Sebastian's face drifted over him, white against the darkness, the dagger raised in his hand. Something bright gold glittered at Sebastian's wrist, as if he were wearing a bracelet. But it wasn't a bracelet, because it was moving. Sebastian looked toward his hand, surprised, as the dagger fell from his loosened grasp and struck the mud with an audible sound.

Then the hand itself, separated from his wrist, thumped to the ground beside it.

Jace stared wonderingly as Sebastian's severed hand bounced and came to rest against a pair of high black boots. The boots were attached to a pair of delicate legs, rising to a slender torso and a familiar face capped with a waterfall of black hair. Jace raised his eyes and saw Isabelle, her whip soaked with blood, her eyes fastened on Sebastian, who was staring at the bloody stump of his wrist with openmouthed amazement.

Isabelle smiled grimly. "That was for Max, you bastard."

"Bitch," Sebastian hissed—and sprang to his feet as Isabelle's whip came slashing at him again with incredible speed. He ducked sideways and was gone. There was a rustle—he must have vanished into the trees, Jace thought, though it hurt too much to turn his head and look.

"Jace!" Isabelle knelt down over him, her stele shining in her left hand. Her eyes were bright with tears; he must seem pretty bad, Jace realized, for Isabelle to look like that.

"Isabelle," he tried to say. He wanted to tell her to go, to run, that no matter how spectacular and brave and talented she was—and she was all those things—she was no match for Sebastian. And there was no way that Sebastian was going to let a little thing like getting his hand sliced off stop him. But all that came out of Jace's mouth was a sort of gurgling noise.

"Don't talk." He felt the tip of her stele burn against the skin of his chest. "You'll be fine." Isabelle smiled down at him tremulously. "You're probably wondering what the hell I'm doing here," she said. "I don't know how much you know—I don't know what Sebastian's told you—but you're not Valentine's son." The *iratze* was close to finished; already Jace could feel the pain fading. He nodded slightly, trying to tell her: *I know.* "Anyway, I wasn't going to come looking for you after you ran off, because you said in your note not to, and I got that. But there was no way I was going to let you die thinking you have demon blood, or without telling you that there's nothing wrong with you, though honestly, how you could have thought anything so stupid in the first place—" Isabelle's hand jerked, and she froze, not wanting to spoil the rune. "And you needed to know that Clary's not your sister," she said, more gently. "Because—because you just did. So I got Magnus to help me track you. I used that little wooden soldier you gave to Max. I don't think Magnus would have done it normally, but let's just say he was in an *unusually* good mood, and I may have told him Alec wanted him to do it—although that wasn't *strictly* true, but it'll be a while before he finds that out. And once I knew where you were, well, he'd already set up that Portal, and I'm *very* good at sneaking—"

Isabelle screamed. Jace tried to reach for her, but she was beyond his grasp, being lifted, flung to the side. Her whip fell from her hand. She scrambled to her knees, but Sebastian was already in front of her. His eyes blazed with rage, and there was a bloody cloth tied around the stump of his wrist. Isabelle darted for her whip, but Sebastian moved faster. He spun and kicked out at her, hard. His booted foot connected with her rib cage. Jace almost thought he could *hear* Isabelle's ribs crack as she flew backward, landing awkwardly on her side. He heard her cry out—Isabelle, who never cried out in pain—as Sebastian kicked her again and then caught up her whip, brandishing it in his hand.

Jace rolled onto his side. The almost finished *iratze* had helped, but the pain in his chest was still bad, and he knew, in a detached sort of way, that the fact that he was coughing up blood probably meant that he had a punctured lung. He wasn't sure how long that gave him. Minutes, probably. He scrabbled for the dagger where Sebastian had dropped it, next to the grisly remains of his hand. Jace staggered to his feet. The smell of blood was everywhere. He thought of Magnus's vision, the world turned to blood, and his slippery hand tightened on the hilt of the dagger.

He took a step forward. Then another. Every step felt like he was dragging his feet through cement. Isabelle was screaming curses at Sebastian, who was laughing as he brought the whip down across her body. Her screams drew Jace forward like a fish caught on a hook, but they grew fainter as he moved. The world was spinning around him like a carnival ride.

One more step, Jace told himself. One more. Sebastian had his back to him; he was concentrating on Isabelle. He probably thought Jace was already dead. And he nearly was. *One step*, he told himself, but he couldn't do it, couldn't move, couldn't bring himself to drag his feet one more step forward. Blackness was rushing in at the edges of his vision—a more profound blackness than the darkness of sleep. A blackness that would erase everything he had ever seen and bring him a rest that would be absolute. Peaceful. He thought, suddenly, of Clary—Clary as he had last seen her, asleep, with her hair spread across the pillow and her cheek on her hand. He had thought then that he had never seen anything so peaceful in his life, but of course she had only been sleeping, like anyone else might sleep. It hadn't been her peace that had surprised him, but his own. The peace he felt at being with her was like nothing he had ever known before.

Pain jarred up his spine, and he realized with surprise that somehow, without any volition of his own, his legs had moved him forward that last crucial step. Sebastian had his arm back, the whip shining in his hand; Isabelle lay on the grass, a crumpled heap, no longer screaming—no longer moving at all. "You little Lightwood bitch," Sebastian was saying. "I should have smashed your face in with that hammer until I was sure you weren't breathing any more—"

And Jace brought his hand up, with the dagger in it, and sank the blade into Sebastian's back.

Sebastian staggered forward, the whip falling out of his hand. He turned slowly and looked at Jace, and Jace thought, with a distant horror, that maybe Sebastian really wasn't human, that he was unkillable after all. Sebastian's face was blank, the hostility gone from it, and the dark fire from his eyes. He no longer looked like Valentine, though. He looked—scared.

He opened his mouth, as if he meant to say something to Jace, but his knees were already buckling. He crashed to the ground, the force of his fall sending him sliding down the incline and into the river. He came to rest on his back, his eyes staring sightlessly up at the sky; the water flowed around him, carrying dark threads of his blood downstream on the current.

He taught me there's a place on a man's back where, if you sink a blade in, you can pierce his heart and sever his spine, all at once, Sebastian had said. *I guess we got the same birthday present that year, big brother,* Jace thought. *Didn't we?*

"Jace!" It was Isabelle, her face bloody, struggling into a sitting position. "*Jace!*"

He tried to turn toward her, tried to say something, but his words were gone. He slid to his knees. A heavy weight was pressing on his shoulders, and the earth was calling him: down, down, down. He was barely aware of Isabelle crying his name as the darkness carried him away.

Simon was a veteran of countless battles. That is, if you counted battles engaged in while playing Dungeons and Dragons. His friend Eric was the military history buff and he was the one who usually organized the war part of the games, which involved dozens of tiny figurines moving in straight lines across a flat landscape drawn on butcher paper.

That was the way he'd always thought of battles—or the way they were in movies, with two groups of people advancing at each other across a flat expanse of land. Straight lines and orderly progression.

This was nothing like that.

This was chaos, a melee of shouting and movement, and the landscape wasn't flat but a mass of mud and blood churned into a thick, unstable paste. Simon had imagined that the Night Children would walk to the battlefield and be greeted by someone in charge; he imagined he'd see the battle from a distance first and be able to watch as the two sides clashed against each other. But there was no greeting, and there were no sides. The battle loomed up out of the darkness as if he'd wandered by accident from a deserted side street into a riot in the middle of Times Square—suddenly there were crowds surging around him, hands grabbing him, shoving him out of the way, and the vampires were scattering, diving into the battle without even a glance back for him.

And there were demons—demons everywhere, and he'd never imagined the kind of sounds they'd make, the screaming and hooting and grunting, and what was worse, the sounds of tearing and shredding and hungry satisfaction. Simon wished he could turn his vampire hearing off, but he couldn't, and the sounds were like knives piercing his eardrums.

He stumbled over a body lying half in and half out of the mud, turned to see if help was needed, and saw that the Shadowhunter at his feet was gone from the shoulders up. White bone gleamed against the dark earth, and despite Simon's vampire nature, he felt nauseated. *I must be the only vampire in the world sickened by the sight of blood*, he thought, and then something struck him hard from behind and he went over, skidding down a slope of mud into a pit.

Simon's wasn't the only body down there. He rolled onto his back just as the demon loomed up over him. It looked like the image of Death from a medieval woodcut—an animated skeleton, a bloodied hatchet clutched in one bony hand. He threw himself to the side as the blade thumped down, inches from his face. The skeleton made a disappointed hissing noise and hoisted the hatchet again—

And was struck from the side by a club of knotted wood. The skeleton burst apart like a piñata filled with bones. They rattled into pieces with a sound like castanets clacking before vanishing into the darkness.

A Shadowhunter stood over Simon. It was no one he'd ever seen before. A tall man, bearded and blood-splattered, who ran a grimy hand across his forehead as he stared down at

Simon, leaving a dark streak behind. "You all right?"

Stunned, Simon nodded and began scrambling to his feet. "Thanks."

The stranger leaned down, offering a hand to help Simon up. Simon accepted—and went flying up out of the pit. He landed on his feet at the edge, his feet skidding on the wet mud. The stranger offered a sheepish grin. "Sorry. Downworlder strength—my partner's a werewolf. I'm not used to it." He peered at Simon's face. "You're a vampire, aren't you?"

"How did you know?"

The man grinned. It was a tired sort of grin, but there was nothing unfriendly about it. "Your fangs. They come out when you're fighting. I know because—" He broke off. Simon could have filled in the rest for him: *I know because I've killed my fair share of vampires.* "Anyway. Thanks. For fighting with us."

"I—" Simon was about to say that he hadn't exactly fought yet. Or contributed anything, really. He turned to say it, and got exactly one word out of his mouth before something impossibly huge and clawed and ragged-winged swept down out of the sky and dug its talons into the Shadowhunter's back.

The man didn't even cry out. His head went back, as if he were looking up in surprise, wondering what had hold of him—and then he was gone, whipping up into the empty black sky in a whir of teeth and wings. His club thumped to the ground at Simon's feet.

Simon didn't move. The whole thing, from the moment he'd fallen into the pit, had taken less than a minute. He turned numbly, staring around him at the blades whirling through the darkness, at the slashing talons of demons, at the points of illumination that raced here and there through the darkness like fireflies darting through foliage—and then he realized what they were. The gleaming lights of seraph blades.

He couldn't see the Lightwoods, or the Penhallows, or Luke, or anyone else he might recognize. He wasn't a Shadowhunter. And yet that man had thanked him, thanked him for fighting. What he'd told Clary was true—this was his battle too, and he was needed here. Not human Simon, who was gentle and geeky and hated the sight of blood, but vampire Simon, a creature he barely even knew.

A true vampire knows he is dead, Raphael had said. But Simon didn't feel dead. He'd never felt more alive. He turned as another demon loomed up in front of him: this one a lizard-thing, scaled, with rodent teeth. It swept down on Simon with its black claws extended.

Simon leaped. He struck the massive side of the thing and clung, his nails digging in, the scales giving way under his grip. The Mark on his forehead throbbed as he sank his fangs into the demon's neck.

It tasted awful.

When the glass stopped falling, there was a hole in the ceiling, several feet wide, as if a meteor had crashed through it. Cold air blew in through the gap. Shivering, Clary got to her feet, brushing glass dust from her clothes.

The witchlight that had lit the Hall had been doused: It was gloomy inside now, thick with shadows and dust. The faint illumination of the fading Portal in the square was just visible, glowing through the open front doors.

It was probably no longer safe to stay in here, Clary thought. She should go to the Penhallows' and join Aline. She was partway across the Hall when footsteps sounded on the marble floor. Heart pounding, she turned and saw Malachi, a long, spidery shadow in the half-light, striding toward the dais. But what was he still doing here? Shouldn't he be with the rest of the Shadowhunters on the battlefield?

As he drew closer to the dais, she noticed something that made her put her hand to her mouth, stifling a cry of surprise. There was a hunched dark shape perched on Malachi's shoulder. A bird. A raven, to be exact.

Hugo.

Clary ducked to crouch behind a pillar as Malachi climbed the dais steps. There was something unmistakably furtive in the way he glanced from side to side. Apparently satisfied that he was unobserved, he drew something small and glittering from his pocket and slipped it onto his finger. A ring? He reached to twist it, and Clary remembered Hodge in the library at the Institute, taking the ring from Jace's hand . . .

The air in front of Malachi shimmered faintly, as if with heat. A voice spoke from it, a familiar voice, cool and cultured, now touched with just the faintest annoyance.

"What is it, Malachi? I'm in no mood for small talk right now."

"My Valentine," said Malachi. His usual hostility had been replaced with a slimy obsequiousness. "Hugin visited me not a moment ago, bringing news. I assumed you had already reached the Mirror, and therefore he sought me out instead. I thought you might want to know."

Valentine's tone was sharp. "Very well. What news?"

"It's your son, lord. Your *other* son. Hugin tracked him to the valley of the cave. He may even have followed you through the tunnels to the lake."

Clary clutched the pillar with whitened fingers. They were talking about Jace.

Valentine grunted. "Did he meet his brother there?"

"Hugin says that he left the two of them fighting."

Clary felt her stomach turn over. Jace, fighting Sebastian? She thought of the way Sebastian had lifted Jace at the Gard and flung him, as if he weighed nothing. A wave of panic surged over her, so intense that for a moment her ears buzzed. By the time the room swam back into focus, she had missed whatever Valentine had said to Malachi in return.

"It is the ones old enough to be Marked but not old enough to fight, that concern me," Malachi was saying now. "They didn't vote in the Council's decision. It seems unfair to punish them in the same way that those who are fighting must be punished."

"I did consider that." Valentine's voice was a bass rumble. "Because teenagers are more lightly Marked, it takes them longer to become Forsaken. Several days, at least. I believe it may well be reversible."

"While those of us who have drunk from the Mortal Cup will remain entirely unaffected?"

"I'm busy, Malachi," said Valentine. "I've told you that you'll be safe. I am trusting my own life to this process. Have some faith."

Malachi bowed his head. "I have great faith, my lord. I have kept it for many years, in silence, serving you always."

"And you will be rewarded," said Valentine.

Malachi looked up. "My lord—"

But the air had stopped shimmering. Valentine was gone. Malachi frowned, then marched down the dais steps and toward the front doors. Clary shrank back against the pillar, hoping desperately that he wouldn't see her. Her heart was pounding. What had all that been about? What was all this about Forsaken? The answer glimmered at the corner of her mind, but it seemed too horrible to contemplate. Even Valentine wouldn't—

Something flew at her face then, whirling and dark. She barely had time to throw her arms up to cover her eyes when something slashed along the back of her hands. She heard a fierce caw, and wings beat against her upraised wrists.

"Hugin! Enough!" It was Malachi's sharp voice. "*Hugin*!" There was another caw and a thump, then silence. Clary lowered her arms and saw the raven lying motionless at the Consul's feet—stunned or dead, she couldn't tell. With a snarl Malachi kicked the raven savagely out of his way and strode toward Clary, glowering. He caught hold of her by a bleeding wrist and hauled her to her feet. "Stupid girl," he said. "How long have you been there listening?"

"Long enough to know that you're one of the Circle," she spat, twisting her wrist in his grasp, but he held firm. "You're on Valentine's side."

"*There is only one side.*" His voice came out in a hiss. "The Clave is foolish, misguided, pandering to half men and monsters. All I want is to make it pure, to return it to its former glory. A goal you'd think every Shadowhunter would approve of, but no—they listen to fools and demon-lovers like you and Lucian Graymark. And now you've sent the flower of the Nephilim to die in this ridiculous battle—an empty gesture that will accomplish nothing. Valentine has already begun the ritual; soon the Angel will rise, and the Nephilim will become Forsaken. All those save the few under Valentine's protection—"

"That's murder! He's murdering Shadowhunters!"

"Not murder," said the Consul. His voice rang with a fanatic's passion. "Cleansing. Valentine will make a new world of Shadowhunters, a world purged of weakness and corruption."

"Weakness and corruption isn't in the *world*," Clary snapped. "It's in *people*. And it always will be. The world just needs good people to balance it out. And you're planning to kill them all."

He looked at her for a moment with honest surprise, as if he were astonished at the force in her tone. "Fine words from a girl who would betray her own father." Malachi jerked her toward him, yanking brutally on her bleeding wrist. "Perhaps we should see just how much Valentine would mind if I taught you—"

But Clary never found out what he wanted to teach her. A dark shape shot between them—wings outspread and claws extended.

The raven caught Malachi with the tip of a talon, raking a bloody groove across his face. With a cry the Consul let go of Clary and threw up his arms, but Hugo had circled back and was slashing at him viciously with beak and claws. Malachi staggered backward, arms flailing, until he struck the edge of a bench, hard. It fell over with a crash; unbalanced, he sprawled after it with a strangled cry—quickly cut off.

Clary raced to where Malachi lay crumpled on the marble floor, a circle of blood already pooling around him. He had landed on a pile of glass from the broken ceiling, and one of the jagged chunks had pierced his throat. Hugo was still hovering in the air, circling Malachi's body. He gave a triumphant caw as Clary stared at him—apparently he hadn't appreciated the Consul's kicks and blows. Malachi should have known better than to attack one of Valentine's creatures, Clary thought sourly. The bird was no more forgiving than its master.

But there was no time to think about Malachi now. Alec had said that there were wards up around the lake, and that if anyone Portaled there, an alarm would go off. Valentine was probably already at the mirror—there was no time to waste. Backing slowly away from the raven, Clary turned and dashed toward the front doors of the Hall and the glimmer of the Portal beyond.

20
Weighed in the Balance

Water struck her in the face like a blow. Clary went down, choking, into freezing darkness; her first thought was that the Portal had faded beyond repairing, and that she was stuck in the whirling black in-between place.

Her second thought was that she was already dead.

She was probably only actually unconscious for a few seconds, though it felt like the end of everything. When she came awake, it was with a shock that was like the shock of breaking through a layer of ice. She had been unconscious and now, suddenly, she wasn't; she was lying on her back on cold, damp earth, staring up at a sky so full of stars it looked like a handful of silver pieces had been flung across its dark surface. Her mouth was full of brackish liquid; she turned her head to the side, coughed and spat and gasped until she could breathe again.

When her stomach had stopped spasming, she rolled onto her side. Her wrists were bound together with a faint band of glowing light, and her legs felt heavy and strange, prickling all over with intense pins and needles. She wondered if she'd lain on them strangely, or perhaps it was a side effect of nearly drowning. The back of her neck burned as if a wasp had stung her. With a gasp she heaved herself into a sitting position, legs stretched out awkwardly in front of her, and looked around.

She was on the shore of Lake Lyn, where the water gave way to powdery sand. A black wall of rock rose behind her, the cliffs she remembered from her time here with Luke. The sand itself was dark, glittering with silver mica. Here and there in the sand were witchlight torches, filling the air with their silvery glow, leaving a tracery of glowing lines across the surface of the water.

By the shore of the lake, a few feet away from where she sat, stood a low table made out of flat stones piled one on the other. It had clearly been assembled in haste; though the gaps between the stones were packed in with damp sand, some of the rocks were slipping away at angles. Placed on the surface of the stones was something that made Clary catch her breath—the Mortal Cup, and laid crossways atop it, the Mortal Sword, a tongue of black flame in the witchlight. Around the altar were the black lines of runes carved into the sand. She stared at them, but they were jumbled, meaningless—

A shadow cut across the sand, moving fast—the long black shadow of a man, made wavering and indistinct by the flickering light of the torches. By the time Clary raised her head, he was already standing over her.

Valentine.

The shock of seeing him was so enormous that it was almost no shock at all. She felt nothing as she stared up at her father, whose face hovered against the dark sky like the moon: white, austere, pitted with black eyes like meteor craters. Over his shirt were looped a number of leather straps holding a dozen or more weapons. They bristled behind him like a porcupine's spines. He looked huge, impossibly broad, the terrifying statue of some warrior god intent on destruction.

"Clarissa," he said. "You took quite a risk, Portaling here. You're lucky I saw you appear in the water between one minute and the next. You were quite unconscious; if it weren't for me, you would have drowned." A muscle beside his mouth moved slightly. "And I wouldn't concern yourself overmuch with the alarm wards the Clave put up around the lake. I took those down the moment I arrived. No one knows you're here."

I don't believe you! Clary opened her mouth to fling the words in his face. There was no sound. It was like one of those nightmares where she would try to scream and scream and nothing would happen. Only a dry puff of air came from her mouth, the gasp of someone trying to scream with a cut throat.

Valentine shook his head. "Don't bother trying to speak. I used a Rune of Silence, one of those that the Silent Brothers use, on the back of your neck. There's a binding rune on your wrists, and another disabling your legs. I wouldn't try to stand—your legs won't hold you, and it'll only cause you pain."

Clary glared at him, trying to bore into him with her eyes,

cut him with her hatred. But he took no notice. "It could have been worse, you know. By the time I dragged you onto the bank, the lake poison had already started its work. I've cured you of it, by the way. Not that I expect your thanks." He smiled thinly. "You and I, we've never had a conversation, have we? Not a real conversation. You must be wondering why I never really seemed to have a father's interest in you. I'm sorry if that hurt you."

Now her stare went from hateful to incredulous. How could they have a conversation when she couldn't even speak? She tried to force the words out, but nothing came from her throat but a thin gasp.

Valentine turned back to his altar and placed his hand on the Mortal Sword. The sword gave off a black light, a sort of reverse glow, as if it were sucking the illumination from the air around it. "I didn't know your mother was pregnant with you when she left me," he said. He was speaking to her, Clary thought, in a way he never had before. His tone was calm, even conversational, but it wasn't that. "I knew there was something wrong. She thought she was hiding her unhappiness. I took some blood from Ithuriel, dried it to a powder, and mixed it with her food, thinking it might cure her unhappiness. If I'd known she was pregnant, I wouldn't have done it. I'd already resolved not to experiment again on a child of my own blood."

You're lying, Clary wanted to scream at him. But she wasn't sure he was. He still sounded strange to her. Different. Maybe it was because he was telling the truth.

"After she fled Idris, I looked for her for years," he said. "And not just because she had the Mortal Cup. Because I loved her. I thought if I could only talk to her, I could make her see reason. I did what I did that night in Alicante in a fit of rage, wanting to destroy her, destroy everything about our life together. But afterward I—" He shook his head, turning away to look out over the lake. "When I finally tracked her down, I'd heard rumors she'd had another child, a daughter. I assumed you were Lucian's. He'd always loved her, always wanted to take her from me. I thought she must finally have given in. Have consented to have a child with a filthy Downworlder." His voice tightened. "When I found her in your apartment in New York, she was still barely conscious. She spat at me that I'd made a monster out of her first child, and she'd left me before I could do the same to her second. Then she went limp in my arms. All those years I'd looked for her, and that was all I had with her. Those few seconds in which she looked at me with a lifetime's worth of hate. I realized something then."

He lifted Maellartach. Clary remembered how heavy even the half-turned Sword had been to hold, and saw as the blade rose that the muscles of Valentine's arm stood out, hard and corded, like ropes snaking under the skin.

"I realized," he said, "that the reason she left me was to protect you. Jonathan she hated, but you—she would have done anything to protect you. To protect you from *me*. She even lived among mundanes, which I know must have pained her. It must have hurt her never to be able to raise you with any of our traditions. You are half of what you could have been. You have your talent with runes, but it's been squandered by your mundane upbringing."

He lowered the Sword. The tip of it hung, now, just by Clary's face; she could see it out of the corner of her eye, floating at the edge of her vision like a silvery moth.

"I knew then that Jocelyn would never come back to me, because of you. You are the only thing in the world she ever loved more than she loved me. And because of you she hates me. And because of that, I hate the sight of you."

Clary turned her face away. If he was going to kill her, she didn't want to see her death coming.

"Clarissa," said Valentine. "Look at me."

No. She stared at the lake. Far out across the water she could see a dim red glow, like fire sunk away into ashes. She knew it was the light of the battle. Her mother was there, and Luke. Maybe it was fitting that they were together, even if she wasn't with them.

I'll keep my eyes on that light, she thought. *I'll keep looking at it no matter what. It'll be the last thing I ever see.*

"Clarissa," Valentine said again. "You look just like her, do you know that? Just like Jocelyn."

She felt a sharp pain against her cheek. It was the blade of the Sword. He was pressing the edge of it against her skin, trying to force her to turn her head toward him.

"I'm going to raise the Angel now," he said. "And I want you to watch as it happens."

There was a bitter taste in Clary's mouth. *I know why you're so obsessed with my mother. Because she was the one thing you thought you had total control over that ever turned around and bit you. You thought you owned her and you didn't. That's why you want her here, right now, to witness you winning. That's why you'll make do with me.*

The Sword bit farther into her cheek. Valentine said, *"Look at me, Clary."*

She looked. She didn't want to, but the pain was too much—her head jerked to the side almost against her will, the blood dripping in great fat drops down her face, splattering the sand. A nauseous pain gripped her as she raised her head to look at her father.

He was gazing down at the blade of Maellartach. It, too, was stained with her blood. When he glanced back at her, there was a strange light in his eyes. "Blood is needed to complete this ceremony," he said. "I intended to use my own, but when I saw you in the lake, I knew it was Raziel's way of telling me to use my daughter's instead. It's why I cleared your blood of the lake's taint. You are purified now—purified and ready. So thank you, Clarissa, for the use of your blood."

And in some way, Clary thought, he meant it, meant his gratitude. He had long ago lost the ability to distinguish between force and cooperation, between fear and willingness, between love and torture. And with that realization came a rush of numbness—what was the point of hating Valentine for being a monster when he didn't even know he was one?

"And now," Valentine said, "I just need a bit more," and Clary thought, *A bit more what?*—just as he swung the Sword back and the starlight exploded off it, and she thought, *Of course. It's not just blood he wants, but death.* The Sword had fed itself on enough blood by now; it probably had a taste for it, just like Valentine himself. Her eyes followed Maellartach's black light as it sliced toward her—

And went flying. Knocked out of Valentine's hand, it hurtled into the darkness. Valentine's eyes went wide; his gaze flicked down, fastening first on his bleeding sword hand—and then he looked up and saw, at the same moment that Clary did, what had struck the Mortal Sword from his grasp.

Jace, a familiar-looking sword gripped in his left hand,

stood at the edge of a rise of sand, barely a foot from Valentine. Clary could see from the older man's expression that he hadn't heard Jace approach any more than she had.

Clary's heart caught at the sight of him. Dried blood crusted the side of his face, and there was a livid red mark at his throat. His eyes shone like mirrors, and in the witchlight they looked black—black as Sebastian's. "Clary," he said, not taking his eyes off his father. "Clary, are you all right?"

Jace! She struggled to say his name, but nothing could pass the blockage in her throat. She felt as if she were choking.

"She can't answer you," said Valentine. "She can't speak."

Jace's eyes flashed. "What have you done to her?" He jabbed the sword toward Valentine, who took a step back. The look on Valentine's face was wary but not frightened. There was a calculation to his expression that Clary didn't like. She knew she ought to feel triumphant, but she didn't—if anything, she felt more panicked than she had a moment ago. She'd realized that Valentine was going to kill her—had accepted it—and now Jace was here, and her fear had expanded to encompass him as well. And he looked so . . . *destroyed.* His gear was ripped halfway open down one arm, and the skin beneath was crisscrossed with white lines. His shirt was torn across the front, and there was a fading *iratze* over his heart that had not quite managed to erase the angry red scar beneath it. Dirt stained his clothes, as if he'd been rolling around on the ground. But it was his expression that frightened her the most. It was so—bleak.

"A Rune of Quietude. She won't be hurt by it." Valentine's eyes fastened on Jace—hungrily, Clary thought, as if he were drinking in the sight of him. "I don't suppose," Valentine asked, "that you've come to join me? To be blessed by the Angel beside me?"

Jace's expression didn't change. His eyes were fixed on his adoptive father, and there was nothing in them—no lingering shred of affection or love or memory. There wasn't even any hatred. Just . . . disdain, Clary thought. A cold disdain. "I know what you're planning to do," Jace said. "I know why you're summoning the Angel. And I won't let you do it. I've already sent Isabelle to warn the army—"

"Warnings will do them little good. This is not the sort of danger you can run from." Valentine's gaze flicked down to Jace's sword. "Put that down," he began, "and we can talk—" He broke off then. "That's not your sword. That's a Morgenstern sword."

Jace smiled, a dark, sweet smile. "It was Jonathan's. He's dead now."

Valentine looked stunned. "You mean—"

"I took it from the ground where he'd dropped it," Jace said, without emotion, "after I killed him."

Valentine seemed dumbfounded. "*You* killed Jonathan? How could you have?"

"He would have killed me," said Jace. "I had no choice."

"I didn't mean that." Valentine shook his head; he still looked stunned, like a boxer who'd been hit too hard in the moment before he collapsed to the mat. "I raised Jonathan—I trained him myself. There was no better warrior."

"Apparently," Jace said, "there was."

"But—" And Valentine's voice cracked, the first time Clary had ever heard a flaw in the smooth, unruffled facade of that voice. "But he was your brother."

"No. He wasn't." Jace took a step forward, nudging the blade an inch closer to Valentine's heart. "What happened to my real father? Isabelle said he died in a raid, but did he really? Did you kill him like you killed my mother?"

Valentine still looked stunned. Clary sensed that he was fighting for control—fighting against grief? Or just afraid to die? "I didn't kill your mother. She took her own life. I cut you out of her dead body. If I hadn't done that, you would have died along with her."

"But *why*? Why did you do it? You didn't need a son, you *had* a son!" Jace looked deadly in the moonlight, Clary thought, deadly and strange, like someone she didn't know. The hand that held the sword toward Valentine's throat was unwavering. "Tell me the truth," Jace said. "No more lies about how we're the same flesh and blood. Parents lie to their children, but you—you're not my father. And I want the truth."

"It wasn't a son I needed," Valentine said. "It was a soldier. I had thought Jonathan might be that soldier, but he had too much of the demon nature in him. He was too savage, too sudden, not subtle enough. I feared even then, when he was barely out of infancy, that he would never have the patience or the compassion to follow me, to lead the Clave in my footsteps. So I tried again with you. And with you I had the opposite trouble. You were too gentle. Too empathic. You felt others' pain as if it were your own; you couldn't even bear the death of your pets. Understand this, my son—I loved you for those things. But the very things I loved about you made you no use to me."

"So you thought I was soft and useless," said Jace. "I suppose it will be surprising for you, then, when your soft and useless son cuts your throat."

"We've been through this." Valentine's voice was steady, but Clary thought she could see the sweat gleaming at his temples, at the base of his throat. "You wouldn't do that. You didn't want to do it at Renwick's, and you don't want to do it now."

"You're wrong." Jace spoke in a measured tone. "I have regretted not killing you every day since I let you go. My brother Max is dead because I didn't kill you that day. Dozens, maybe hundreds, are dead because I stayed my hand. I know your plan. I know you hope to slaughter almost every Shadowhunter in Idris. And I ask myself, how many more have to die before I do what I should have done on Blackwell's Island? No," he said. "I don't *want* to kill you. *But I will.*"

"Don't do this," said Valentine. "Please. I don't want to—"

"To die? No one wants to die, Father." The point of Jace's sword slipped lower, and then lower until it was resting over Valentine's heart. Jace's face was calm, the face of an angel dispatching divine justice. "Do you have any last words?"

"Jonathan—"

Blood spotted Valentine's shirt where the tip of the blade rested, and Clary saw, in her mind's eye, Jace at Renwick's, his hand shaking, not wanting to hurt his father. And Valentine taunting him. *Drive the blade in. Three inches—maybe four.* It wasn't like that now. Jace's hand was steady. And Valentine looked afraid.

"Last words," hissed Jace. "What are they?"

Valentine raised his head. His black eyes as he looked at the boy in front of him were grave. "I'm sorry," he said. "I am so sorry." He stretched out a hand, as if he meant to reach out to Jace, even to touch him—his hand turned, palm up, the fingers opening—and then there was a silver flash and something flew by Clary in the darkness like a bullet shot out of a gun. She felt displaced air brush her cheek as it passed, and then Valentine had caught it out of the air, a long tongue of silver fire that flashed once in his hand as he brought it down.

It was the Mortal Sword. It left a tracery of black light on the air as Valentine drove the blade of it into Jace's heart.

Jace's eyes flew wide. A look of disbelieving confusion passed over his face; he glanced down at himself, where Maellartach stuck grotesquely out of his chest—it looked more bizarre than horrible, like a prop from a nightmare that made no logical sense. Valentine drew his hand back then, jerking the Sword out of Jace's chest the way he might have jerked a dagger from its scabbard; as if it had been all that was holding him up, Jace went to his knees. His sword slid from his grasp and hit the damp earth. He looked down at it in puzzlement, as if he had no idea why he had been holding it, or why he had let it go. He opened his mouth as if to ask the question, and blood poured over his chin, staining what was left of his ragged shirt.

Everything after that seemed to Clary to happen very slowly, as if time were stretching itself out. She saw Valentine sink to the ground and pull Jace onto his lap as if Jace were still very small and could be easily held. He drew him close and rocked him, and he lowered his face and pressed it against Jace's shoulder, and Clary thought for a moment that he might even have been crying, but when he lifted his head, Valentine's eyes were dry. "My son," he whispered. "My boy."

The terrible slowing of time stretched around Clary like a strangling rope, while Valentine held Jace and brushed his bloody hair back from his forehead. He held Jace while he died, and the light went out of his eyes, and then Valentine laid his adopted son's body gently down on the ground, crossing his arms over his chest as if to hide the gaping, bloody wound there. "*Ave—*," he began, as if he meant to say the words over Jace, the Shadowhunter's farewell, but his voice cracked, and he turned abruptly and walked back toward the altar.

Clary couldn't move. Could barely breathe. She could hear her own heart beating, hear the scrape of her breathing in her dry throat. From the corner of her eye she could see Valentine standing by the edge of the lake, blood streaming from the blade of Maellartach and dripping into the bowl of the Mortal Cup. He was chanting words she didn't understand. She didn't care to try to understand. It would all be over soon, and she was almost glad. She wondered if she had enough energy to drag herself over to where Jace lay, if she could lie down beside him and wait for it to be over. She stared at him, lying motionless on the churned, bloody sand. His eyes were closed, his face still; if it weren't for the gash across his chest, she could have told herself he was asleep.

But he wasn't. He was a Shadowhunter; he had died in battle; he deserved the last benediction. *Ave atque vale.* Her lips shaped the words, though they fell from her mouth in silent puffs of air. Halfway through, she stopped, her breath catching. What should she say? Hail and farewell, Jace Wayland? That name was not truly his. He had never even really *been* named, she thought with agony, just given the name of a dead child because it had suited Valentine's purposes at the time. And there was so much power in a name. . . .

Her head whipped around, and she stared at the altar. The runes surrounding it had begun to glow. They were runes of summoning, runes of naming, and runes of binding. They were not unlike the runes that had kept Ithuriel imprisoned in the cellars beneath the Wayland manor. Now very much against her will, she thought of the way Jace had looked at her then, the blaze of faith in his eyes, his belief in her. He had always thought she was strong. He had showed it in everything he did, in every look and every touch. Simon had faith in her too, yet when he'd held her, it had been as if she were something fragile, something made of delicate glass. But Jace had held her with all the strength he had, never wondering if she could take it—he'd known she was as strong as he was.

Valentine was dipping the bloody Sword over and over in the water of the lake now, chanting low and fast. The water of the lake was rippling, as if a giant hand were stroking fingers lightly across its surface.

Clary closed her eyes. Remembering the way Jace had looked at her the night she'd freed Ithuriel, she couldn't help but imagine the way he'd look at her now if he saw her trying to lie down to die on the sand beside him. He wouldn't be touched, wouldn't think it was a beautiful gesture. He'd be angry at her for giving up. He'd be so—disappointed.

Clary lowered herself so that she was lying on the ground, heaving her dead legs behind her. Slowly she crawled across the sand, pushing herself along with her knees and bound hands. The glowing band around her wrists burned and stung. Her shirt tore as she dragged herself across the ground, and the sand scraped the bare skin of her stomach. She barely felt it. It was hard work, pulling herself along like this—sweat ran down her back, between her shoulder blades. When she finally reached the circle of runes, she was panting so loudly that she was terrified Valentine would hear her.

But he didn't even turn around. He had the Mortal Cup in one hand and the Sword in the other. As she watched, he drew his right hand back, spoke several words that sounded like Greek, and threw the Cup. It shone like a falling star as it hurtled toward the water of the lake and vanished beneath the surface with a faint splash.

The circle of runes was giving off a faint heat, like a partly banked fire. Clary had to twist and struggle to reach her hand around to the stele jammed into her belt. The pain in her wrists spiked as her fingers closed around the handle; she pulled it free with a muffled gasp of relief.

She couldn't separate her wrists, so she gripped the stele awkwardly in both hands. She pushed herself up with her elbows, staring down at the runes. She could feel the heat of them on her face; they had begun to shimmer like witchlight. Valentine had the Mortal Sword poised, ready to throw it; he was chanting the last words of the summoning spell. With a final burst of strength Clary drove the tip of the stele into the sand, not scraping aside the runes Valentine had drawn but tracing her own pattern over them, writing a new rune over the one that symbolized his name. It was such a small rune, she thought, such a small change—nothing like her immensely powerful Alliance rune, nothing like the Mark of Cain.

But it was all she could do. Spent, Clary rolled onto her side just as Valentine drew his arm back and let the Mortal Sword fly.

Maellartach hurtled end over end, a black and silver blur that joined soundlessly with the black and silver lake. A great plume went up from the place where it splashed down:

a flowering of platinum water. The plume rose higher and higher, a geyser of molten silver, like rain falling upward. There was a great crashing noise, the sound of shattering ice, a glacier breaking—and then the lake seemed to blow apart, silver water exploding upward like a reverse hailstorm.

And rising with the hailstorm came the Angel. Clary was not sure what she'd expected—something like Ithuriel, but Ithuriel had been diminished by many years of captivity and torment. This was an angel in the full force of his glory. As he rose from the water, her eyes began to burn as if she were staring into the sun.

Valentine's hands had fallen to his sides. He was gazing upward with a rapt expression, a man watching his greatest dream become reality. "*Raziel,*" he breathed.

The Angel continued to rise, as if the lake were sinking away, revealing a great column of marble at its center. First his head emerged from the water, streaming hair like chains of silver and gold. Then shoulders, white as stone, and then a bare torso—and Clary saw that the Angel was Marked all over with runes just as the Nephilim were, although Raziel's runes were golden and alive, moving across his white skin like sparks flying from a fire. Somehow, at the same time, the Angel was both enormous and no bigger than a man: Clary's eyes hurt trying to take all of him in, and yet he was all that she could see. As he rose, wings burst from his back and opened wide across the lake, and they were gold too, and feathered, and set into each feather was a single golden staring eye.

It was beautiful, and also terrifying. Clary wanted to look away, but she wouldn't. She would watch it all. She would watch it for Jace, because he couldn't.

It's just like all those pictures, she thought. The Angel rising from the lake, the Sword in one hand and the Cup in the other. Both were streaming water, but Raziel was dry as a bone, his wings undampened. His feet rested, white and bare, on the surface of the lake, stirring its waters into small ripples of movement. His face, beautiful and inhuman, gazed down at Valentine.

And then he spoke.

His voice was like a cry and a shout and like music, all at once. It contained no words, yet was totally comprehensible. The force of his breath nearly knocked Valentine backward; he dug the heels of his boots into the sand, his head tilted back as if he were walking against a gale. Clary felt the wind of the Angel's breath pass over her: It was hot like air escaping from a furnace, and smelled of strange spices.

It has been a thousand years since I was last summoned to this place, Raziel said. *Jonathan Shadowhunter called on me then, and begged me to mix my blood with the blood of mortal men in a Cup and create a race of warriors who would rid this earth of demonkind. I did all that he asked and told him I would do no more. Why do you summon me now, Nephilim?*

Valentine's voice was eager. "A thousand years have passed, Glorious One, but demonkind are still here."

What is that to me? A thousand years for an angel pass between one blink of an eye and another.

"The Nephilim you created were a great race of men. For many years they valiantly battled to rid this plane of demon taint. But they have failed due to weakness and corruption in their ranks. I intend to return them to their former glory—"

Glory? The Angel sounded faintly curious, as if the word were strange to him. *Glory belongs to God alone.*

Valentine didn't waver. "The Clave as the first Nephilim created it exists no more. They have allied themselves with Downworlders, the demon-tainted nonhumans who infest this world like fleas on the carcass of a rat. It is my intention to cleanse this world, to destroy every Downworlder along with every demon—"

Demons do not possess souls. But as for the creatures you speak of, the Children of Moon, Night, Lilith, and Faerie, all are souled. It seems that your rules as to what does and does not constitute a human being are stricter than our own. Clary could have sworn the Angel's voice had taken on a dry tone. *Do you intend to challenge heaven like that other Morning Star whose name you bear, Shadowhunter?*

"Not to challenge heaven, no, Lord Raziel. To *ally* myself with heaven—"

In a war of your making? We are heaven, Shadowhunter. We do not fight in your mundane battles.

When Valentine spoke again, he sounded almost hurt. "Lord Raziel. Surely you would not have allowed such a thing as a ritual by which you might be summoned to exist if you did not *intend* to be summoned. We Nephilim are your children. We need your guidance."

Guidance? Now the Angel sounded amused. *That hardly seems to be why you brought me here. You seek rather your own renown.*

"Renown?" Valentine echoed hoarsely. "I have given everything for this cause. My wife. My children. I have not withheld my sons. I have given everything I have for this—*everything*."

The Angel simply hovered, gazing down at Valentine with his weird, inhuman eyes. His wings moved in slow, undeliberate motions, like the passage of clouds across the sky. At last he said, *God asked Abraham to sacrifice his son on an altar much like this one, to see who it was that Abraham loved more, Isaac or God. But no one asked you to sacrifice your son, Valentine.*

Valentine glanced down at the altar at his feet, splashed with Jace's blood, and then back up at the Angel. "If I must, I will compel this from you," he said. "But I would rather have your willing cooperation."

When Jonathan Shadowhunter summoned me, said the Angel, *I gave him my assistance because I could see that his dream of a world free of demons was a true one. He imagined a heaven on this earth. But you dream only of your own glory, and you do not love heaven. My brother Ithuriel can attest to that.*

Valentine blanched. "But—"

Did you think that I would not know? The Angel smiled. It was the most terrible smile Clary had ever seen. *It is true that the master of the circle you have drawn can compel from me a single action. But you are not that master.*

Valentine stared. "My lord Raziel—there is no one else—"

But there is, said the Angel. *There is your daughter.*

Valentine whirled. Clary, lying half-conscious in the sand, her wrists and arms a screaming agony, stared defiantly back. For a moment their eyes met—and he *looked* at her, really looked at her, and she realized it was the first time her father had ever looked her in the face and *seen* her. The first and only time.

"Clarissa," he said. "What have you done?"

Clary stretched out her hand, and with her finger she wrote in the sand at his feet. She didn't draw runes. She drew words: the words he had said to her the first time he'd seen what she could do, when she'd drawn the rune that had destroyed his ship.

MENE MENE TEKEL UPHARSIN.

His eyes widened, just as Jace's eyes had widened before he'd died. Valentine had gone bone white. He turned slowly to face the Angel, raising his hands in a gesture of supplication. "My lord Raziel—"

The Angel opened his mouth and spat. Or at least that was how it seemed to Clary—that the Angel spat, and that what came from his mouth was a shooting spark of white fire, like a burning arrow. The arrow flew straight and true across the water and buried itself in Valentine's chest. Or maybe "buried" wasn't the word—it *tore* through him, like a rock through thin paper, leaving a smoking hole the size of a fist. For a moment Clary, staring up, could look *through* her father's chest and see the lake and the fiery glow of the Angel beyond.

The moment passed. Like a felled tree, Valentine crashed to the ground and lay still—his mouth open in a silent cry, his blind eyes fixed forever in a last look of incredulous betrayal.

That was the justice of heaven. I trust that you are not dismayed.

Clary looked up. The Angel hovered over her, like a tower of white flame, blotting out the sky. His hands were empty; the Mortal Cup and Sword lay by the shore of the lake.

You can compel me to one action, Clarissa Morgenstern. What is it that you want?

Clary opened her mouth. No sound came out.

Ah, yes, the Angel said, and there was gentleness in his voice now. *The rune.* The many eyes in his wings blinked. Something brushed over her. It was soft, softer than silk or any other cloth, softer than a whisper or the brush of a feather. It was what she imagined clouds might feel like if they had a texture. A faint scent came with the touch—a pleasant scent, heady and sweet.

The pain vanished from her wrists. No longer bound together, her hands fell to her sides. The stinging at the back of her neck was gone too, and the heaviness from her legs. She struggled to her knees. More than anything, she wanted to crawl across the bloody sand toward the place where Jace's body lay, crawl to him and lay down beside him and put her arms around him, even though he was gone. But the Angel's voice compelled her; she remained where she was, staring up into his brilliant golden light.

The battle on Brocelind Plain is ending. Morgenstern's hold over his demons vanished with his death. Already many are fleeing; the rest will soon be destroyed. There are Nephilim riding to the shores of this lake at this very moment. If you have a request, Shadowhunter, speak it now. The Angel paused. *And remember that I am not a genie. Choose your desire wisely.*

Clary hesitated—only for a moment, but the moment stretched out as long as any moment ever had. She could ask for anything, she thought dizzily, anything—an end to pain or world hunger or disease, or for peace on earth. But then again, perhaps these things weren't in the power of angels to grant, or they would already have been granted. And perhaps people were supposed to find these things for themselves.

It didn't matter, anyway. There was only one thing she could ask for, in the end, only one real choice.

She raised her eyes to the Angel's.

"Jace," she said.

The Angel's expression didn't change. She had no idea whether Raziel thought her request a good one or a bad one, or whether—she thought with a sudden burst of panic—he intended to grant it at all.

Close your eyes, Clarissa Morgenstern, the Angel said.

Clary shut her eyes. You didn't say no to an angel, no matter what it had in mind. Her heart pounding, she sat floating in the darkness behind her eyelids, resolutely trying not to think of Jace. But his face appeared against the blank screen of her closed eyelids anyway—not smiling at her but looking sidelong, and she could see the scar at his temple, the uneven curl at the corner of his mouth, and the silver line on his throat where Simon had bitten him—all the marks and flaws and imperfections that made up the person she loved most in the world. *Jace.* A bright light lit her vision to scarlet, and she fell back against the sand, wondering if she was going to pass out—or maybe she was dying—but she didn't want to die, not now that she could see Jace's face so clearly in front of her. She could almost hear his voice, too, saying her name, the way he'd whispered it at Renwick's, over and over again. *Clary. Clary. Clary.*

"Clary," Jace said. "Open your eyes."

She did.

She was lying on the sand, in her torn, wet, and bloodied clothes. That was the same. What was not the same was that the Angel was gone, and with him the blinding white light that had lit the darkness to day. She was gazing up at the night sky, white stars like mirrors shining in the blackness, and leaning over her, the light in his eyes more brilliant than any of the stars, was Jace.

Her eyes drank him in, every part of him, from his tangled hair to his bloodstained, grimy face to his eyes shining through the layers of dirt; from the bruises visible through his torn sleeves to the gaping, blood-soaked tear down the front of his shirt, through which his bare skin showed—and there was no mark, no gash, to indicate where the Sword had gone in. She could see the pulse beating in his throat, and almost threw her arms around him at the sight because it meant his heart was beating and that meant—

"You're alive," she whispered. "Really alive."

With a slow wonderment he reached to touch her face. "I was in the dark," he said softly. "There was nothing there but shadows, and I was a shadow, and I knew that I was dead, and that it was over, all of it. And then I heard your voice. I heard you say my name, and it brought me back."

"Not me." Clary's throat tightened. "The Angel brought you back."

"Because you asked him to." Silently he traced the outline of her face with his fingers, as if reassuring himself that she was real. "You could have had anything else in the world, and you asked for me."

She smiled up at him. Filthy as he was, covered in blood and dirt, he was the most beautiful thing she'd ever seen. "But I don't want anything else in the world."

At that, the light in his eyes, already bright, went to such a blaze that she could hardly bear to look at him. She thought of the Angel, and how he had burned like a thousand torches, and that Jace had in him some of that same incandescent blood, and how that burning shone through him now, through his eyes, like light through the cracks in a door.

I love you, Clary wanted to say. And, *I would do it again. I would always ask for you*. But those weren't the words she said.

"You're not my brother," she told him, a little breathlessly, as if, having realized she hadn't yet said them, she couldn't get the words out of her mouth fast enough. "You know that, right?"

Very slightly, through the grime and blood, Jace grinned. "Yes," he said. "I know that."

Epilogue

Across the Sky in Stars

I loved you, so I drew these tides of men into my hands
and wrote my will across the sky in stars.

—T. E. Lawrence

The smoke rose in a lazy spiral, tracing delicate lines of black across the clear air. Jace, alone on the hill overlooking the cemetery, sat with his elbows on his knees and watched the smoke drift heavenward. The irony wasn't lost on him: These were his father's remains, after all.

He could see the bier from where he was sitting, obscured by smoke and flame, and the small group standing around it. He recognized Jocelyn's bright hair from here, and Luke standing beside her, his hand on her back. Jocelyn had her head turned aside, away from the burning pyre.

Jace could have been one of that group, had he wanted to be. He'd spent the last couple of days in the infirmary, and they'd only let him out this morning, partly so that he could attend Valentine's funeral. But he'd gotten halfway to the pyre, a stacked pile of stripped wood, white as bones, and realized he could go no farther. He'd turned and walked up the hill instead, away from the mourners' procession. Luke had called after him, but Jace hadn't turned.

He'd sat and watched them gather around the bier, watched Patrick Penhallow in his parchment white gear set the flame to the wood. It was the second time that week he'd watched a body burn, but Max's had been heartbreakingly small, and Valentine was a big man—even flat on his back with his arms crossed over his chest, a seraph blade gripped in his fist. His eyes were bound with white silk, as was the custom. They had done well by him, Jace thought, for the sake of Clary and Jocelyn, though his ashes would never be used to build the Silent City. Instead they would be scattered at a crossroads, where lost souls were thought to reside.

They hadn't buried Sebastian. A group of Shadowhunters had gone back to the valley, but they hadn't found his body—washed away by the river, they'd told Jace, though he had his doubts.

He had looked for Clary in the crowd around the bier, but she wasn't there. It had been almost two days now since he'd seen her last, at the lake, and he missed her with an almost physical sense of something lacking. It wasn't her fault they hadn't seen each other. She'd been worried he wasn't strong enough to Portal back to Alicante from the lake that night, and she'd turned out to be right. By the time the first Shadowhunters had reached them, he'd been drifting into a dizzy unconsciousness. He'd woken up the next day in the Basilias with Magnus Bane staring down at him with an odd expression—it could have been deep concern or merely curiosity, it was hard to tell with Magnus. Magnus told him that though the Angel had healed Jace physically, it seemed that his spirit and mind had been exhausted to the point that only rest could heal them. In any event, he felt better now. Just in time for the funeral.

A wind had come up and was blowing the smoke away from him. In the distance he could see the glimmering towers of Alicante, their former glory restored. He wasn't totally sure what he hoped to accomplish by sitting here and watching his father's body burn, or what he would say if he were down there among the mourners, speaking their last words to Valentine. *You were never really my father*, he might say, or *You were the only father I ever knew*. Both statements were equally true, no matter how contradictory.

When he'd first opened his eyes at the lake—knowing, somehow, that he'd been dead, and now wasn't—all Jace could think about was Clary, lying a little distance away from him on the bloody sand, her eyes closed. He'd scrambled to her in a near panic, thinking she might be hurt, or even dead—and when she'd opened her eyes, all he'd been able to think about then was that she wasn't. Not until there were others there, helping him to his feet, exclaiming over the scene in amazement, did he see Valentine's body lying crumpled near the lake's edge and feel the force of it like a punch in the stomach. He'd known Valentine was dead—would have killed him himself—but still, somehow, the sight was painful. Clary had looked at Jace with sad eyes, and he'd known that even though she'd hated Valentine and had never had any reason not to, she still felt Jace's loss.

He half-closed his eyes and a flood of images washed across

the backs of his eyelids: Valentine picking him up off the grass in a sweeping hug, Valentine holding him steady in the prow of a boat on a lake, showing him how to balance. And other, darker memories: Valentine's hand cracking across the side of his face, a dead falcon, the angel shackled in the Waylands' cellar.

"Jace."

He looked up. Luke was standing over him, a black silhouette outlined by the sun. He was wearing jeans and a flannel shirt as usual—no concessionary funeral white for him. "It's over," Luke said. "The ceremony. It was brief."

"I'm sure it was." Jace dug his fingers into the ground beside him, welcoming the painful scrape of dirt against his fingertips. "Did anyone say anything?"

"Just the usual words." Luke eased himself down onto the ground beside Jace, wincing a little. Jace hadn't asked him what the battle had been like; he hadn't really wanted to know. He knew it had been over much quicker than anyone had expected—after Valentine's death, the demons he had summoned had fled into the night like so much mist burned off by the sun. But that didn't mean there hadn't been deaths. Valentine's hadn't been the only body burned in Alicante these past days.

"And Clary wasn't—I mean, she didn't—"

"Come to the funeral? No. She didn't want to." Jace could feel Luke looking at him sideways. "You haven't seen her? Not since—"

"No, not since the lake," Jace said. "This was the first time they let me leave the Basilias, and I had to come here."

"You didn't *have* to," Luke said. "You could have stayed away."

"I wanted to," Jace admitted. "Whatever that says about me."

"Funerals are for the living, Jace, not for the dead. Valentine was more your father than Clary's, even if you didn't share blood. You're the one who has to say good-bye. You're the one who will miss him."

"I didn't think I was allowed to miss him."

"You never knew Stephen Herondale," said Luke. "And you came to Robert Lightwood when you were only barely still a child. Valentine was the father of your childhood. You *should* miss him."

"I keep thinking about Hodge," Jace said. "Up at the Gard, I kept asking him why he'd never told me what I was—I still thought I was part demon then—and he kept saying it was because he didn't know. I just thought he was lying. But now I think he meant it. He was one of the only people who ever even knew there *was* a Herondale baby that had lived. When I showed up at the Institute, he had no idea which of Valentine's sons I was. The real one or the adopted one. And I could have been either. The demon or the angel. And the thing is, I don't think he ever knew, not until he saw Jonathan at the Gard and realized. So he just tried to do his best by me all those years anyway, until Valentine showed up again. That took a sort of faith—don't you think?"

"Yes," Luke said. "I think so."

"Hodge said he thought maybe upbringing might make a difference, regardless of blood. I just keep thinking—if I'd stayed with Valentine, if he hadn't sent me to the Lightwoods, would I have been just like Jonathan? Is that how I'd be now?"

"Does it matter?" said Luke. "You are who you are now for a reason. And if you ask me, I think Valentine sent you to the Lightwoods because he knew it was the best chance for you. Maybe he had other reasons too. But you can't get away from the fact that he sent you to people he knew would love you and raise you with love. It might have been one of the few things he ever really did for someone else." He clapped Jace on the shoulder, a gesture so paternal that it almost made Jace smile. "I wouldn't forget about that, if I were you."

Clary, standing and looking out Isabelle's window, watched smoke stain the sky over Alicante like a smudged hand against a window. They were burning Valentine today, she knew; burning her father, in the necropolis just outside the gates.

"You know about the celebration tonight, don't you?" Clary turned to see Isabelle, behind her, holding up two dresses against herself, one blue and one steel gray. "What do you think I should wear?"

For Isabelle, Clary thought, clothes would always be therapy. "The blue one."

Isabelle laid the dresses down on the bed. "What are you going to wear? You are going, aren't you?"

Clary thought of the silver dress at the bottom of Amatis's chest, the lovely gossamer of it. But Amatis would probably never let her wear it.

"I don't know," she said. "Probably jeans and my green coat."

"Boring," Isabelle said. She glanced over at Aline, who was sitting in a chair by the bed, reading. "Don't you think it's boring?"

"I think you should let Clary wear what she wants." Aline didn't look up from her book. "Besides, it's not like she's dressing up for anyone."

"She's dressing up for Jace," Isabelle said, as if this were obvious. "As well she should."

Aline looked up, blinking in confusion, then smiled. "Oh, right. I keep forgetting. It must be weird, right, knowing he's not your brother?"

"No," Clary said firmly. "Thinking he was my brother was weird. This feels—right." She looked back toward the window. "Not that I've really seen him since I found out. Not since we've been back in Alicante."

"That's strange," said Aline.

"It's not strange," Isabelle said, shooting Aline a meaningful look, which Aline didn't seem to notice. "He's been in the hospital. He only got out today."

"And he didn't come to see you right away?" Aline asked Clary.

"He couldn't," Clary said. "He had Valentine's funeral to go to. He couldn't miss that."

"Maybe," said Aline cheerfully. "Or maybe he's not that interested in you anymore. I mean, now that it's not forbidden. Some people only want what they can't have."

"Not Jace," Isabelle said quickly. "Jace isn't like that."

Aline stood up, dropping her book onto the bed. "I should go get dressed. See you guys tonight?" And with that, she wandered out of the room, humming to herself.

Isabelle, watching her go, shook her head. "Do you think she doesn't like you?" she said. "I mean, is she jealous? She did seem interested in Jace."

"Ha!" Clary was briefly amused. "No, she's not interested in Jace. I think she's just one of those people who say whatever they're thinking whenever they think it. And who knows, maybe she's right."

Isabelle pulled the pin from her hair, letting it fall down

around her shoulders. She came across the room and joined Clary at the window. The sky was clear now past the demon towers; the smoke was gone. "Do *you* think she's right?"

"I don't know. I'll have to ask Jace. I guess I'll see him tonight at the party. Or the victory celebration or whatever it's called." She looked up at Isabelle. "Do you know what it'll be like?"

"There'll be a parade," Isabelle said, "and fireworks, probably. Music, dancing, games, that sort of thing. Like a big street fair in New York." She glanced out the window, her expression wistful. "Max would have loved it."

Clary reached out and stroked Isabelle's hair, the way she'd stroke the hair of her own sister if she had one. "I know he would."

Jace had to knock twice at the door of the old canal house before he heard quick footsteps hurrying to answer; his heart jumped, and then settled as the door opened and Amatis Herondale stood on the threshold, looking at him in surprise. She looked as if she'd been getting ready for the celebration: She wore a long dove gray dress and pale metallic earrings that picked out the silvery streaks in her graying hair. "Yes?"

"Clary," he began, and stopped, unsure what exactly to say. Where had his eloquence gone? He'd always had that, even when he hadn't had anything else, but now he felt as if he'd been ripped open and all the clever, facile words had poured out of him, leaving him empty. "I was wondering if Clary was here. I was hoping to talk to her."

Amatis shook her head. The blankness had gone from her expression, and she was looking at him intently enough to make him nervous. "She's not. I think she's with the Lightwoods."

"Oh." He was surprised at how disappointed he felt. "Sorry to have bothered you."

"It's no bother. I'm glad you're here, actually," she said briskly. "There was something I wanted to talk to you about. Come into the hall; I'll be right back."

Jace stepped inside as she disappeared down the hallway. He wondered what on earth she could have to talk to him about. Maybe Clary had decided she wanted nothing more to do with him and had chosen Amatis to deliver the message.

Amatis was back in a moment. She wasn't holding anything that looked like a note—to Jace's relief—but rather she was clutching a small metal box in her hands. It was a delicate object, chased with a design of birds. "Jace," Amatis said. "Luke told me that you're Stephen's—that Stephen Herondale was your father. He told me everything that happened."

Jace nodded, which was all he felt called on to do. The news was leaking out slowly, which was how he liked it; hopefully he'd be back in New York before everyone in Idris knew and was constantly staring at him.

"You know I was married to Stephen before your mother was," Amatis went on, her voice tight, as if the words hurt to say. Jace stared at her—was this about his mother? Did she resent him for bringing up bad memories of a woman who'd died before he was ever born? "Of all the people alive today, I probably knew your father best."

"Yes," Jace said, wishing he were elsewhere. "I'm sure that's true."

"I know you probably have feelings about him that are very mixed," she said, surprising him mainly because it was true. "You never knew him. He wasn't the man who raised you. You don't even look that much like him, except for your fair hair—but those eyes of yours, I don't know where you got those. So maybe I'm being crazy, bothering you with this. Maybe you don't really want to know about Stephen at all. But he *was* your father, and if he'd known you—" She thrust the box at him then, nearly making him jump back. "These are some things of his that I saved over the years. Letters he wrote, photographs, a family tree. His witchlight stone. Maybe you don't have questions now, but someday perhaps you will, and when you do—when you do, you'll have this." She stood still, giving him the box as if she were offering him a precious treasure. Jace reached out and took it from her without a word; it was heavy, and the metal was cold against his skin.

"Thank you," he said. It was the best he could do. He hesitated, and then said, "There is one thing. Something I've been wondering."

"Yes?"

"If Stephen was my father, then the Inquisitor—Imogen—was my grandmother."

"She was . . ." Amatis paused. "A very difficult woman. But yes, she was your grandmother."

"She saved my life," said Jace. "I mean, for a long time she acted like she hated my guts. But then she saw this." He drew the collar of his shirt aside, showing Amatis the white star-shaped scar on his shoulder. "And she saved my life. But what could my scar possibly mean to her?"

Amatis's eyes had gone wide. "You don't remember getting that scar, do you?"

Jace shook his head. "Valentine told me it was an injury from when I was too young to remember, but now—I don't think I believe him."

"It's not a scar. It's a birthmark, of sorts, and a Herondale family secret. The story Stephen told me was that years ago, a Herondale ancestor encountered an angel. The angel touched him on the shoulder, and the touch left a mark like a star. It is the mark of one who has had contact with an angel. The mark was passed on through his blood: all his male descendants have it as well."

Jace thought of Ithuriel, tortured and dying in the cellars of the Wayland mansion. He had told no one of that encounter, and suspected Clary hadn't either. It was too raw, too private and painful. "So anyone who has had contact with an angel—a real, living angel—might have one? Not just a Herondale?"

Amatis looked puzzled. "I suppose, but I've never heard of anyone else having contact like that. You know the Clave says no one but Jonathan Shadowhunter has ever seen an angel face to face. But that's what your father told me." She touched her right upper arm. "His scar was here. I have never heard of anyone who wasn't a Herondale having a mark like it. Imogen must have seen it and guessed who you really were."

Jace stared at Amatis, but he wasn't seeing her: He was seeing that night on the ship; the wet, black deck and the Inquisitor dying at his feet. "She said something to me," he said. "While she was dying. She said, 'Your father would be proud of you.' I thought she was being cruel. I thought she meant Valentine. . . ."

Amatis shook her head. "She meant Stephen," she said softly. "And she was right. He would have been."

Clary pushed open Amatis's front door and stepped inside, thinking how quickly the house had become familiar to her. She no longer had to strain to remember the way to the front door, or the way the knob stuck slightly as she pushed it open. The glint of sunlight off the canal was familiar, as was the view of Alicante through the window. She could almost imagine living here, almost imagine what it would be like if Idris were home. She wondered what she'd start missing first. Chinese takeout? Movies? Midtown Comics?

She was about to head for the stairs when she heard her mother's voice from the living room—sharp, and slightly agitated. But what could Jocelyn have to be upset about? Everything was fine now, wasn't it? Without thinking, Clary dropped back against the wall near the living room door and listened.

"What do you mean, you're staying?" Jocelyn was saying. "You mean you're not coming back to New York at all?"

"I've been asked to remain in Alicante and represent the werewolves on the Council," Luke said. "I told them I'd let them know tonight."

"Couldn't someone else do that? One of the pack leaders here in Idris?"

"I'm the only pack leader who was once a Shadowhunter. That's why they want me." He sighed. "I started all this, Jocelyn. I should stay here and see it out."

There was a short silence. "If that's how you feel, then of course you should stay," Jocelyn said at last, but her voice didn't sound sure.

"I'll have to sell the bookstore. Get my affairs in order." Luke sounded gruff. "It's not like I'll be moving right away."

"I can take care of that. After everything you've done . . ." Jocelyn didn't seem to have the energy to maintain her bright tone. Her voice trailed off into silence, a silence that stretched out so long that Clary thought about clearing her throat and walking into the living room to let them know she was there.

A moment later she was glad she hadn't. "Look," Luke said, "I've wanted to tell you this for a long time, but I didn't. I knew it would never matter, even if I did say it, because of what I am. You never wanted that to be part of Clary's life. But she knows now, so I guess it doesn't make a difference. And I might as well tell you. I love you, Jocelyn. I have for twenty years." He paused. Clary strained to hear her mother's response, but Jocelyn was silent. At last Luke spoke again, his voice heavy. "I have to get back to the Council and tell them I'll stay. We don't ever have to talk about this again. I just feel better having said it after all this time."

Clary pressed herself back against the wall as Luke, his head down, stalked out of the living room. He brushed by her without seeming to see her at all and yanked the front door open. He stood there for a moment, staring blindly out at the sunshine bouncing off the water of the canal. Then he was gone, the door slamming shut behind him.

Clary stood where she was, her back against the wall. She felt terribly sad for Luke, and terribly sad for her mother, too. It looked like Jocelyn really didn't love Luke, and maybe never could. It was just like it had been for her and Simon, except she didn't see any way that Luke and her mother could fix things. Not if he was going to stay here in Idris. Tears stung her eyes. She was about to turn and go into the living room when she heard the sound of the kitchen door opening and another voice. This one sounded tired, and a little resigned. Amatis.

"Sorry I overheard that, but I'm glad he's staying," Luke's sister said. "Not just because he'll be near me but because it gives him a chance to get over *you*."

Jocelyn sounded defensive. “Amatis—”

“It’s been a long time, Jocelyn,” Amatis said. “If you don’t love him, you ought to let him go.”

Jocelyn was silent. Clary wished she could see her mother’s expression—did she look sad? Angry? Resigned?

Amatis gave a little gasp. “Unless—you *do* love him?”

“Amatis, I can’t—”

“You do! You *do*!” There was a sharp sound, as if Amatis had clapped her hands together. “I knew you did! I always knew it!”

“It doesn’t matter.” Jocelyn sounded tired. “It wouldn’t be fair to Luke.”

“I don’t want to hear it.” There was a rustling noise, and Jocelyn made a sound of protest. Clary wondered if Amatis had actually grabbed hold of her mother. “If you love him, you go right now and tell him. Right now, before he goes to the Council.”

“But they want him to be their Council member! And he wants to—”

“All Lucian wants,” said Amatis firmly, “is you. You and Clary. That’s all he ever wanted. Now go.”

Before Clary had a chance to move, Jocelyn dashed out into the hallway. She headed toward the door—and saw Clary, flattened against the wall. Halting, she opened her mouth in surprise.

“Clary!” She sounded as if she were trying to make her voice bright and cheerful, and failing miserably. “I didn’t realize you were here.”

Clary stepped away from the wall, grabbed hold of the doorknob, and threw the door wide open. Bright sunlight poured into the hall. Jocelyn stood blinking in the harsh illumination, her eyes on her daughter.

"If you don't go after Luke," Clary said, enunciating very clearly, "I, personally, will kill you."

For a moment Jocelyn looked astonished. Then she smiled. "Well," she said, "if you put it like *that*."

A moment later she was out of the house, hurrying down the canal path toward the Accords Hall. Clary shut the door behind her and leaned against it.

Amatis, emerging from the living room, darted past her to lean on the windowsill, glancing anxiously out through the pane. "Do you think she'll catch him before he gets to the Hall?"

"My mom's spent her whole life chasing me around," Clary said. "She moves *fast*."

Amatis glanced toward her and smiled. "Oh, that reminds me," she said. "Jace stopped by to see you. I think he's hoping to see you at the celebration tonight."

"*Is* he?" Clary said thoughtfully. *Might as well ask. Nothing ventured, nothing gained.* "Amatis," she said, and Luke's sister turned away from the window, looking at her curiously.

"Yes?"

"That silver dress of yours, in the trunk," said Clary. "Can I borrow it?"

The streets were already beginning to fill with people as Clary walked back through the city toward the Lightwoods' house. It was twilight, and the lights were beginning to go on, filling the air with a pale glow. Bunches of familiar-looking white flowers hung from baskets on the walls, filling the air with their spicy smells. Dark gold fire-runes burned on the doors of the houses she passed; the runes spoke of victory and rejoicing.

There were Shadowhunters out in the streets. None were

wearing gear—they were in a variety of finery, from the modern to what bordered on historical costumery. It was an unusually warm night, so few people were wearing coats, but there were plenty of women in what looked to Clary like ball gowns, their full skirts sweeping the streets. A slim dark figure cut across the road ahead of her as she turned onto the Lightwoods' street, and she saw that it was Raphael, hand in hand with a tall dark-haired woman in a red cocktail dress. He glanced over his shoulder and smiled at Clary, a smile that sent a little shiver over her, and she thought that it was true that there really was something alien about Downworlders sometimes, something alien and frightening. Perhaps it was just that everything that was frightening wasn't necessarily also bad.

Although, she had her doubts about Raphael.

The front door of the Lightwoods' house was open, and several of the family were already standing out on the pavement. Maryse and Robert Lightwood were there, chatting with two other adults; when they turned, Clary saw with slight surprise that it was the Penhallows, Aline's parents. Maryse smiled at her past them; she was elegant in a dark blue silk suit, her hair tied back from her severe face with a thick silver band. She looked like Isabelle—so much so that Clary wanted to reach out and put a hand on her shoulder. Maryse still seemed so sad, even as she smiled, and Clary thought, *She's remembering Max, just like Isabelle was, and thinking how much he would have liked all this.*

"Clary!" Isabelle bounded down the front steps, her dark hair flying behind her. She was wearing neither of the outfits she'd showed to Clary earlier, but an incredible gold satin dress that hugged her body like the closed petals of a flower.

Her shoes were spiked sandals, and Clary remembered what Isabelle had once said about how she liked her heels, and laughed to herself. "You look *fantastic*."

"Thanks." Clary tugged a little self-consciously at the diaphanous material of the silver dress. It was probably the girliest thing she'd ever worn. It left her shoulders uncovered, and every time she felt the ends of her hair tickle the bare skin there, she had to quell the urge to hunt for a cardigan or hoodie to wrap herself in. "You too."

Isabelle bent over to whisper in her ear. "Jace isn't here."

Clary pulled back. "Then where—?"

"Alec says he might be at the square, where the fireworks are going to be. I'm sorry—I have no idea what's up with him."

Clary shrugged, trying to hide her disappointment. "It's okay."

Alec and Aline tumbled out of the house after Isabelle, Aline in a bright red dress that made her hair look shockingly black. Alec had dressed like he usually did, in a sweater and dark pants, though Clary had to admit that at least the sweater didn't appear to have any visible holes in it. He smiled at Clary, and she thought, with surprise, that actually he *did* look different. Lighter somehow, as if a weight were off his shoulders.

"I've never been to a celebration that had Downworlders at it before," said Aline, looking nervously down the street, where a faerie girl whose long hair was braided with flowers—no, Clary thought, her hair *was* flowers, connected by delicate green tendrils—was plucking some of the white blossoms out of a hanging basket, looking at them thoughtfully, and eating them.

"You'll love it," Isabelle said. "They know how to party."

She waved good-bye to her parents and they set off toward the plaza, Clary still fighting the urge to cover the top half of her body by crossing her arms over her chest. The dress swirled out around her feet like smoke curling on the wind. She thought of the smoke that had risen over Alicante earlier that day, and shivered.

"Hey!" Isabelle said, and Clary looked up to see Simon and Maia coming toward them up the street. She hadn't seen Simon for most of the day; he'd gone down to the Hall to observe the preliminary Council meeting because, he said, he was curious who they'd choose to hold the vampires' Council seat. Maia looked out of place wearing anything as girly as a dress, and indeed she was clad in low-slung camo pants and a black T-shirt that said CHOOSE YOUR WEAPON and had a design of dice under the words. It was a gamer tee, Clary thought, wondering if Maia was really a gamer or was wearing the T-shirt to impress Simon. If so, it was a good choice. "You heading back down to Angel Square?"

Maia and Simon acknowledged that they were, and they headed toward the Hall together in a companionable group. Simon dropped back to fall into step beside Clary, and they walked together in silence. It was good just to be close to Simon again—he had been the first person she'd wanted to see once she was back in Alicante. She'd hugged him very tightly, glad he was alive, and touched the Mark on his forehead.

"Did it save you?" she'd asked, desperate to hear that she hadn't done what she had to him for no reason.

"It saved me," was all he'd said in reply.

"I wish I could take it off you," she'd said. "I wish I knew what might happen to you because of it."

He'd taken hold of her wrist and drawn her hand gently back down to her side. "We'll wait," he'd said. "And we'll see."

She'd been watching him closely, but she had to admit that the Mark didn't seem to be affecting him in any visible way. He seemed just as he always had. Just like Simon. Only he'd taken to brushing his hair slightly differently, to cover the Mark; if you didn't already know it was there, you'd never guess.

"How was the meeting?" Clary asked him now, giving him a once-over to see if he'd dressed up for the celebration. He hadn't, but she hardly blamed him—the jeans and T-shirt he had on were all he had to wear. "Who'd they choose?"

"*Not* Raphael," Simon said, sounding as if he were pleased about it. "Some other vampire. He had a pretentious name. Nightshade or something."

"You know, they asked me if I wanted to draw the symbol of the New Council," Clary said. "It's an honor. I said I'd do it. It's going to have the rune of the Council surrounded by the symbols of the four Downworlder families. A moon for the werewolves, and I was thinking a four-leaf clover for the faeries. A spell book for the warlocks. But I can't think of anything for the vampires."

"How about a fang?" Simon suggested. "Maybe dripping blood." He bared his teeth.

"Thank you," Clary said. "That's very helpful."

"I'm glad they asked you," Simon said, more seriously. "You deserve the honor. You deserve a medal, really, for what you did. The Alliance rune and everything."

Clary shrugged. "I don't know. I mean, the battle barely went on for ten minutes, after all that. I don't know how much I helped."

"I was *in* that battle, Clary," Simon said. "It may have been about ten minutes long, but it was the worst ten minutes of my life. And I don't really want to talk about it. But I will say that even in that ten minutes, there would have been a lot more death if it hadn't been for you. Besides, the battle was only part of it. If you hadn't done what you did, there would be no New Council. We would be Shadowhunters and Downworlders, hating each other, instead of Shadowhunters and Downworlders, going to a party together."

Clary felt a lump rising in her throat and stared straight ahead, willing herself not to tear up. "Thanks, Simon." She hesitated, so briefly that no one who wasn't Simon would have noticed it. But he did.

"What's wrong?" he asked her.

"I'm just wondering what we do when we get back home," she said. "I mean, I know Magnus took care of your mom so she hasn't been freaking out that you're gone, but—school. We've missed a ton of it. And I don't even know . . ."

"You're not going back," Simon said quietly. "You think I don't know that? You're a Shadowhunter now. You'll finish up your education at the Institute."

"And what about you? You're a vampire. Are you just going to go back to high school?"

"Yeah," Simon said, surprising her. "I am. I want a normal life, as much as I can have one. I want high school, and college, and all of that."

She squeezed his hand. "Then you should have it." She smiled up at him. "Of course, everyone's going to freak out when you show up at school."

"Freak out? Why?"

"Because you're so much hotter now than when you left." She shrugged. "It's true. Must be a vampire thing."

Simon looked baffled. "I'm hotter now?"

"Sure you are. I mean, look at those two. They're both totally into you." She pointed to a few feet in front of them, where Isabelle and Maia had moved to walk side by side, their heads bent together.

Simon looked up ahead at the girls. Clary could almost swear he was blushing. "Are they? Sometimes they get together and whisper and *stare* at me. I have no idea what it's about."

"Sure you don't." Clary grinned. "Poor you, you have two cute girls vying for your love. Your life is hard."

"Fine. You tell me which one to choose, then."

"No way. That's on you." She lowered her voice again. "Look, you can date whoever you want and I will *totally* support you. I am all about support. Support is my middle name."

"So *that's* why you never told me your middle name. I figured it was something embarrassing."

Clary ignored this. "But just promise me something, okay? I know how girls get. I know how they hate their boyfriends having a best friend who's a girl. Just promise me you won't cut me out of your life totally. That we can still hang out sometimes."

"Sometimes?" Simon shook his head. "Clary, you're crazy."

Her heart sank. "You mean . . ."

"I *mean* that I would never date a girl who insisted that I cut you out of my life. It's non-negotiable. You want a piece of all *this* fabulousness?" He gestured at himself. "Well, my best friend comes along with it. I wouldn't cut you out of my life, Clary, any more than I would cut off my right hand and give it to someone as a Valentine's Day gift."

"Gross," said Clary. "Must you?"

He grinned. "I must."

Angel Square was almost unrecognizable. The Hall glowed white at the far end of the plaza, partly obscured by an elaborate forest of huge trees that had sprung up in the center of the square. They were clearly the product of magic—although, Clary thought, remembering Magnus's ability to whisk furniture and cups of coffee across Manhattan at the blink of an eye, maybe they were real, if transplanted. The trees rose nearly to the height of the demon towers, their silvery trunks wrapped with ribbons, colored lights caught in the whispering green nets of their branches. The square smelled of white flowers, smoke, and leaves. All around its edges were placed tables and long benches, and groups of Shadowhunters and Downworlders crowded around them, laughing and drinking and talking. Yet despite the laughter, there was a somberness mixed with the air of celebration—a present sorrow side by side with joy.

The stores that lined the square had their doors thrown open, light spilling out onto the pavement. Partygoers streamed by, carrying plates of food and long-stemmed glasses of wine and brightly colored liquids. Simon watched a kelpie skip past, carrying a glass of blue fluid, and raised an eyebrow.

"It's not like Magnus's party," Isabelle reassured him. "Everything here ought to be safe to drink."

"*Ought* to be?" Aline looked worried.

Alec glanced toward the mini-forest, the colored lights reflecting in the blue irises of his eyes. Magnus stood in the shadow of a tree, talking to a girl in a white dress with a cloud of pale brown hair. She turned as Magnus looked toward them, and Clary locked eyes with her for a moment across the distance that separated them. There was something familiar about her, though Clary couldn't have said what it was.

Magnus broke away and came toward them, and the girl he'd been talking to slipped into the shadows of the trees and was gone. He was dressed like a Victorian gentleman, in a long black frock coat over a violet silk vest. A square pocket handkerchief embroidered with the initials M.B. protruded from his vest pocket.

"Nice vest," said Alec with a smile.

"Would you like one exactly like it?" Magnus inquired. "In any color you prefer, of course."

"I don't really care about clothes," Alec protested.

"And I love that about you," Magnus announced, "though I would also love you if you owned, perhaps, one designer suit. What do you say? Dolce? Zegna? Armani?"

Alec sputtered as Isabelle laughed, and Magnus took the opportunity to lean close to Clary and whisper in her ear. "The Accords Hall steps. Go."

She wanted to ask him what he meant, but he'd already turned back to Alec and the others. Besides, she had a feeling she knew. She squeezed Simon's wrist as she went, and he turned to smile at her before returning to his conversation with Maia.

She cut through the edge of the glamour forest to cross the square, weaving in and out of the shadows. The trees reached up to the foot of the Hall stairs, which was probably why the steps were almost deserted. Though not entirely. Glancing toward the doors, Clary could make out a familiar dark outline, seated in the shadow of a pillar. Her heart quickened.

Jace.

She had to gather her skirt up in her hands to climb the stairs, afraid she'd step on and tear the delicate material. She almost wished she had worn her normal clothes as she approached Jace, who was sitting with his back to a pillar, staring out over the square. He wore his most mundane clothes—jeans, a white shirt, and a dark jacket over them. And for almost the first time since she'd met him, she thought, he didn't seem to be carrying any weapons.

She abruptly felt overdressed. She stopped a slight distance away from him, suddenly unsure what to say.

As if sensing her there, Jace looked up. He was holding something balanced in his lap, she saw, a silvery box. He looked tired. There were shadows under his eyes, and his pale gold hair was untidy. His eyes widened. "Clary?"

"Who else would it be?"

He didn't smile. "You don't look like you."

"It's the dress." She smoothed her hands down the material self-consciously. "I don't usually wear things this . . . pretty."

"You always look beautiful," he said, and she remembered the first time he'd called her beautiful, in the greenhouse at the Institute. He hadn't said it like it was a compliment, but just as if it were an accepted fact, like the fact that she had red hair and liked to draw. "But you look—distant. Like I couldn't touch you."

She came over then and sat down next to him on the wide top step. The stone was cold through the material of her dress. She held her hand out to him; it was shaking slightly, just enough to be visible. "Touch me," she said. "If you want to."

He took her hand and laid it against his cheek for a moment. Then he set it back down in her lap. Clary shivered a little, remembering Aline's words back in Isabelle's bedroom. *Maybe he's not that interested in you anymore. I mean, now that it's not forbidden.* He had said *she* looked distant, but the expression in his eyes was as remote as a faraway galaxy.

"What's in the box?" she asked. He was still clutching the silver rectangle tightly in one hand. It was an expensive-looking object, delicately carved with a pattern of birds.

"I went to Amatis's earlier today, looking for you," he said. "But you weren't there. So I talked to Amatis. She gave me this." He indicated the box. "It belonged to my father."

For a moment she just looked at him uncomprehendingly. *This was Valentine's?* she thought, and then, with a jolt, *No, that's not what he means.* "Of course," she said. "Amatis was married to Stephen Herondale."

"I've been going through it," he said. "Reading the letters, the journal pages. I thought if I did that, I might feel some sort of connection to him. Something that would leap off the pages at me, saying, *Yes, this is your father.* But I don't feel anything. Just bits of paper. Anyone could have written these things."

"Jace," she said softly.

"And that's another thing," he said. "I don't have a name anymore, do I? I'm not Jonathan Christopher—that was someone else. But it's the name I'm used to."

"Who came up with Jace as a nickname? Did you come up with it yourself?"

Jace shook his head. "No. Valentine always called me Jonathan. And that's what they called me when I first got to the Institute. I was never supposed to think my name was Jonathan Christopher, you know—that was an accident. I got the name out of my father's journal, but it wasn't me he was talking about. It wasn't my progress he was recording. It was Seb— It was Jonathan's. So the first time I ever told Maryse that my middle name was Christopher, she told herself that she'd just remembered wrong, and Christopher had been Michael's son's middle name. It had been ten years, after all. But that was when she started calling me Jace: It was like she wanted to give me a new name, something that belonged to her, to my life in New York. And I liked it. I'd never liked Jonathan." He turned the box over in his hands. "I wonder if maybe Maryse knew, or guessed, but just didn't want to know. She loved me . . . and she didn't want to believe it."

"Which is why she was so upset when she found out you *were* Valentine's son," said Clary. "Because she thought she ought to have known. She kind of *did* know. But we never do want to believe things like that about people we love. And, Jace, she was right about you. She was right about who you really are. And you *do* have a name. Your name is Jace. Valentine didn't give that name to you. Maryse did. The only thing that makes a name important, and yours, is that it's given to you by someone who loves you."

"Jace what?" he said. "Jace Herondale?"

"Oh, please," she said. "You're Jace *Lightwood*. You know that."

He raised his eyes to hers. His lashes shadowed them thickly, darkening the gold. She thought he looked a little less remote, though perhaps she was imagining it.

"Maybe you're a different person than you thought you were," she went on, hoping against hope that he understood what she meant. "But no one becomes a totally different person overnight. Just finding out that Stephen was your biological father isn't going to automatically make you love him. And you don't have to. Valentine wasn't your real father, but not because you don't have his blood in your veins. He wasn't your real father because he didn't *act* like a father. He didn't take care of you. It's always been the Lightwoods who have taken care of you. *They're* your family. Just like Mom and Luke are mine." She reached to touch his shoulder, then drew her hand back. "I'm sorry," she said. "Here I am lecturing you, and you probably came up here to be alone."

"You're right," he said.

Clary felt the breath go out of her. "All right, then. I'll go." She stood up, forgetting to hold her dress up, and nearly stepped on the hem.

"Clary!" Setting the box down, Jace scrambled to his feet. "Clary, wait. That wasn't what I meant. I didn't mean I wanted to be alone. I meant you were right about Valentine—about the Lightwoods—"

She turned and looked at him. He was standing half in and half out of the shadows, the bright, colored lights of the party below casting strange patterns across his skin. She thought of the first time she'd seen him. She'd thought he looked like a lion. Beautiful and deadly. He looked different to her now. That hard, defensive casing he wore like armor was gone, and he wore his injuries instead, visibly and proudly. He hadn't even used his stele to take away the bruises on his face, along the line of his jaw, at his throat where the skin showed above the collar of his shirt. But he looked beautiful to her still, more than before, because now he seemed human—human, and real.

"You know," she said, "Aline said maybe you wouldn't be interested anymore. Now that it *isn't* forbidden. Now that you could be with me if you wanted to." She shivered a little in the flimsy dress, gripping her elbows with her hands. "Is that true? Are you not . . . interested?"

"*Interested?* As if you were a—a book, or a piece of news? No, I'm not *interested*. I'm—" He broke off, groping for the word the way someone might grope for a light switch in the dark. "Do you remember what I said to you before? About feeling like the fact that you were my sister was a sort of cosmic joke on me? On both of us?"

"I remember."

"I never believed it," he said. "I mean, I believed it in a way—I let it drive me to despair, but I never *felt* it. Never felt you were my sister. Because I didn't feel about you the way you're supposed to feel about your sister. But that didn't mean I didn't feel like you were a part of me. I've always felt that." Seeing her puzzled expression, he broke off with an impatient noise. "I'm not saying this right. Clary, I hated every second that I thought you were my sister. I hated every moment that I thought what I felt for you meant there was something wrong with me. But—"

"But *what?*" Clary's heart was beating so hard it was making her feel more than a little dizzy.

"I could see the delight Valentine took in the way I felt about you. The way you felt about me. He used it as a weapon against us. And that made me hate him. More than anything else he'd ever done to me, that made me hate him, and it made me turn against him, and maybe that's what I needed to do. Because there were times I didn't know if I wanted to follow him or not. It was a hard choice—harder than I like to remember." His voice sounded tight.

"I asked you if I had a choice once," Clary reminded him. "And you said, 'We always have choices.' You chose against Valentine. In the end that was the choice you made, and it doesn't matter how hard it was to make it. It matters that you did."

"I know," Jace said. "I'm just saying that I think I chose the way I did in part because of you. Since I've met you, everything I've done has been in part because of you. I can't untie myself from you, Clary—not my heart or my blood or my mind or any other part of me. And I don't want to."

"You don't?" she whispered.

He took a step toward her. His gaze was fastened on her face, as if he couldn't look away. "I always thought love made you stupid. Made you weak. A bad Shadowhunter. *To love is to destroy.* I believed that."

She bit her lip, but she couldn't look away from him, either.

"I used to think being a good warrior meant not caring," he said. "About anything, myself especially. I took every risk I could. I flung myself in the path of demons. I think I gave Alec a complex about what kind of fighter he was, just because he wanted to live." Jace smiled unevenly. "And then I met you. You were a mundane. Weak. Not a fighter. Never trained. And then I saw how much you loved your mother, loved Simon, and how you'd walk into hell to save them. You *did* walk into that vampire hotel. Shadowhunters with a decade of experience wouldn't have tried that. Love didn't make you weak, it made you stronger than anyone I'd ever met. And I realized I was the one who was weak."

"*No.*" She was shocked. "You're not."

"Maybe not anymore." He took another step, and now he was close enough to touch her. "Valentine couldn't believe I'd killed Jonathan," he said. "Couldn't believe it because I was the weak one, and Jonathan was the one with more training. By all rights he probably should have killed me. He nearly did. But I thought of *you*—I saw you there, clearly, as if you were standing in front of me, watching me, and I knew I wanted to live, wanted it more than I'd ever wanted anything, if only so that I could see your face one more time."

She wished she could move, wished she could reach out and touch him, but she couldn't. Her arms felt frozen at her sides. His face was close to hers, so close that she could see her own reflection in the pupils of his eyes.

"And now I'm looking at you," he said, "and you're asking me if I still want you, as if I could stop loving you. As if I would want to give up the thing that makes me stronger than anything else ever has. I never dared give much of myself to anyone before—bits of myself to the Lightwoods, to Isabelle and Alec, but it took years to do it—but, Clary, since the first time I saw you, I have belonged to you completely. I still do. If you want me."

For a split second longer she stood motionless. Then, somehow, she had caught at the front of his shirt and pulled him toward her. His arms went around her, lifting her almost out of her sandals, and then he was kissing her—or she was kissing him, she wasn't sure, and it didn't matter. The feel of his mouth on hers was electric; her hands gripped his arms, pulling him hard against her. The feel of his heart pounding through his shirt made her dizzy with joy. No one else's heart beat like Jace's did, or ever could.

He let her go at last and she gasped—she'd forgotten to breathe. He cupped her face between his hands, tracing the curve of her cheekbones with his fingers. The light was back in his eyes, as bright as it had been by the lake, but now there was a wicked sparkle to it. "There," he said. "That wasn't so bad, was it, even though it wasn't forbidden?"

"I've had worse," she said, with a shaky laugh.

"You know," he said, bending to brush his mouth across hers, "if it's the lack of *forbidden* you're worried about, you could still forbid me to do things."

"What kinds of things?"

She felt him smile against her mouth. "Things like this."

After some time they came down the stairs and into the square, where a crowd had begun to gather in anticipation of the fireworks. Isabelle and the others had found a table near the corner of the square and were crowded around it on benches and chairs. As they approached the group, Clary prepared to draw her hand out of Jace's—and then stopped herself. They could hold hands if they wanted to. There was nothing wrong with it. The thought almost took her breath away.

"You're here!" Isabelle danced up to them in delight, carrying a glass of fuchsia liquid, which she thrust at Clary. "Have some of this!"

Clary squinted at it. "Is it going to turn me into a rodent?"

"Where is the trust? I think it's strawberry juice," Isabelle said. "Anyway, it's yummy. Jace?" She offered him the glass.

"I am a man," he told her, "and men do not consume pink beverages. Get thee gone, woman, and bring me something brown."

"Brown?" Isabelle made a face.

"Brown is a manly color," said Jace, and yanked on a stray lock of Isabelle's hair with his free hand. "In fact, look—Alec is wearing it."

Alec looked mournfully down at his sweater. "It was black," he said. "But then it faded."

"You could dress it up with a sequined headband," Magnus suggested, offering his boyfriend something blue and sparkly. "Just a thought."

"Resist the urge, Alec." Simon was sitting on the edge of a low wall with Maia beside him, though she appeared to be deep in conversation with Aline. "You'll look like Olivia Newton-John in *Xanadu*."

"There are worse things," Magnus observed.

Simon detached himself from the wall and came over to Clary and Jace. With his hands in the back pockets of his jeans, he regarded them thoughtfully for a long moment. At last he spoke.

"You look happy," he said to Clary. He swiveled his gaze to Jace. "And a good thing for you that she does."

Jace raised an eyebrow. "Is this the part where you tell me that if I hurt her, you'll kill me?"

"No," said Simon. "If you hurt Clary, she's quite capable of killing you herself. Possibly with a variety of weapons."

Jace looked pleased by the thought.

"Look," Simon said. "I just wanted to say that it's okay if you dislike me. If you make Clary happy, I'm fine with you." He stuck his hand out, and Jace took his own hand out of

Clary's and shook Simon's, a bemused look on his face.

"I don't dislike you," he said. "In fact, because I actually *do* like you, I'm going to offer you some advice."

"Advice?" Simon looked wary.

"I see that you are working this vampire angle with some success," Jace said, indicating Isabelle and Maia with a nod of his head. "And kudos. Lots of girls love that sensitive-undead thing. But I'd drop that whole musician angle if I were you. Vampire rock stars are played out, and besides, you can't possibly be very good."

Simon sighed. "I don't suppose there's any chance you could reconsider the part where you didn't like me?"

"Enough, both of you," Clary said. "You can't be complete jerks to each other forever, you know."

"Technically," said Simon, "I can."

Jace made an inelegant noise; after a moment Clary realized that he was trying not to laugh, and only semi-succeeding.

Simon grinned. "Got you."

"Well," Clary said. "This *is* a beautiful moment." She looked around for Isabelle, who would probably be nearly as pleased as she was that Simon and Jace were getting along, albeit in their own peculiar way.

Instead she saw someone else.

Standing at the very edge of the glamoured forest, where shadow blended into light, was a slender woman in a green dress the color of leaves, her long scarlet hair bound back by a golden circlet.

The Seelie Queen. She was looking directly at Clary, and as Clary met her gaze, she lifted up a slender hand and beckoned. *Come.*

Whether it was her own desire or the strange compulsion of the Fair Folk, Clary wasn't sure, but with a murmured excuse she stepped away from the others and made her way to the edge of the forest, wending her way through riotous partygoers. She became aware, as she drew close to the Queen, of a preponderance of faeries standing very near them, in a circle around their Lady. Even if she wanted to appear alone, the Queen was not without her courtiers.

The Queen held up an imperious hand. "There," she said. "And no closer."

Clary, a few steps from the Queen, paused. "My lady," she said, remembering the formal way that Jace had addressed the Queen inside her court. "Why do you call me to your side?"

"I would have a favor from you," said the Queen without preamble. "And of course, I would promise a favor in return."

"A favor from *me*?" Clary said wonderingly. "But—you don't even like me."

The Queen touched her lips thoughtfully with a single long white finger. "The Fair Folk, unlike humans, do not concern themselves overmuch with *liking*. Love, perhaps, and hate. Both are useful emotions. But *liking* . . ." She shrugged elegantly. "The Council has not yet chosen which of our folk they would like to sit upon their seat," she said. "I know that Lucian Graymark is like a father to you. He would listen to what you asked him. I would like you to ask him if they would choose my knight Meliorn for the task."

Clary thought back to the Accords Hall, and Meliorn saying he did not want to fight in the battle unless the Night Children fought as well. "I don't think Luke likes him very much."

"And again," said the Queen, "you speak of *liking*."

"When I saw you before, in the Seelie Court," Clary said, "you called Jace and me brother and sister. But you knew we weren't really brother and sister. Didn't you?"

The Queen smiled. "The same blood runs in your veins," she said. "The blood of the Angel. All those who bear the Angel's blood are brother and sister under the skin."

Clary shivered. "You could have told us the truth, though. And you didn't."

"I told you the truth as I saw it. We all tell the truth as we see it, do we not? Did you ever stop to wonder what untruths might have been in the tale your mother told you, that served her purpose in telling it? Do you truly think you know each and every secret of your past?"

Clary hesitated. Without knowing why, she suddenly heard Madame Dorothea's voice in her head. *You'll fall in love with the wrong person,* the hedge-witch had said to Jace. Clary had come to assume that Dorothea had only been referring to how much trouble Jace's affection for Clary would bring them both. But still, there were blanks, she knew, in her memory—even now, things, events, that had not come back to her. Secrets whose truths she'd never know. She had given them up for lost and unimportant, but perhaps—

No. She felt her hands tighten at her sides. The Queen's poison was a subtle one, but powerful. Was there anyone in the world who could truly say they knew every secret about themselves? And weren't some secrets better left alone?

She shook her head. "What you did in the Court," she said. "Perhaps you didn't lie. But you were unkind." She started to turn away. "And I have had enough unkindness."

"Would you truly refuse a favor from the Queen of the Seelie Court?" the Queen demanded. "Not every mortal is granted such a chance."

"I don't need a favor from you," Clary said. "I have everything I want."

She turned her back on the Queen and walked away.

When she returned to the group she had left, she discovered that they had been joined by Robert and Maryse Lightwood, who were—she saw with surprise—shaking hands with Magnus Bane, who had put the sparkly headband away and was being the model of decorum. Maryse had her arm around Alec's shoulder. The rest of her friends were sitting in a group along the wall; Clary was about to move to join them, when she felt a tap on her shoulder.

"Clary!" It was her mother, smiling at her—and Luke stood beside her, his hand in hers. Jocelyn wasn't dressed up at all; she wore jeans, and a loose shirt that at least wasn't stained with paint. You couldn't have told from the way Luke was looking at her, though, that she looked anything less than perfect. "I'm glad we finally found you."

Clary grinned at Luke. "So you're *not* moving to Idris, I take it?"

"Nah," he said. He looked as happy as she'd ever seen him. "The pizza here is terrible."

Jocelyn laughed and moved off to talk to Amatis, who was admiring a floating glass bubble filled with smoke that kept changing colors. Clary looked at Luke. "Were you ever *actually* going to leave New York, or were you just saying that to get her to finally make a move?"

"Clary," said Luke, "I am shocked that you would suggest such a thing." He grinned, then abruptly sobered. "You're all right with it, aren't you? I know this means a big change in your life—I was going to see if you and your mother might want to move in with me, since your apartment's unlivable right now—"

Clary snorted. "A big change? My life has *already* changed totally. Several times."

Luke glanced over toward Jace, who was watching them from his seat on the wall. Jace nodded at them, his mouth curling up at the corner in an amused smile. "I guess it has," Luke said.

"Change is good," said Clary.

Luke held his hand up; the Alliance rune had faded, as it had for everyone, but his skin still bore the white telltale trace of it, the scar that would never entirely disappear. He looked thoughtfully at the Mark. "So it is."

"Clary!" Isabelle called from the wall. "Fireworks!"

Clary hit Luke lightly on the shoulder and went to join her friends. They were seated along the wall in a line: Jace, Isabelle, Simon, Maia, and Aline. She stopped beside Jace. "I don't see any fireworks," she said, mock-scowling at Isabelle.

"Patience, grasshopper," said Maia. "Good things come to those who wait."

"I always thought that was 'Good things come to those who do the wave,'" said Simon. "No wonder I've been so confused all my life."

"'Confused' is a nice word for it," said Jace, but he was clearly only somewhat paying attention; he reached out and pulled Clary toward him, almost absently, as if it were a reflex. She leaned back against his shoulder, looking up at the sky. Nothing lit the heavens but the demon towers, glowing a soft silver-white against the darkness.

"Where did you go?" he asked, quietly enough that only she could hear the question.

"The Seelie Queen wanted me to do her a favor," said Clary. "And she wanted to do me a favor in return." She felt Jace tense. "Relax. I told her no."

"Not many people would turn down a favor from the Seelie Queen," said Jace.

"I told her I didn't need a favor," said Clary. "I told her I had everything I wanted."

Jace laughed at that, softly, and slid his hand up her arm to her shoulder; his fingers played idly with the chain around her neck, and Clary glanced down at the glint of silver against her dress. She had worn the Morgenstern ring since Jace had left it for her, and sometimes she wondered why. Did she really want to be reminded of Valentine? And yet, at the same time, was it ever right to forget?

You couldn't erase everything that caused you pain with its recollection. She didn't want to forget Max or Madeleine, or Hodge, or the Inquisitor, or even Sebastian. Every memory was valuable; even the bad ones. Valentine had wanted to forget: to forget that the world had to change, and Shadowhunters had to change with it—to forget that Downworlders had souls, and all souls mattered to the fabric of the world. He had wanted to think only of what made Shadowhunters different from Downworlders. But what had been his undoing had been the way in which they were all the same.

"Clary," Jace said, breaking her out of her reverie. He

tightened his arms around her, and she raised her head; the crowd was cheering as the first of the rockets went up. "Look."

She looked as the fireworks exploded in a shower of sparks—sparks that painted the clouds overhead as they fell, one by one, in streaking lines of golden fire, like angels falling from the sky.

Acknowledgments

When you look back on writing a book, you can't help but realize what a group effort it all is, and how quickly the whole thing would sink like the *Titanic* if you didn't have the help of your friends. With that in mind: Thanks to the NB Team and the Massachusetts All-Stars; thanks to Elka, Emily, and Clio for hours of plotting help, and to Holly Black for hours of patiently reading the same scenes over and over. To Libba Bray for providing bagels and a couch to write on, Robin Wasserman for distracting me with clips from *Gossip Girl*, Maureen Johnson for staring at me in a frightening way while I was trying to work, and Justine Larbalestier and Scott Westerfeld for forcing me to get off the couch and go somewhere to write. Thanks also to Ioana for helping me with my (nonexistent) Romanian. Thanks as always to my agent, Barry Goldblatt; my editor, Karen Wojtyla; the teams at Simon & Schuster and Walker Books for getting behind this series; and Sarah Payne for making changes long past deadline. And of course to my family—my mother, my father, Jim and Kate, the Esons clan, and of course Josh, who still thinks Simon is based on him (and he may be right).

Continue Clary and Jace's adventures in

City of Fallen Angels,

BOOK FOUR OF THE MORTAL INSTRUMENTS.

FALLING

"So, did you have fun with Isabelle tonight?" Clary, her phone jammed against her ear, maneuvered herself carefully from one long beam to another. The beams were set twenty feet up in the rafters of the Institute's attic, where the training room was located. Walking the beams was meant to teach you how to balance. Clary hated them. Her fear of heights made the whole business sickening, despite the flexible cord tied around her waist that was supposed to keep her from hitting the floor if she fell. "Have you told her about Maia yet?"

Simon made a faint, noncommittal noise that Clary knew meant "no." She could hear music in the background; she could picture him lying on his bed, the stereo playing softly as he talked to her. He sounded tired, that sort of bone-deep tired she knew meant that his light tone didn't reflect his mood. She'd asked him if he was all right several times at the beginning of the conversation, but he'd brushed away her concern.

She snorted. "You're playing with fire, Simon. I hope you know that."

"I don't know. Do you really think it's such a big deal?" Simon sounded plaintive. "I haven't had a single conversation with Isabelle—or Maia—about dating exclusively."

"Let me tell you something about girls." Clary sat down on a beam, letting her legs dangle out into the air. The attic's half-moon windows were open, and cool night air spilled in, chilling her sweaty skin. She had always thought the Shadowhunters trained in their tough, leatherlike gear, but as it turned out, that was for later training, which involved weapons. For the sort of training she was doing—exercises meant to increase her flexibility, speed, and sense of balance—she wore a light tank top and drawstring pants that reminded her of medical scrubs. "Even if you haven't had the exclusivity conversation, they're still going to be mad if they find out you're dating someone they know and you haven't mentioned it. It's a dating rule."

"Well, how am I supposed to know that rule?"

"Everyone knows that rule."

"I thought you were supposed to be on my side."

"I am on your side!"

"So why aren't you being more sympathetic?"

Clary switched the phone to her other ear and peered down into the shadows below her. Where was Jace? He'd gone to get another rope and said he'd be back in five minutes. Of course, if he caught her on the phone up here, he'd probably kill her. He was rarely in charge of her training—that was usually Maryse,

Kadir, or various other members of the New York Conclave pinch-hitting until a replacement for the Institute's previous tutor, Hodge, could be found—but when he was, he took it very seriously. "Because," she said, "your problems are not real problems. You're dating two beautiful girls at once. Think about it. That's like . . . rock-star problems."

"Having rock-star problems may be the closest I ever get to being an actual rock star."

"No one told you to call your band Salacious Mold, my friend."

"We're Millennium Lint now," Simon protested.

"Look, just figure this out before the wedding. If they both think they're going to it with you and they find out at the wedding that you're dating them both, they'll kill you." She stood up. "And then my mom's wedding will be ruined, and she'll kill you. So you'll be dead twice. Well, three times, technically . . ."

"I never told either of them I was going to the wedding with them!" Simon sounded panicked.

"Yes, but they're going to expect you to. That's why girls have boyfriends. So you have someone to take you to boring functions." Clary moved out to the edge of the beam, looking down into the witchlight-illuminated shadows below. There was an old training circle chalked on the floor; it looked like a bull's-eye. "Anyway, I have to jump off this beam now and possibly hurtle to my horrible death. I'll talk to you tomorrow."

"I've got band practice at two, remember? I'll see you there."

"See you." She hung up and stuck the phone into her bra; the light training clothes didn't have any pockets, so what was a girl to do?

"So, are you planning to stay up there all night?" Jace stepped into the center of the bull's-eye and looked up at her.

He was wearing fighting gear, not training clothes like Clary was, and his fair hair stood out startlingly against the black. It had darkened slightly since the end of summer and was more a dark gold than light, which, Clary thought, suited him even better. It made her absurdly happy that she had now known him long enough to notice small changes in his appearance.

"I thought you were coming up here," she called down. "Change of plans?"

"Long story." He grinned up at her. "So? You want to practice flips?"

Clary sighed. Practicing flips involved flinging herself off the beam into empty space, and using the flexible cord to hold her while she pushed off the walls and flipped herself over and under, teaching herself to whirl, kick, and duck without worrying about hard floors and bruises. She'd seen Jace do it, and he looked like a falling angel while he did, flying through the air, whirling and spinning with beautiful, balletic grace. She, on the other hand, curled up like a potato bug as soon as the floor approached, and the fact that she intellectually knew she wasn't going to hit it didn't seem to make any difference.

She was starting to wonder if it didn't matter that she'd been born a Shadowhunter; maybe it was too late for her to be made into one, or at least a fully functional one. Or maybe the gift that made her and Jace what they were had been somehow distributed unequally between them, so he had gotten all the physical grace, and she had gotten—well, not a lot of it.

"Come on, Clary," Jace said. "Jump." She closed her eyes and jumped. For a moment she felt herself hang suspended, free of everything. Then gravity took over, and she plunged toward the floor. Instinctively she pulled her arms and legs in, keeping her eyes squeezed shut. The cord pulled taut and she rebounded, flying back up before falling again. As her velocity slowed, she opened her eyes and found herself dangling at the end of the cord, about five feet above Jace. He was grinning.

"Nice," he said. "As graceful as a falling snowflake."

"Was I screaming?" she asked, genuinely curious. "You know, on the way down."

He nodded. "Thankfully no one's home, or they would have assumed I was murdering you."

"Ha. You can't even reach me." She kicked out a leg and spun lazily in midair.

Jace's eyes glinted. "Want to bet?"

Clary knew that expression. "No," she said quickly. "Whatever you're going to do—"

But he'd already done it. When Jace moved fast, his individual movements were almost invisible. She saw his hand go to his belt, and then something flashed in the air. She heard the sound of parting fabric as the cord above her head was sheared through. Released, she fell freely, too surprised to scream—directly into Jace's arms. The force knocked him backward, and they sprawled together onto one of the padded floor mats, Clary on top of him. He grinned up at her.

"Now," he said, "that was much better. You didn't scream at all."

"I didn't get the chance." She was breathless, and not just from the impact of the fall. Being sprawled on top of Jace, feeling his body against hers, made her hands shake and her heart beat faster. She had thought maybe her physical reaction to him—their reactions to each other—would fade with familiarity, but that hadn't happened. If anything, it had gotten worse the more time she'd spent with him—or better, she supposed, depending on how you thought about it.

He was looking up at her with dark golden eyes; she wondered if their color had intensified since his encounter with Raziel, the Angel, by the shores of Lake Lyn in Idris. She couldn't ask anyone: Though everyone knew that Valentine had summoned the Angel, and that the Angel had healed Jace from injuries Valentine had inflicted on him, no one but Clary and Jace knew that Valentine had done more than just injure his adopted son. He had stabbed Jace through the heart as part of the summoning ceremony—stabbed him, and held him while he died. At Clary's wish Raziel had brought Jace back from death. The enormity of it still shocked Clary, and, she suspected, Jace as well. They had agreed never to tell anyone that Jace had actually *died*, even for a brief time. It was their secret.

He reached up and pushed her hair back from her face. "I'm joking," he said. "You're not so bad. You'll get there. You should have seen Alec do flips at first. I think he kicked himself in the head once."

"Sure," said Clary. "But he was probably eleven." She eyed him. "I suppose you've always been amazing at this stuff."

"I was born amazing." He stroked her cheek with the tips of his fingers, lightly but enough to make her shiver. She said nothing; he was joking, but in a sense it was true. Jace had been born to be what he was. "How long can you stay tonight?"

She smiled a little. "Are we done with training?"

"I'd like to think that we're done with the part of the evening where it's absolutely required. Although there are a few things I'd like to practice. . . ." He reached up to pull her down, but at that moment the door opened, and Isabelle came stalking in, the high heels of her boots clicking on the polished hardwood floor.

Before Clary and Jace there were Tessa,
Will, and Jem. Discover their story in

Clockwork Angel,

BOOK ONE OF THE INFERNAL DEVICES.

Southampton, May.

Tessa could not remember a time when she had not loved the clockwork angel. It had belonged to her mother once, and her mother had been wearing it when she died. After that it had sat in her mother's jewelry box, until her brother, Nathaniel, took it out one day to see if it was still in working order.

The angel was no bigger than Tessa's pinky finger, a tiny statuette made of brass, with folded bronze wings no larger than a cricket's. It had a delicate metal face with shut crescent eyelids, and hands crossed over a sword in front. A thin chain that looped beneath the wings allowed the angel to be worn around the neck like a locket.

Tessa knew the angel was made out of clockwork because if she lifted it to her ear she could hear the sound of its machinery, like the sound of a watch. Nate had exclaimed in surprise that it was still working after so many years, and he had looked in vain for a knob or a screw, or some other method by which the angel might be wound. But there had been nothing to find. With a shrug he'd given the angel to Tessa. From that moment she had never taken it off; even at night the angel lay against her chest as she slept, its constant *ticktock, ticktock* like the beating of a second heart.

She held it now, clutched between her fingers, as the *Main* nosed its way between other massive steamships to find a spot at the Southampton dock. Nate had insisted that she come to Southampton instead of Liverpool, where most transatlantic steamers arrived. He had claimed it was because Southampton was a much pleasanter place to arrive at, so Tessa couldn't help being a little disappointed by this, her first sight of England. It was drearily gray. Rain drummed down onto the spires of a distant church, while black smoke rose from the chimneys of ships and stained the already dull-colored sky. A crowd of people in dark clothes, holding umbrellas, stood on the docks. Tessa strained to see if her brother was among them, but the mist and spray from the ship were too thick for her to make out any individual in great detail.

Tessa shivered. The wind off the sea was chilly. All of Nate's letters had claimed that London was beautiful, the sun shining every day. Well, Tessa thought, hopefully the weather there was better than it was here, because she had no warm clothes with her, nothing more substantial than a woolen shawl that had belonged to Aunt Harriet, and a pair of thin gloves. She had sold most of her clothes to pay for her aunt's funeral, secure in the knowledge that her brother would buy her more when she arrived in London to live with him.

A shout went up. The *Main*, its shining black-painted hull gleaming wet with rain, had anchored, and tugs were plowing their way through the heaving gray water, ready to carry baggage and passengers to the shore. Passengers streamed off the ship, clearly desperate to feel land under their feet. So different from their departure from New York. The sky had been blue then, and a brass band had been playing. Though, with no one there to wish her good-bye, it had not been a merry occasion.

Hunching her shoulders, Tessa joined the disembarking crowd. Drops of rain stung her unprotected head and neck like pinpricks from icy little needles, and her hands, inside their insubstantial gloves, were clammy and wet with rain. Reaching the quay, she looked around eagerly, searching for a sight of Nate. It had been nearly two weeks since she'd spoken to a soul, having kept almost entirely to herself on board the *Main.* It would be wonderful to have her brother to talk to again.

He wasn't there. The wharves were heaped with stacks of luggage and all sorts of boxes and cargo, even mounds of fruit and vegetables wilting and dissolving in the rain. A steamer was departing for Le Havre nearby, and damp-looking sailors swarmed close by Tessa, shouting in French. She tried to move aside, only to be almost trampled by a throng of disembarking passengers hurrying for the shelter of the railway station.

But Nate was nowhere to be seen.

"You are Miss Gray?" The voice was guttural, heavily accented. A man had moved to stand in front of Tessa. He was tall, and was wearing a sweeping black coat and a tall hat, its brim collecting rainwater like a cistern. His eyes were peculiarly bulging, almost protuberant, like a frog's, his skin as rough-looking as scar tissue. Tessa had to fight the urge to cringe away from him. But he knew her name. Who here would know her name except someone who knew Nate, too?

"Yes?"

"Your brother sent me. Come with me."

"Where is he?" Tessa demanded, but the man was already walking away. His stride was uneven, as if he had a limp from an old injury. After a moment Tessa gathered up her skirts and hurried after him.

He wound through the crowd, moving ahead with purposeful speed. People jumped aside, muttering about his rudeness as he shouldered past, with Tessa nearly running to keep up. He turned abruptly around a pile of boxes, and came to a halt in front of a large, gleaming black coach. Gold letters had been painted across its side, but the rain and mist were too thick for Tessa to read them clearly.

The door of the carriage opened and a woman leaned out. She wore an enormous plumed hat that hid her face. "Miss Theresa Gray?"

Tessa nodded. The bulging-eyed man hurried to help the woman out of the carriage—and then another woman, following after her. Each of them immediately opened an umbrella and raised it, sheltering themselves from the rain. Then they fixed their eyes on Tessa.

They were an odd pair, the women. One was very tall and thin, with a bony, pinched face. Colorless hair was scraped back into a chignon at the back of her head. She wore a dress of brilliant violet silk, already spattered here and there with splotches of rain, and matching violet gloves. The other woman was short and plump, with small eyes sunk deep into her head; the bright pink gloves stretched over her large hands made them look like colorful paws.

"Theresa Gray," said the shorter of the two. "What a delight to make your acquaintance at last. I am Mrs. Black, and this is my sister, Mrs. Dark. Your brother sent us to accompany you to London."

Tessa—damp, cold, and baffled—clutched her wet shawl tighter around herself. "I don't understand. Where's Nate? Why didn't he come himself?"

"He was unavoidably detained by business in London. Mortmain's couldn't spare him. He sent ahead a note for you, however." Mrs. Black held out a rolled-up bit of paper, already dampened with rain.

Tessa took it and turned away to read it. It was a short note from her brother apologizing for not being at the docks to meet her, and letting her know that he trusted Mrs. Black and Mrs. Dark—*I call them the Dark Sisters, Tessie, for obvious reasons, and they seem to find the name agreeable!*—to bring her safely to his house in London. They were, his note said, his landladies as well as trusted friends, and they had his highest recommendation.

That decided her. The letter was certainly from Nate. It was in his handwriting, and no one else ever called her Tessie. She swallowed hard and slipped the note into her sleeve, turning back to face the sisters. "Very well," she said, fighting down her lingering sense of disappointment—she had been so looking forward to seeing her brother. "Shall we call a porter to fetch my trunk?"

"No need, no need." Mrs. Dark's cheerful tone was at odds with her pinched gray features. "We've already arranged to have it sent on ahead." She snapped her fingers at the bulging-eyed man, who swung himself up into the driver's seat at the front of the carriage. She placed her hand on Tessa's shoulder. "Come along, child; let's get you out of the rain."

As Tessa moved toward the carriage, propelled by Mrs.

Dark's bony grip, the mist cleared, revealing the gleaming golden image painted on the side of the door. The words "The Pandemonium Club" curled intricately around two snakes biting each other's tails, forming a circle. Tessa frowned. "What does that mean?"

"Nothing you need worry about," said Mrs. Black, who had already climbed inside and had her skirts spread out across one of the comfortable-looking seats. The inside of the carriage was richly decorated with plush purple velvet bench seats facing each other, and gold tasseled curtains hanging in the windows.

Mrs. Dark helped Tessa up into the carriage, then clambered in behind her. As Tessa settled herself on the bench seat, Mrs. Black reached to shut the carriage door behind her sister, closing out the gray sky. When she smiled, her teeth gleamed in the dimness as if they were made out of metal. "Do settle in, Theresa. We've a long ride ahead of us."

Tessa put a hand to the clockwork angel at her throat, taking comfort in its steady ticking, as the carriage lurched forward into the rain.

Discover Emma and Julian's story in

Lady Midnight,

THE FIRST BOOK IN CASSANDRA CLARE'S

NEW SERIES, THE DARK ARTIFICES.

Emma took her witchlight out of her pocket and lit it—and almost screamed out loud. Jules's shirt was soaked with blood and worse, the healing runes she'd drawn had vanished from his skin. They weren't working.

"Jules," she said. "I have to call the Silent Brothers. They can help you. I *have* to."

His eyes screwed shut with pain. "You can't," he said. "You know we can't call the Silent Brothers. They report directly to the Clave."

"So we'll lie to them. Say it was a routine demon patrol. I'm calling," she said, and reached for her phone.

"No!" Julian said, forcefully enough to stop her. "Silent Brothers know when you're lying! They can see inside your head, Emma. They'll find out about the investigation. About Mark—"

"You're not going to bleed to death in the backseat of a car for Mark!"

"No," he said, looking at her. His eyes were eerily blue-green, the only bright color in the dark interior of the car. "You're going to fix me."

Emma could feel it when Jules was hurt, like a splinter lodged under her skin. The physical pain didn't bother her; it was the terror, the only terror worse than her fear of the ocean. The fear of Jules being hurt, of him dying. She would give up anything, sustain any wound, to prevent those things from happening.

"Okay," she said. Her voice sounded dry and thin to her own ears. "Okay." She took a deep breath. "Hang on."

She unzipped her jacket, threw it aside. Shoved the console between the seats aside, put her witchlight on the floorboard. Then she reached for Jules. The next few seconds were a blur of Jules's blood on her hands and his harsh breathing as she pulled him partly upright, wedging him against the back door. He didn't make a sound as she moved him, but she could see him biting his lip, the blood on his mouth and chin, and she felt as if her bones were popping inside her skin.

"Your gear," she said through gritted teeth. "I have to cut it off."

He nodded, letting his head fall back. She drew a dagger from her belt, but the gear was too tough for the blade. She said a silent prayer and reached back for Cortana.

Cortana went through the gear like a knife through melted butter. It fell away in pieces and Emma drew them free, then sliced down the front of his T-shirt and pulled it apart as if she were opening a jacket.

Emma had seen blood before, often, but this felt different. It was Julian's, and there seemed to be a lot of it. It was smeared up and down his chest and rib cage; she could see where the arrow had gone in and where the skin had torn where he'd yanked it out.

"Why did you pull the arrow out?" she demanded, pulling her sweater over her head. She had a tank top on under it. She patted his chest and side with the sweater, absorbing as much of the blood as she could.

Jules's breath was coming in hard pants. "Because when someone—shoots you with an arrow—" he gasped, "your immediate response is not—'Thanks for the arrow, I think I'll keep it for a while.'"

"Good to know your sense of humor is intact."

"Is it still bleeding?" Julian demanded. His eyes were shut.

She dabbed at the cut with her sweater. The blood had slowed, but the cut looked puffy and swollen. The rest of him, though—it had been a while since she'd seen him with his shirt off. There was more muscle than she remembered. Lean muscle pulled tight over his ribs, his stomach flat and lightly ridged. Cameron was much more muscular, but Julian's spare lines were as elegant as a greyhound's. "You're too skinny," she said. "Too much coffee, not enough pancakes."

"I hope they put that on my tombstone." He gasped as she shifted forward, and she realized abruptly that she was squarely in Julian's lap, her knees around his hips. It was a bizarrely intimate position.

"I—am I hurting you?" she asked.

He swallowed visibly. "It's fine. Try with the *iratze* again."

"Fine," she said. "Grab the panic bar."

"The what?" He opened his eyes and peered at her.

"The plastic handle! Up there, above the window!" She pointed. "It's for holding on to when the car is going around curves."

"Are you sure? I always thought it was for hanging things on. Like dry cleaning."

"Julian, *now is not the time to be pedantic.* Grab the bar or I swear—"

"All right!" He reached up, grabbed hold of it, and winced. "I'm ready."

She nodded and set Cortana aside, reaching for her stele. Maybe her previous *iratzes* had been too fast, too sloppy. She'd always focused on the physical aspects of Shadowhunting, not the more mental and artistic ones: seeing through glamours, drawing runes.

She set the tip of it to the skin of his shoulder and drew, carefully and slowly. She had to brace herself with her left hand against his shoulder. She tried to press as lightly as she could, but she could feel him tense under her fingers. The skin on his shoulder was smooth and hot under her touch, and she wanted to get closer to him, to put her hand over the wound on his side and heal it with the sheer force of her will. To touch her lips to the lines of pain beside his eyes and—

Stop. She had finished the *iratze.* She sat back, her hand clamped around the stele. Julian sat up a little straighter, the ragged remnants of his shirt hanging off his shoulders. He took a deep breath, glancing down at himself—and the *iratze* faded back into his skin, like black ice melting, spreading, being absorbed by the sea.

He looked up at Emma. She could see her own reflection in his eyes: she looked wrecked, panicked, with blood on her neck and her white tank top. "It hurts less," he said in a low voice.

The wound on his side pulsed again; blood slid down the side of his rib cage, staining his leather belt and the waistband of his jeans. She put her hands on his bare skin, panic rising up inside her. His skin felt hot, too hot. Fever hot.

"I have to call," she whispered. "I don't care if the whole world comes down around us, Jules, the most important thing is that you *live.*"

"Please," he said, desperation clear in his voice. "Whatever is happening, we'll fix it, because we're *parabatai.* We're forever. I said that to you once, do you remember?"

She nodded warily, hand on the phone.

"And the strength of a rune your *parabatai* gives you is special. Emma, you can do it. You can heal me. We're *parabatai* and that means the things we can do together are . . . extraordinary."

There was blood on her jeans now, blood on her hands and her tank top, and he was still bleeding, the wound still open, an incongruous tear in the smooth skin all around it.

"Try," Jules said in a dry whisper. "For me, try?"

His voice went up on the question and in it she heard the voice of the boy he had been once, and she remembered him smaller, skinnier, younger, back pressed against one of the marble columns in the Hall of Accords in Alicante as his father advanced on him with his blade unsheathed.

And she remembered what Julian had done, then. Done to protect her, to protect all of them, because he always would do everything to protect them.

She took her hand off the phone and gripped the stele, so tightly she felt it dig into her damp palm. "Look at me, Jules," she said in a low voice, and he met her eyes with his. She placed the stele against his skin, and for a moment she held still, just breathing, breathing and remembering.

Julian. A presence in her life for as long as she could remember, splashing water at each other in the ocean, digging in the sand together, him putting his hand over hers and them marveling at the difference in the shape and length of their fingers. Julian singing, terribly and off-key, while he drove, his fingers in her hair carefully freeing a trapped leaf, his hands catching her in the training room when she fell, and fell, and fell. The first time after their *parabatai* ceremony when she'd smashed her hand into a wall in rage at not being able to get a sword maneuver right, and he'd come up to her, taken her still-shaking body in his arms and said, "Emma, Emma, don't hurt yourself. When you do, I feel it, too."

Something in her chest seemed to split and crack; she marveled that it wasn't audible. Energy raced along her veins, and the stele jerked in her hand before it seemed to move on its own, tracing the graceful outline of a healing rune across Julian's chest. She heard him gasp, his eyes flying open. His hand slid down her back and he pressed her against him, his teeth gritted.

"Don't *stop*," he said.

Emma couldn't have stopped if she'd wanted to. The stele seemed to be moving of its own accord; she was blinded with memories, a kaleidoscope of them, all of them Julian. Sun in her eyes and Julian asleep on the beach in an old T-shirt and her not wanting to wake him, but he'd woken anyway when the sun went down and looked for her immediately, not smiling till his eyes found her and he knew she was there. Falling asleep talking and waking up with their hands interlocked; they'd been children in the dark together once but now they were something else, something intimate and powerful, something Emma felt she was touching only the very edge of as she finished the rune and the stele fell from her nerveless fingers.

"Oh," she said softly. The rune seemed lit from within by a soft glow.

Turn the page to read the
letter Jace left for Clary.

Clary,

Despite everything, I can't bear the thought of this ring being lost forever, any more than I can bear the thought of leaving you forever. And though I have no choice about the one, at least I can choose about the other. I'm leaving you our family ring because you have as much right to it as I do.

I'm writing this watching the sun come up. You're asleep, dreams moving behind your restless eyelids. I wish I knew what you were thinking. I wish I could slip into your head and see the world the way you do. I wish I could see myself the way you do. But maybe I don't want to see that. Maybe it would make me feel even more than I already do that I'm perpetuating some kind of Great Lie on you, and I couldn't stand that.

I belong to you. You could do anything you wanted with me and I would let you. You could ask anything of me and I'd break myself trying to make you happy. My heart tells me this is the best and greatest feeling I have ever had. But my mind knows the difference between wanting what you can't have and wanting what you shouldn't want. And I shouldn't want you.

All night I've watched you sleeping, watched the

moonlight come and go, casting its shadows across your face in black and white—I've never seen anything more beautiful. I think of the life we could have had if things were different, a life where this night is not a singular event, separate from everything else that's real, but every night. But things aren't different, and I can't look at you without feeling like I've tricked you into loving me.

The truth no one is willing to say out loud is that no one has a shot against Valentine but me. I can get close to him like no one else can. I can pretend I want to join him and he'll believe me, up until that last moment where I end it all, one way or another. I have something of Sebastian's; I can Track him to where my father's hiding. And that's what I'm going to do. So I lied to you last night. I said I just wanted one night with you. But I want every night with you. And that's why I have to slip out of your window now, like a coward. Because if I had to tell you this to your face, I couldn't make myself go.

I don't blame you if you hate me, I wish you would. As long as I can still dream, I will dream of you.

—Jace

CASSANDRA CLARE'S

#1 *New York Times* Bestselling Series

THE MORTAL INSTRUMENTS
THE INFERNAL DEVICES
THE DARK ARTIFICES

A thousand years ago, the Angel Raziel mixed his blood with the blood of men and created the race of the Nephilim. Human-angel hybrids, they walk among us, unseen but ever present, our invisible protectors.

They call themselves Shadowhunters.

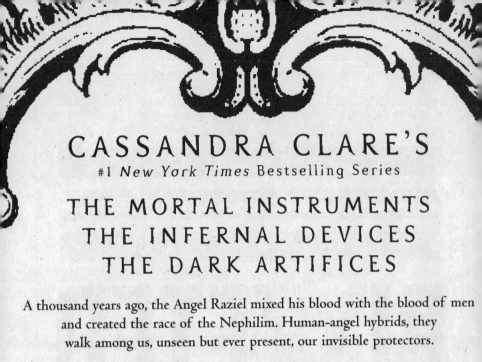

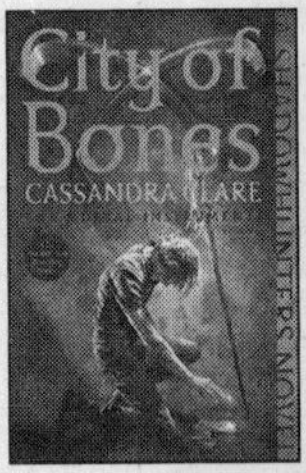

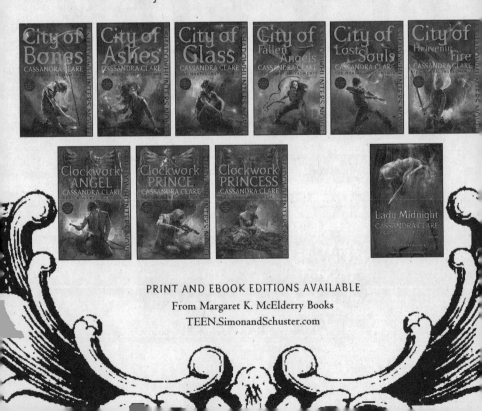

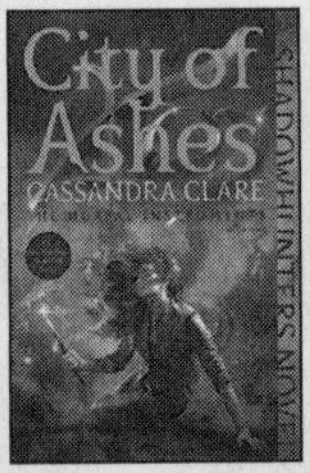

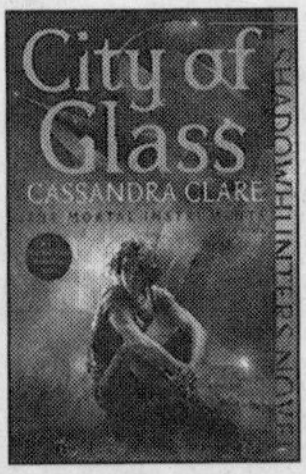

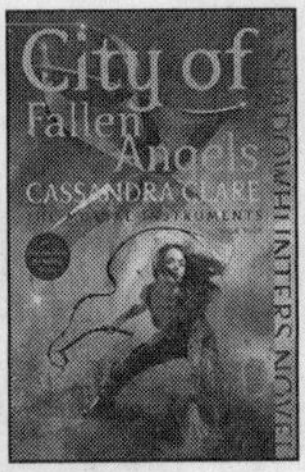

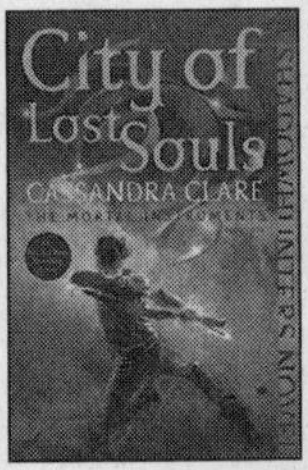

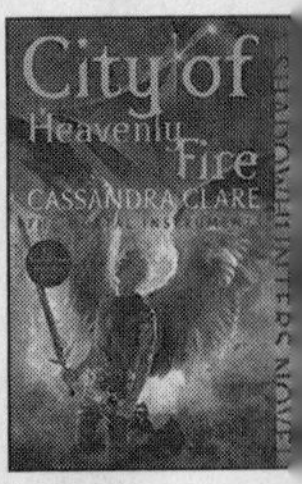

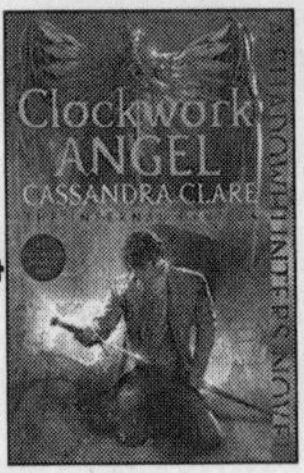

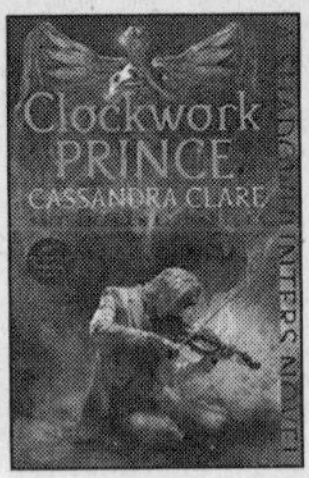

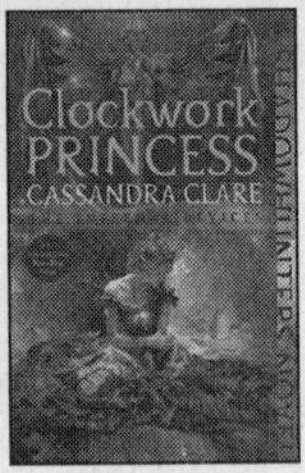

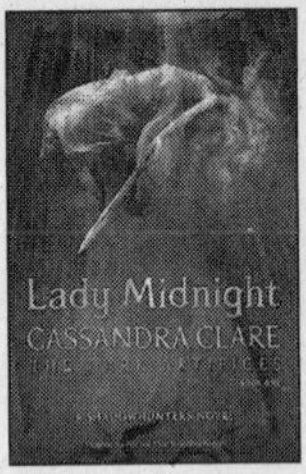

PRINT AND EBOOK EDITIONS AVAILABLE

From Margaret K. McElderry Books

TEEN.SimonandSchuster.com

ALL THE STORIES ARE TRUE
THE
Shadowhunter's
Codex
AS COMPILED BY
Cassandra Clare
and Joshua Lewis

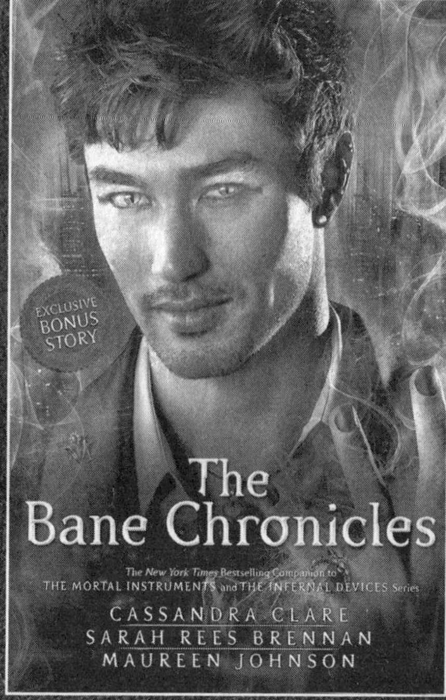
EXCLUSIVE
BONUS
STORY
The
Bane Chronicles
The New York Times Bestselling Companion to
THE MORTAL INSTRUMENTS and THE INFERNAL DEVICES Series
CASSANDRA CLARE
SARAH REES BRENNAN
MAUREEN JOHNSON

Companion to the bestselling series
THE MORTAL INSTRUMENTS and THE INFERNAL DEVICES
CASSANDRA CLARE
SARAH REES BRENNAN
TALES FROM THE SHADOWHUNTER ACADEMY
Welcome to Shadowhunter Academy

Companion to the bestselling series
THE MORTAL INSTRUMENTS and THE INFERNAL DEVICES
CASSANDRA CLARE
ROBIN WASSERMAN
TALES FROM THE SHADOWHUNTER ACADEMY
The Lost Herondale